P9-CFJ-828

Winter Park
PUBLIC LIBRARY
Presented by
The
Rachel D. Murrah
Fiction
Endowment Book Fund

THE *Trial* AND

OF THE *Traitor* GEORGE WASHINGTON

Also by Charles Rosenberg

Death on a High Floor
Long Knives
Paris Ransom
Write to Die

THE *Trial* AND *Execution* OF THE *Traitor* GEORGE WASHINGTON

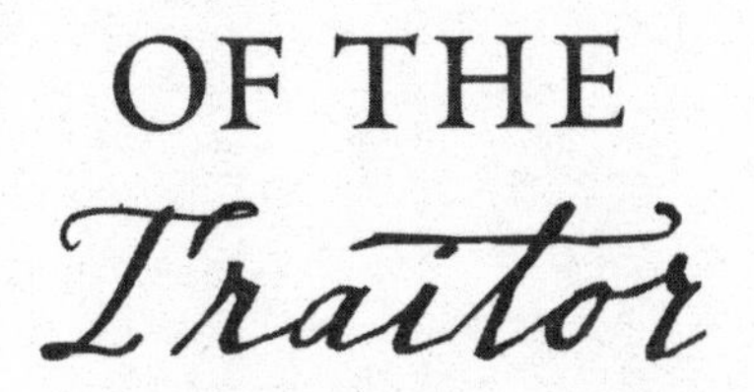

a novel

CHARLES ROSENBERG

HANOVER
SQUARE
PRESS

ISBN-13: 978-1-335-20032-7

The Trial and Execution of the Traitor George Washington

For questions and comments about the quality of this book, please contact us at CustomerService@Harlequin.com.

HanoverSqPress.com
BookClubbish.com

Printed in U.S.A.

This book is dedicated to my wife, Sally Anne, and my son, Joe, who, many years ago, when I first imagined this novel, bugged me repeatedly to get started on it, and to my agent, Erica Silverman, who encouraged me to finish it once I had begun.

THE *Trial*

AND

Execution

OF THE

Traitor

GEORGE WASHINGTON

PART I

Late Fall 1780

1

The almost seven-week voyage westbound across the North Atlantic had not gone well. Black had been seasick on and off since the day the sloop-of-war HMS *Peregrine* had sailed out of Portsmouth. Some weeks, when the wind and waves had been relatively calm, he'd been fine. But each time the weather roughened he'd had to rush for the bucket all over again. Some cruel sailor had even painted his name on it. It had all seemed to amuse the crew, and they had snickered openly in front of him. If he'd been able to wear his uniform, with rank and campaign medals on display, they would never have dared. But on this voyage, as testified to by the name splashed on the bucket, he was travelling as "Mr. Smith." He was billeted as a civilian supposedly being transported to New York at the request of the Admiralty, for reasons not revealed to the crew or the more junior officers. And so they treated him with disdain, as if he were a clerk in a counting house.

Even the ship's captain, Charles Ingram, had seemed at least mildly amused by his discomfort, despite Ingram having assured him that the sea was rather calm for the North Atlantic in late fall. The Captain, of course, was aware not only of his true name—Jeremiah Black—but also of his rank, and where he was actually going to be put ashore. He had not been entrusted, however, with the true nature of Black's assignment. Once or twice, in the guise of seeming to commiserate with him about his seasickness, the Captain had tried to worm out of him the purpose of his mission. Black had steadfastly refused to be drawn in or to share his orders.

Those orders had been handed to Black by none other than the First Minister of Great Britain, Lord North himself, in a small meeting room on the second floor of 10 Downing Street. There, after reading them, Black had been made to understand that, aside from North and the military aide who briefed him on the more detailed plans as North stood by, only two other people in all of England were privy to them. North had named only one—the First Lord of the Admiralty. Black had gained the distinct impression, perhaps erroneously, that the second person who'd been told of the plan was the man whose large portrait hung on the wall—George III, King by the Grace of God, of England, Scotland and Wales, and, more recently, of Ireland, too.

He had also been given to understand that his promotion to the rank of full colonel was temporary, done so that he would outrank Captain Ingram during the voyage. Ingram, although captain of the ship, was only a navy commander by rank, the army equivalent of a lieutenant colonel. Should Black fail in his mission, he would be busted back to major, posthumously if necessary. Should he succeed, much glory and a general's star awaited him. Or so he allowed himself to imagine.

As the meeting was coming to an end, North had shown him a copy of Captain Ingram's orders. Ingram was to deliver him to a deserted beach well north of Philadelphia, not far south of where the Raritan River met the sea. The drop-off was to be done, if possible, on one of ten nights in mid- to late November between the hours of midnight and 4:00 a.m. If at all possible, he was to be put ashore on a night when the beach was not bright with moonlight. Should the ship fail to make landfall by one of those ten nights, Ingram was to take the ship into New York for reprovisioning. Then sail it back to England, with *Mr. Smith* still on board.

If good fortune prevailed, and the ship was able to land him on the beach on one of the ten appointed nights, Captain Ingram was to wait no more than eight days for Black to return to the same beach. If he failed to make it back on time, he was to be abandoned to his fate.

Black had asked why the rescue attempt was to be limited to only eight nights. North had looked away, and his aide, instead of answering Black's question in detail, had said only, "Longer too much risks your discovery. But in any case, if you fail, no one in the United Kingdom will ever acknowledge that you were on an official mission, and if discovered you will be labelled a rogue officer attempting unsanctioned heroics."

After that, standing there before Lord North, he had read through his orders once more and asked, "Minister, will Captain Ingram know what I hope to be carrying on my return?"

"No, he will not. Are there any other questions, Colonel?"

"I have two, my Lord."

"I am listening."

"First, I am deeply honoured to be entrusted with this mission, but—"

North interrupted. "You want to know why we are sending you when the loyal colonists have already planned your mission in such detail? Why can't they do it themselves?"

"With all respect, Minister, the question is more, what do you hope I can add to what already seems a well-planned mission?"

North walked over to a window, clasped his hands behind his back and looked out, seeming to focus on something in the far distance. His face looked puffy and worn. It was perhaps not surprising. The "American war," as it was often called, had not proved the easy victory originally predicted. Instead, it had dragged on for more than four years, with France giving more and more aid to the rebellion.

After a moment, North turned back to face him. "You are being sent as the embodiment of the King's justice. The Loyalists over there—" he waved an arm towards the windows, as if to send his hand flying across the Atlantic "—are no doubt good men, but we do not wish this supreme traitor taken by—" he paused, searching for the words "—a ragtag group with no formal authority. Whereas you, an officer in His Majesty's service, dressed in the scarlet of a British uniform, will carry out a lawful arrest."

"I see," Black said, but the Prime Minister was not done.

"That arrest, carried out in the very heart of the rebellion, will tell all that, whatever the grievances of the colonists, King and Parliament are still sovereign in the colonies. Sovereign!"

North was breathing hard and becoming red in the face. Black decided not to pursue it further. "Thank you, my Lord," he said. "I think I understand." Although in reality, he did not.

"You said you had *two* questions, Colonel."

"If I apprehend him, but for whatever reason cannot return him here, what are my orders?"

North stared at him. "Your orders are to sail there, capture him and return him here. That is all."

He thought of pressing the issue, but North had already walked back to a green-felt table laden with documents and begun to examine them. "You are dismissed, Colonel," he said, without turning around. "My aide will show you out."

"Thank you, my Lord."

Black and the aide had almost reached the door when North once again turned towards them and said, "God speed you on your way, young man."

Young? He didn't feel all that young. Black had undertaken his first secret mission for the army when he was but twenty years old, and it had felt like an adventure. Now, at age thirty-three, the idea of travelling three thousand miles across an ocean to a land he'd never been to before, seizing a commanding general from the middle of his own troops and returning him to London, alive, seemed not so much an adventure as a likely death sentence. At least for him. Perhaps for both of them.

2

On their forty-eighth day at sea Captain Ingram called Black to the bridge. It was late afternoon, and the sun was already low in the sky.

Ingram was holding a long spyglass to his eye. "We are no doubt close to shore," he said.

"Can you see it through the glass?"

"Not yet. But there are shore signs. Green leaves in the water, more flotsam than normal, shorebirds in the sky, and the depth is dropping off rapidly."

"Anything else, Captain?"

"A well-honed sense of the sea."

"Where are we, then?"

"If our navigator has well calculated our latitude, and our maps and charts are correct, off the coast of His Majesty's Colony of New Jersey, somewhat south of the mouth of the Raritan River."

"How sure are you of either?"

"I'm confident in our navigator. Whether the latitude of the beach in question as marked on our charts is accurate is anyone's guess."

"You have no tools to help you, Captain?"

"Yes. For charts of this coast, we have the *Atlantic Neptune.* The Admiralty paid one hundred thousand pounds to have it created just four years ago. At that price, it ought to be good, eh?"

"I would hope."

"But it hasn't been corrected since this lunatic war began. And who is to say it doesn't need correcting?"

"Can we get closer before choosing a place to land? If I land on the wrong beach, there will be no one to greet me."

"Colonel, I will be candid. We will be lucky to find the right beach, although it is favourable to us that the beach in question has two distinctive rock formations."

"What is unfavourable?"

"If our calculation of where we are is off by even a few minutes of latitude, we may miss the beach by miles."

"Is the only choice to try to head straight in?"

"No. The usual way would be to locate the mouth of the Raritan—not that difficult—and head down the coast, constantly checking latitude and looking for the rock formations. But that route takes us very close to New York, with a lot of shipping nearby. We'd be more likely to be spotted."

"By American warships?"

"Not likely. We have largely swept the sea of the ships of the so-called Continental Navy. My main worry will be the privateers they have licensed, but they will be mainly off of Philadelphia. I hope."

"So overall, this may not be easy."

"Put it this way, Colonel. Whoever thought up the idea of bringing you from England to land—in the midst of what is very much a naval war—on a particular beach at night without first going into a known port and acquiring a pilot familiar with the coastline must be an idiot."

"You may be speaking of the First Lord of the Admiralty."

"Perhaps I am. Idiocy is not unknown in such high places. But in any case, we cannot get much closer to shore now lest we be seen."

"Understood."

"When we put you ashore, we will, of course, have no choice but to come in closer, and hope that the dark hides us from unfriendly eyes. And that brings me to the reason I asked you to come up here."

"Which is?"

"Tonight is the first night of the ten nights we should prefer, according to my orders, to put you ashore. Do you wish to go tonight or wait?"

"The sea is rough now. Perhaps I should wait a day or two."

"Perhaps. But it is equally likely it will get much rougher in the days ahead."

"What will the moon be like tonight?"

"Using the longitude of the town of Tom's River as our guide, which we have in our charts, the moon will not rise until after 2:00 a.m."

"So if you put me ashore before 2:00 there will be no moon on the beach."

"That is right."

"May I borrow your spyglass, Captain?"

"Of course." Ingram handed it to him, and he put it to his eye and aimed it at the horizon. He saw only water—not that he had really expected to see land—but he had somehow felt the need to confirm that the shore could not yet be seen.

He handed it back. "I think, Captain, to avoid the sea getting any rougher, I will go tonight. How close in can you get me?"

"This is a small, fast ship with a shallow draught, but even so, with the uncertainty of the bottom charts, we dare not come too close to shore. We will use a longboat to take you in."

"How long will that take?"

"We will want to put the boat in the water at least two miles out. If things go well, it should take less than an hour to row you in."

"Or more if things don't go well?"

"Yes, or less, as I just said, especially if we dare get closer. Although the closer in we get, the greater the chance that someone on the beach or on a high hill will see us, even at night in very weak moonlight. Not to mention the noise the chains of the capstan make as we weigh anchor."

"How far out would you have to anchor so as to not be seen at all?"

"With the height of our mast, about twelve miles. And there's one more thing."

"Which is?"

"In a sea like today's the trip in a small boat will not be easy on your stomach. You'll be deathly ill with seasickness by the time you reach shore, even though we are lucky to have men good with small boats in our crew."

Black didn't know what Ingram meant, so he did what he often did when what was said didn't make good sense to him. He just asked directly. "I don't understand. Aren't all sailors good with such boats?"

"Most sailors hate small boats. They think climbing into one is the step right before drowning. But a fair dozen of our men were impressed into His Majesty's Navy from whalers, and they're used to small boats, where they get up close to harpoon the whales."

"That sounds very good for me, then, even in a rough sea."

"Only in the sense that they won't likely swamp or capsize the boat and probably won't be sick themselves." He paused. "But you will be. Very. Unless a calm day should come along."

Black was silent, weighing what Ingram was saying.

"In case I'm not being clear," Ingram said. "I advise you go tonight, Colonel, because bad as it may be, the sea could become even worse tomorrow and the following days."

Black thought about it for a few more seconds. "All right. Tonight it is."

As Ingram was about to leave, Black said, "I have one more question, Captain."

"What is it?"

"I understand your orders are to send a boat to pick me up for each of eight nights."

"Correct."

"I worry about this because I don't know how long this mission will take or what problems I will encounter along the way."

"And?"

"If I am not here by the eighth night, are you willing to come back for a ninth night? In case I am delayed."

Ingram sighed. "I fear not. My orders are quite strict on this point. I would be court-martialled for violating them." He looked at Black and grimaced. "I don't want to be shot."

Black knew that Ingram was referring to the fact that, only a little over twenty years earlier, the navy had infamously executed Admiral John Byng on the quarterdeck of his own flagship for failing to relieve a besieged British garrison.

Black raised his eyebrows and widened his eyes, a look he knew tended to endear him to people. "I would not wish to see you shot, Captain."

Ingram laughed, if perhaps a bit uneasily, and changed the subject back to the weather. "So you will for sure go tonight, Colonel, despite the rough sea?"

"Yes, Captain. Taking extraordinary risks in the service of my country is what my life as a soldier has turned out to be about. The risk of getting even more seasick than I have already been is small compared to what is to come."

3

Black was rowed ashore just after midnight amidst boiling seas and pelting rain, which had begun in the evening. The slicker they gave him to wear over his peacoat kept him more or less dry, but hardly warm.

It took almost two hours for six sailors to get him in. On the way, the small boat pitched and rolled, and he vomited constantly, then got the dry heaves when his stomach finally had nothing left to bring up. When they reached shore, the sailors grabbed him under the arms, swung him out of the boat and stood him up in the surf. He watched them row away until, within seconds, they disappeared into the rain.

As he turned to stumble away from the water's edge, a breaker caught him from behind and knocked him down. His face was pitched into the ground, and he could taste wet sand in his mouth. It made his stomach heave yet again.

Suddenly, he felt arms pulling him up and heard a voice say, "Passerby! Who might you be?"

It was the code words he had been told to expect. He coughed, spit the sand out of his mouth and got out the required pass phrase: "A Patriot indeed!"

Then came the confirming answer from the voice. "Be welcome amongst us!"

The voice, he could now see, came from a barely made-out tall, thin man of middle years. He was wearing a rolled-up knit cap that dripped water and a full-length dark wool coat. He wore no slicker, but the coat seemed somehow to shed the rain.

"I am Rufus," the man said. "We should go quickly. People walk upon this beach at night, even at this hour in this weather." Rufus took him by the elbow and led him a few dozen feet to a muddy trail that seemed to hug the beach. There were two horses waiting, tethered to a tree. As they approached, the horses gave a shake, trying to throw off the rain.

"Do you ride?" Rufus asked.

"Yes, of course." He had on the tip of his tongue to remind him that he was an officer in the British Army, so it was a given that he could ride. As the words were forming on his lips, he thought the better of it. The less the Americans, Loyalists or not, knew about him the better, at least for now.

"What is your name?" the man asked.

"Simon Smith."

Rufus smiled a crooked smile and revealed a broken front tooth. "I need your real name."

"Why?"

"We have been told the real name of the person whom we are to meet on this beach. If you don't know the correct name, we will assume you have replaced the real man, and we will kill you."

"I could have intercepted that person and learned his real name before taking his place. You wouldn't be able to tell."

"So true. Now tell me your name."

"Jeremiah Black."

Rufus stared at him for a few seconds, as if trying to figure out if he had spoken the right name. A chill went through Black. Had there been some mix-up? Was that not the name they expected?

"And what is your rank, sir?"

"I'm a colonel in the King's Guard." He smiled to himself as he said it. So much for keeping his military connections secret.

Finally, Rufus said, "Welcome, Colonel Black. We have been expecting you, although you have picked a godforsaken night to arrive."

Just then Black heard a muffled sound and the sharp, high-pitched bark of a dog. Once, then twice. Rufus put his hand on his shoulder, pushed him down and slapped the other hand over his mouth. He put his mouth to Black's ear. "Make no sound."

A voice at some distance, hard to make out, said, "It's nothing, old fellow. No one else would be fool enough to walk here in this weather."

Black waited, crouched down and tense, his knees beginning to ache. The dog barked again. Could the animal smell them, even in the rain?

Perhaps five minutes passed before they heard the man move off down the beach. And then the bark, twice more, clearly now much further away. He imagined the dog, wanting to go back and find what he smelled—them. But the master, thank God, was in control and no doubt wanting to get out of the rain.

Rufus pulled him back up, leaned close and said, "Let's go."

"Do you think that was truly just a man and his dog?"

"I know not. I do know we need to leave here. Let's mount and ride."

One of the waiting horses was large, the other hardly bigger than a pony. "Take the smaller one," Rufus said. He mounted the larger of the two and headed down a narrow trail that branched off the road. Black mounted and followed.

Rufus had taken Black's statement that he could ride at face value. Despite the dark night and the wet, muddy soil, Rufus rode quickly. It reminded Black of the night rides on the moors that he had taken as a very young officer, all in preparation for deployment to America to fight in the war with the French—a war that had ended not long before he was to have shipped out to help fight it.

The task of following Rufus was made slightly easier by a light that came from a tiny lantern that hung to the side of one of the saddlebags. It was easy enough to follow but small enough—perhaps—not to give them away. He gave it only momentary thought, with his attention mainly taken up by the task of riding a strange, too small horse on an unfamiliar trail in the dark.

After about fifteen minutes, they came to a clearing, and he could see the ghostly outline of a barn on the other side. When they were halfway across, Rufus brought his horse to a sudden stop, then reached down, grabbed the lantern, raised it above his head, held it there a few seconds and then dropped it down again as far as his arm could reach. He next raised it up again, and then repeated the actions on the other side.

For a few seconds, nothing happened, and Black had the sinking feeling that perhaps things were already going awry, as they had on his last overseas mission. Finally, an answering light appeared high on the side of the barn, blinked three times and went dark. Then it blinked three times again. Rufus seemed satisfied and moved his horse ahead, slowly this time. Black followed.

When they got up to the barn, they rode through an already open door. He wrinkled his nose at the smell. It was not the odour of manure that he had expected, but a powerful blast of mould. The barn had clearly been abandoned some time ago. Now, he thought, I'm going to find out if Rufus is really a Loyalist sent to fetch me, or if he is an enemy who intercepted the real messenger and beat the code words and my name out of him.

He heard the door close behind him with a bang. It was suddenly pitch-black.

4

"Good morning to you, Colonel Black," a voice said. "Welcome to His Majesty's Colony of New Jersey."

Rufus, still astride his horse, opened a door on the side of the lantern and held it up high so that it gave off slightly more light. It illuminated a solitary figure standing in front of them. He was middle-aged, short but solid, with a large mop of hair. Even in the dim light, Black could see that the man's hair was almost flame red.

"Good morning to you, sir," Black responded. "May I have the honour of knowing your name?"

"Those who have planned this say that the less we all know about each other the better, despite the fact that I must of necessity know your name. But that all seems so unchivalrous, don't you agree?"

The man said it with a kind of infectious mirth, and Black could not help but like him even without knowing him. He didn't know whether he agreed with the sentiment or not, but, caught up in the man's charm, found himself saying, "It would be so, yes." Then he said, "And, again, your name is?"

"Dr. Horatio Stevens."

"Pleased to make your acquaintance, Dr. Stevens. I apologize, but while I was told that I would meet a person of that name, I have also been instructed, upon first setting eyes on you, to ask for proof that you are who you say you are."

"Certainly," Dr. Stevens said. He rolled up his left shirtsleeve to above the elbow and presented his upper arm for inspection.

Black peered at it and saw that it was what he had been told to expect: a roughly inked tattoo of Patrick Henry's famous words, "Give me liberty or give me death," wrapped around the man's arm in a double band.

"That seems, Dr. Stevens, an odd sentiment for a Loyalist."

"It is a sentiment I still believe in deeply, Colonel. But while this Revolution was once about liberty, and garnered my support, it no longer is. It has become instead a Revolution for merchants, bankers and planters. Not to mention France. We who love liberty will in the long run be better off staying with our king."

Black didn't know quite how to reply to that, so he just grunted. But what he remembered was what had been drummed into his head during the special training he had received prior to an earlier confidential mission: a man who has betrayed someone once will easily do it again if it profits him.

Dr. Horatio Stevens fit the bill. Likeable as he was, he had first betrayed his King and was now betraying his Revolution. Black wondered how Lord North had picked Stevens for the American end of the operation. But that was a foolish thought. Lord North had no doubt picked someone who picked someone who picked Dr. Stevens. In any case, Stevens would bear watching.

It was time to get on with it. "Dr. Stevens, do you have a plan? I was told you would have a plan with details far beyond what has already been told to me."

"Yes, Colonel, I have a new plan. Since the original plans were made, the target has unexpectedly moved. Dismount and I will tell you about it."

He hesitated. It might well be safer to stay mounted, but then again, if they wanted to do him harm, it would make little difference. The barn door was closed, and he had little idea where he was. He steeled himself, dismounted and walked slowly over to Stevens.

5

"Dr. Stevens, before we get to the plan, would you cease to call me colonel for now?" Black said. "I think you must know the reason."

"Yes, you are out of uniform. If you are caught while wearing your real one, you could argue that you should be treated as a prisoner of war. Without one..."

"I will be hanged as a spy if it becomes known that I am a soldier."

"Do you have papers that show that you are something other than a soldier?"

"Yes." He reached into his waistcoat pocket and pulled out a set of papers wrapped in oilskin. He unbundled them and handed them to Stevens. To Black's amazement, they were still dry.

Stevens read quickly through them. "These say that you have been apprenticed to an inventor in Charleston."

"Yes, and I will tell anyone who asks that because of the war and the marauding of rebel ships, I was landed in New York instead of Charleston and became lost while making my way south."

"What kind of inventor?"

"He is a man skilled at machinery who is trying, I will say, to invent a machine to separate cotton fibres from the seeds."

"Have you ever even seen any machine that does that?"

"No. That is no doubt why the man can be said to want to invent it. The patent would make him wealthy. But I have always been a good mechanic, and in my youth I worked in my father's blacksmith shop and tinkered with things. I could be of use to such a man, and I can make that story stick if pressed."

"Your youth? Good God, how old are you now?"

"Thirty-three."

"From my perspective, at an age much closer to fifty than to forty, you are still young. But be that as it may, if you are caught in the midst of this operation, Mr. Black, that cotton story will do you little good."

Stevens turned to Rufus, who had remained on his horse, and said, "Please give me the lantern."

Rufus handed Stevens the lantern, whereupon Stevens took the papers Black had given him, used the flame to light them on fire and dropped them on the ground. The papers burned and curled to ash. With his boot, Stevens ground the blackened remains into the dirt.

"There, the ridiculous cotton machine story is no more, and I will give you shortly something to replace it."

He turned once again to Rufus and said, "Rufus, you may leave us now. I will be quite safe with Mr. Black. It's best you get ahead of us, as we talked about."

Rufus nodded, turned his mount around and headed out.

After he had left, Black said, "Dr. Stevens, I am not so much wet as bone cold. Are we able to risk a fire?"

"No. But I have brought more appropriate clothes for you and they will be warmer." He pulled a shirt, pants and a jacket out of his saddlebags. "Put these on and you will be not only warmer, but less suspicious looking."

Black took them, examined them and said, "This is an American uniform, showing the rank of corporal."

"Yes, of the 1st Pennsylvania and using your real name. With it you can travel openly during the first part of the operation. The papers I will give you say you were on leave to visit your dying mother."

"This takes away any claim that I am a civilian."

"That claim was ridiculous on its face, and would not save you."

"Before we get to our final goal, I will need the uniform of a British officer. Have you been told that?"

"Yes, it was in the plan from the start, and we are working on it. For the moment, though, please put these on."

Once he had reclothed himself in what he had been handed—a dark green military-style coat with buff lapels, waistcoat and knee breeches—Black asked, "Do you have a gun for me?"

"No. You will have no need of a gun right now. I will get you one later. If you are asked, just say that you left your gun with your regiment."

Not having a gun made Black uncomfortable. He was an expert marksman and had always felt most at ease, when in the field, with a musket or pistol in his hands. But it was the Loyalists who had planned all of this, so he had no choice but to accept it for the moment.

"You mentioned we might now do this differently than I was told?" Black said.

"Ah, yes." Dr. Stevens took a long stick and began to sketch a map in the dirt floor of the barn.

"This is the shoreline—from New York to Philadelphia—and this is the small inlet where you landed." He made an X. "Washington and his staff are now headquartered in New Jersey, in a small town called Totowa, inside the Dey Mansion." He made another mark.

"I was told in England his headquarters were elsewhere."

"Since that plan of attack was sent to England, he has moved his headquarters at least twice."

"How far is Totowa?"

"About four days' hard ride. Maybe a little longer."

"The same amount of time to get back?"

"Yes."

"This could be a problem. The ship will come back for me on only eight nights. If it takes us more than eight days round trip, I will be out of luck."

"Surely, if you have Washington by then, they will come back for you anyway."

"How do you propose I let them know I have him?"

Stevens rubbed his stick back and forth in the dirt, clearly thinking, and finally said, "I see your point."

"I suppose we will just have to hurry. In any case, how are we to accomplish our goal when we get to Totowa?"

"We have acquired plans of the house in which he is staying." He drew a square in the dirt beside the first map. "It faces south down a valley. The man's office and bedroom are both on the ground floor, here, in the southeast corner." He marked a large W in the corner.

"What kind of security does he have?"

"The house and the General himself are guarded by the elite of what some call his Life Guard. Officially the Commander-in-Chief Guard."

"How many of them are there?"

"Most are out patrolling. But in and around the house, there are twenty-four. Each one of them young, tall and big. And fierce. Each one born in America. Washington doesn't trust those who were born elsewhere."

"Three watches?"

"Yes, eight soldiers in each watch. Most stationed to the east of the house, towards the British lines."

"What about the others, who aren't on watch?"

"At night, the ones who are not on duty sleep on planks laid on the rafters in the attic, above the second floor."

"What is our plan?"

"We have fifteen Loyalists who will meet us there, five sharp-shooters—two of them also excellent with a bow—and five men very good with knives."

"And the other five, who are they?"

"Rough customers. We can make use of them however it suits us."

"How will we get away?" Black said.

"They will have fresh horses with them for our use."

"We will likely be followed."

"Yes, as soon as his guard realizes Washington is gone, they will surely follow us quickly and in force. I have a ruse that I think will send them elsewhere."

"Tell me about it."

Stevens described it, and Black said, "It could work. For at least a little while. Now, if you would, tell me more details."

"We will come in from north and west of the house. The sentries are much less vigilant in that direction because the American lines are to the east of the house, and the British lines even further east, over high hills. The commanders of the guard think any attempt will likely come from the east, in an effort to flank the American lines."

"Is there anyone else in the house besides Washington and his guards?"

"Yes, the family that has lent him the house is still living there, including children."

"What will we do with them?"

"They live on the west side of the house, Washington on the east. The rough men will tie them and gag them and keep them locked in their rooms. By the time they are freed, we will be well away."

Black took a deep breath and said, "This adds much risk. And I do not wish to kill people who have not taken up arms against us. Nor children ever."

"The husband is in the militia and fights against us."

"I am not much mollified by that, but I suppose there is nothing to be done about it."

"No, there is not, but we hope not to have to kill them."

"How did you get all this information, Dr. Stevens?"

"From a spy in the ranks. A senior enlisted man."

"Why is he motivated to tell us these things?"

"The usual. Not enough to eat. No pay. Harsh officers. Thinking his enlistment has expired, but they won't let him go. There are even rumours of a coming mutiny of the Pennsylvania Line."

"This man was paid for his information?"

"Yes."

"Were you paid to change sides?"

Stevens stiffened. "No."

Black took the stick from him. "Under your plan, we have to ride four days from here—" he poked the landing site "—all the way to Totowa—" he dragged the stick between the two, leaving a deep furrow in the soil "—and then back again for four days—" he dragged the stick backwards "—with the Americans in hot pursuit."

"What is the alternative?"

Black drew a short line from Totowa to New York. "Take him to New York—it can't be more than half a day's march to the British lines, and then seek General Clinton's assistance in getting the prisoner to the ship and transporting him back to London."

"Two problems with that."

"Which are?"

"We would have to pass through American lines to reach the British, and scouts even faster than us will have been sent out to alert them to stop us."

"What else?"

"If General Clinton gets his hands on Washington he will probably hang the man himself. He is angry about Washington hanging Major Andre."

"Who is Major Andre?"

"General Benedict Arnold came over to the British side in September and tried to give the plans for the American fort at West Point to General Clinton. But his plan was foiled."

"He was caught?"

"No. But Major Andre, the British officer who was his intermediary, *was* caught—with the plans for the fort in his boot."

"Was he not just a soldier doing his duty to suborn a soldier of the other side? The rules of war permit that."

"Unfortunately, he was in civilian clothes when caught and carrying false papers, using a false name. He was judged a spy by a court martial and hanged. He was Clinton's favourite aide."

"Just as I am now wearing the clothing of the wrong army and using fake papers."

"Yes. If we are caught, perhaps it will please Clinton to have you and Washington swing together from the same gibbet."

"Along with you."

"I will be far too minor a fellow for them to waste a rope. I will be dispatched in some back alley."

After that sobering exchange Dr. Stevens said, "I have stopped hearing rain on the roof, so we'd best get under way. We have a long way to go, and we must not look like we are too much in a hurry. A soldier returning to his regiment is never anxious to get back."

"We are going to travel in the open, by day after the sun rises?"

"Yes, at least getting there. Along the way, I will school you in the politics of this rebellion and you can tell me about your mother."

"My mother?"

"Yes, the one you just took leave to visit because she was near death."

6

By the time the sun began to rise, they had left the barn behind by many miles and ridden through two small villages, both eerily quiet. Black had half-expected that they would be challenged as they passed by, but the towns had lain dead-asleep, not a lamp showing or a person stirring, and no watchman had stepped into the road to ask their business. They also came upon several small streams, but they were shallow and the horses crossed them without difficulty. Once in a while, where the water was deeper or faster, they traversed the stream via a crude bridge, or at least the bridges seemed crude to Black when he compared them to bridges he had ridden across in the English countryside.

Along the way, Stevens talked to Black about what the doctor continued to call "this rebellion" and of the strains it had brought to all, especially the shortages of everything imported, which was almost everything, but even of locally grown food.

"How is the population in these parts divided in loyalty?" Black asked.

"There are about an equal number on both sides of the argument, with many others in the middle. But those in favour of independence have seized control of the governmental machinery, so Loyalists who used to speak out openly against the so-called Revolution now stay largely silent for fear of being tarred and feathered or worse."

"Where are these Loyalists, then? They are the people I must depend on if things go awry."

"Many have left for New York, where the British still reign, or for England or Canada, so not many are left hereabouts. I will tell you who they are when you need to know. But right now I need to tell you who you are."

Stevens then told Black the story he had made up about Black's own background, in case he was challenged.

"What about you, Dr. Stevens?" Black asked. "Who are you in this charade?"

"I am your cousin, and I accompanied you to see your mother, my beloved aunt. Her name, by the way, is Constance—Constance Black."

"What if someone wants to talk to me about my experiences in battle?"

"The answer is that you joined up only at the start of the year, and that, but for a few skirmishes, you have seen almost no action except for guard duty—tedious and boring, by the way."

"I see."

"You're an officer in the British Army. Have you been in actual battles?"

"Yes."

"If it comes to that and you must describe the skirmishes, draw on that experience. No one will know the difference."

They rode on for a while. From time to time they passed men going the other way, usually on foot but twice on horseback. Black felt himself stiffen each time someone passed, but other than offering a tip of the hat and a wary "Good day," no one tried to speak to them.

As they rode along, the road—really more of a rutted cart track than what Black considered a true road—had been bordered by thick woodlands. Suddenly, it emerged into unploughed fields, where Black could see the stubble of old cornstalks protruding from the ground.

"Are you hungry, Corporal Black?" Stevens asked.

"Yes, quite starved really."

"We will soon come upon another village, where there is an inn. We can stop there and eat."

"Do you know the leanings of this village?"

"No, but it doesn't matter. You are wearing the uniform of a regiment of George Washington's army. People will know your leanings without the need to ask. If their views are contrary to yours, they will likely stay silent."

"This town you have mentioned, Dr. Stevens, the one I am to be from. What if someone else hails from thereabout?"

"It's seventy miles away in another colony. It's most unlikely."

The sign marking the inn, a two-story, red-sided clapboard structure, said, *THE LION*. The letters were painted in black on a weather-beaten wooden plaque that protruded into the road from a second-story window. Under *LION* someone had carved an outline of the very beast mentioned.

"Have you ever seen an actual lion, Dr. Stevens?" Black asked, as they dismounted.

"No."

"Well, neither had the man who carved this one, since it looks nothing like a real lion."

"You have seen one, then?"

"Yes, once, when I was but a lad. On the grounds of the Tower of London, where at one time they kept a sort of menagerie, although it is mostly gone now."

"Your family must have been of high rank to be allowed in there."

"No, much of the place was open to whoever wanted to visit there."

As they were about to go in, Stevens touched Black on the arm. "Do not forget, no one here drinks tea anymore. If you don't want beer or ale, ask for coffee."

"Thank you for reminding me."

Stevens pulled open the door and they walked inside. The place was already crowded with travellers, seated on benches pushed up to crude wooden tables, of which there were six. A fire roared in the fireplace, giving off both heat and smoke. The smell of bacon filled the room.

They looked around for a place they might be alone, but found none. They seated themselves across from one another at the end of a table at which six other men were already seated. One of the men looked over at them, nodded his head in seeming acknowledgement and turned back to the food on his plate. The other five gave no indication that they had even noted their arrival.

Soon a plump woman in a stained apron, wearing a matronly cap and carrying a pitcher of ale, appeared and said, "What will it be, gentlemen?"

"What is being served?" Dr. Stevens asked.

"We have pork and biscuits and gravy. And if you want to afford it, bacon. We have no eggs. The hens are not laying."

"And to drink?" Black asked.

"Why, ale—" she raised the pitcher as if to show it "—and coffee. And we still serve tea here, although by the looks of ye, you'll not be wanting that."

"You'd be right about that," Black said. "I'll have pork and biscuits, please, and ale."

"The same," Dr. Stevens said. "But coffee instead."

"And I will change my mind and have the coffee instead of ale, too," Black said.

She looked at Black. "You don't sound like you're from around here, Corporal."

"I'm not. I'm from near the town of Axel, in Pennsylvania. I was home on leave just now, visiting my mother, who is not long for this world, I fear."

He hoped that his statement of near bereavement would deflect the conversation from his origins.

One of the men down the table, who had not previously deigned to acknowledge them, looked up from his plate. "I myself come from near to Axel. But you don't sound as if you're from there." He paused. "You sound English."

Black saw no reason to hide it. Nor could he have done so even if he had wanted to. Instead he put a broad smile on his face, as if he'd been paid a compliment. "Indeed I am. I came here when I was eleven, apprenticed to a blacksmith in Charleston. He was cruel, and I ran away."

The others at the table had now stilled their forks and turned their attention towards him. Not, he sensed, in a friendly way. He felt a need to elaborate on his story.

"I ended in Axel, where the Blacks, who are Friends—good Quaker people—took me in and taught me to farm."

"What of your indenture to the smith?" one of the men asked. "What about that, eh?"

"Mr. Black, whose last name I took in gratitude and whom I call my father, paid off the indenture. And I am now repaying the debt to my new country."

He realized, as he spoke, that he was taking a risk. On the one hand, his thinly woven tale now had a more substantial warp and woof to it and so was perhaps more believable. On the other hand, its details would be much easier to check. He sensed Stevens, sitting next to him, wishing him to be silent.

Stevens said, "Madame, I will change my drink to ale, for I'd like to raise a toast."

She took the pitcher she still carried and filled the empty glass that had been sitting next to Stevens on the table. Black held up his own glass, indicating that she should fill it.

Stevens held his glass aloft. "To the glorious cause," he said, "and to the independence of these United States of America, and to those who fight for them." He turned to Black and bowed slightly.

There were huzzahs all around, and then all returned abruptly to eating, as if the matter were at an end.

Stevens and Black were served and finished their pork, biscuits and gravy. Stevens paid the bill, and they left. Once they were mounted and out of town, Stevens said, "You made a mistake in there."

"How?"

"Quakers oppose British taxation of the colonies, but most do not approve of war, and only a few have signed up to fight in this rebellion on either side. So they are mistrusted by all. And now you have brought that mistrust on yourself."

"What am I to do, then?"

"There is a group of Quakers called the Free Quakers, who fight in the war on the side of the so-called Patriots. If you are asked again, it is that group you are aligned with. Although it would be best if you simply left that story behind."

"Perhaps we should avoid public inns, then."

"Perhaps."

Just then, Black said, "Do you hear someone behind us?"

Dr. Stevens brought his horse to a halt and stayed Black's at the same time. They remained still and listened.

"Someone is indeed following us," Stevens said. "Take that path there—" he pointed towards a narrow side path "—and ride till you are out of sight. I will wait here for whoever is following."

"Do you have a pistol?"

"I won't need one. Now go."

7

Black urged his horse down a small trail that led off the road. After not too many yards, he edged into a thick copse of trees and pulled the horse up short. He could still see Stevens through the branches, but doubted he could be seen himself.

Not more than a minute later, the man who had challenged him at the inn rode up behind Stevens and pulled even. The two men sat talking for a moment and then began gesticulating at one another. Black strained to hear what they were saying, but caught only rising voices; clearly it was an argument. Suddenly, the man's arm shot forward, twice, and Black caught the glint of sunlight on metal. Stevens toppled from his horse onto his back and lay unmoving.

The man looked around, stopped, stared directly at the trees where Black was hiding and began to gallop directly towards him, holding the reins in one hand and the knife aloft in the other. Black broke off a stout, dry branch from a tree and rode out of the copse, spurring his horse ever faster. As the man bore down and they were about to pass each other, Black swung the tree branch like a cudgel, aiming for the man's midsection, but then, at the very last second, flipped the branch upward and connected instead with his head.

He heard the sharp crack of the man's skull breaking, followed almost instantaneously by a sound like a stick squashing a plum. The man fell onto the trail and lay there, twitching, brains oozing from his shattered head and blood pouring out of his mouth.

Black rode back to where Stevens still lay in the road, dismounted, bent down to him, opened his shirt and spread it apart. There were two large stab wounds, one in his abdomen and one on the right side of his chest, both bleeding profusely.

"I am not dead," Stevens said in a weak voice, barely above a whisper. "But I soon will be."

"I will take you back to the inn, and they will fetch a doctor."

"No, there will be too many questions. Someone will come this way soon and help me, if I can be helped, which I doubt. Take my horse. The map you will need is in the saddlebag, along with food and money. Rufus will meet you near Totowa."

"I must stay and help you."

"You must not."

And so he went. But it was with a heavy heart. He had known Stevens only briefly, but had come to like him. It was not the first time, though, that he had had to leave a dead friend behind. If, against all odds, he succeeded in this mission, he hoped to make it his last.

He rode on for several hours and managed, without dismounting, to pull the map from the saddlebag and glance at it. The route was clear enough, marked out in blue ink. The line stopped at a town called Totowa, which was circled.

He passed through several villages and nodded at the few people he came upon, wished them a good day and rode on. To his relief, they merely nodded back and returned his greeting.

He stopped twice along the way, each time riding a few hundred yards off the road into the woods and each time finding a stream where both he and the horse could drink their fill. The horse grazed on the grass by the stream bank while he supped from the meagre provisions he found in the saddlebags—hard tack and stale, coarse bread.

During his stops he took time to explore what else was in the saddlebags. There wasn't much—a well-worn copy of the Lord's Prayer, printed on foolscap, and a long, double-edged knife with a bone handle. He examined the blade, but saw no dried blood. Either it had not been recently used or had been thoroughly cleaned.

There was also a set of handwritten orders that purported to be from the commanding officer of his regiment, granting him leave to visit his mother. The papers were creased and stained, as if he'd had to produce them for inspection more than once. The orders said that he was due to report back for duty two days hence "where the regiment will be." He wondered how he was supposed to know where it would be, but pushed the question aside.

After feeling around some more inside the saddlebags, he found a small pouch sewn into a side wall. He loosened the threads at the top, burrowed his hand inside and pulled out a heavy lump of something rolled in cloth. He unwrapped it and watched six silver coins, all Spanish pieces of eight, tumble into his hand. They'd obviously been wrapped to keep them from jingling.

He dipped his hand further in and found, stuffed at the very bottom, a wad of paper bills. He unfolded them and counted six bills, each one a fifty-five-dollar note issued by the Continental Congress and dated 1780. Each said on its face that the bearer was entitled to receive the equivalent amount in Spanish milled dollars or an equal sum in gold or silver. It seemed far too large an amount for a poor soldier to be carrying. He put one bill in a waistcoat pocket and shoved the other bills and the coins back in the pouch. He pulled the threads tight and hoped there'd be no jingle as he rode. If the money—he assumed it to be a veritable fortune in a land racked by war—were discovered he'd quickly be unmasked as something more than a simple soldier.

At the end of his second foray into the woods, he looked at the position of the sun in the sky, which he could just make out through a small gap in the trees. He judged that it would be dark in less than two hours. Not that he had any kind of timepiece to measure the exact passage of the hours.

It was going to be far too cold to sleep outside, and in any case the saddlebags contained no blankets. He looked again at the map and saw that there was a nearby town on the blue line. Perhaps he could reach it before dark and find an inn and a bed for the night, which surely would have been Dr. Stevens's plan in any case. He returned to the road and set off at as fast pace as the horse, who'd already carried him a far piece, was willing to go. The increasingly rutted track did not make the trip easier.

He reached the town just as the sun was setting and came immediately upon an inn and tavern called The Oaks. He noticed there was a blank space between the words *The* and *Oaks*. Looking more closely, he could see that the word *Royal*, which had once been in between, had been painted over, along with the image of a crown above it. It seemed a good place for a soldier fighting on the side of the Revolution to spend the night.

He tied his horse to a hitching post in front, took the saddlebag off and knocked on the door. A comely young woman, neither short nor tall, with blue eyes and with blonde hair wrapped in a bun atop her head, greeted him. He judged her no more than twenty years of age.

"Good evening, soldier."

"Good evening, ma'am. I am Jeremiah Black. I would like dinner and a room for the night if you have it."

"We have both dinner and a room. The hot dinner is one and

ninety, the room is two—you will share with three others—and breakfast in the morning, if wanted, is another one."

"I wish a room for myself only if that can be done." As soon as he said it, he realized he had set himself apart from a mere soldier. But it was now too late to take it back.

She raised her eyebrows. "If you are the last guest we get for the night we will have a room for you alone, at six. If other guests by chance come later and share the room, I will reduce the price."

"That is without problem."

She looked over his shoulder and regarded the horse. "Pasture for the horse for twenty-four hours is four."

"Just pasturage?"

"We can also give him a bucket of oats for another two."

It occurred to him that he should not agree to the prices too easily.

"We will be here only until the morning," he said. "We will not need the pasture for many hours."

She smiled. "A fair point. I will give you the pasturage for early morning anyway if you want it, a barn for the horse for the night *and* the oats, all for four."

"Agreed."

"How do you propose to pay, soldier? We do not take barter here." She looked him up and down, then glanced at the saddlebags in his hand and again at the horse. "Not that you appear to have any pig or such to barter with."

"I have notes of the Continental Congress."

She gave him a strange look. "Most people call them Continentals."

"Of course" was all he could think of to say.

She pursed her lips. "The prices I quoted you were in shillings and pence, which is what most people hereabouts have, although the few who are very wealthy use Spanish gold or silver milled dollars."

Black felt relief that he had not taken out the Spanish coins, which would have raised questions about where he came upon such wealth. And he was also glad he had taken the time to read the text on the notes. "Continentals are equal to Spanish milled dollars," he said. "They say so." He took one from his waistcoat pocket and held it out to her.

She made no effort to take the proffered bill from him. "That may be what is written on them, but so many have been printed that they are now close to worthless. Surely you know that."

He decided not to try to explain away his ignorance. "I will need to go elsewhere, then."

"No, since you are a soldier, and in support of our glorious Revolution—" she paused as if to emphasize that she had said it with sarcasm "—I will take them. But you must pay in advance. It totals to twelve and ninety, assuming breakfast."

He gave her a broad smile and raised his eyebrows. "Do you recommend the breakfast?"

"Why yes, since I make it myself." She smiled back at him.

With the thought that he might later need her help for something—and she was not an unattractive woman—he replied, "If you make it, I'm sure it is indeed excellent."

He watched her blush and again handed her the fifty-five-dollar note. This time she took it. "I will have change," he said.

When she had the bill in hand, she turned it over a few times and said, "Where did you get this note, soldier? It looks almost new."

"I have just come from my mother's deathbed. This and a little more was all she left me. My brother took the bedstead, the pots and the dresser."

"You got the raw end of that deal."

"Yes, I did. Having the room to myself will be little enough to salve the hurt."

"I have kept you standing here in the doorway long enough," she said. "I will show you to your room, and then I will get your change, which will buy you almost nothing. Except from me." She smiled at him.

Black wondered, briefly, why she was being so accommodating, but pushed the thought aside. Perhaps she was attracted to him.

She led him up a rickety stairway to the second level. The room was small, but clean, and it had four narrow beds, each with homespun sheets somewhat the worse for wear, and two rough woollen blankets, folded at the bottom of the bed. There was a bowl and pitcher on the dresser.

"Is there hot water?" he asked.

"It can be boiled up for another…"

"Continental?"

"Yes, but because you are a soldier, I will do it for free." She smiled at him again, and he thought that if he had not been on a mission, he might have arranged to stay another night.

She grabbed the pitcher and headed for the door. "Dinner is in one hour."

"If you don't mind, I prefer to eat alone. I am in grief and do not want to have to talk to others about my mother. Or the war, for that matter."

"We can do that," she said. "There is a small table to the side where I can seat you."

"What is your name, miss?"

"Mary. Mary White. That makes us black and white." She gave him still another smile and left.

She returned after not very long with a pitcher of hot water. He washed up and went down to dinner, taking his saddlebags with him. She seated him at a side table, as promised. Glancing at the saddlebags, she said, "You fear theft?"

"I fear the loss of the few small things of my mother's that I brought away with me."

"I see. And I understand."

He placed the saddlebags under his chair and waited to be

served. He looked over at the main table, where six rather rough-looking men were seated. They paid him no attention. Which was fortunate; he didn't want to try out his story again. Soon after, a new group of four entered the room and seated themselves at another table. They, too, paid him no attention.

The meal, when it came, was hot and filling—biscuits, beef with gravy and peas. He wondered how the inn had come by the food, since Dr. Stevens had told him, while educating him about the political situation, that such things, especially beef, were in short supply.

When he was done, Mary approached him, holding a plate which held a large piece of pie. "I have made an apple-rhubarb and have a piece for you in honour of your service. Free."

"Thank you, Mary White. I have a great love for pie. It reminds me of my mother."

"You are most welcome, Corporal Black." She set the pie down in front of him, and he devoured it. He had always loved the combination of sweet and tart that the apple and rhubarb combination brought, although this one had perhaps too much rhubarb. He thought to ask for another piece, but thought better of it since he was getting sleepy.

Back in his room, he decided to leave his uniform on lest he needed to flee in the middle of the night. Once he lay down it struck him that he ought not leave his saddlebags on the floor, for the room had no lock. He reached down to lift them up and put them under his head, even then struggling to stay awake long enough to do it. The last thought he had before sleep took him was that he had liked Dr. Stevens and was sorry he was gone.

8

Black awoke in the dead of night, groggy and with a great ache on the back of his head, as if he'd been clubbed. He was enough awake to realize that something sharp was pushed against his throat and that the saddlebags were no longer under his head. He tried to raise his arms to push the sharp thing away, but found they were tied rightly around his waist. He tried to jump up, but his legs were tightly bound at the ankles.

He could feel the hot breath of someone hovering over him. "What did you do with Dr. Stevens?" a voice asked. "Did you kill him?" When the voice spoke that second time, he realized it was Mary.

To admit to knowing Dr. Stevens would be to admit much, so he said nothing.

"If you don't answer me, Corporal, I will slit your throat from ear to ear."

He tried to speak but his throat was dry, and only a croak came out. He tried again. "What would you do with my body?"

"If you are the Englishman I think you, the men at dinner will help me bury you and whistle while they do it."

"There were other men at the second table last night. If I scream, they will come to investigate."

"They also enjoyed my pie. And ate more of it. Now tell me where Dr. Stevens is. Or I will slit you and be done with it."

Clearly, he needed to admit to knowing Stevens. The question was how much to admit. "We were on our way here," he said. "We were waylaid on the road, just after lunch. He was mortally wounded."

There was a long pause, and he heard her suck in her breath. Finally, she said, "Why didn't you stay with him?"

"He told me to ride on."

"To go where?"

A half-truth might do for now. "He gave me the map in the saddlebags, and this town was circled, so I rode here. Yours was the first inn I came upon."

She said nothing for a moment, as if considering his answer. "I looked at your map. Totowa is also circled."

"That it is."

"Tell me why." She pressed the blade more tightly against his throat. Any harder and he would bleed.

If she is a Patriot, he thought, the truth will surely kill me. If a Loyalist, the truth might save me. He sensed her somehow false to the Patriot cause, but it was in reality nothing more than a desperate hunch.

"My mission is in Totowa."

He felt the knife ease up slightly. "What mission, exactly?"

"To take George Washington back to England to stand trial for high treason. I am an officer of His Majesty's Army sent by His Majesty to carry out that mission." He thought briefly of adding that he could instead choose to kill Washington because his orders didn't expressly forbid it. But he decided to keep that to himself. Perhaps because he had thought increasingly about that option, and how much easier it would be to carry out than getting Washington back to the ship.

The knife left his throat, but she made no move to untie him. He waited silently, sensing that his life was still in the balance. Finally, she spoke. "We will go to Totowa together."

"Will you untie me now, then?"

"We will need to talk more first."

"What about?"

"About whether you are who you say you are."

"Who else would I be? I've just told you things that would see me hanged from a tree if they were revealed to many hereabouts. I am in a false uniform."

"You could be an agent of the rebellion, sent to infiltrate the Loyalist resistance. With a faked map and a pretty story."

He thought for a moment. "I see no way to persuade you by mere words, and a man's loyalties are hardly engraved on his forehead." He paused. "Nor a woman's, for that matter."

"This is true," she said.

"So, we are at an impasse."

She laughed. "Hardly that. You are still tied. I still have your knife, and I can still use it."

"Have you ever killed anyone, Mary?"

"Not yet."

"It is a messy business, especially up close."

"This entire rebellion has proved a messy business. You would not be the first to die messily in it."

"Have many died hereabouts?"

She snorted. "Ha! Many Loyalists have died. Or lost their property. These so-called Revolutionaries are nothing more than the low classes, those without property who wish to take our property for themselves. Had I let my true feelings be known, we would have lost this inn."

"We?"

"My husband and I."

"Where is your husband?"

"He is away. And according to you, dead."

"Dr. Stevens is your husband?"

"Yes."

"So you are not Mary White, but Mary Stevens."

"I was once Mary White. But that matters not. Now tell me more of what you say happened to him."

He told her, and when he was done, he heard her quietly crying. "I would comfort you if you would release me, Mary."

"I need not your comfort, and I dare not release you without someone else here because I don't know whether to trust your story or not." She got up and said, "It would be foolish for you to try to escape or make a sound." She left the room.

He tested the ropes that bound his hands and legs. They were still tight. Even if he could somehow loosen them, he would have little chance of getting away. The best thing he could do was to ride to Totowa with Mary—if she was really planning to go there—and somehow be rid of her on the way or just after he got there. Rufus had ridden ahead, so perhaps he would be there, too. And there were the fifteen Loyalists Dr. Stevens had promised would meet up with them.

Minutes passed, and he heard only the faint chirping of the birds that begin to sing just before dawn. Perhaps Mary was simply gathering up a group to bury him.

His increasingly morbid thoughts were interrupted by the sound of the door opening. The room was still mostly dark, but he could make out Mary and several men she had brought back with her. She carried a lit candle and he saw they were three of the six men who had been at dinner the night before. One man was a true giant, well over six feet tall and burly.

"Bear," Mary said, addressing the giant, "untie him. If he tries anything, hit him with this." She handed the man a wooden cudgel. "I used it on him last night after the pie took him down but left him still stirring."

"What are we to do with him?" Bear asked.

"We'll go to Totowa, as Dr. Stevens planned. And meet up there with the others. If this man is who he says he is, we will need him."

"How do you know to trust him?" Bear asked.

"We don't, but Rufus is to be at an inn nearby, and he will tell us if this man is who he says he is since Rufus was to be at the beach."

Black said nothing. What would happen if Rufus failed to show up?

Bear asked the same question, except out loud. "And if Rufus doesn't come, Mary, then what?"

"What would *you* have us do in that case?" Mary asked.

"Kill him," Bear said.

Black had been listening to their discussion with mounting apprehension. The more they talked about him as if he were an object, the more danger he was in. He had also noticed that the other three men were clenching and unclenching their fists.

Black decided to make himself part of the conversation. "There is also a question why I should trust *you*," he said.

"Yes, there is that," Mary said. "But if neither of us can trust the other, you are the one tied up in the bed. If we kill you, we might eliminate the good to be gained from you, but we will also take away the risk."

"I will offer you something," Black said. "I will tell you how Washington is to be gotten back to England—which beach is the pickup beach. Without that information, your whole venture on behalf of your king will be useless."

"Some of us are of the opinion," Bear said, "that the rebellion will collapse if the General is shot dead. A trial in London of Washington might make our good King George smile, but it will do us no good here. So why kidnap him? It would be so much simpler to kill him. I would enjoy doing it with my own hands."

"And some of us are of a different opinion," Mary said.

"And what opinion is that?" Bear asked.

"That the authorities in London know what they are about, and that putting Washington on trial there for treason will bring the rebels to bargain for a settlement. Then Loyalists like us can live in peace, and with our properties intact."

Black interrupted. "I have spoken of this very thing with Lord North himself," he said. Which was a lie because Lord North had mentioned no such thing to him. But it seemed the right thing to say.

Mary, who had been facing Bear, whirled and looked hard at him. "You met with the First Minister?"

"Yes. It is he who gave me my direct orders. And while there is disagreement in the government over whether Washington is more help to us dead or on trial, or whether his absence from the rebellion will make any difference at all, the King wants to see him tried—and watch him suffer a traitor's death. You are all loyal subjects of the Crown and should do as your king commands. As I am doing."

No one said anything. As he waited for someone to speak, Black knew that his invocation of the King might be thought false in itself. What proof did he have that he had met with Lord North? To these people he might as well have said that he'd met with Moses.

Finally, Mary said to Bear, "Untie him, but keep a close eye on him, and search him for small knives and any orders he may carry."

Once his hands were freed, she turned to Black and said, "One false move and we will kill you." Hardly had she finished speaking than she began to weep, and he heard her say aloud, amidst copious tears, "All this killing. So many friends, and now my husband, too. What will end this war?"

9

They rode out at dawn—Black, Mary, Bear and the two other men, who'd yet to identify themselves by name. Bear carried a long gun, and he assumed the others carried hidden knives or pistols. Before they mounted, Bear had clamped a heavy brass ring around his right ankle and pulled his legging over it to conceal it, which it did poorly. "You won't be able to run far with that," he had said. "And if you try, I will catch you and carve you up."

They'd given him the horse he'd ridden in on the day before, which seemed refreshed. His saddlebags had been put back in place, although he didn't know if any of their contents had been restored. He assumed the money was gone. And Mary had the knife.

For the first little while, they rode in silence, passing people on foot, two or three people on horseback and a few small carts bumping over the ruts, all heading the other way. Mary rode beside him, with the others trailing behind. Finally, he said, "Why is everyone else going the other way?"

"It's a market day in town."

"How long a ride between here and Totowa?"

"Likely three days of riding if we make good progress without interruption, to a town a few miles short of Totowa itself. Beyond that town, we will be challenged."

"What could interrupt us, Mary?"

"Soldiers of Washington's Life Guard riding the countryside on patrol to see what is what."

"How will I know if we come upon them?"

"They have an arrogance about them hard to miss. Most wear tall leather or bearskin helmets with a white feather plume tipped in blue. Always on the left. They might as well be guarding a king."

No sooner had she finished speaking than a soldier in an American uniform approached on foot and caught his eye. Black stiffened, but the man merely saluted. Black returned the salute, and the man walked on.

"Where do you think that soldier is heading, Mary?"

"Probably to break into a farm to steal chickens. Washington's army is ill fed, and the soldiers pillage what they need. Usually at night, though, so perhaps he has a different mission today."

"That cannot build loyalty from local folks."

"It's why so many hereabouts, while they shout loyalty to the rebel cause, pine, in this fifth year of war, for the British to return."

"If the soldiers pillage, then the army is not well led."

"Have you ever led hungry men?"

"No. But what is the opinion of people here about Washington? The papers in England say he is a great leader, and that he is indispensable to the cause. The most famous person in the world, some call him."

She paused for a moment, then said, "Others are of the opinion that he just looks good on a horse."

Black laughed. "Surely there is more to it than that."

"We shall see," she said, "how he leads from the Tower when he is in London and how indispensable he is there."

"Tell me about Washington's Life Guard," he said. "In England, they told me this guard is more than two hundred men, each one strong and loyal."

"That is so, but not all are there at once, and they are now more relaxed because they are further from British lines than where Washington was headquartered before, and they have high hills surrounding them."

"Who is their commander?"

"We are in luck there because their Captain-Commandant, William Colfax, is on leave to see his ailing son. His second-in-command is also away, and so they are left with Rufus Gilbert in charge for the moment. He is a less careful man. And tends to the drink."

"How do you know all this, Mary?"

She turned, looked at him and shrugged. "Spies. There are spies everywhere in this war. On both sides, and sometimes on both sides at the same time."

"Everyone thinks you a Patriot?"

"I hope so. Certainly, we attend all of the Patriot town meetings and such."

"How did you know that I was not a Patriot soldier?"

"It is in part the way you carry yourself. The way you move. You are clearly not from here or anywhere even close to here."

"Then I must, perhaps, learn to carry myself otherwise."

"Perhaps. But I also had a sense of you as foreign. You came as if from nowhere, and you were carrying too much money for a mere soldier on leave. And you didn't even know what to call the paper bills." She laughed.

"Is that all?" He smiled in a way to try to make light of it. But she had named too many things that set him apart. He would have to be even more on guard about it. And maybe try to say even less.

"No, that was not all," she said. "I also knew my husband was to meet a man at the beach and bring him back."

"I see."

They rode on in silence for a while after that, and she asked, "Do you think there is any chance that my husband survived his wounds?"

He thought for a moment how to answer, for he didn't want to give her false hope. Finally, he said, "I fear to say I think it unlikely."

She said nothing, and after a few moments, he said, "Do you have children, Mary?"

"I had three," she said. "They all died before the age of two. I blame it on this war. My milk did not come in, and wet nurses were hard to find. And, well, it doesn't matter now."

"How old are you, Mary?"

"Twenty-nine."

"You look much younger."

"So I am oft told."

They rode on for a while in silence until he felt it grow awkward. Mary must have, too, because she said, "I need to find a way for a few moments not to think of my husband. Tell me some about yourself."

"What is it you wish to know?"

"Are you married?"

"No."

"That surprises." She turned her head and smiled at him. "There must be many a woman back in England who would find you handsome, with your dark hair and blue eyes."

Black felt himself blushing. "There may be a few, but much of my life as a soldier has been spent away from England, on the Continent, and I have not thought it right to visit my many absences upon a wife. Perhaps when this mission is over."

"That is another thing I have wondered. How came you to this thing?"

"When I first became an officer, there was a mission that needed a lieutenant who was both fast of foot and strong. I am indeed fast, and even though short, very strong."

"I saw that when, even after eating my pie, you struggled to get up, and I had to push you back down."

He rubbed the back of his head, which was still sore. "And then hit me with a club of some sort."

"No, rather with a large book."

He expected her to apologize, but she did not.

"And so you now are chosen often for duties of this sort?" she asked.

"Yes."

They rode on again in silence. Finally, she made a motion with her hand towards the rear and dropped back, quickly replaced by Bear, who gave him a curt nod but did not utter a word.

A sense of foreboding suddenly descended on him. Lord North's aide had told him that he would meet up with a group that had made the detailed plans that were needed. His task would be only to arrest Washington and get him back to the waiting ship. Instead he found himself with a group of people who might be Loyalists or might just be taking him to Totowa to turn him in, collect reward money and stay to see him hanged.

Bear had apparently been thinking, too, because, after a while, he said, "I have been thinking on how to know if you be true or false."

"And?"

"With Dr. Stevens dead, there is no sure way to know. And Rufus, if he has survived, is still days ahead of us."

"He can identify me then."

"Yes, unless you are false, in which case, you may be leading Rufus and the rest of us to our doom—for the rebels to hang all in a row."

Suddenly, Black saw, cantering towards them, a soldier sitting tall in the saddle and wearing the helmet Mary had described—dark leather with, on the left side, a white feather plume tipped in blue. The man pulled up sharply only a few feet in front of them, causing their own horses to rear up. Three other soldiers on horseback were close behind the first, but hung back a few feet. They were all big men, dressed identically, and indistinguishable except for the leader, who had a vivid red scar across his cheek. Unlike the others, he also had a small red feather stuck amidst the white ones in his plume.

When the horses had settled, the man with the scar looked at Black and said, "Who are you, soldier, and what is your business in these parts?"

"I am Jeremiah Black. I have been on leave from the 1st Pennsylvania to visit my dying mother. I am on my way back to my unit."

"And who are these people with you?"

"Owners and friends of an inn at which I stayed last night. They were riding the same way as I, and we chose to ride together."

"That is a nice story," the soldier said.

"It was also for companionship. And for me, so I can push my mother's death out of my mind."

The man squinched his eyes up, as if weighing the tale. He appeared to be unarmed, but the three men behind him all had their hands on their sword hilts. Black feared the soldier questioning him would notice the bulge of the brass ring beneath his leggings, but the man kept his focus on his face.

"Let me see your orders," he said.

Black didn't know if Mary had left his fake orders in his saddlebags. There was nothing but to try it. He reached down, found with relief that they were there and pulled them out. "Here," he said.

The man made a show of examining the papers, turning his head this way and that as if trying to judge their authenticity.

He finally handed them back and said, "They appear genuine. But you are approaching the territory we protect for the safety of His Excellency, General Washington, and his staff."

"I did not know," Black said. "I am sorry."

"Good. If after tomorrow we see you anywhere other than on the direct route back to your unit, we will have cause to detain you and investigate this further."

Without a word of goodbye, he turned and rode off, followed by the other three. When they had gotten perhaps twenty feet away, the leader turned briefly to stare back at Black, as if to fix his face in his memory.

After they had left, Black said, "Why does the man with the scar on his cheek have a red feather in his plume, whereas the others do not?"

"I don't know," Mary said. "A sign of leadership, maybe. Or he's just a dandy and they permit it."

"Bear, have you ever seen a red feather like that before?" Black asked.

"Never."

"I have an uneasy feeling about this," Black said. "Because if we come upon those four again, we will be even closer to Washington's headquarters, and we will look even more suspicious. My soldier-on-leave story will no longer persuade them."

"What do you suggest?" Bear asked.

"Try to kill them if we can." He paused. "Mary, please give me the knife back."

Without a word, she handed it to him.

10

The following days of travel proved uneventful. The first night, Black, Mary and Bear—the other two had disappeared before nightfall, and he got no answer as to where they had gone—stayed at an inn called The Crow, where no one paid them much notice. In the morning Bear paid the bill, explaining to the innkeeper that Black was his cousin and telling the usual story. The second night, they stayed in a barn, because there were not many towns and even fewer inns.

As the next day dawned, they rode out of the barn, saying almost nothing to one another. The road, which had now deteriorated from a rutted cart track into a narrow trail, passed through deep woods. They were challenged twice by roving patrols, all wearing the blue-tipped, white-feathered cockade of Washington's personal guard. They did not run into the original patrol again, and Black's papers, which were given only a cursory look, seemed to pass muster without problem even though they were not truly on a path back to the lines of the 1st Pennsylvania.

As they rode away from the second patrol, Bear said, "Whoever forged those orders did a good job."

"It was my husband," Mary said. "May he rest in peace."

"Amen," they all said in almost the same breath, then rode on again in silence. Black could hear Mary crying quietly to herself. He wished again that there was a way to comfort her.

At the end of that day, they stopped at The Tankard, a run-down place with a mug of ale stencilled on a faded wooden sign that hung above the front door. A crudely lettered wooden plank nailed to the gate said, "Closed." Mary ignored it and pushed through. They rode their horses around to the back and left them inside a tumbledown barn, inside of which someone had left fresh hay and water.

They went into the inn through a back entrance. In the dim light—no lanterns were lit—Black immediately spotted Rufus sitting and looking at something on the run-down table.

"Mary, this is Rufus," Black said.

"I already know him," Mary said.

Rufus looked up at the three of them. "Mary, if you and Bear could leave us alone for a few minutes?"

Mary nodded, and they left the room.

Rufus turned and fixed Black with a cold stare. "Where is Dr. Stevens?"

"Dead, or at least I assume he is."

"What happened?"

Black told the story again and ended by saying, "I have seen many injuries, and I doubt any man could survive such a wound, even with the best surgeon to tend to him."

Rufus grunted. "He was a good man. And this war is such a gruesome thing, setting one good man against another. Six or seven years ago the man who killed him would have been drinking to his health or seeking him out to doctor his sick child."

"Why did you send Mary and Bear out of the room?" Black asked.

"They know certain things but not other things."

"Do I know all the things *I* need to know, Rufus?"

"You will, soon enough. We are only a few miles from Totowa."

"Thus, this is the night?" Black said.

"Yes, and a good one it is because the word is out that they will very soon move the headquarters elsewhere."

"I am more than agreeable to go tonight. This is the end of the fourth day since I was landed on the beach. If we delay and come upon anything unexpected, I may lack time to get back to the beach by the eighth night. They are not coming back for me after that."

A look of surprise passed across Rufus's face. "I did not know that."

"Dr. Stevens knew."

"You must have told him after I left the barn," Rufus said. "Why did they put that condition on your mission? It is foolish."

"I do not know. Although I have my suspicions."

"What are they?"

"They are not anxious for me to succeed. They may instead want Washington to die in the attempt. And perhaps us along with him."

Rufus said nothing for a while. Finally, he spoke. "This has been too long and carefully planned on this side of the Atlantic, guided by London, for that to be true. Or so I think. But this night is in any case a good night for another reason. Washington has reduced the personal guard immediately around him from twelve to eight, in order to grant more leaves, both to the guard and to others."

"Why?"

"We have a man in Washington's retinue. He reports to us that Washington's spies in New York have told him that Clinton has given up on capturing him."

"Why would Washington believe that?"

"Because General Clinton has known for almost two weeks exactly where Washington is but has made no move to come after him."

"Do you have confidence, then, in your own man? That this story is not bait for a trap?"

Rufus shrugged. "He has not led us astray before."

"When precisely does your man say Washington is moving his headquarters?"

"In a day or two. They will begin packing up tomorrow."

"All right. Tell me the plan."

Rufus walked towards a fireplace, the bottom of which was covered with a fine layer of white ash. He grabbed a stick that was leaning to the side and began to draw in the ash, much as Dr. Stevens had drawn in the dirt of the barn.

"This," he said, drawing a small square, "is the headquarters building. It's a two-story house, known locally as Dey house, lent to the General by the wealthy merchant John Hackett. Washington's bedroom is on the bottom floor, in the southwest corner." He drew an X in the proper place.

"What time will we strike?" Black asked.

"At 1:00 a.m."

"Is that not too early? Washington may still be awake when we arrive."

"True, but more important is that the guard shift changes at 2:00 a.m. By 1:00 the guards on duty will be tired."

"What of the guards who are not on duty?"

"They sleep on a platform in the rafters above the second floor. Our man says it is hard to hear from there what is happening far below."

"Won't they be stirring, Rufus, in preparation for their shift?"

"According to what he has told us, the guards seize every minute of sleep that belongs to them."

"Where are Washington's senior officers?"

"Our man says Hamilton and the rest of them are down in

the valley with the army, and that the less senior officers sleep in a different house."

"You rely a lot on this one man," Black said.

"I have little choice."

"All right. Do go on."

Rufus took the stick and placed eight dots around the house. "There are eight pickets in all. Usually three behind and five in front. They are supposed to patrol, but our man says that late at night, they do not. They just stand their station."

"Why only three behind?"

"The short of it is that the commander of the guard believes that if the British punch through the American lines and reach the house, they will have to come from the front."

"Why not from the back?"

"The British would come in at least company strength—a minimum of fifty men—and the terrain behind is too rough for that."

"Won't we need to pass through that same terrain?"

"No. Because we pass easily for Patriots, we can take the trail that goes through the low part of the valley for a good part of the way and then, before we reach the bottom of the valley, go up and then down a very large hill and flank the house from the rear. I have reconnoitred the trail twice, both times pretending to gather firewood."

"Do you have a plan to overcome the guards?"

Before Rufus could answer, the door opened and five men, led by Mary, entered. Each wore darkened clothes and had blackened their faces and the backs of their hands with soot. All were tall, but lithe. They nodded at Black.

"These men will overcome the guards," Rufus said. "I thought it best they see you and you them so you will not kill each other. The password, if you are challenged, is Liberty."

"The noise these men make as they shoot the guards will rouse everyone in the house," Black said.

Almost as one, the men pulled long knives from their belts and held them aloft.

"If God is with us, no guns will be needed," Rufus said.

"Will these men have no guns at all, then?"

"They will have pistols but hope not to use them."

"And as for me?"

"We have both a knife and a pistol for you. I will give them to you after these men leave."

"I see. You said when we were in the barn that there would be fifteen men in all, including five sharpshooters."

"They will also be there. Mainly to cover our retreat. We have told them not to use their guns unless it can't be helped."

"How will you coordinate the time of the attack?"

Rufus pulled out a pocket watch. It was gold, about two inches wide. He held it up.

"I have this watch, and the leader of these men has one, too."

The largest of the men raised his hand. "I am Horst," he said and used his other hand to pull out an identical watch. He held it up for all to see.

"In England I have only seen those in the hands of the rich," Black said.

"Here, too. But we have been planning this for many months, and we have put together what we need."

"Can you make them tell the same time?"

"Yes, we matched the time on the two watches before you arrived," Rufus said. "They gain or lose minutes easily over a day's time, but they should stay together for the next few hours."

"When will they strike?" Black asked.

"At 12:45. God willing, we will arrive at 1:00 and find they have eliminated the pickets behind the house."

"And what of the guards in front?" Black asked.

"They are a hundred yards to the front. If all goes well, they won't even know we were there."

Black waited a moment, then said, "And the guards at the doors and inside?"

"We will deal with them when we get there. These five gentlemen will be with us."

"Rufus, I now have some things to discuss with you in private," Black said. He looked over at Mary and the five men. "I do not mean to offend."

Rufus turned to them and said, "We will see you at the house. Godspeed." They left wordlessly.

Rufus got up and began to pace the room. "What do you want to know, Colonel?"

"Bear didn't return with Mary. Where is he?"

"He has left to scout the Totowa house. He'll be used as needed. Why do you ask?"

"I think he's a danger to my mission. *Our* mission."

"Why?"

"He wants to kill Washington. My orders are to take him prisoner."

"Bear will follow orders."

"Whose orders? He is not subject to some military command."

"My orders. I have known him since he was a small boy. He talks big, but he does as he's told."

"I hope you are right."

"What else?"

"You have known from the beginning that to do this in the way the Prime Minister desires—to have it be an official act of the King bringing a traitor to justice—I need a British officer's uniform. Do you have it?"

"Is that the only reason?"

"Of course not. As you know, if I'm caught in this American uniform, I'll be hanged as a spy. If I'm wearing a British uniform, I have a right under the laws of war to attempt sabotage behind enemy lines. I must be treated as a prisoner of war."

Rufus laughed. "Colonel, if you're caught trying to harm His

Excellency, as they all call him, you will likely be killed on the spot. British uniform or no British uniform. Law or no law."

"Still..." Black said.

Rufus interrupted him. "I have planned for this. Come with me."

He led Black to a back room, where the red coat of a British officer's uniform was laid out.

Black walked over to it. "Where did you get it?"

"Yesterday, from a dead redcoat. By luck a dead colonel, whom I judged to have been about your size."

"How did he die? There are no marks on it."

"We don't know."

Black had the sense he was lying but decided not to press it. "What about my old American uniform?"

"We might need it in the escape. Let's keep it. Go change into the new one. When the sun sets we'll get on towards Totowa. While we wait, we can talk about the plans we have to get His Excellency back to the beach once we have him in hand. I will also work on preparing the ruse we discussed."

When Black returned to the room some time later, resplendent in his borrowed red jacket, Rufus looked him over and said, "You look every inch the British officer."

Black smiled. "That's because I am one. And how goes the ruse?"

Rufus held up a scroll of parchment. "I've finished it and hope it will work."

"Let us pray it will work," Black said. "Or this will all have been for naught."

"It's time to go now," Rufus said.

They gathered what they needed—which included a pistol and knife for each of them—and set off into the night. Rufus led the way.

11

They had walked for hours along rough trails bordered by deep woods, when, suddenly, Black heard voices. Rufus grabbed his arm and jerked him into the trees. He held his breath as a patrol of soldiers wearing the blue-tipped feathers walked by—strolled really—talking amongst themselves and heading in the direction from which he and Rufus had just come.

He heard one say, "Why are we doing this? If the redcoats come, they will come overland in formation from the east, like they always do."

"Yah," someone else said.

He was grateful that, before they left The Tankard, he had donned an overcoat Rufus had given him to protect against the cold. He knew it was irrational, but Black feared that otherwise the red of his coat would have been visible, even through the trees.

They waited there for at least ten minutes, until they were sure the patrol had moved on.

"Let's go," Rufus said. "We need to hurry because it smells

and feels as if there will soon be rain. We must shortly cross a river, using a ford, rather than the nearby bridge. The ford will be easy to use now because the water is likely low, but a hard rain will make it much more difficult."

Black looked up, but couldn't see the sky. "If the smells of rain are the same here as in England, it does indeed seem as if rain is on the way."

Rufus seemed to know the intricate way from trail to trail, including the location of the ford, which turned out to have not much water in it. After a while, he used a flint to light a candle inside a small, triangular lantern he'd been carrying. He leaned towards Black and said, in a voice so low Black had to strain to hear, "We have to take even rougher side paths now and hope no one sees this light. I don't think we're likely to run into any more patrols back here. The guard will assume redcoats will stick to the main trails."

Their progress was slow because the lantern gave little light. The path had been so little used that branches overhung it in many places, and rains had exposed rocks under foot. After a while, the trail began to climb, which slowed their progress even more.

Eventually, the trail sloped downward at a sharp angle and then crossed on the level through thick woods. After not too long, Rufus took out his pocket watch and consulted it by the light of the lantern. He leaned close and whispered in Black's ear, "It's 12:30. Around the next bend, we will be able to see the house." He reached into the lantern and snuffed out the candle with his fingers.

They reached the edge of the trees and saw, at a distance of several hundred yards across cleared land, a barely made-out two-story stone house with a mansard roof. A single light shone in one of the windows.

Rufus sat down on the ground and gestured that Black should do the same. "We will wait till 1:00," he said.

The night was utterly still. Black's thoughts flew to the bloody work that Rufus's men were carrying out, at least if all was going according to plan. Had they been using guns, he would have heard the shots. The sound of a knife slitting someone's throat wouldn't carry. He was a hardened soldier, and yet he felt for the young men who were to die that night.

Finally, as the cold of the night seemed to be settling into his bones, Rufus leaned towards him and said, "To the house now. The task is either done or it's not. If not, we'll be caught no matter what we do, so there's little point in sneaking up."

They rose and walked openly towards the house. When they reached it, the back door was hanging open. A dead soldier lay to one side, the blood from his throat staining the white plume on his helmet. Not far away, another soldier was sprawled on his back, close by a wall of the house, an arrow buried deep in his chest. Black assumed he had tumbled from the steep roof. Black dropped his overcoat, removed the pistol Rufus had given him from the small sack in which he had been carrying it, charged it with powder, loaded in the ball and walked boldly in, followed by Rufus.

Black found himself in a wood-planked entry hall, at the end of which was the front door to the house. In a corner to the left of the door stood a large grandfather clock. The door was guarded by a man with a long gun. The man seemed to know who Rufus and Black were since he didn't challenge them.

"Where is the family that lives here?" Black said. "Have you locked them away or did you kill them, too?"

"Neither," the man said. "We have luck tonight because all of the family are at a funeral in another town and won't return until tomorrow." Then, with a nod of his head, he motioned them through an open doorway in the left-hand wall. Rufus started to go through, but Black put out his hand and blocked his way. Whatever risk there might be on the other side, Black would take first.

He walked through the door and saw a tall, stately man standing calmly beside an elegant rosewood writing desk, which was pushed against the wall. He was wearing silver-framed reading glasses. Rufus's five hired killers—which was how Black had come to think of them—stood post around the room. Three had pistols at the ready, and one of those had a bow slung over his shoulder and a quiver of arrows on his back. The other two held long guns. One said, "We told him if he makes a sound we'll kill him." To Black's surprise and distress, Bear was also in the room.

He had not expected to be awed by Washington, and yet he was. The man had an aura of command about him that somehow exceeded his size, which was not small in any case. Black judged him as at more than six feet tall, with broad shoulders. There was something about his presence that fit how the London papers had described him: a man raising up a new nation.

Washington pushed the glasses down on his nose, fixed him with an icy stare and said, "Are you sent by General Clinton, Colonel?"

"I am sent by your king, with a warrant for your arrest on a charge of high treason."

"He is not my king. If you have a warrant, where is it?"

"In a safe place, to which we will be taking you. I will serve it on you there."

"In New York?"

"We are taking you where we are taking you."

"You will not make it through our lines."

"We will see about that, Excellency."

He had surprised himself by using the term of respect. After all, Washington had not been appointed a general by any sovereign state or any power he or his King recognized. And yet.

"There are men sleeping upstairs," Washington said. "And many armed pickets around this house, as well as a watch on the roof. The best of my men. You will not get away."

"They are all dead," Rufus said. "As you will be if you fail to go quietly with us."

Washington turned his head to regard Rufus. "Sir, if I must die in the defence of my country, my life will be forfeit in a noble cause, for this great nation will be independent of England, with or without me."

Out of the corner of his eye, Black sensed motion. He snapped his head around to see Bear raise a pistol and point it at Washington.

"You deserve to die, you son of a dog. You've killed thousands in your unholy cause."

Black instantly pointed his own pistol at Bear. But in that split second when time seems to slow to a crawl, he knew that the retort of the gun would wake the soldiers sleeping above. He grabbed the pistol by the barrel, imagined Bear's ear the target on a shooting range and hurled it, hoping it wouldn't go off. It didn't, but flew true. Bear staggered back and dropped to the floor, unmoving.

Rufus looked to the others and said, "Get the pistol, restrain him and take him with you. Don't release him until well after we're gone."

Suddenly, Bear rolled partly off the floor and again took aim at Washington. Black leapt, hurled himself on top of Bear, grabbed his head in both hands and smashed it violently against the floor, twice. He felt the body go limp.

Rufus looked down at Bear and said, "He wouldn't actually have shot. You didn't have to kill him."

"Yes, he would have, and, yes, I did, assuming he is truly dead," Black said. He instantly realized that attacking Bear had transferred the leadership of the mission to him. He also realized that getting the General back to the ship would entail keeping the man from being killed by someone else on the way there.

He turned to look again at Washington. During the melee, he had neither ducked nor moved. He remained standing behind his desk, as before. Black could see in his eyes that he had decided to let fate decide if he was to live or die.

"Sir," Black said, "you are my prisoner. You have my word as an officer in His Majesty's Service that if you cooperate no harm will come to you." He paused. "If you try to flee we *will* shoot you."

"I will cooperate, Colonel. Your forces clearly have the upper hand for the moment, and I don't wish more of my men to die tonight needlessly. My thanks to you for saving my life."

"You are welcome. Now we need to go. Rufus, put the document on the desk."

Rufus unrolled the parchment he had prepared earlier and laid it down on the rosewood desk, anchoring it top and bottom with inkwells so that it lay open and prominent.

"May I know what it says?" Washington asked, pushing his reading glasses back up and squinting down. "I cannot read it from up here, even with these spectacles."

Black pondered only a second. "Read it to him, Rufus."

Rufus read aloud, "'To the Continental Army. If you want your Commander back, you will find him in New York City. We will bargain with you for his release, the price of which is treating with me and our admiral in good faith to settle this rebellion.' It is signed, 'With my compliments, Major General William Clinton.'"

"Ah, so that is what this concerns," Washington said.

Rufus walked up behind him and said, "Apologies, but I must gag you." He paused for a split second and added, "Excellency." He took a long cloth from a waistcoat pocket, twisted it through Washington's mouth and tied it behind his head, then handed him a hat that he took from a hat rack on the wall. Rufus looked to Black.

"We need to go," Black said again. "We've already tarried here too long."

They marched the most famous man in the world out the back door and into the night. No one had stirred in the house. The dead soldier by the door was still dead.

12

As they walked across the field and left the house behind, the rain that Rufus had promised began. It brought with it a ground-hugging mist that blocked sight and muffled sound.

Washington walked just ahead of him, but Black could barely make out the General's back. Three others walked immediately in front, with Rufus—just a shadow really—leading the way.

If ever the man were going to run for it, this was the time.

"Men," Black said, "guard the prisoner close."

Two of the three who'd been in front dropped back immediately, one on each side. It still did not seem adequate to him.

Shortly after they reached the woods, where the mist began to clear, they were joined by five more men—just as Rufus had promised—who seemed to appear out of nowhere. Each was wearing an American army uniform. They immediately reinforced the guard around Washington.

Black sighed in relief. His prisoner was not going to escape tonight, even though Black had chosen not to bind his hands, thinking that on the rough terrain, Washington might fall and would then have no way to catch himself. Bringing a dead or injured man back to London was not his plan. He also removed the gag, because the man seemed to be choking and gagging badly on it.

Rufus seemed to know a way back with fewer towns and led on without hesitation, despite the dark and the rain. As they walked, Washington said nothing, but slogged along with the rest of them. The trail was turning to mud, and their boots were soon covered with it, while their coats and hats dripped a steady stream of water. Washington had no coat, and Black could see that he had hunched his shoulders up against the cold.

Black stopped from time to time to try to listen, letting the others get a few yards ahead. He expected to hear pursuers—perhaps a shout or a shot—but all he heard was the rain. They marched for what seemed like hours, yet no one accosted them. Perhaps the ruse had worked.

They stopped a few times to eat and drink. The new men had brought hard tack, bread and beer. At one point, when they were sitting across from one another, Washington asked him, "Where are we really going?"

There was no reason now not to tell him. "To London."

"To what end?"

"Your sovereign will have you tried for high treason."

Washington paused a moment and said, "He is perhaps your sovereign, but he is no longer mine. He has forfeited the right. We made that clear in our declaration."

Black had always been uncomfortable with political argument, and he didn't wish to begin arguing now. He said only, "This is something you can argue in London, Excellency."

"Assuming you get me there."

"Yes, assuming that."

He became aware that several of the men had clustered around them and had to have overheard the conversation. There was muttering and cursing amongst them. If they shared Bear's views, there was nothing he would be able to do to stop them from killing the General and burying him in the woods. Or leaving him for the vultures.

Rufus had apparently much the same fear. He appeared out of the crowd and said, "We need to move on."

They stopped that night at an abandoned barn, which had been stocked with food and drink, stacks of dry clothes and horses for all. Black admired the planning that had gone into the mission and wondered how many people were involved. The more there were, the more chance someone would sell them out.

Rufus approached him and said, "Despite the risk, I think we must build a fire, or we shall all die of consumption. Especially him." He pointed at Washington, who had yet to remove his soaked clothes. "General," he said, handing Washington some clothes, "these clothes are not wet."

Washington stared at them and said, "I will not replace the uniform of my country with these civilian rags."

"You may catch your death of cold, Excellency," Rufus said.

"Then so be it. I am prepared to die for my country here and now. Such a death might well be preferable to being taken to London. Others will carry on the glorious struggle without me. My own fate matters not."

"If we build a fire, will you at least agree to sit by it?" Black asked.

Washington didn't answer even though he was shivering.

They built the fire, and in the end Washington sat by it and dried out. He also accepted an overcoat that had been left for them. Black assumed his choice not to fall ill and to accept the coat meant that he was still of a mind to escape if he could.

He pointed out to Rufus that a more regulation way to guard the prisoner would be to gird him about with an inner circle of men, and then position the others at some distance in an outer circle. That way, if he managed to break free of the inner circle, he could still be quickly caught. Shortly after, Black saw that Rufus had repositioned the men as he had suggested.

The next day went better. The rain abated to an occasional drizzle and the temperature warmed a little. That second night, they slept in another old barn that someone had again presupplied with food, water and fresh horses. Earlier in the day, they also acquired two outriders, who rode ahead of them and came back from time to time to warn them of people on the road, whereupon they would ride a ways into the woods so as to not be seen. And if they were seen, well, they were most of them in American army uniforms, including Black, who had changed back.

Washington no longer looked ill and no longer shivered. He still said little, and responded to questions only in monosyllables. Attempts to engage him in conversation failed.

Black kept a close eye on him. On several occasions, when Washington thought no one was paying attention, Black caught him looking around intently, especially as they passed through or near a town. But he made no effort to bolt.

Towards the end of the second day, Black rode up next to Rufus, who was mounted that day on a horse that was tethered to Washington's horse, and said, "Too many people now know about this. The outriders, the people who have supplied the barns for us, these guards." He waved towards the men girding their prisoner.

"Perhaps. But there was no way to get this done without support."

"You're confident in these people to keep quiet?"

"For now. Once we have him on the ship and away, they will probably brag to people about their role."

"Which would be at their peril."

"Yes, and mine."

Washington spoke for the first time that day. "Both your army and mine are riddled with spies. And people who talk. None of this is likely secret even at this moment. You will not get me on whatever ship you have brought without a fierce fight."

"I think we will, Excellency."

"I have thought about what this is all about," he said. "I assume you are taking me to London, not to hang me, but to force a negotiation."

"About what?" Black asked.

"About the offer of settlement that was made last year by a commission you sent to Philadelphia. Which was rejected out of hand, with my blessing."

Black thought quickly. There was no point in telling him what he knew about Lord North's actual plans. "I am of too lowly a rank for their plans to be shared with me," he said. "I am simply to get you to London, and I will."

Washington went quiet and seemed lost in thought as they rode along. Black assumed he had finished what he had to say. Finally, though, he said, "If you release me, I will promise you on my honour as a soldier and a gentleman that I will try to persuade the Continental Congress to treat with any peace delegation your country sends."

Rufus broke in. "You have not the power to make that happen."

"I can be persuasive. And your having captured me and then let me go will be taken as a sign of good faith."

"I hear the Continental Congress does not trust you," Rufus said. "And that many there dislike you and think you power hungry."

Washington glowered at him. "You hear wrong." The words had practically exploded out of his mouth. Perhaps the General wasn't used to hearing such direct criticism.

Shortly after, they stopped for a break. Black left Washington on the horse, guarded by one of the soldiers, and beckoned Rufus to a small grove of trees where they could talk without being overheard. "I am surprised he has made no move to escape," Black said.

"He's probably biding his time till he sees a good opportunity."

"Perhaps we should secure him further, Rufus. A boot on his leg, as the one Mary put on me?"

"No. For if we must at some point make a quick getaway on foot, he will be too much hobbled, whereas a gun at his back will move him along quite nicely."

"Unless he wishes to die," Black said.

"A man who has come this far in life and done what he has done will have no wish to die, to my thinking."

Their conversation was interrupted by the crack of a gun and the sound of a ball thudding into a tree nearby.

13

The gunshot was close by, and the horses startled. Black reined his mount in hard to stop him from bolting. Before he could turn to see if anyone was to their rear—the shot sounded as if it had come from directly behind—Washington had managed to turn his horse and take off into the woods, in the apparent direction of the gunshot, yelling, "It's General Washington! Give aid!"

Black gestured at the three men on horseback who had been surrounding Washington but had nonetheless let him escape. "Find the gunman. Take him alive if you can. Rufus and I will go after the General."

As he said it, he plunged his horse into the woods, with Rufus close behind.

"Why didn't you send the others after him?" Rufus asked.

"I don't want him shot."

"What's your plan?"

"Follow the broken branches. He can't have gone far. Or maybe he'll shout out again."

They continued to push through the trail of broken branches

for many minutes, forcing them out of the way as they passed. Every few minutes they stopped to listen, but heard nothing. Then they heard more shots. Three of them. Almost at the same moment, they came upon Washington. He was still on his horse, but his coat was torn and his face was badly scratched. His progress had clearly been arrested by the steep bank of a stream that lay directly in front of him.

He turned and looked at them. "You have caught me, it appears."

"Why did you try this?" Black asked. "You had little chance of success."

"I am a soldier. It's a soldier's duty to try to escape, Colonel. My guards seemed distracted by the sudden gunshot. I thought it might have come from one of my own guard coming after me. I rode back from whence we came, towards where I thought they might be."

"We're going to ride back to the place we were," Black said, "with one of us in front of you and one of us behind. If you flee again, I will find you again and shoot you." Even as he said it, he realized that he probably wouldn't, but he thought it worth saying.

"We should tie his hands," Rufus said. "Or he will surely try again."

"I don't want to, for the same reasons as before. Maybe another way will work." He turned to Washington. "Excellency, will you give me your word—as an officer and a gentleman—that you will not try to escape again? If you will do that, I will leave you untied and without a heavy boot on your leg."

Washington thought a moment. "I will give you my word while we are here in America. If you manage to get me to London, I make no such pledge."

"That will do for now."

"I still don't trust him," Rufus said.

"It's enough for me," Black said.

They reversed their path through the branches, but heard no more gunshots. When they arrived at the clearing from which they'd started out, they helped Washington down from his horse. Just then the three men that Black had sent in pursuit of the gunman returned. There was a body slung sideways over one of the horses.

Black dismounted and walked over. It was Bear.

Two of the other men came over to the horse, hoisted Bear up and laid him on his back on the ground. Black could see that the man was close to finished. His breathing was laboured and raspy, and blood soaked his shirt. Black pulled Bear's shirt from his belt, which revealed a gaping, bloody hole in his stomach.

"Why did you have to shoot him?" he asked. "We might have learned something from him about those who may be pursuing us."

"There was no choice," one of the men said. "It was him or one of us."

Black said nothing in response. He had had enough experience of battle to know that if you weren't there when it happened, you had no right to ask the details. Men did what they thought they had to do to live.

He bent down until he was almost in Bear's face. "How long have you been following us?"

"It doesn't matter," he said. His voice was faint, almost impossible to hear.

"I thought you were dead."

"I wasn't." His breath was coming harder.

"You should kill him," Rufus said.

"Which way did the soldiers go to look for the General?"

"Most went towards New York."

"What about the rest?"

Bear struggled to answer, but his body went suddenly limp, and only a rattle emerged. The first time Black had seen death take a man, he had been surprised that a rattle actually came out. Now he knew to expect it. He got up and said, "He's gone."

"There is something you should see," one of the men said. He reached into his saddlebag and pulled out two leather helmets, each topped by a white feather plume, tipped in blue. On one of them, a small red feather had been stuck amidst the white ones. "These must have fallen from their heads, maybe taken off by overhanging branches, and were left behind in their haste to leave."

"Where did you find them?" Black asked.

"Just off the trail, a few feet from where the dead man fell."

"Where exactly?"

"Behind him, from the direction he'd come."

"Did you see any footprints leading away?"

The man looked embarrassed. "I'm sorry. We didn't look."

"Why does this matter?" Rufus asked.

"I've seen helmets like these before on the heads of men patrolling as part of the Commander-in-Chief Guard. One of them even had the small red feather. This means that Bear wasn't alone. We need to worry where the men who were with him—or maybe they were following him—went."

"If they're part of the Guard, why did they let Bear shoot at Washington?" Rufus asked.

"Maybe Bear wasn't the shooter, and maybe Washington wasn't the target. Maybe it was me. Or you, Rufus."

Washington, who had been sitting propped against a tree, spoke up. "I can tell you about the red feather. It's given to men in my Guard in whom I place special trust. The fact that one of them is on our trail is good reason for you to let me go now—if you value your life."

Black laughed. "I think not."

"Laugh now, but when you're caught and are about to swing from a gibbet, it will be no laughing matter."

"We need to go," Black said.

Rufus pointed at Bear's body and said, "We owe him a burial before we go."

"There's no time, Rufus. Anyway, we owe him nothing." He looked over at the men who had brought Bear's body in. "Drag him into the woods as far as you can go and cover him up with wet leaves. On your way out, take branches and smooth over your tracks." He paused. "But before you cover him over, put a bullet in his head. I want to be sure this time."

He turned to Washington. "Excellency, as we reach more populated areas, we may come upon more people and some may recognize you. If you call out to them for help, and they respond, we're going to shoot them."

"To harm them would be a violation of the laws of war."

"Perhaps so. But many hereabouts are involved in traitorous acts, and they are within the sovereignty jurisdiction of His Majesty, King George III. How he chooses to deal with them is not covered by the laws of war. This is an unlawful rebellion, not a war."

Washington stared at him for a moment then said, "This is a just Revolution that will sound down the ages. In the moment, though, if you harm a hair on the heads of the people we may come upon, I will see you hanged."

"Their safety is in your hands, General."

Washington nodded, but didn't otherwise respond, and continued to hold Black in his gaze.

Black broke the stare off first and looked away, then turned to two of the men in uniform, who, along with everyone else in their entourage, had been frozen in place, watching the confrontation.

"You two," he said, "take the helmets with the feathers and wear them for the duration. If anyone asks, you're part of the Commander-in-Chief's Life Guard."

Fifteen minutes later—Bear's body disposed of in the woods as ordered—they mounted and left. As they rode out, Black could not help but look back over his shoulder. He had the sense they were being followed, but couldn't say exactly why, other than to dwell on the apparent escape of the men who had somehow lost their helmets.

Overall, the ride to the beach, which had required still one more night's stay in a barn, turned out to be surprisingly free of new problems. Black had even begun to relax about being followed—partly because he had twice sent riders back to check the trail behind them. They returned each time saying that they had seen nothing of note and no one of interest. Partly he felt more at ease simply because, since Bear's death, no additional trouble had come. The latter reason was foolish, of course. Trouble, when it came, oft came unheralded.

Black had worried that some interaction between Washington and residents of the area would lead to trouble. As it turned out, though, they met relatively few people along the way, partly because they were frequently able to make progress after dark and thus avoid much travel at the height of the day. Too, the steady rain seemed to have kept many people off the road. On the few occasions when they did come upon someone, people seemed to shrink back. Black assumed that at least some of them did recognize Washington, both by his height and his uniform, but wanted to stay as far as possible from the soldiers with the special helmets. The Life Guards' fierce reputation apparently preceded them.

Nor, to Black's relief, did Washington himself take the opportunity to shout out who he was. Perhaps the General had taken to heart Black's threat to harm civilians. Or maybe Washington feared dying in the melee that would surely erupt if someone tried to intervene? Black dismissed the thought out of hand. Whatever Washington was, he had surely demonstrated himself to be no coward. Most likely, Washington just assumed there would be a better opportunity to escape later. Black had never quite believed his pledge not to try.

Black understood, though, that they had also been the beneficiaries of simple good fortune. Now the question was whether their luck would continue once they reached the beach, which they came upon towards nightfall on the fourth day. They recognized it at a distance by spying the more or less straight line of trees that bordered it. Once they saw them, Black and Rufus rode forward, leaving Washington behind, closely guarded, and Black was quickly able to spot the sand through the bare branches of the trees. "Rufus, are you certain we've come back to the right beach?" he asked.

"Yes. I can make out the two huge rocks that mark it."

"Ah, yes. I see them now."

"Colonel, by my count, this is the eighth night, is it not?"

"Yes. Assuming the ship is still out there."

"So you've made it."

Rufus looked out to sea. "A very large storm is brewing. Look at the size of the breakers and the swell of the sea. I wonder if a rowboat can land at all."

Black peered out towards the ocean. "Well, if they cannot get in tonight, perhaps they will come back for me tomorrow night, the ninth night but what would be only the eighth attempt."

"That would mean staying here another night."

"Yes."

"When the boat arrives, Colonel, do you intend to take men with you other than Washington?"

"No. The rowers are young and strong and can supply all the help I will need to control Washington." He paused. "Wait. Do you want to come with me, Rufus? You can if you wish."

"Ah, no. This is my country. There would be nothing for me in England. Win or lose, here I stay."

Black suddenly stiffened. "Rufus, there are men walking from the tree line out onto the beach."

"They are ours, I am quite sure."

"How do you know?"

"I sent a messenger ahead, that first night we spent in the barn after taking the General, and asked that they come here at dusk each night for a week. There are many towns around here that are Loyalist through and through."

"Do these people know what we are about?"

"No, of course not."

"How can you be sure that's who these men are? That there are not rebels mixed in amongst them?"

Rufus sighed. "To put your mind at ease, I will go and check." He moved off down the beach.

He came back a few minutes later. "All ours, Colonel."

"I continue to have the feeling we are being followed."

"I saw no one except those I know, and they will not bother us or the boat when it comes in."

Just then, a very large wave smashed onto the beach with a roar. Black felt its spray on his face, even though it broke at least a hundred feet away.

Rufus looked out to sea again. "The wind is still rising and the rain is starting to come down in buckets. This is going to be a gale. Even if they do get a boat in, I fear it will capsize or be swamped on the way back to the ship."

"Let us hope not. But assuming the boat arrives, I have no choice but to get in." He looked out again at the boiling sea. "If they come at all."

"Can you swim, Colonel?"

"Not very well."

"Can Washington?"

He shook his head back and forth. "I have no idea."

14

PHILADELPHIA

Two days later, Samuel Huntington of Connecticut, the President of the Continental Congress—a tall man with a thin face, an aquiline nose and greying hair that cascaded down the back of his neck in a profusion of curls—glanced out the window of his small office on the second floor of the Pennsylvania State House in Philadelphia, the meeting place of the Continental Congress, and saw something he'd not seen before: a horse and rider thundering up Chestnut Street, which ran in front of the building and was usually filled only with elegant carriages. He continued to watch as the rider pulled up directly in front, dismounted and appeared to search for a place to hitch his horse, which was lathered up from hard riding. The man failed to find a hitch since no one in recent memory had ridden a horse directly up to the front door of the elegant, three-story brick building.

A few seconds later, he saw a small boy approach the man. They exchanged words, the man handed the boy a coin and the lad led the horse away. Looking more closely, he could see that the man, like the horse, had been riding hard—his face and neck were covered with sweat.

The man walked up the brick sidewalk and knocked on the large front door, which someone, presumably the porter, opened to admit him.

When Huntington had first assumed the presidency of the Congress the year before, his immediate predecessor, Rufus Jay, had shown him that his office contained a very convenient spy-hole in one wall, large enough to see what was happening in the building's lower entrance hall, but cleverly concealed so that it wasn't visible from the other side. If he pressed his eye against the hole and the people spoke loudly enough, he could not only see but also hear what was happening below.

He moved immediately to the peephole, pressed his eye against it and saw the visitor speaking to the porter, a small man who was almost entirely bald but declined to wear a wig. He had been specifically hired for his refusal to be impressed by anyone, and his ability to turn away most office seekers.

The visitor had a loud voice, and Huntington heard him say, quite clearly, "I have news of His Excellency, George Washington, and I must see President Huntington as soon as possible."

The porter did not appear impressed. "As he is the President of the Continental Congress, you will need an appointment. He is an important man and—"

"When you tell him what I have come to talk about, I'm sure he will see me. But I appreciate your trouble in finding him, if he's here." He handed the man a coin.

The porter took the coin, looked at it, pocketed it and said, "Thank you for that. Please come back tomorrow morning, and in the meantime I will see if Mr. Huntington will be able to make time to see you. But he may not be able to."

Huntington burst out of his office and ran down the nearby set of stairs to the ground floor. "Sir, if you have news of General Washington, I will be pleased to see you now. Mr. Bartholomew here—" he gestured at the porter "—tries hard to protect me from crazed people and Loyalists, who are sometimes one and the same."

"I thought he was one such," Bartholomew said. "I most certainly did."

"I understand, Excellency," the visitor said. "And take no offence. I'm Herman Atwood. I've just come from south of the Raritan River, and I have news of General Washington's fate."

"I'm anxious to hear it. Others have already told us he was taken, and news about the kidnapping is spreading as fast as the fastest horses can ride. As is the outrage amongst the people. But reports of what exactly happened to him are ever more confused. Some even say he is dead."

Atwood cast a glance at the porter.

Taking his meaning, Huntington said, "You can speak candidly in front of Mr. Bartholomew. The fact that General Washington was kidnapped from his headquarters is already well-known here. It's been almost six days. The riddle as to exactly where he might have been taken is a matter of everyone's concern."

"Very well, then. Sir, I was part of a small group of men who followed the General and his kidnappers from near his headquarters, where he was first seized, to a beach in New Jersey."

"Why didn't you attempt to rescue him along the way?"

"There were too many of them, too well armed. Also, we feared harming His Excellency in any attempt."

"Did not Patriots along the way volunteer to help?"

"Many in those parts are Loyalists. The Patriots we approached closed their doors to us. They are sick of war, it seems."

"And at the beach?"

"It was long past midnight, with heavy wind and rain, when a large wooden boat came in. There were eight sailors. It was pitching bad. The General tried to get away, but they grabbed him and shoved him in."

"Did anyone else get on?"

"Yes, one other man."

"What else do you know, Mr. Atwood?"

"Very little. May I have some beer, please, if you have it? I have not had drink in several hours of hard riding."

Bartholomew nodded in acknowledgement of the request and left the room.

"I didn't want to say this in front of him, Mr. Huntington, lest I start a poisonous rumour. But I fear General Washington didn't survive the trip in that small boat."

"Why?"

"The storm was rising fast and the boat was pitching and rolling very bad. I saw two waves overtop it, and three sailors were bailing with buckets while the others rowed."

"How long could you see it?"

"Not long. Every little while it disappeared into the bottom of a trough, and then it disappeared entirely into the rain and the mist. I thought I heard shouting, but I couldn't tell for sure, so loud was the rain and the wind."

"Were any bodies washed up?"

"I don't know. I left to come here within the hour."

Bartholomew returned with a large mug of beer and handed it to Atwood, who said, "Excuse me," and drank down almost the entire thing without stopping.

When Atwood had slaked his thirst, Huntington said, "Did you see or hear anything that would tell you if they were planning to take him to New York or to England or somewhere else?"

"No. Do you know?"

"We sent a fast messenger to General Clinton's headquarters in New York under a flag of truce. Clinton claims to know nothing about it and says it was done on no authority of his. He is now looking for Washington, too, and hoping to find him before we do."

Atwood wrinkled his nose. "Odd. Very odd," he said.

"Yes," Huntington said. "Unless you assume His Excellency is being taken to London on a British warship, and the plan was hatched without Clinton's knowledge."

"I think there was a name on the side of the longboat," Atwood said.

"What was it?"

He squinted, clearly thinking hard. Finally, he said, "I just cannot recall. It was dark and raining. I'm very sorry."

"When you are alone somewhere, sit quietly and try to fix your mind's eye on it," Huntington said. "Sometimes that works. And if you do come up with it, Mr. Atwood, please let me know right away."

"I will."

"In the meantime, we've established an emergency committee to try to deal with this. Washington is only one man, but he has become the heart and soul of this Revolution. We fear if we fail to get him back, everything will collapse into chaos. By happenstance, we are meeting in about two hours. Will you join us?"

"Yes. But I need a place to eat and then stay the night. Perhaps you could direct me."

Huntington looked to Bartholomew. "Mr. Bartholomew, please take Mr. Atwood to the City Tavern. Then help him find an inn for the night. Both the meal and the inn should be charged to the account of the Congress."

"Thank you, sir," Atwood said.

"You're most welcome. We will see you back here when the bell in the tower tolls six. There are others who need to hear what you saw."

15

Huntington had cobbled the emergency committee together—he named it the Committee on Repatriation—from amongst those delegates who were still in Philadelphia, many having already departed to begin the long journey home so that they might spend Christmas with their families. He also persuaded Charles Thompson, locally famous as one of the leaders of the Philadelphia branch of the Sons of Liberty, to attend. Thompson had not been a delegate, but rather served in the perhaps more powerful position of permanent secretary to the Congress.

Atwood arrived as the bell tolled six, and repeated for the members what he had told Huntington earlier in the day.

"Have you as yet remembered the name of the ship that you saw on the longboat?" Huntington asked. Then he paused and added, "But perhaps all ships don't paint the ship's name on their longboats."

"This one did, I'm certain. I just can't recall it."

"If you do, please find me and tell me. I am in touch with our navy, such as it is these days."

"I will do that, sir."

Finally, Huntington said, "Mr. Atwood, I, for one, thank you for doing your patriotic duty in coming to explain to us what has happened to His Excellency. It is most helpful. What are your plans now?"

"To return to New Jersey after a good night's sleep."

"Which you richly deserve." He rose and extended his hand. "You have the thanks of the entire nation."

Atwood, realizing that he was being dismissed, rose and shook Huntington's proffered hand. "I am pleased to have been of service to my country." He stepped towards the door, but just before reaching it, he turned and said, "What are you going to do?"

"Why, try to rescue him," Huntington said.

After Atwood had left, Thompson said, "Surely, you cannot be serious. Especially without the name of the ship. There are no doubt dozens of British warships out there."

"I didn't mean a rescue at sea. We will instead start by trying to negotiate his release in London."

"In exchange for what?"

"We will need to work that out," Huntington said.

They quickly agreed that whatever the strategy might be, whomever they sent to negotiate should be sent quickly, followed by more people later. Yet the need for speed left out three of their very best.

John Adams was already in France as a special representative to try to bring about a more formal alliance with France, as was Benjamin Franklin. Even if they were able to be notified and make their way to England amidst the French war with England, there would be no way to instruct them. But perhaps, someone pointed out, it was just as well. Adams, if the London papers which they had seen were to be believed, was the patriot leader whom George III disliked the most.

Thomas Jefferson was another possibility, but he was at that moment two hundred fifty miles away in Virginia serving as its governor. Virginia was at least a week's travel each way. In addition, he owned slaves, and slavery had already been effectively abolished in England several years earlier, which might make him a poor choice. And, as one member of the committee put it—whether seriously or not, it was hard to tell—"He might not really work all that hard to prevent Washington being put to death."

They also discarded the names of various generals, as well as a few well-regarded colonels and majors.

In the end, they chose Ethan Abbott, thirty-nine years old, not a delegate, but a war hero and a well-known and well-regarded lawyer in Philadelphia. He already knew many of the members of Congress well, including every member of the committee, because he'd represented them on personal and business matters while they were in Philadelphia. He had even briefly represented Benjamin Franklin before he left for France.

On some level, Huntington said, it didn't matter whom they chose. The British were going to do with Washington what they were going to do, and the representative sent from the Congress would likely make little difference. What mattered, he said, based on his careful reading of the London papers they received, the reports of the parliamentary debates that came his way, and his meetings with the Carlisle Commission, when they had spent six futile months in Philadelphia in 1778 trying to get someone in the Patriot camp interested in negotiating a settlement to the war, was whether Lord North or the King ended up winning the argument about how the war should end.

"What about Mr. Abbott's missing leg?" one of the delegates asked. "Won't having only half a leg hinder him in getting around?"

Huntington laughed. "No, and when they find out exactly how he lost it, the British will respect him. With regard to those men in Parliament and at court who have not themselves been in any war, it will give him a leg up." He smiled at the pun.

"He is also something of a dandy," one of them said.

"No, he simply dresses a great deal better than you," one of the men, who had spent time in London, said. "And that, too, will go over quite well in London and especially in court. Have you ever seen court dress, with its velvet and lace and gold buttons and medallions? He will fit right in."

And so Ethan Abbott was selected to travel to London and represent the Continental Congress in negotiations with the British, with a larger, supporting delegation to follow within the week. Perhaps Dr. Franklin could later be dispatched from France as well if needed, but that would take much longer to arrange and might put Franklin, wanted for treason for having signed the Declaration, at personal risk.

Now there remained only to let Abbott know he'd been chosen and persuade him to go. Huntington had gone to visit with Abbott before their current meeting to let him know he planned to put his name in contention. Abbott had reluctantly consented, but he did so, he had said, only because he knew he would never be chosen.

When Huntington went immediately to Abbott's home to tell him the news, he resisted. "I have not the talent for this."

"I think you do, Mr. Abbott. I think you are perfect."

"I was a soldier, and now I have returned to being a lawyer. What talents do I have for this? I think I have none."

"I know well your reputation as a negotiator, sir. You are measured and polite most of the time. But when needed you can be blunt. It is the very combination of talents which we need in this endeavour. That your country needs."

"My tendency to be blunt on occasion? I consider that a flaw in my character. When I feel it start to rise up in me, I try to beat it down."

Huntington smiled. "Try not to beat it down too much, Mr. Abbott. I have no doubt you will need it in London."

Neither of them said anything for a moment. Finally, Huntington broke the silence and said, "And there is one more thing. If you do this and are successful—or even if you're not—you will be famous for the rest of your life."

"I'm already quite famous enough."

"Only in a minor way for your exploits on the battlefield. That will all fade quickly. I am talking about wider fame, of the kind that I have no doubt is well worth having. Amongst other things, you can more easily acquire a wife."

"I'm not sure I want a wife."

"Everyone should have one, Mr. Abbott. It doesn't preclude you from— Well, never mind."

"General Washington has no idea who I am."

"I will give you a glowing letter of introduction. And since Washington does not consider me a competitor, it will go much further than something from Adams or Jefferson. Only a letter from Hamilton would do better, but he is at the moment at best two days' ride from here, and you must leave quickly."

"It makes no sense to send only one man."

"We will dispatch a small delegation shortly after you leave to arrive in London, we hope, not long after you do. And we can perhaps find a way to get Dr. Franklin to France to come to your assistance should things seem not to be going well."

"I still don't see how this is all going to work."

Over a bottle of fine port—two, actually—that Huntington had brought with him, they argued back and forth well into the night. Finally, Abbott gave up and accepted.

At the very end, as Huntington was preparing to leave, there was a loud knock at the door. Abbott opened it, and there stood Herman Atwood.

"Mr. Huntington, they told me I'd find you here." He looked to Abbott. "Pardon the intrusion, sir, but I didn't want to wait to tell the news." He was breathing hard, as if he'd run there from his inn. "I finally remembered the name of the ship. It was on the side of the longboat. HMS *Peregrine*."

16

TWO DAYS EARLIER

Aboard the HMS Peregrine *three miles off the coast of New Jersey*

Captain Ingram stood on the rolling deck, feet braced wide apart, talking with his first officer, Lieutenant Joshua Lansford, and looking shoreward.

"Mr. Lansford, what do you make of the weather?"

"You know the old saying, 'Red sky at night, sailors' delight, red sky at morning...'"

Ingram laughed and finished it for him. "'...sailors take warning.'"

"Yes, and the sky was blood red at dawn. Now, at sunset, it's not. But whether that old ditty is right or wrong, we must take warning because all the other signs—the swells, the wind, the smell—say a huge storm is in the making. And the rain is starting to come down hard."

"I agree," Ingram said. "That means tonight is likely the last night we will be able to launch a boat towards shore, and even then that boat will be at great risk. Once it has returned, we must get out of here and head for the open sea."

"I have looked at the charts," Lansford said. "There is no port nearby to take shelter in, at least not one our forces are likely to control."

"And the bottom here is very shallow."

"Yes, so as the wind rises, we are at risk of being blown aground. Unless we leave now."

"Agreed again," Ingram said. "But here's the thing. We are obligated to send a boat in again tonight to see if our mysterious friend has returned. If he isn't there tonight—as I suspect he will not be—we won't be able to try again. Our orders are not to try for more than eight nights."

"Captain, we must surely sail from here within the next few hours or risk losing the ship without sending in a boat. If we sail without Black we can decide later if we should return for him and call *that* the eighth night."

"No. Launch the boat towards the beach at the appropriate time as usual, and then get us ready to sail as soon as it comes back in. In the meantime, I will get some badly needed hours of sleep. Wake me when the boat is back."

He walked over to his bunk, pulled back the heavy curtain that provided a modicum of privacy and climbed in, not even bothering to remove his boots. He pulled the drapes closed. If he were the captain of a larger ship, he might well have a separate cabin to himself. The thought followed him into sleep.

He was in the midst of a wonderful dream—he was in a pub with his wife in the small village of Chedworth, in which they had met and courted, toasting an old friend's retirement—when a loud voice dragged him rudely out of sleep. "Captain! The boat is back!"

He threw back the curtain and heaved himself to his feet beside the bunk. The voice belonged to Lansford.

"Then we must put to sea at once and leave our friend to his fate."

"No, no. Smith has returned with another man, who is wearing an American uniform."

"You know nothing else about the second man?"

"Not yet. The man is in sickbay, near to death with cold and wet. And to boot, Smith is seasick again, poor man."

"He has not said who the second man is?"

"No."

"Take me to them."

17

Ingram had not set foot in the sickbay—a small, cramped room deep in the bowels of the ship—since his inspection of the ship just before they set sail. His conversations with the naval surgeon, Mr. Arbuthnot, had been perfunctory. They had not yet been in battle, so there had been no grievous wounds to discuss. Nor had anyone fallen out of the rigging. And since they had not made landfall anywhere, no sailor had come down with the clap. Indeed, the crew assigned to the ship by the Navy Board had seemed an unusually healthy lot for a group of British seamen. To his astonishment, many seemed, except for drinking the usual allotment of grog, downright abstemious. He had attributed it to the luck of the draw. Certainly, he'd captained ships on which his luck had run hard the other way.

He and Lansford entered the sickbay, a small room with an iron stove in the corner set atop bricks and a layer of sand to protect the wooden deck from the heat. Curtains had been hung on the walls—well away from the stove—to reduce draughts. He immediately spotted a man laid out in a bunk against the wall, on his back and wrapped chin to toe in blankets. From what he could see of his face, the man was of late middle years. Arbuthnot was leaning over him.

Ingram glanced over and saw Black with his arms folded, his shoulders pushed back into a corner, no doubt trying to brace himself against the increasing roll of the ship. His clothing was damp, and he had the green look of someone who has been seasick for hours.

"Mr. Arbuthnot," Ingram said, "may I have your report please?"

Arbuthnot looked up and said, "Welcome to sickbay, Captain. This man—" he pointed to the body on the bunk "—is near to death from cold and exposure. I'm told he fell overboard. He also has a bruise on the side of his head."

"What can you do for him?"

"For the cold we're heating bricks." He pointed to the surgical mate, who was crouched in front of the sickbay stove, in which a blaze was roaring. "As soon as they're hot enough, we'll place them around his body and try to warm him up gradually. If done too quickly, he will certainly die."

"Is there nothing else you can do...with all your education?"

Ingram assumed Arbuthnot would understand that he was making sly reference to the fact that most navy surgeons didn't receive their training and degree from the Royal College of Physicians. Most went instead to a lower prestige, barber-related program. Indeed, Ingram had asked Arbuthnot, when he had first come aboard, if his assignment by the Navy Board to such a small, insignificant ship—normally a physician with his fancy Royal College credentials would be posted to an admiral's flagship—was a punishment of some sort. Arbuthnot had shrugged and replied that he had no idea why he'd been assigned to Ingram's ship, but he was pleased to be of service.

Arbuthnot ignored Ingram's reference to his fancy education. "Rum might be of help to him," he said. "But he has to be conscious, or he'll choke. If he survives there might be some other things I could give him to help him recover from the cold. As for the head bruise, it's hard to say. It may or may not be serious. It will have to heal itself if it can."

The Captain looked at Black. "Who is the man in the bunk?"

"His Excellency, General George Washington."

"I don't think this is the time for levity, Mr. Smith. Who is he?"

"I intend no levity, Captain. That's who he is. My mission was to arrest him and bring him back to London to face the King's justice. He is a leader of the rebellion and thus a traitor."

There was a long silence in the room as Ingram, Lansford and Arbuthnot turned, almost as one, to stare down at Washington's face.

"I suppose it could be him," Ingram said. "I've seen a few drawings in magazines, and the face is perhaps the same. Mr. Smith, how do you know for certain it's Washington?"

"I captured him myself."

"What? Where?"

"At his headquarters."

He raised his eyebrows. "And you did this alone?"

"Of course not. I had aid from Loyalists, much of it preplanned. And you no longer need to call me Smith. My true name, which is Colonel Black, will do from now on."

The surgeon's mate spoke up. "Mr. Arbuthnot, the bricks are warm enough now. And perhaps it's not my place, but if you still have any doubts as to who this man is, his uniform speaks for his high station." He pointed to a heap of clothes piled in the corner.

Lansford walked over, picked up the largest piece and hoisted up a dripping-wet military-style waistcoat. The buttons and epaulettes were gold. Or at least Ingram could make out that they had once been gold, even if they were now a dirty brown.

"I took the coat off him when he was brought in," the mate said.

Black unlimbered himself from the corner and spoke in a tone of command Ingram had not heard before. “Captain, if you still have doubts, I will show you my orders, and you will believe who this is. The question now, though, is whether he will survive.” He looked to the doctor.

The mate had begun handing the hot bricks to Arbuthnot, wrapping each first in thick cloth to prevent them burning their own hands or the patient. As he answered, Arbuthnot was bent over his patient placing the bricks around his body, beneath the blanket. “Only God knows,” he said. “But I will do my best, as I would for any man, general or no.”

“Colonel, let’s return to the Great Cabin,” Ingram said. “I want to see those orders you referred to.”

“Of course, Captain. In the meantime, may I suggest you station four marines here to make sure he doesn’t escape?”

Ingram laughed. “Even if he lives, where would he go?”

“I don’t know. But he tried to escape once on our way to the beach. And I’m still not convinced he fell accidentally off the boat. He may well have been intending to try to swim back to shore.”

“We don’t have a lot of marines on board, given the small size of our boat. I can spare only two, at least for now.”

“I must insist on four,” Black said.

“Who is the captain of this ship, Colonel Black?”

“You are, sir, but I remind you that I outrank you.”

“Any time you want to take command, Colonel, do let me know. In the meantime, I will continue to make these kinds of decisions that immediately affect the ship and its safety. I will send two only.”

Arbuthnot cleared his throat, clearly uneasy at the confrontation. “Pray send two who don’t have colds,” he said. “This patient is in bad enough condition as it is.”

“You really believe that one person can give a cold to another, Mr. Arbuthnot? That it is not just foul vapours that all breathe in?"

"I do believe that."

Ingram laughed again. "I suppose it's your fancy education speaking."

"Yes, and now we know why, with that fancy education, I was assigned to this ship, Captain."

Ingram headed for the door. "Follow me, Colonel Black. I would like you to show me your orders." The ship was by then rolling steeply enough that Black had visible difficulty holding on to the ladders as well as climbing through the hatches that led from deck to deck. At one point, Ingram, who led the way, reached a hand down to help hoist him up and said, "I thought you had gotten better at this on the voyage over."

"No, Captain, I fear I will never get better on ships. After we return to London, I hope never to board one again."

When they reached the Great Cabin, Ingram pulled his sea trunk out from under his bunk, opened it and extracted two envelopes—one fat and one thin—each sealed with red wax. He handed both to Black. "These are the documents you left with me for safekeeping, Colonel."

Black broke the seal on the fat one, extracted a sheaf of papers, some of them folded up, and handed the top sheet back to Ingram.

Ingram read it and said, without looking up, "All right, these order you to arrest Washington and bring him back to London for trial, and to use 'all lawful means.'"

"Do you see who has signed it?"

"Yes. The Prime Minister and the First Lord of the Admiralty, with their seals." He looked up. "Wouldn't it have made sense to let me in on the secret? I came close to leaving you on the beach. I would not even have thought of it had I known what you were doing here."

"I wished to tell you, Captain, but was ordered not to. I don't know the reasons."

"Perhaps it's because I have never been a favourite of the Admiralty."

"Be that as it may, do you still have any doubts the man in sickbay is General Washington? Or do you think I would dare to bring an impostor back to London?"

"I believe you," Ingram said.

"Good," Black said. "And speaking of London, when we finally get there, we will have to send a messenger to Lord North for instructions."

"All right. And the other envelope, what's in there, Colonel?" Ingram frowned. "Only if you're permitted to tell me, of course."

"It's an arrest warrant for the General."

"Won't do you much good now."

"When he wakes up, I will serve it on him."

"*If* he wakes up," Ingram said.

18

To Ingram's surprise, Washington did wake up. On their third day at sea—after the storm had finally abated—Arbuthnot appeared in the Great Cabin and said, "The General—if that's who he really is—began to stir and moan yesterday, then sat up this morning and asked where he was."

"What did you tell him?"

"The truth. He seemed not to comprehend it, and immediately fell back on the bunk and seemed again unconscious, or at least in a deep sleep."

"How did you cure him?"

"I did nothing other than put warm bricks around him, day and night, but did nothing for the head wound except bandage it. His own body did the rest. He is apparently of a very strong constitution."

"If he recovers fully, will he be of sound mind?"

Arbuthnot shrugged. "Most people who come as near to freezing to death as he did do not recover at all. I have seen only two other cases in my career where they awoke."

"And?"

"One, after a few weeks, seemed good as new. The other... was no better than stupid. Good only for eating and babbling. He didn't last long. In this case, there is nothing to do but wait."

"When you think he can walk, let me know, and I will double the marine guard."

"Very good, Captain."

After he left, Ingram went in search of Black and found him sitting on the fantail, watching some dolphins who were playing in the ship's wake. He looked up as Ingram arrived and stood. "Captain, I have not seen you in several days."

"You have not been eating in the wardroom with the rest of the officers."

"I have been eating—when I can—with a bucket. I thought to spare you all."

"That is kind of you, Colonel. But I have sought you out because I have news."

"Is the General dead?"

"No, to the contrary. Your prisoner is awake, although not yet able to walk."

"When will he be able to walk and talk?"

"Mr. Arbuthnot didn't say exactly. But the question is not so much that as what condition his mind will be in when he can walk again."

"Oh?"

"Our surgeon says there is a chance he may be as a person without much of a mind."

Black walked to the railing and gazed out to sea. Then he said, without turning around, "If that happens, Captain, I don't want to take him back to London as the walking dead."

"Colonel, if I understand your thought, you should know that no living man will ever be thrown overboard from my ship, mind or no mind."

"Understood."

"Good. I will keep you posted on his condition. I bid you good day." He turned and walked away. Black would have to be watched if the General didn't recover all of his faculties.

Two days later, Arbuthnot again appeared in the Great Cabin. "The General is not only awake, but eating well."

"And his mind?"

"It seems intact. Although he claims no memory of how he got on this ship. I have talked to two members of the longboat crew, and they tell me he tried to swim back to shore, despite the sea."

"Has he tried to leave the sickbay?"

"No. And there are two marines outside to prevent that, as you ordered."

"Has the man said who he is?"

"Yes. General George Washington, Commander-in-Chief of the Army of the Continental States of America."

"Do you believe him?"

"Yes."

"Very good. I will visit the General soon."

"I suggest you wait a day or two. He is still weak."

"Will you let me know when you think he's ready to be seen?"

"Of course, Captain."

"Sooner will be better than later, Mr. Arbuthnot."

"Understood, Captain."

"Very good."

Ingram started to leave the room, then turned and said, "Have you told Colonel Black yet that the General is awake?"

"No. You're the captain, and I owe the information to you first. Do you want me to tell him?"

"Not yet."

"Yes, sir."

Upon leaving Arbuthnot, he went to look for Black and once again found him sitting on the fantail, watching the dolphins.

"They're fascinating to watch, aren't they, Colonel?"

"Yes."

"You're lucky to see them. They are almost never this far north in the winter. Perhaps it means we will have currents favourable for a quick trip."

"I hope so."

"I watch the dolphins myself at times. I sometimes wonder if they enjoy life more than we do."

Black laughed. "Yes. They probably don't have military missions they have to worry about."

"Are you worried about your mission?"

"Of course. I fear having to take a man without a mind back to my king. I will have failed in my mission if Washington has no mind. Although I suppose they might hang him anyway."

"I have good news for you, then. Arbuthnot reports that the General is awake, eating, and seems of sound mind. Except he doesn't remember how he got here."

"Just as well perhaps," Black said. "If he is awake and in his right mind, I would like to see him now."

"Mr. Arbuthnot says we need to wait a few days," Ingram said. "And I will see him first, then you."

"He is my prisoner."

"Yes, and this is still my ship, even if you outrank me."

"This is a delicate matter, Captain. I do outrank you, and it matters here because this is not a matter of shipboard safety. It is a matter of my mission."

Ingram just stared at him.

"Why don't we see him together?" Black said.

"Fine. We will do that."

"Good."

"Now I have something to discuss with you, Colonel. What are your plans for Washington's time on this ship? If the weather stays with us, we will be at least four more weeks before we reach Portsmouth."

"He should be confined to quarters, and well guarded."

"I have been thinking about that, and I don't fully agree. He is the commanding general of an army and as such, under the rules of war, is a prisoner of war and entitled to the courtesies due his rank."

Black stood up. "It is a rebel army. Not recognized by our king."

"I can't fully agree with you, Colonel. From what I read, it's an army made up of thousands of men. One that has actually won battles against our vaunted military. And one to which our government has sent plenipotentiaries to try to open negotiations."

"This is your ship, Captain, so there's not much I can do to change your attitude. But what does this mean as a practical matter?"

"I will cause the marines to guard him at all times, as you wish, but he will eat in the wardroom with the officers and be accorded privileges of rank."

Black just looked at him. "You're going to salute him?"

"Most likely, yes."

"That is your choice, sir. I will not."

19

The next day, Ingram looked up from his table in the Great Room, where he'd been working on updating his ship's log, and saw Arbuthnot come in.

"The General is much better today," the surgeon said. "He has asked to speak to the captain of the ship." He smiled. "That would be you, I believe."

"Good. I will go immediately to see him. He's still in sick-bay?"

"Yes. Shall I ask Colonel Black to join us?"

"Yes. I will send someone to fetch him. But in the meantime, let us go see him and Colonel Black will catch up." Ingram gave an order to find Black to a seaman, and they headed down to sickbay.

On the way, Arbuthnot briefed him on Washington's condition: finally awake most of the day, no longer shivering, pulse rate steady, skin not clammy anymore and back to a normal colour. Eating voraciously.

At the door to sickbay, they encountered the two marines

who were guarding the entrance. They saluted Ingram, and he saluted back. Then he stopped in his tracks, turned, faced them directly and said, "Starting now, no one besides Mr. Arbuthnot and his mate is to enter the room without my permission. Colonel Black may come in if someone else is here."

"Aye, aye, sir!" they said in unison and saluted again.

When they walked in, Washington was sitting in a chair at a small table, eating. He was wearing his uniform, which had been restored to a semblance of clean. He looked directly at Ingram's shoulder boards, where his commander's rank was displayed, and wobbled to his feet.

"Good morning, Captain," he said and said nothing more, clearly waiting, Ingram thought, for him to initiate a salute to acknowledge Washington's superior rank.

"Before I salute you, sir, please tell me who you are."

"General George Washington, Commander-in-Chief of the Continental Army of the United States."

"How do I know this to be true?"

"I suggest you enquire of Colonel Black, who I now seem to recall captured me, and I am told is on this ship."

A voice from the doorway said, "I captured him at his headquarters. Unless they were using a double, he speaks the truth as to who he is. But I see no reason to salute him, Captain. His army is not the army of a country recognized by anyone."

A wry smile swept across Washington's face. "Unless, Colonel Black, you don't consider France to be a country. They recognized *my* country three years ago."

Ingram glanced briefly at Black, looked back to Washington, raised his hand to his forehead and saluted. "Welcome aboard, General. Unfortunately, you are a prisoner, so we will need to establish some rules of conduct while you are aboard my ship."

"What type of prisoner am I?"

"A prisoner of war, as far as I am concerned. But Colonel

Black—" he gestured at him "—believes you are simply a captured rebel."

"What do you propose with regard to rules of conduct, Captain?" Washington said.

"First, when you are feeling well again, you are most welcome to dine with me and my officers in the wardroom."

"Thank you."

"Second, you will be given a berth commensurate with your rank, but you will be guarded at all times by at least two marines, sometimes four."

"I give you my word, if you will parole me to go when and where I wish unguarded, that I will not try to escape, damage your ship or crew or otherwise harm your mission."

"Perhaps in time," Ingram said. "But for now the marines must go with you. We have at least four weeks to work out a different arrangement."

"I understand, Captain. But I will nevertheless pledge, on my honour, not to try to escape the ship, in the hope that you will soon parole me to go where I wish."

"Thank you, General. I will count on your pledge. Now I must take my leave. I trust that Mr. Arbuthnot has been taking good care of you?"

"Indeed he has."

He saluted Washington. "Good day, General."

As they left sickbay, Black said, "Captain, there's something I want to say to you, and it is with all due respect."

"What?"

"Washington tried to escape when we were bringing him to the beach. And when he supposedly fell out of the boat in rough sea, I think he actually jumped out and was trying to swim back to shore."

"I have heard that. And so?"

"I have a sense that he is up to something."

"Like what?"

"I wish I knew."

"Well, one thing I know for sure. There is absolutely no way for him to escape from here." He gestured at the ship's hull. "Yonder lies only the sea."

Each day since his visit to sickbay, Ingram had seen Arbuthnot in the wardroom at least once a day when the officers sat down to their evening meal. And each day, he had asked the surgeon the same question: "How goes General Washington?" Each day he had received the same response: "Ever stronger, eating well, gaining weight."

On their eighth day at sea, Ingram was standing on the bridge, looking out to sea and wondering how long their good weather and good winds would last. Suddenly, Arbuthnot appeared beside him. He saluted and said, "Captain, General Washington has asked me to convey a message to you."

"What is it?"

"He says that if your invitation to dine with the officers in the wardroom is still open, he would like to accept for this evening."

"Please tell him he is most welcome. We will expect him for the evening meal."

"He asks, also, if his marine guards must accompany him everywhere."

"Inhospitable as it is, the answer is yes."

"Will you notify Colonel Black?"

"I suppose it's only proper." He grinned. "After all, he does outrank me."

"I've noticed that he's not been joining us for meals."

"I know. I think on the days when he's sick, the sight of food makes him ill at times. Have you been able to do anything for his condition?"

"I told him to spend as much time as possible on deck, in the breeze and looking out to sea. I also offered him a syrup made from five roots that has helped some people in the past, but he has declined to take it."

"Did he say why?"

"Something about being poisoned at one point when he was seeking out Washington."

Ingram raised his eyebrows. "Did he say by whom?"

"He declined to say."

"I will have to discuss this with him. But come to think of it, why don't you let him know about tonight's dinner with General Washington. It would save me the duty and would be much appreciated."

"I'd prefer you do it, Captain."

"All right, I will."

Ingram went to look for Black and found him again on the fantail. "Colonel Black," Ingram said, "I want you to know that General Washington will be joining us in the wardroom for dinner this evening. I hope you will join, although if your seasickness prevents that, I would understand."

"I'm at least somewhat better now that the sea is calmer, thank you," Black said. "I will attend."

"Good. I will meet you there, Colonel."

Ingram walked away and went to look for his steward. He found him in the Great Room. "Please set the table tonight with the china mess plates."

"They're packed away in straw, Captain. We usually use the china only in port. Otherwise, as you know, we use the wooden plates, even for the officers."

"I think the sea is calm enough to risk it."

"Aye, aye, sir. I will get it done."

20

Ingram thought the setting on the long oak table in the Great Cabin looked splendid. The stewards had set out white china plates, a crown in blue at the center with twisted vines on the rim. To the side of each lay gold cutlery with the fouled-anchor navy seal engraved on each handle. All were laid out on a white tablecloth, or at least as white as it could be kept while at sea.

The cutlery was his personal set. He had, on a lark, bought it from a high-born friend who had made it to admiral and retired to the countryside, saying that he no longer felt the need for such frivolous things. Ingram had been carting it from command to command ever since, hoping against hope to someday make it to admiral himself, with his own flagship. But he now understood better than ever that his origins in the merchant class—his father had been a prosperous wool merchant—would likely preclude him from ever wearing the shoulder boards of an admiral.

His musings were interrupted by the arrival of his officers—Lansford, the three lieutenants not on watch, four midshipmen and Arbuthnot. Colonel Black had indeed come, looking less green than usual. Washington, however, had not yet arrived. All of them, he noticed, kept glancing at the door.

A few minutes after they'd all taken their seats, the General appeared, accompanied by his two marine guards. Ingram didn't imagine that Washington's late appearance was by accident. He started to enter the room, and the marines started to enter with him.

"You marines may wait outside," Ingram said.

They saluted and withdrew.

He had been thinking for some time what level of respect to accord Washington when he arrived. It had been one thing to salute him in sickbay. It was quite another to do it here, with most of his officers present. But as he rose from his seat, he knew there had never truly been a question as to what he would do. He snapped his hand to his forehead and gave the regulation palm down salute. His action caused all the others, including, to his surprise, Black, to rise and do the same. Washington returned the salute and bowed slightly to all.

"Welcome, Your Excellency," Ingram said. "Please take a seat." He himself had been seated, as protocol for a ship's captain dictated, at the head of the table, and he gestured for Washington to take the seat to his left. After all were seated, he gestured to the stewards to fill the wine glasses with port, which he had authorized to be withdrawn from the special stores in the hold.

He took his wine glass in hand and rose to give a toast, realizing that it was a bit inappropriate given the guest, but gave it anyway. "To the King! To our ships at sea! A willing foe and sea room!"

His officers rose and toasted, as did Washington, who had a bemused smile on his face.

Then Washington made his own toast. "When I had the pleasure of travelling on one of His Majesty's ships as a very young man, I was always fond of this one," he said, raising his glass. "To our wives and sweethearts, may they never meet!"

They all burst into laughter. Even Black smiled. Washington's toast set a festive tone for the remainder of the meal.

After the first course had been served—dried beef in a heavy sauce—Ingram asked of Washington, "When were you on one of His Majesty's ships?"

"Ah," Washington said, "I have exaggerated a bit. It was not a ship of the line, but actually a merchantman. That toast was, though, given many times. At the time I had neither sweetheart nor wife. Now I have a most loyal and wonderful wife, and no sweetheart at all." He smiled.

"Where were you going?"

"I sailed from Richmond to Barbados with my brother, who was seeking a cure for his consumption."

"Did that help?"

"Perhaps in the short term. He passed away not long after we returned."

"I'm sorry to hear that."

"There has been so much death in this war, Captain, that a single death in my family matters little at this point."

A lieutenant overhearing the conversation said, "Was your brother in the navy?"

"No. I was almost, though. I had my bags packed to leave to become a midshipman, but at the last moment didn't go."

"Was there a reason?" the lieutenant asked.

Washington laughed. "Yes, my mother. She objected, and if my mother objected, you didn't move forward. At least not at the age that I was then—fifteen!"

Black, who was sitting quite far down the table, asked, "So you are comfortable on ships, then?"

"Yes, but hardly experienced. And at times have the same difficulties you have with the motion, Colonel. Today has been better, though."

Washington had, Ingram thought, tried to ingratiate himself with Black by pretending to share his misery. The type of thing a true leader did instinctually. He assumed Washington was pretending, however, because no one had reported to him that the General was suffering from seasickness.

"Seasick or not, what of this so-called Revolution?" one of the other lieutenants, who had no doubt had his share of rum before the meal began, asked. "Why are you colonists not content with the blessings our king bestows on his subjects? Which are many."

Washington paused, as if he'd been asked the question many times before.

"We have declared our own, independent nation because the blessings you speak of have been bestowed only on men who live in England."

"What do you mean?" the lieutenant asked.

"I mean you have the right to vote to choose your representatives to Parliament. And that same Parliament, whom you Englishmen elect, places taxes on us over which we have no say. All we wish is to have these very blessings you speak of for ourselves."

"Why don't you ask for them?" Black said.

"Surely you are joking, Colonel. Surely you must know that we have asked for our rights many times and have not only been rejected again and again but punished for asking."

"Surely," Black said, "throwing tea into a harbour is not asking for anything. It is just thuggery."

"I did not countenance that," Washington said. "It was done in New England, where the hand of your ministers and Parliament has been particularly heavy, so perhaps it can be understood as an outburst grown of frustration."

"What you colonists do not understand," Black said, "is that the members of that Parliament you mention have your interests at heart as they govern. You are like our children and the Parliament like a distant, but caring, parent."

Washington stiffened. "If you will excuse me, we are not

children, and even if we were, a parent who is three thousand miles away can hardly be a good parent." He paused. "Do you understand, Colonel Black, how long this distant Parliament has treated us as children?"

Without waiting for a response, Washington answered his own question. "We've been treated as children for more than one hundred fifty years, Colonel. Indeed some families have lived in our land for three, four, five, even seven or eight generations. I myself am the third generation to be born on the soil of Virginia and carry the name Washington."

While Ingram was musing to himself about that, Colonel Black had responded to Washington, lambasting the colonies for not having paid what he considered their fair share of the defence in the French and Indian War. Lieutenant Crisp, meanwhile, who'd by then had far too much wine, was, to Ingram's surprise, joining Washington's complaint, but focusing on the fact that so many men in England itself lacked the right to vote. Black was getting red in the face, Washington had his arms crossed across his chest and Crisp was gesticulating wildly.

The dinner was not turning out as Ingram had hoped. Perhaps naively, he had expected it to be a pleasant meal amongst officers and gentlemen about which he could someday regale his grandchildren—of whom he already had four. He decided to try to bring it back to the way he wanted it.

He stood, tapped on his glass till all were silent and said, "Gentlemen, I propose a toast to the land of General Washington's birth, Virginia!" Everyone huzzahed and clinked glasses.

Then Washington rose. "And I propose a toast to the land of *your* birth, Captain, or so I assume… England!"

All clinked and huzzahed again.

Hoping to continue the spirit of it, Ingram said, "And finally, to *our* king." He hoped that if Black were to report the toasts up the chain of command, he would not note that Ingram had said *our* king rather than the usual *the* king, thus leaving Washington an opening not to object since he could have been referring only to the Englishmen at the table.

Washington, clearly understanding his point, rose again and said, "*We* do not have a king, sir, but we do have many statesmen. I propose a toast to an illustrious Virginia statesman, Thomas Jefferson!"

There was suddenly a stone-cold silence around the table. "Jefferson? Why Jefferson?" the second lieutenant—who to that point had been silent—asked. "Isn't he the one who slandered our king in your so-called Declaration of Independence?"

Washington paused, as if carefully considering his response, and said, "Mr. Jefferson could be something of a hothead at times, and in any case I was not present at the gathering that wrote and approved the Declaration." He smiled a close-lipped smile.

Ingram's respect for Washington rose still higher. The man had to know that he was being taken to London to be tried for treason. And while it was one thing openly to declare the independence of the colonies for various political reasons, it was quite another to attack the King personally. Washington had just distanced himself from that. No one at the table would be able to testify at his trial that Washington had sat there in the wardroom of one of the King's ships and personally insulted him.

His thoughts were interrupted by a loud bang, followed a minute later by shouts and cries of anguish.

The door was flung open.

21

It was one of the crew who gave only the most perfunctory of salutes. "Captain! A ship to port! It came out of the mist. They are trying to board us."

Ingram jolted himself from his chair, along with every other officer, and rushed for the door. As he passed through the doorway, he yelled at the marines stationed just outside, "Guard the prisoner!"

The marines moved immediately into the cabin and stood one to each side of Washington, bayonets fixed.

Only Black and Washington remained in the cabin, still seated at the table.

"Are you concerned I might try to escape, Colonel?" Washington asked him.

"You have tried at least twice, both times at peril to yourself."

"How would you propose I escape from this room and these two marines, even assuming the ship that's trying to board us is American?"

"Even if I knew, I wouldn't suggest to you how to do it."

The door banged open again and Captain Ingram burst back in and pointed at the marines. "Every man on deck. Leave the prisoner!" He pointed at Black. "*Every* man!" Black hesitated, then got up and followed the Captain and the marines out onto the deck. Just as he went through the door he glanced back at Washington. The man was still sitting calmly at the table.

When Black emerged onto the deck it was thick with mist, but he could nevertheless make out four iron grappling hooks slung over the gunwale, and four men, none wearing a uniform, clambering over the rail onto the deck to join others who had arrived. Black saw two boarders brandishing swords, another swinging a large club above his head and one man with a long knife. That man lunged at a *Peregrine* crew member, but his target stepped nimbly aside, seized the knife and plunged it into the boarder's throat.

The clash of metal on metal, mixed with screams, was becoming deafening, and the deck was growing slippery with blood.

Black barely had time to take it all in when a man ran directly at him and swung a broadsword at his head. He ducked and felt a whoosh of air as the weapon passed just above him. Black lunged at his attacker, caught him around the waist and flung him backwards. They fell to the deck together, with Black on top. They landed, hard, and he heard the man's sword skitter away. But the man was huge. With only one try, he flipped Black over and began pounding his head on the deck. Then the man stood up, lifting Black up with him, grabbed him in a bear hug and began walking them both towards the rail. Black struggled to free himself but was powerless to break the man's grip. Suddenly, the man went limp in his arms. Instinctively, he wrapped his arms around the man to keep him from falling. Black looked over the man's shoulder and saw Captain Ingram standing there, holding up a sword, its tip covered with blood.

"You can let him go," Ingram said. "If he's not dead, he soon will be."

Black released the man and heard rather than saw him hit the deck. He realized that all had gone quiet. He looked around and saw bodies everywhere, most of them ununiformed, a few wearing the blue of the British Navy.

"There weren't many of them," Black said.

"When the boarding party is small, the goal is to seize the commander of the ship and trade his life for something of great value and leave," Ingram said.

A voice behind him said, "It appears you have repulsed their effort to board you, Captain."

Black turned and saw that it was Washington.

"I thought you had promised not to try to escape," Ingram said.

"I made no attempt to escape, Captain. I merely stood near the rail. After all, I made no promise to avoid being rescued."

Ingram actually laughed. "General Washington, you should perhaps have been a lawyer."

"You should lock him up for the rest of the voyage," Black said.

"I don't think so," Ingram said. "I don't know whether the men who tried to board us were privateers or Americans trying to rescue the General, and who by some miraculous stroke of luck managed to find us on the open ocean. But either way, I don't think it is likely to happen again."

"You will take no action against him, then?" Black asked.

"He seems to me not to have done anything to dishonour his pledge," Ingram said. "But I'll increase his guard." He paused. "Just to be sure."

For the balance of the voyage, Captain Ingram gave Washington the liberty of his ship—so long as his guards went with him. They shared many convivial dinners together—none attended by Colonel Black, although he was always invited.

At their final dinner, Ingram raised a toast: "To an end to this war, and your quick return to your country."

Washington responded: "To a *just* end to this war and all wars."

When the *Peregrine* docked in Portsmouth, they had to wait more than four days for Lord North to be notified and for a contingent of marines to arrive.

As the gangplank was finally lowered, Ingram turned to Washington and said, "General, I fear that what you face will not be pleasant, to say the least. I wish you the best of luck."

"Captain, you have been every inch an officer and a gentleman. Godspeed to you and your ship."

Colonel Black, who had been standing to the side, listening, together with two of the ship's marines, said, "General, you are my prisoner. Please put your hands behind your back so that I might secure them. I will be taking you down as soon as the gangplank is secured."

PART II

January 9, 1781

22

10 DOWNING STREET
LONDON

The First Minister was not in the best of moods. The war in the rebellious American colonies had, he supposed, been going well enough. General Cornwallis had been pressing the agreed-upon southern strategy in the Carolinas and reported winning almost every battle. But he had yet to deliver a true knockout blow to the rebels, and he was now reporting being constantly harried by colonial militia.

Cornwallis's very latest report, which North had not received until November, reported that a month earlier, at a place called King's Mountain, a rebel militia had engaged a British militia of Loyalists personally recruited and led by one of Cornwallis's officers, Major Ferguson. The Loyalists had been roundly defeated, with more than 1,100 men killed, wounded or captured out of an initial force of 1,200. One of the dead was Major Ferguson himself. North hardly knew whether the defeat was simply a misfortune in the course of a long and bloody war or a calamity.

For that kind of military interpretation, he relied on Lord

Germain, Secretary of State for the American colonies, who had actual experience as both a soldier and a general in the field and so was vastly better informed on things military. Indeed, against his better judgement, North had turned over direct command of the armies in the colonies to Germain. And Germain's view was that the loss at King's Mountain was regrettable but nothing to worry overly about. Still, the report was causing North anxiety.

Worse, it was now January and, given the five-week or longer travel time from the Carolinas to England, for all he knew the war had already been won. Or lost. The delays in receiving current news was maddeningly frustrating.

Meanwhile, the costs of supplying an army three thousand miles away were taking a large toll on the treasury, and Parliament was restive, with more and more members questioning the value of spending blood and treasure to defeat the ingrates across the sea, especially when the ongoing war with France seemed much more important. And then there was the King. Far from wanting to give up or soften his views, he was impatient to see the rebellion put down once and for all. North's informants in the palace had even told him that the King was having vivid dreams of Washington, Adams, Franklin and the rest of them swinging on the gallows at Tyburn. He hoped it was a false rumour.

He took another sip of the camomile tea his physician had prescribed for anxiety. Perhaps it helped, but he was sick of the stuff. Just then, his private secretary, Hartleb, knocked and said, "There is a messenger come from Portsmouth with a note for you. Do you wish to receive him now or shall I just take the note?"

Portsmouth was where His Majesty's ships docked, so it might well be news from Cornwallis.

"Show him in, please."

A moment later, the messenger, who was dressed from head to toe in brown leather and sweating—whether from the journey or nervousness, North couldn't tell—entered, bowed slightly and said, "Your Lordship, I have this note for you from the Captain of HMS *Peregrine*, which docked early this morning in Newport."

"Thank you," North said and nodded at his young assistant, Hartleb, who gave the messenger a coin. As the man was about to turn and depart, North said, "Wait. Did you read the message?"

"Of course not, my Lord. I would never do such a thing."

"And yet you seem excited. Do you know its contents?"

The man paused and took a deep breath. "Yes. Or at least I suspect what it says."

"How did you come by this information?"

"I overheard the captain of the ship talking to another man."

"What did he say to this man?"

"That on the ship is the traitor George Washington, under arrest." He smiled broadly. "And if this be true, congratulations to you, sir. You will soon have the blaggard in hand."

North ignored the proffered congratulations. "Did he mention a Colonel Black?"

"Yes, my Lord. He mentioned he is on the ship."

"Have you told anyone else?"

"Certainly not."

"Good."

"But..."

"But what?"

"I think others nearby also heard the captain speaking about it. And they ran off shortly after hearing it."

"Even so, will you keep it to yourself for now?"

"Yes, my Lord."

North nodded again to his aide, who dug into his small purse and handed the messenger a larger coin.

"Young man," North said, "if you keep your mouth absolutely closed about this until the day after tomorrow at dawn, you may return here for another coin. If not, I will see to it that you have great trouble finding work." He paused. "Or send you to one of the prison hulks for revealing a state secret."

"Of course, my Lord. I will not mention it." He bowed again, more deeply this time, turned on his heel and left, almost running out of the room.

North looked at Hartleb. "We must get this news to the King before he hears it from someone else. Please order my carriage immediately."

"You are going without an appointment for an audience?"

"If I arrange for one, it will surely be tomorrow before it is done. In the meantime, if that young man who was just here already knows the news, many others in London may already know it, too."

"I will send for your carriage."

"Good. Also send a trusted messenger on a fast horse to Portsmouth. Black has instructions as to what to do now and will be awaiting the messenger."

"What is to be done by us?" Hartleb asked.

"Arrange for a contingent of marines to go to Portsmouth, take charge of Washington and bring him to London as soon as they can. Black will be expecting them. They are to stop just on the other side of London Bridge and await my further orders. Tell the Warder at the prison hulk *Justicia* that a special prisoner is coming and is to be housed in a separate cell, far from the ordinary prisoners. We don't want him harmed."

"Not imprisoned in the Tower, like the other American who is there now?"

North knew that Hartleb was referring to Henry Laurens, a former President of the Continental Congress who had been captured at sea, apparently on the way to try to negotiate a loan from the Dutch. "For one thing, I think he is quite different," North said. "Laurens may be a well-known rebel in the colonies, but he is virtually unknown here. He has little political value for us. Thus, where we hold him makes no difference."

"And for the other thing?"

"The Americans have shown little interest in bargaining for his release."

"Why not, do you think?"

"They don't seem to care what happens to him. The General will be quite different, I suspect. Which is why I want him in a real prison with a bad reputation. That way, the Americans will *think* he is going to suffer a traitor's death on the gallows at Tyburn. Sending him to a hotel like the Tower will send the wrong message."

"I have been to the Tower only twice, but it hardly seems a hotel."

"Close enough, compared to a prison hulk."

"I have heard the prison hulks are rife with typhus. Do you not risk his dying there?"

"Tell the Warder to put him in a cell segregated from other prisoners. The Americans will be anxious enough to get him back that I doubt he will be there long enough to contract anything."

"Very well. I will see to it."

"Good. Now go."

North put his chin on his hands. Dear God, he thought. I had no hope to succeed in this. If it proves to be true, I must tell the King. And persuade him not to undertake anything rash.

23

The King was living at the Queen's House—more formally Buckingham House—with Queen Charlotte and their thirteen children, including Prince William, who had just been born. (Good God, North asked himself. Would there soon be even more children?) While the palace was officially at St. James, the King was often at home at Buckingham. North had no appointment for an audience—the first time he had ever arrived to see the King without one—but he wanted to lose no time, lest the rumour, which he was sure was already winging its way to London, reach the King before he did. The risk was real because the King had informants everywhere.

On arriving at Buckingham House by carriage, he bid his coachmen to wait. As he got out, he noted that the King's colours were flying on the flagpole over the House, which meant the King was in residence.

He climbed down from his carriage and approached the guard booth, which was staffed by two royal marines with fixed bayonets. An army major was also present.

"Good afternoon, Major," North said. "I am Lord North, the First Minister, here to see the King on a most urgent matter."

The man actually reared back slightly, so surprised was he to see the First Minister at the gate. Recovering, he peered hard at North, clearly trying to determine if the gentleman standing in front of him was truly the First Minister or just a lunatic. After a moment, he said, "How am I to tell if you are really Lord North?"

North gestured at his highly polished carriage, still standing only a few steps away, with four horses, two liveried coachmen in front and a soldier standing guard on the running board. The major looked, clearly taking in all of that plus the Royal Arms—the crown with rampant lion and standing, chained unicorn—emblazoned on the side of the carriage.

"What beggar or fool do you think arrives in that?" North asked.

"All right, I will enquire. Please wait."

North paced up and down for a few minutes, but it was not long before some pedestrians seemed to become aware of him and his carriage and began pointing at him and edging closer. He was rescued by the return of the major. "The King's equerry, who happens to be here, too, will see you and vouch for you—if that is possible." He left unsaid what would happen if he could not be vouched for, but North imagined that it would not be good.

Fortunately, he had met and dealt with the King's equerry many times. They met in a courtyard beyond the guard gate. The equerry, Lord Salisbury, looked at first startled, then said, "It is indeed you, North. I take it you do not have an appointment with His Majesty."

"No, I do not. I have never before come to see the King in this fashion, but I have news for him of the utmost urgency."

"It is most irregular, but I will enquire if he will grant you an audience on such short notice. May I tell him whether this news is good or bad?"

"Good. Excellent, in fact."

Lord Salisbury led him to an anteroom, where he waited, trying to think how best to put the whole matter to the King, whom he had kept in the dark about the whole project. And now, by coming to the Queen's House without court dress, and without an appointment, he was breaching every protocol. He had, in fact, been to the Queen's House only one other time, when the King, the year before, had invited the cabinet on the spur of the moment to join him for a meeting in his private library.

Finally, after what seemed like hours but was probably only minutes, he was led in to see the King in that very same library. He was sitting in a large chair at the head of the table, dandling his newborn son on his lap and making cooing noises. Upon seeing North, he passed the baby to a nearby maid, who whisked the child out of the room. With a hand gesture, he dismissed three other servants, who backed out of the room and closed the door quietly behind them.

"This is most unusual, my Lord. Unheard of, even. What brings you here so informally, without court dress, and with no appointment for an audience or even an hour's notice?" He frowned.

North, standing in front of him, but a respectable distance back, bowed and said, "Good afternoon, Your Majesty. I apologize for so informal an appearance, but I wanted you to hear the good news from your First Minister before you might hear it from the street."

"The Americans have surrendered all of their armies? That horrible man John Adams has died of the pox?" The King laughed uproariously.

"No, Sire. The news is that George Washington has been captured."

"What, what? Are you serious?"

"Very."

"Where is he? In New York in Clinton's hands? Or did Cornwallis seize him down in the South, where I hear our campaign is going well."

"Neither. He is just arrived here."

"What? Here in London?" A broad smile lit his face from one side to the other and North felt his own face light up in response. The King, albeit only forty-two, had recently, in North's view, begun on his face to show the cares of the monarchy, despite the recent victories against the Americans.

"No, Sire. He is aboard one of your ships in the harbour at Portsmouth, but I have ordered him transported to one of the prison hulks in the Thames, under guard by two marine detachments."

"Why not to Newgate?"

"Newgate, like the Clink, was destroyed by the mobs last June. And none of the remaining prisons is convenient. Besides, a prison hulk should frighten him and he can be moved someplace better in exchange for concessions."

"Can we not just hang the traitor there in Portsmouth, on the spot? I can travel there easily."

He knew the King was joking since during the last year or two he had evinced great interest in the laws of war as they applied to prisoners captured by both sides during the conflict. He thus was no doubt aware of the legal process to be followed.

"No, Sire. He must be brought here to London for trial, probably at the Old Bailey. We will need to notify the prosecutor and begin the process."

"He will be charged with high treason, I assume. And with his guilt so obvious, the trial for high treason will just be a formality, correct? How long will it take before we can watch him swing? I have never attended a public hanging, but there is always a first time."

"Sire, it will take some time. It is important to make the process look fair. All the world will be watching."

"True, true."

"There is also his defence to be considered."

"What defence can there be?"

"He will contend that he cannot be criminally prosecuted. That he is a prisoner of war, and that under the laws of war, he must be released at the end of hostilities or exchanged for another prisoner. Unless he has committed an actual crime, such as murder. Of which there is no evidence here."

"The laws of war be damned! I want him executed. That is, after all, what they did to poor Major Andre."

"Yes, they did. But the claim was that he was captured behind their lines out of uniform so he was no better than a spy."

The King rose from his chair, which North had never seen him do before during an audience with him, and began to pace, hands clasped behind his back.

"Let me ask you this, First Minister. These Americans are not a country. They are our colonies, and colonies I have formally proclaimed to be in a state of rebellion, is that not right?"

"Yes, you did that in 1775 as to at least some colonies."

"And so why should we recognize their army as anything other than a band of rebels, who are not subject to the laws of war? Were the rioters who burned Newgate and the Clink this past June an army entitled to plead the laws of war in their defence?"

"No. But as applied to the rebels in the colonies, that is an excellent question, Sire. But one reason to apply them, surely, is that we want our own soldiers treated fairly. If we ignore the laws of war, the rebels may have excuse to do so, too. We have tens of thousands of men in the colonies, and hundreds are already prisoners of the Americans."

"Very well. But you now know my wishes. You are a clever man, and I'm sure you will figure out how to carry them out."

North did not want to engage the King in a pointless debate about who had what powers. The King was well aware that the Parliament made the laws in the name of the King, and that the monarch could either sign them or abdicate. And the King was also well aware that the government carried out those laws, albeit always in the King's name, without much regard as to how he wished them carried out. And so North tried to distract him with some details, which the King was usually interested in pursuing.

"Sire, do you wish to know how the capture was carried out?"

"Of course. I was distracted from that by the fact of the capture, but I am most anxious to learn the details. Was it Clinton's men who captured him? Or Cornwallis's?"

"Neither. I sent a special agent, a Colonel Black, to seize him at his headquarters and bring him back here, outside the normal military chain of command."

"I am very pleased. But why not have him taken to New York?"

"I feared that if he were captured by our forces, bringing him back here might prove difficult and, with the time it takes to communicate back and forth, that General Clinton, who is still very angered by the hanging of his young aide Major Andre, might find an excuse to hang Washington himself in New York, thus taking away his true value."

"What true value?"

"To use as a bargaining chip to bring the rebellion to a quick and satisfactory end."

The King was silent for a moment. "I see. Well, I would prefer to hang him even if that causes the rebellion to last a little longer, frankly. And in any case, as you know, I don't believe the rebels will ever settle. They will settle only for their independence unless our fist smashes them."

"I understand, Sire."

"Was this your personal doing?"

"Yes, Sire, it was."

"My heartiest congratulations, then. Did you involve Lord Germain in it?"

"No."

The King stroked his chin. "I see. Well, perhaps leaving him out made sense."

"With your permission, Sire, I need to go and arrange for him to be taken to one of the prison hulks."

"I think he should go instead to the Tower," the King said.

"Why, Sire? The Tower is no longer fully a prison, and it will be too easy for him to escape from there, even if he is very closely held there, as Henry Laurens is."

"The Tower is where, for centuries, important traitors have been imprisoned before their execution."

"The highborn and titled government officials have been executed there. Not commoners."

"I don't know if that's true, but I nevertheless want to see him in the Tower. The thought pleases me somehow. Be sure to put him in a room where he can see the stone on which Anne Boleyn lost her head. And let the Governor and Warder of the Tower know that the General is to be made aware of its use."

"Of course, Sire." North had, in fact, no idea if anyone knew where the stone was on which the Queen had been beheaded, if it even still existed. Or was it a block of wood? The King was far from crazy, but the conversation was rapidly descending into farce. North tried again to reason with him. "Sire, it has been over thirty years since anyone was beheaded. And, again, it's a fate traditionally reserved for the highborn. It is a death that confers prestige."

"Washington's head on a pike on London Bridge might make it worthwhile to find an exception to that tradition."

North didn't think it worthwhile to remind the King that he wasn't Henry VIII and that, as a monarch with limited powers, he couldn't make that kind of thing happen. Or could he?

24

After North left the King, he returned briefly to 10 Downing, where he asked Hartleb to send a messenger to notify Solicitor General James Mansfield—the man in charge of preparing Crown prosecutions—that North would shortly be coming to see him. Usually, ministers whom he wanted to see would, if their offices were elsewhere, call upon North at 10 Downing. But Mansfield and his predecessors in office had of late proved prickly about their supposed independence from the government. North had no desire to stand on ceremony. He needed to be sure that the investigation of Washington would proceed at a slow pace—long enough to use him to negotiate an end to the war.

After about an hour, the messenger returned to say that Mansfield was in his office and would be pleased to see North as soon that day as might be convenient. North called for his coachman and got immediately under way.

As his carriage rocked along, North reminded himself of the two things that gave him the upper hand over Mansfield. First, only three months earlier, he had recommended Mansfield's appointment to the King. Second, Mansfield's ultimate goal in life was to be a judge. Judicial appointments might formally be made by the King, but they were in fact controlled by the First Minister. There would be no need to mention either of those things, of course. They would perfume the very air of the room.

The greeting was effusive. Mansfield, a tall man in his late forties with a long nose and a receding hairline, rose upon North being announced and said, "My Lord, what an honour that you have come personally to see me in my humble office."

The rather large office to which he referred was hardly humble, but it was certainly cluttered. Every surface, including all the chairs, was piled high with briefs, most bound up with flat white ribbons to indicate their status as prosecution briefs in criminal cases.

"My apologies there are so few places to sit, my Lord."

"It is not a problem for me to remain standing. This should not take a long time."

Mansfield moved to the conference table, cleared the paper stacks from two of the chairs and said, "Making you stand would be terribly rude. Please do sit down. Would you like some tea, my Lord? I have something special from Richard Twining's establishment, just arrived from India."

"No, thank you. I've just come from 10 Downing, and I thought it appropriate, Mr. Solicitor, to let you know formally who will soon be a prisoner in the Tower."

"I already know. My sources told me early this morning he had been captured. But I was not aware until now where he would be imprisoned. If it is to be the Tower, we will soon add General Washington to the other American rebel who is now held there."

North tried to cover up his surprise. "How did you know that Washington has been captured, if I might ask?"

"I am friends with a man who is friends with the Admiral who superintends the Portsmouth naval base."

"I see" was all North said out loud. To himself, he praised God he had gotten to the King before the news had spread all over London, as it must already be doing. Or maybe the King had in fact heard it all before North got there. Although if he had, he had certainly given no sign of it. It also reminded him, as if he needed reminding, that there were no real secrets in London.

North tried to turn the conversation back to where he wanted it to go—delay, including the time and effort that would need to be expended on the Gordon Trial. "Mr. Solicitor, as you well know, Lord George Gordon is also a prisoner in the Tower."

"That he is. We will be trying him very soon for high treason for his role in fomenting the terrible riots and the resulting fires of this last June. And, I devoutly hope, escorting him shortly thereafter to the gallows at Tyburn."

"Yes, that is to be hoped," North said. "Lord Gordon is a traitor, not only to his King, but to his class."

The Solicitor General, though, was not yet ready to discuss the Gordon trial. He was instead intent on learning more about Washington. "I am most curious to know, my Lord, how Washington's capture was accomplished. I assume that he was not taken on the high seas like the hapless Mr. Laurens. Was it Clinton or Cornwallis?"

"Neither. I went outside the procedure by which orders are usually given in the military. With the aid of a certain Admiral and a certain General whom I will not name, I got it accomplished, complete with arrest warrant."

Mansfield chuckled. "I see. Why did you feel you even needed a warrant?"

"Because when I looked into it, Mr. Solicitor, I was surprised to find that although the colonies had been declared in a general state of rebellion and sedition in 1775, only two arrest warrants had ever been issued for any of the leaders of the rebellion, Washington not amongst them. I wanted to give no one the idea that Washington, once captured, would be a prisoner of war rather than an arrested traitor."

"When did you set this all in motion, my Lord?"

"A little over a year ago I sent a mission to start the arrangements, involving Loyalists, of course. And then I sent another mission after that one to finalize things, and this final time, a specially trained man—a Colonel in the army—who carried out the plan."

"You were at the time not sanguine about our prospects?"

"No. We are spending vast sums of money on the effort and copiously shedding the blood of our young soldiers. We'd had almost ten thousand deaths to that point."

North paused, surprised at himself for needing to push back tears.

"I know the war has been a heavy burden for you, my Lord."

"Yes, it has. I thought that having Washington in our hands would make it a great deal easier to bring the rebels to the bargaining table and work out a reasonable peace short of full independence."

"I don't mean to be unkind in saying this, my Lord, but that is something which you've so far failed to accomplish, despite several attempts."

"Two more or less serious attempts before I conceived this latest mission, yes. Although they were both badly bungled by those sent to carry them out."

"But now, my Lord—" Mansfield paused and his face lit up "—I have heard we are on the verge of winning, and we can transport all of the rebel leaders here in chains, try them for treason and hang them high."

He raised his hand in front of his face, pointed it downward and waggled his first and middle fingers back and forth, clearly intending to imitate a man's legs kicking as he strangled on the rope.

North did not respond.

Mansfield, perhaps realizing that North was not all that pleased with his finger puppetry, said, "My Lord, I assume that you must have a purpose in coming here, else you would simply have let me know of Washington's capture through one of your assistants. You must want something." He paused. "I should be inclined to provide it. So long as it is just."

"I do want something."

"What might that be?"

"Before Washington can be charged, there must be an investigation. I would like it to be thorough…and slow."

"I'm not sure what there is to investigate. All we need do is read the jury their bloody independence declaration, in which they insult the King personally, make many false allegations against him, call him a tyrant and declare they are independent."

"Washington didn't sign that document."

"But he has conspired with those who did to carry out its purpose."

"Then, as you can see, Mr. Solicitor, there *is* something complicated to investigate. This conspiracy you mention, plus your work on the upcoming Gordon trial."

"Well, it's true that I am right now very busy finishing the preparation for Lord Gordon's trial, which is to start shortly in the Old Bailey. The preparation is a great deal of work because the mob he encouraged to burn the better part of Westminster, in supposed protest of the relaxation of restrictions on Catholics, had many rioters in it. Some are now imprisoned, some not, and interviewing them and preparing them to be witnesses at his trial has proved time-consuming and complicated."

"I can understand, Mr. Solicitor, that that might consume you for many weeks."

"Yes. I suppose that our work on the Gordon matter could indeed delay the investigation of General Washington. Is that all you want for him, a slower walk to the gallows?"

"Certainly."

"There is something else I should tell you, then, my Lord," the Solicitor General said.

"What is that?"

"Despite my earlier statement, the trial of Washington may not be so simple. We will need witnesses to his treason."

"Surely there are plenty of officers here in London who served in America and can testify to his efforts to defeat His Majesty's Army, the very essence of treason."

"Well, this morning I managed to talk to two who happen to be resident here of London and live quite nearby. They are reluctant—deeply reluctant—to testify against Washington."

"Why?"

"Two reasons. First, they respect him greatly. They did not when he assumed command in '75, but they do now that he has fought them to a stalemate."

"And the second?"

"They insist he is a prisoner of war and nothing more, as they say they would be if captured by the Americans. That status would, of course, mean imprisonment until the war's end, but no punishment as such."

"How will we overcome that?"

"There may be officers here in London who have different attitudes. Or if not, there may be some officers still serving in America who do. But we will have to send someone over there to look for them and bring them back."

"Which means Washington's trial cannot take place for months."

"Exactly."

"Will you undertake the effort to find the appropriate witnesses?"

"Yes."

North stood up. "Thank you, Mr. Solicitor. I very much appreciate your assistance in a matter of such high importance to

King and country. Now I must go to the Tower to inform the Warder of the arrival of his new prisoner."

As his carriage rolled towards the Tower, North could not help but wonder if, in seizing Washington, he had not been far too clever. What if the rebels did not come to the bargaining table, but Cornwallis went on to win decisively and defeat the rebellion? And what if Washington and the other leaders ended up being executed, as both the King and Mansfield wished? The King would have triumphed.

"And then?" he asked himself and knew the answer: the constraints that bound the King to behave like a monarch of limited powers, subject to an elected government, might well be loosened for good. Which meant that instead of being remembered as the man who lost America—a thought that often kept him up at night—he would instead be remembered as the man who lost English democracy.

25

As North approached the Tower walls, with the White Tower looming above them from within, he thought, as he did every time he saw it, about all those who had died inside, from the two young princes murdered by their uncle, Richard III, to Henry VIII's wife of three years, Anne Boleyn, and many others, before and since. North's enemies, for whom he was a man lacking in emotion, would have been surprised to know that he shivered slightly every time he laid eyes on the place. Once at the Tower, North located both the Governor, Major Gore, who oversaw the Tower's operations, and the Warder, who was charged with the well-being of those who were staying there. Both men were clearly astounded to see him. First Ministers did not usually visit.

"Gentlemen, I will soon be sending you a special prisoner," he said. "Someone suspected of high treason, but not yet indicted."

"May we know his name?" the Governor asked.

"You will learn his name when he arrives, which will probably be within two days, maybe sooner." Although North well knew, of course, that they would probably read it in the newspapers within the day.

"I understand, Excellency," the Warder said. "I will not enquire further for now. Is the man to be treated as a prisoner or a guest?"

"I do not understand the difference."

"We have some sections of the Tower containing rooms which are more like apartments. They have no bars and the people living in them are accused of no crime. They are simply living here, day in and day out. We might better call them residents."

"And others?"

"There are prisoners who are given more or less the run of the Tower, except that they may not leave entirely freely, or are restricted only to certain areas. They are locked in only at night. Still other sections have cells, with bars, in which the prisoner is more closely guarded and sometimes not permitted to leave the cell at all. This man Laurens, of whom I trust you are aware, is in two small rooms, formerly an apartment, to which we have added bars. They overlook the parade, where he may be stared at by those who walk by. He is largely confined to the rooms."

"Those in the first group you call guests?"

"It is more my own term to help distinguish one from the other, my Lord." He grinned.

"I see. I think the King would like to see him treated more as a guest for now, with some possible restrictions I will later suggest to you."

"If I might ask, my Lord, if the man who will shortly be delivered here is suspected of high treason, why is he to be treated as a guest of any kind?"

"I didn't mean that he is to undergo no stresses. He should be permitted, for example, to walk about, but only where people can see him and jeer at him. My goal is to humble him. Also, we can perhaps influence him later by taking away some of the liberties he comes to enjoy."

"The King giveth and the King taketh away?" the Warder asked.

"Precisely."

"Is he to be permitted visitors? Lord Gordon, for example, has been permitted visitors from time to time, although Laurens's visitors are very restricted."

"Yes, we may learn important things by seeing who comes to visit him."

"All right, my Lord, we will put him in a room with bars, as we have done with Laurens, but not restrict him so much. Are people to be permitted to throw things at him? Offal and rotten fruit and eggs and the like? There is a building on the parade to which the public might be given access during the day. If the prisoner—excuse me, the guest—could be restricted to walking only upon that area of the parade, he might be a target of items thrown from the windows of that structure."

"Is that something that has been done here in recent times?"

"Not that I know of, my Lord, but it is done in other places in England, and if you wish him to be humbled..." He raised his eyebrows and shrugged his shoulders.

North thought a moment. "All right, but only with small, soft things. With larger things, there would be too much chance of injury."

"We will see it done properly."

"And there is one other thing, Governor. Do you have a room from which the prisoner will be able to see the stone on which Anne Boleyn lost her head?"

The Governor gave him a strange look. "I have never heard that we still have such a stone, if it even was a stone rather than a wood block. But I think it was more likely a block. A stone would dull or break the executioner's sword."

"Well, nevertheless, find a big, flat stone and put it someplace where the prisoner can see it. If he asks, tell him it's where the Queen lost her head. The King wishes it done."

"And if the prisoner doesn't ask?"

"Tell him nothing."

"All right, my Lord. I will be sure to do so."

He bid them good afternoon and walked to his carriage, which was waiting in a courtyard. He glanced up and saw three ravens peering down at him from a high wall. It did not seem a good omen.

He climbed into the carriage and bid his driver take him back to Number 10. When he arrived there, it was already late in the day. With the exception of Hartleb, the staff had gone, his wife was out of town and the two of his children who still lived with them, ages fifteen and twenty, were out and about. He felt the fatigue and despondency from which he sometimes suffered coming upon him and wandered into the garden at the back of the house. The garden was still very much in winter, but nevertheless a place he liked to go and sit and think. His favourite spot was a weathered oak bench built around an old holly tree. He sat there and let the usual thoughts run through his head: that he was stuck in a life he increasingly found not to his liking and wished fervently to cease being First Minister if only the King could be persuaded to let him go. So far His Majesty had not agreed.

He had been active as a young man and enjoyed clubbing and playing at sports. Now, although he was only forty-eight, he felt like an old man, and he had become increasingly inactive and, as the kinder opposition papers described him, corpulent. He rarely got to go out and do anything, let alone observe anything first-hand or close-up. Instead, he spent his days listening to the Members of Parliament whine and his ministers complain.

He had even tired of meeting with the King, whom he had known since childhood, when his father was the King's tutor.

Next month would mark the tenth anniversary of his accession to his current office. At first, meeting one-on-one with George III about affairs of state had been fascinating. But the

King's idiosyncrasies—including his constant desire to shape political events and, since the revolt in the American colonies began, his desire to win the war no matter the cost—had begun to wear on him.

From the bench he could see the small wooden door that led through the garden wall into an alleyway. He had often thought of just walking through it and leaving it all behind.

He suddenly had an idea. He heaved himself up from the bench and went to find Hartleb to see if they could make it happen.

Several days later, in the afternoon, Hartleb approached North and said, "We have received word that the marines and their prisoner have reached the south side of London Bridge and await instructions."

"Very good. Send a messenger to let them know that when the sun has just begun to set they should start to proceed across the bridge and then to the Tower. Is there any other information?"

"Yes. Crowds have begun to gather. Word has spread that someone important is being brought in. But there are different rumours as to who it is. They are shielding him with a hood, so no one is certain."

"Let them know to take the hood off when they proceed across the bridge and let people know who it is. But have him gagged. I've heard that he doesn't speak often, but when he does, he has a silver tongue."

"Your Lordship, is that not risky? Ruffians may hurl stones at him."

"I earlier thought that risk too great to take, but I think I will take it for now in order to enjoy the humiliation he is certain to feel by being paraded in public like a common criminal. We can take greater precautions later, when he is in the Tower."

"Yes, my Lord."

"If Colonel Black is there with his prisoner, as I suspect he must be, ask that he call on me first thing tomorrow morning at Number 10."

"Yes, my Lord."

"And when you return, let us put our plan in motion."

26

North's first thought had been that they should station themselves directly across from Traitors Gate, the main entrance into the Tower, which a military contingent would need to use to get inside. In the end, he had chosen to be taken, along with Hartleb, to the front of the church of St. Magnus the Martyr, which faced the road that led directly to London Bridge. The sun was just setting when they arrived.

"Wait behind the church for us," he said to the coachman. "We will return to you within the hour."

"Of course, my Lord. But perhaps it would be better if you were to wait with the carriage over there." He pointed to an archway just up the block. "It would be safer. This is not a genteel neighbourhood."

"Thank you," North said. "But I prefer to remain here by the church."

With that, he walked up the steps to the church and pressed himself into a dark niche near the large wooden door, which was closed. Hartleb quickly joined him. North could see the street, but no one could see them. Or so he hoped.

"Might not someone come through this door, Mr. Hartleb?" he asked.

"Unlikely this time of night, my Lord. The vespers were already two hours ago." He pointed to a hand-lettered sign on the door setting out the church's schedule.

"Do you think my disguise adequate?" North asked.

Hartleb looked him over. "The hood, drawn tight like that, covers most of your face, and the rough cloth of the coat perhaps covers your status."

North looked down at his shoes. "My boots do not look right."

Hartleb looked down at his own. "Nor mine. But it is not something I thought of. Perhaps we could..."

He was interrupted by North. "Look! People are beginning to gather along the roadway. I can't see the bridge, but I can hear the babble of people on it."

"Word must have spread, sir. Perhaps this will not be an unruly group, though. I see nothing in their hands."

"In the riots, the ruffians were very good at concealing things until they wanted to use them. That's why so many constables were injured until we finally called in the army."

"I was not in your service at the time."

"More's the pity."

"Oh, wait, sir. That one man there—" he pointed "—is carrying a small bag at his side, which bulges suspiciously."

"I hope it is offal and not rocks. But look, here they come."

They watched as the marines came down from the bridge onto the roadway in front of the church. North pressed his back against the stone wall, the better to protect himself from being seen. As he waited, he realized that he had not felt so alive in years.

"There he is," Hartleb said, pointing. "On the horse, in the middle of the formation!"

"I had heard he was tall," North said, "but he sits even taller in the saddle than I had expected."

As the procession began to pass directly in front of them, the man with the bag darted in amongst the marines, followed by two more men. They reached into their bags and began throwing something at Washington.

"Whatever are they throwing?" North asked.

"Flower petals, I think."

"Flower petals? Where would they get those this time of year?"

"I don't know. Perhaps they were dried in the summer and saved."

Suddenly, the crowd began to shout, but the sound was initially muffled. Then it came clear.

"Long live George Washington!" And then it was repeated over and over, louder each time, a chant taken up all and down the road, where more people waited.

Without warning, the door to the church opened and a silver-haired man in clerical garb stepped out. "Excuse me for startling you," he said. "I came out to see what all the noise is about. Do you know who the man on the horse is?"

"Yes," North said. "It's General George Washington."

"Really? That is remarkable. It seems the crowd is pleased to see him. Do you know what brings him here?"

North hesitated. "No, not really."

The man had been looking away from them, towards the procession. As it moved out of sight, he turned fully towards them and said, "It's a cold night. May I offer you gentlemen a hot tea?"

"We are well situated, thank you," Hartleb said.

"Let me at least introduce myself," he said. "I'm Cedric Smith, the rector of this church. And who might you gentlemen be?"

He glanced at their faces, stared a few seconds at North's,

then bolted back in surprise. "Your Lordship, excuse me. I did not expect you here."

"These are unusual times. I hope I can prevail upon you to keep our presence here to yourself. It is something of a state secret."

"Of course. Of course. But I must ask, was that man on the horse really George Washington?"

"Yes, we believe so."

"I will not ask whether you know how he got here or what he is doing here, but it would be a great blessing if it might help bring an end to the war."

"It could do that," North said. "It could indeed."

"If you will excuse me, Excellency, I have work to do inside." He made a slight bow, opened the door and disappeared back into the interior.

North looked at Hartleb. "So much for the efficacy of the disguise."

They both laughed.

As they headed back to the carriage, North said, "Mr. Hartleb, what do you think the chances are of his keeping our presence here a secret, whether a state secret or just an ordinary secret?"

"About the same as cows reading Greek."

"You are probably right. Is that a phrase they used at Oxford back when you were there?"

"Yes, and more colourful expressions, too."

North smiled. "Perhaps you will tell them to me sometime."

"I could never—"

"Don't worry. I will not ask. But in any case, who do you think all those people are who are cheering Washington?"

"I really don't know."

"It seems likely to me they are American rebels who are secreted here in London. How many Americans are in this city, do you think?"

"Quite a few, but they are almost all Loyalists who have fled the colonies. And certainly no Loyalist is a friend to Washington. They regard him as someone who has destroyed their erstwhile comfortable lives."

They had reached the carriage, and the coachman held the open door for them. As he stepped inside, he said to Hartleb, "Somehow, the rebels got wind of this and came out to greet their leader. I don't know how they found out, but it must be so."

"That is certainly possible, my Lord."

"I can see no other explanation."

27

North returned to his apartment, which consisted of seven well-appointed rooms on the second floor of Number 10, climbed into bed and fell into a deep, if troubled, sleep.

The next morning, when he returned to the state floor, where the cabinet room was located, he spied Hartleb, already at work at his desk.

"Good morning, Excellency. I trust you are well today."

"Very, thank you, Mr. Hartleb. And you?"

"The same, sir."

"Very good. Let's discuss my schedule for the day."

"Colonel Black is already here, as you requested. He is waiting in the anteroom."

"Please show him in."

Black entered a few minutes later. North rose from his chair and went to greet him, extending his hand and, when taken, pumping Black's hand vigorously.

"Colonel Black, my heartfelt congratulations on having accomplished your mission. I must tell you..."

"...that you didn't think I would succeed?"

North smiled. "No, but I knew that if anyone could succeed, you could. You were selected from amongst our best young officers. I also knew, of course, that no matter how competent and courageous you are, your mission involved great risks."

Black laughed. "There were a few, Excellency, here and there."

"I'm sure there were. This afternoon, I'd like you to tell my staff the details. Tomorrow, I'd like also for you to attend a cabinet meeting to describe your activities to the ministers. My secretary will let you know the time of the meeting."

"Of course."

"My military adviser, Lord Germain, will be present tomorrow. I assume you know who he is."

"Yes, the Secretary of State for the American colonies."

"Exactly. As you may also know, up till now, I have put him directly in charge of our armies in America, and our forces at sea, as well. He will no doubt be unhappy with me because I kept him in the dark about your mission."

"He was not aware?"

"No. And that is his complaint. That I went outside his chain of command."

"I'm not currently attached to any army unit that is in America, nor to the sea forces that are there."

"The very point I have made to him. Nonetheless, he is an ambitious man, and he thinks that the fact that this was done without his participation reflects poorly on him. He wants to sit where I sit, you see."

"Is there some particular way I should comport myself, then, to avoid giving offence?"

"No, I simply want you to be aware that if he flies into a rage, it is nothing you have done or said."

"Understood, my Lord."

"Good. Now let me ask you, how was the trip from Portsmouth to the Tower?"

"It went well enough, especially at the beginning, when we were near Portsmouth. Washington rode a horse, closely guarded, and the marines put a strong perimeter in place. When we got close to London, though, word had somehow got out and there were crowds along the way."

"I have heard they were unruly."

"I cannot say for sure, my Lord. We were inside three ranks of marines. I could hear people shouting, but I could hardly see them."

"Were the crowds friendly or hostile?"

"Largely friendly, so far as I could hear, but perhaps as much from curiosity as anything else."

"Is he now safely in the Tower?" North asked.

"Yes."

"Very good. In a few weeks, we will be having a ceremony here at 10 Downing for you."

"A ceremony, sir?"

"Yes, for your promotion to Brigadier General. It is not something I can do on my own, but I will strongly urge it upon the Promotions Board and I'm sure the King will support it with enthusiasm. Which reminds me that the King would enjoy an audience with you."

"I'm honoured, sir, both at the promotion if it occurs and at the opportunity to meet the sovereign. But it was enough for me just to serve my king and my country."

"You have honoured and aided your king and country more than you know, Colonel. What are your plans now?"

"I hope to obtain a leave of perhaps a month to return to Bibury, where my sister and her children still live. I have not seen them in almost a year."

"That sounds a wonderful plan. I wonder, though, if you

might consider doing one more favour for your country before you take your leave, which I will plan to extend to two months."

"What is that, sir?"

"Move into the Tower. I am concerned it is somehow not secure for Washington there."

Black realized that Lord North was not really making a request of him. He expected him simply to agree to do it. Nonetheless, Black said, "If I may be so bold, my Lord, why is he being held there in lieu of a more secure place?"

"The King wants him there. For what I might call political reasons. It is as simple as that."

"I will accept the assignment and hope to do my best."

28

Abbott sailed to England aboard the civilian sloop *Lily Rose*, captained by Roger Chittum and flying a white flag. It was a relatively smooth voyage. Other than bumping his head several times on a bulkhead—they were designed for shorter men—he suffered no ill effects from the voyage.

On the way, they were boarded three times—once two days off the coast of Philadelphia, where the ships of the British blockade seemed thick in the water, once in mid-ocean and once as they made landfall on the southwest tip of Ireland. On the first two occasions, the officer in charge of the boarding party had briefly inspected their papers, including the commission appointing Abbott as Ambassador Plenipotentiary. Each time, the officer had handed the papers back, saluted Captain Chittum, wished them fair sailing and departed.

The third time was different. The officer in charge of the boarding party had been openly hostile and had insisted Abbott and Captain Chittum board his longboat and return with him to his own ship, HMS *Duke*, a three-decker 98-gun ship of the line. Abbott had never before laid eyes on such a huge vessel.

Once aboard *Duke*, the British captain and two of his officers had interrogated them for more than two hours, before finally acknowledging that perhaps they were who they said they were and permitting them to return to their own ship. But the Captain of *Duke* had icily instructed Captain Chittum that the *Lily Rose* was to remain in place for twenty-four hours to give the British ship time to make port and advise the authorities of the imminent arrival of the American ship. So Captain Chittum sailed *Lily Rose* back and forth for a day off the Irish coast. Even in winter, Abbott found it beautiful.

Four weeks earlier, Charles Thompson had been present when Huntington had given Abbott his ambassadorial instructions. Whether to record them for the records of the Congress in his job as Secretary, or for some other reason, Abbott was unsure.

After Huntington had left the room, Thompson said, "I know you have been told your powers are limited and that you may do this, but not that."

"True."

"My advice? Promise what you need to get Washington back. From what I have heard in the Congress these many months, day in and day out, we are currently losing the war. With Washington to lead us, we can still win it. Without him, I fear we will not."

"What if I promise something beyond my authority?"

"I'd not worry about it. Just get Washington released as part of the agreement you make while they wait for confirmation from Congress—which you will assure them is only a formality. It will all work out."

"Why would they let him go before the agreement is confirmed?"

"He can be paroled, if we are lucky, to some neutral country, and promise on his honour to come back if the agreement is not confirmed. We'll then spirit him out of that country."

"You're certain, then, that this strategy will work?"

"If the reports the Congress has received of what is being said in Parliament are correct. North, who initiated the intolerable taxes and restrictions visited upon us, has more recently become desperate to end the war and get on with the task of defeating France. He simply has yet to convince the King."

"Do you know if the King can be convinced?"

"I would have no way of knowing. But in the end the decision belongs to the government."

"If the King opposes the deal?"

He shrugged. "He can abdicate."

"I am still concerned about exceeding my authority."

"If you have to exceed your authority, you can use Dr. Franklin as your model. He has never paid much attention to such boundaries."

"I know him, of course, but only as a sometime client, and then only briefly. Do you know him well?"

"Fairly well, yes, although we have not always been political friends."

"I will try to emulate him, sir. But I have a question of you."

"Of course, Colonel. What is it?"

"What will you be doing on this side of the ocean to respond to this outrage? Surely, the Congress and the generals will not just sit here and think that sending me is a solution."

"We are recalling to Philadelphia all the delegates who have already left to spend Christmas at home. For those who are many days away, we have sent fast horsemen." He paused and laughed. "From the look on your face, Colonel, you don't think that is adequate."

"I don't. Is there anything else?"

"Many of our best generals are in the Carolinas, fighting Cornwallis and his troops. But we still have considerable forces near New York, and we are talking now with the generals who are nearby about doing something audacious." He paused. "As soon as a temporary commander-in-chief is named."

"Who might that be?"

"By talent and success it should be—likely will be—Major General Nathanael Greene. But he is on his way to North Carolina to take command of our southern army. He will need to be recalled, and that will take weeks."

Abbott was incredulous. "So the audacious thing you think of may be delayed by weeks?"

"It might. Sometimes this war grinds exceedingly slow."

"Even so, what kind of thing might that be to retaliate for this outrage?"

Thompson stood there for a moment, saying nothing.

"Do you not trust me, Mr. Thompson?"

Thompson laughed again. "We do. Indeed we are entrusting you with perhaps the most important thing, getting General Washington back here. It's just that we have no plan as yet. We are awaiting the arrival of several men and generals important to anything we might do. They should be here within days. I assume that some kind of new military thrust will be the result."

"I see. Perhaps you will find a way to let me know."

"We will write to you regularly, and we will assume that you will send us your reports regularly. But you will be many weeks away and in the midst of the enemy. It would be hard to assure the secrecy of what we might tell you or what you might tell us. You may need to go for long periods without any further formal instructions from us. And your communicating back to us may end up being just as general in nature."

"You could send a person to me with the instructions in his head."

"Of course, and we may. Is there anything else you wish to ask, Colonel?"

"No. Is there anything else you might want to tell me?"

"Only that when you see His Excellency please give him my regards and my best wishes for his good health and his prompt return to lead us on to victory."

"I will."

"Godspeed, Colonel."

Almost five weeks after he had said goodbye to Philadelphia, Abbott stood on the deck of the *Lily Rose*, pondering his conversation with Thompson, which by then seemed long ago. He watched as the harbour pilot guided them slowly into port, the long ocean voyage finally behind him. As a foreign ship, they had first been quarantined off the port for five days before being permitted into the harbour, so Abbott fully expected to be met by someone from the government.

He was not disappointed. When they disembarked, he found a squad of British soldiers in dress uniforms waiting for him on the quay. Standing slightly in front of them was a well-dressed civilian wearing a long black coat with silver buttons, a red waistcoat beneath and black breeches, topped off with a white cravat at the neck. His black boots came to mid-calf.

"Greetings, sir," the man said. "We have been expecting you. But I have not yet had the pleasure of learning your name."

"I'm Ethan Abbott, Ambassador Plenipotentiary from the Continental Congress of the American States. I am here with full authority to negotiate the release of His Excellency, General Washington."

"Welcome to England, Mr. Abbott. I'm Jacob Hartleb, first assistant to His Excellency Lord North, First Lord of the Treasury and Chancellor of the Exchequer." He bowed slightly.

"Is he not also the Prime Minister?"

Hartleb smiled. "He prefers not to use that title because he says it doesn't exist in our laws, but he is oft called that, yes. Or sometimes First Minister. In any case, if you are asking if he has authority to negotiate on behalf of His Majesty, he does."

"I see. Now that we have introduced each other, has His Excellency, George Washington, already arrived in England?"

"Yes. He is well and living in the Tower of London."

"He is imprisoned?"

"Yes, in the Tower, but he is not closely held. You might say he is for the moment more of a guest."

"Whatever his status, I should like to see him immediately."

"I'm afraid that will take a while. First your credentials must be examined, the government must decide what status you are to be accorded and so forth. But I'll see what can be done."

Abbott thought to protest that his status was clear—he was an ambassador from a sovereign and independent country—but then thought better of it. This was neither the time nor the place. Instead, he said only, "Thank you. I plan to ask after His Excellency's well-being every day."

Hartleb looked over Abbott's shoulder, as if searching for someone else. After an awkward few seconds, and looking slightly embarrassed, he asked, "Are you the only person of ambassadorial rank in your party?"

Abbott smiled. "Yes. Were you expecting someone else?"

"Candidly, we were expecting Dr. Franklin to arrive from France on a different ship, or even John Adams, although, given His Majesty's disposition with regard to the latter gentleman, it was perhaps wise not to send him."

"I am the only one, and I have as yet had no contact with our representatives in France. I have full authority to negotiate with your government without him." Without a further word, he handed Hartleb his commission. Hartleb gave the papers no more careful examination than had the first two officers who had boarded *Lily Rose*, and handed them back.

"I've never seen such papers before, but they seem in order. I am being rude, however," Hartleb said. "I do not mean to keep you standing here. We have two carriages nearby, one for us and one for whatever baggage you have, which the porters will see to unless something in it is confidential."

"No, there is nothing like that."

"Good. We should go, then. Unfortunately, we were not able to bring either carriage onto the dock." He stared at Abbott's peg, which Abbott had intentionally left visible beneath a pair of culottes, rather than try to strap on a fake boot of wood and leather, made for him by a clever shoemaker in Philadelphia. "Can you…?"

"Fear not, Mr. Hartleb. I can walk a long way on this peg. I have had it quite a while. Sometimes I limp a bit, but please don't worry about it."

"If I might be so bold as to ask a personal question of someone of whom I have only just made the acquaintance, how did you lose it?"

Abbott knew that what he was really asking was whether it was a military wound or something else. He was only too happy to oblige him.

"I lost it at the battle of Saratoga. A ball in the leg."

"Ah, that was a battle we lost, and badly. Indeed, the generals who lost it came back to testify before Parliament as to how it could possibly have happened. Back then, we thought all of you, and your soldiery in particular, were rural bumpkins."

"But we weren't and we are not."

"So true. Well, at least one of your famous generals in that battle, General Arnold, has now come over to us."

"I know Mr. Arnold. I rode beside him. You are most welcome to keep him."

"You don't refer to him as *General* Arnold?"

"No, his name was struck from the records of our army. If he is a general at all, he is your general now, not ours." As soon as the words were out of his mouth, he realized that getting into an argument about who was or was not a traitor wasn't a path it made sense to go down. At least not right then.

Nor, apparently, did Hartleb since he quickly changed the subject. "Let's head to the carriage, then—" he pointed down the dock, where Abbott could see a black carriage waiting, perhaps a hundred yards away "—and be on our way to London."

Abbott didn't usually walk with a limp over short distances, despite his peg, but on that day he chose to limp a bit. Just to drive home who he was and what he stood for.

29

One of the many things that Charles Thompson had discussed with Abbott the day he left was where he might stay in London.

"The government," Thompson had said, "will no doubt offer to put you up in some kind of guest house for important visitors. You should politely decline the invitation because that house will be a den of spies."

"You have provided me with sufficient funds to rent lodging."

"Yes, certainly. But I have an alternative idea that might work out. As you know, Dr. Franklin lived in London for several years in the '50s and again for many years in the '60s and '70s, before returning here. While there, he boarded with the widow Margaret Stevenson and her daughter, Polly, who is also now widowed, as well as, later, Polly's children, at their home. He often spoke of them to me as if they were a second family."

"But Mrs. Stevenson knows neither you nor me," Abbott said. "For although I spent some time with Dr. Franklin upon his return from England, he never mentioned the Stevensons to me."

"In times of war, many niceties fall away. I will give you a letter of introduction to Mrs. Stevenson, explaining my own position, your relationship to the Congress and Dr. Franklin, and I am sure they will make room for you."

"Even though they are on opposite sides from us?"

"From what Dr. Franklin told me, I wouldn't assume that to be the case, although he mentioned that they are discreet."

"If they will take me in—in exchange for rent, I assume—that would be ideal."

"You have great talents, Colonel, so I assume you will negotiate our independence on acceptable terms—amongst other things, we would like to continue to trade with them if we can also trade with others—and come home in triumph."

"I will try my best."

"One more thing. In London you may be in need of assistance at some point. There are men in London, whom we call Friends of America, who may be able to help." He handed him a piece of parchment. "Here are the names and addresses of five of them, including one, Joshua Laden, who is perhaps more inclined to take certain risks than the others. Memorize the list and then tear it up and throw it into the sea."

"How will they know who I am?"

Thompson smiled. "You just tell them you know me and ask them to confirm my middle name, which is Elihu. Very few people know that. Except them, and now you. I think that makes it a better code than the usual Greek and Roman names, which in my view are too easily guessed."

"Cannot someone easily find out your middle name?"

"No. It is indeed my middle name, but to learn it they would have to find the baptismal records of the church into which I was born. It has otherwise never been used."

The trip from Portsmouth to London took the better part of two days. Along the way, he tried to draw Hartleb out on the political situation, the war and a number of other topics, but the man refused to be drawn. The conversation ended up turning instead to pleasantries.

He did learn that, like himself, Hartleb was a former army officer, who, also like himself, had been mustered out as a colonel, was unmarried and lived for his work. He was devoted to his superior, Lord North, whom he described as a brilliant man, heavily burdened by the cares of office.

As they rumbled along, Abbott again told Hartleb that he had to insist on seeing Washington immediately upon arriving in London.

"Again, I'm afraid that will need to wait a couple of days, Mr. Abbott. Your status and all of that, as I said. And these things always take time no matter what, and it is not as if you had an appointment."

Abbott could no longer see a reason to hold back. "Mr. Hartleb, there is no true question about my status. I am the ambassador from an independent, sovereign nation. I am here to secure the release of a prisoner of war, in exchange for a possible resolution of certain differences between our two countries. It is as simple as that."

"I'm afraid it is not so simple, Colonel. We have well-known differences over the question of sovereignty, and you may yourself also be a subject of His Majesty who has treasonously attempted to overthrow his rule."

"If that is the case, Mr. Hartleb, you should just make me a *guest* in the Tower alongside General Washington. Then our two countries can continue to make war against one another and spend still more blood and treasure until the inevitable result, recognition of our independence."

Hartleb said nothing in response and they rode along in uncomfortable silence for some time. Finally, Abbott said, "I must enquire, is General Washington in good health?"

"Yes, very. Indeed, His Majesty's personal physician has examined him and declared him so. And he is also in good spirits so far as I understand. Although I have not met with him personally."

"Has Lord North?"

"Not so far as I know. And I think I would know."

"What, exactly, are the conditions of his imprisonment?"

"As I said before, he is not exactly a prisoner. He's free, for example, to walk about most parts of the Tower grounds."

"Unguarded?"

"No, he has guards with him at all times, his room has bars on the window and his door is locked at night from the outside. We also have other means of restraint available should he prove…difficult. Which he has so far not."

"If I must wait a day or two to see Washington, I would, as an alternative, to meet with Lord North upon our arrival."

"That, too, will have to wait. His Lordship is quite busy with affairs of state."

Abbott thought—ever so briefly—of demanding an audience with the King, but that seemed ridiculous in the moment, and he resigned himself to waiting. But not for long.

Was making him wait a tactic? Or was something else going on?

Upon their arrival in London, and just as Thompson had predicted, Hartleb took him to a large house in an area called The Strand. He referred to it as a government guest house used for important visitors, and told him that there was a cook, and a manservant, a Mr. Sellars, at his disposal. Abbott had firmly in mind Thompson's advice to seek lodging not supplied by the government, but that would take a few days to arrange, and for the moment he could not see the harm in it. He would need to be cautious, though. He assumed there would be spies and eavesdroppers everywhere.

"Is anyone else staying there at this time, Mr. Hartleb?"

"Not right now. But there might be others in due course."

"Am I free to leave the house?"

"Certainly. You are a guest of the government, and an important one. I assume you have come with money, but if not we will supply it. You should feel free to explore London, to eat where you please. You might even take in a play. As Christmas and New Year's are just behind us, most theatres are dark, but a few are still open. I can recommend something if you like."

"Why, thank you. I might just take you up on that."

"Do take a hansom cab to go back and forth, particularly at night. London's streets are, I regret to say, not the safest, particularly if you are well dressed."

After getting him settled in the house, Hartleb said, "I assume you have things coming from the ship in the carriage."

"Yes. Two trunks."

"Is that all? You may have a long stay here. I would not think that what you need to be an adequate ambassador could fit easily into only two trunks."

Hartleb had a smile on his face as he said it, but Abbott couldn't tell if he was being sarcastic or not. He decided to take what the man said at face value.

"I would certainly have preferred to bring more of my wardrobe with me because I do like to be well dressed. I didn't have sufficient time. It is regrettable because I understand that London is the capital not only of the British Empire, but of fashion, as well."

"The French might contest that, but in any case—" Hartleb looked him up and down "—you are already the best-dressed American I have seen in many a year."

"Why, thank you, but perhaps you have not met the correct Americans. On the other hand, have you ever had occasion to meet Dr. Franklin, Mr. Hartleb?"

"Yes, several times. I assume you mean to suggest that he is not the very picture of sartorial splendour."

"Not hardly." They laughed together.

"I will be going now, sir. But if you should need to contact

Lord North's office, Mr. Sellars can arrange that. Otherwise, we will be back to you in a day or two regarding arrangements to see Washington."

"I should like to see him much sooner than that."

"I understand. Again, I will see what I can do."

Hartleb wished him a good evening and started to depart. At the last second, he stopped, turned around and said, "Mr. Abbott, there is something else I feel I should tell you, as one former army officer to another."

"What is that?"

"I would prefer you not tell anyone you heard this from me, but Washington is going to need a lawyer, and a very good one."

"Why is that?"

"The King is determined to see him brought to trial."

"For what?"

"High treason."

"Then I demand to see him at once."

Hartleb looked startled. "The King?"

"No. Although I would see him, too, if he would grant me an audience. I am referring to His Excellency, General Washington."

"I will do what I can. But sometimes these things take time."

"You continue to say that. What could possibly take more time than has already gone by? Your government has known for at least several days that I would be arriving. I am now here and ready to go to work."

"Well, we do have your letters of appointment now. But they are from a body—this Continental Congress—that we do not recognize. It is in our eyes an illegal assembly. The Foreign Office will, in conjunction with the Secretary of State for the American colonies, Lord Germain, work to decide whether we should negotiate with you or just put you in jail, too."

"Which you have also said before. And which was as ridiculous then as it is now. Two years ago your government sent the

Carlisle Peace Commission to Philadelphia, where they met with numerous members of the Continental Congress—which you now label an illegal assembly—on multiple occasions."

"I'm afraid we view that as having been different. But in any case, I will do what I can to hasten this along. In the meantime, I suggest you use the time to explore this great city."

In truth, Abbott was very anxious to explore London, now that he had finally arrived here, after having desired it for so many years. But he was not about to admit that.

"Perhaps I will," Abbott said. "But first I want to resolve these more important matters. I am not happy about this delay."

"I do understand. But, again, the treason matter is serious, and obtaining a barrister very promptly is important. If you do not know anyone, I can supply you a list of names of men who are accomplished in the area of criminal defence for high crimes."

"Thank you. I may need that list."

"You're very welcome. Now I must go. A good evening to you."

30

Abbott spent a sleepless night and arose in the morning more upset than before at having been refused immediate access to Washington. If there was no progress by the end of the day, he would go directly to the Tower himself the very next day and demand of the jailer to see the man whose freedom he'd been sent to secure.

In the meantime, the question of how to identify the best lawyer was urgent but, at the same time, a puzzle. He could not, of course, represent Washington himself because he wasn't admitted to the bar in England and wouldn't be able to get admitted without undertaking extensive further training in England. Unfortunately, in the haste of his departure from Philadelphia, he had neglected to discuss the topic with either Thompson or Huntington, obvious as the need ought to have seemed.

Benjamin Franklin, having lived in London for so many years, would likely know the best men, but he was in France. The round-trip time for messages was probably measured in weeks, assuming it could even be done efficiently and confidentially in a time of war between England and France.

He was thus on his own in figuring it out, as he was loath to accept the list of suggested barristers that Hartleb had offered. There was no way to know in what way particular lawyers on Hartleb's list might be beholden to the government, or hoping for later favour by giving Washington less than a robust defence. An alternative was to try to locate the few patriotic Americans who were in London—not the thousands of Loyalists who had fled there—and ask them for suggestions.

At one time he might himself have been one of those American Londoners. He had thought of going to London to train as a barrister. He had opted instead, after attending the College of New Jersey in Princeton, to return to Philadelphia, where he apprenticed himself to an older lawyer nearing the end of his career. A man who himself had trained at the Inns of Court in London.

His room, on the second floor of the guest house, looked out on a park and was elegantly furnished. A large feather bed surrounded by embroidered curtains sat next to one wall, and a clearly expensive armoire against another, with a washstand and basin beside it. Against the third wall there was an exquisite cherrywood dresser with drawers on the bottom, surmounted by a drop-down desk and a glass-doored bookcase. A comfortable fire had been lit in a fireplace surrounded by an ornate black marble mantel. Above it hung a large portrait of George III in hunting attire. He stared at it. Perhaps it was meant to suggest to him that his country was prey.

He wandered over to the bookcase, opened the doors and looked through the books, which were mostly Shakespearean plays and recent novels. There was one called *The Sylph*, some of whose pages were still uncut, showing a publication date of 1778. Its author was listed only and oddly as A Young Lady. As he paged through the uncut pages in the front of the book, it seemed a bit racy. He was looking forward to settling down with it when there was a knock on the door.

He opened it, and there stood the house's porter, Mr. Jarvis, to whom he'd been briefly introduced upon his arrival.

Quite seemingly proud to announce it, Jarvis said, "The Right Honourable Edmund Burke, MP, is here and requests to see you. He regrets his lack of an appointment."

"Well, I certainly know of him. He's been one of our largest supporters in Parliament. Please ask him to come up."

"Sir, if I may, it would be more appropriate to meet him in the parlour." He raised his eyebrows and tilted his head back slightly. There was clearly an unspoken "you colonial bumpkin."

"I'll be delighted to do that as well, as soon as I am properly dressed for such a meeting."

"Sir, may I speak freely?"

"Of course, Mr. Jarvis. You may always do so with me. This is not my country, I have a delicate mission and assistance is always of value."

"Sir, Edmund Burke is a famous orator and an important Member of Parliament. I know that he shares many of your countrymen's opinions about matters of how your colonies should be governed."

"I have read some of his speeches, and, yes, he apparently does."

Jarvis pursed his lips and looked down at the floor, clearly trying to decide whether to go further. He looked up and said, "But he is a Whig, and the Whigs are in the minority. Which means he is an opponent of the current government."

"And therefore?"

"It is perhaps not my station to tell you this, but allying yourself too closely with him may not benefit your cause."

"I thank you for telling me. It is much appreciated. And you need not worry about your station."

"Thank you."

"I was a Whig myself, not too long ago, before the Revolution began."

"What are you now?"

"A Patriot. I like to think we have dispensed with parties in my country, at least for the moment."

"We should not keep Mr. Burke waiting."

"No, we should not, but I will first need Mr. Sellars to assist me in dressing for the occasion. What I am wearing currently is not appropriate to meet a Member of Parliament. Please ask Mr. Sellars, if he is available, to come in. I should be ready to go downstairs in about thirty minutes. I'm sure Mr. Burke will understand the needs of a gentleman to be appropriately attired."

Sellars arrived shortly thereafter and helped him select clothing from his trunks—a blue waistcoat with black breeches and, on his left leg, a black leather boot. He also removed the iron peg that was usually attached to his wooden leg—the leg had been amputated just below the knee—and replaced it with a peg of silver. It was impractical for regular use because it wore too quickly, but for show, particularly for a meeting with someone he'd never encountered before, it was perfect.

Jarvis arrived back just as he finished dressing.

"Thank you, Mr. Sellars," he said. "Lead the way, Mr. Jarvis."

Jarvis held the door to the room open for him, and he headed for the stairs. He had long ago learned to navigate a set of steps without clunking his way down. But he chose, this time, to let the silver pin make a very distinct bang, both on the wooden steps and as he stumped his way across the entrance hall towards the parlour doors, which were closed.

31

Jarvis, trailed by Abbott, flung open the doors to the room and announced to whomever might be within, "His Excellency Ethan Abbott, Ambassador of the Continental Congress of the American States."

The announcement startled Abbott. It was not so much being called Excellency as hearing the Continental Congress referred to, here in the heart of London—and despite what Hartleb had said—as the governing body of a country. It made his scalp prickle.

The man who was presumably Burke stood up before Jarvis had an opportunity to perform any introductions and said, "A very good day to you, Excellency. I am Edmund Burke, a Member of Parliament, and I have come to welcome you to London."

He was a short man, with a long nose, a ruddy complexion and red hair, unpowdered. He had a rich Irish accent, which surprised Abbott even though he well knew that Burke was Irish.

"And good day to *you*, sir," Abbott said.

Jarvis interrupted. "May I serve you gentlemen tea? Or perhaps something stronger, given the hour?"

"I think not at the moment," Burke said.

"Nor I, Jarvis. But would you enquire again in a little while?"

"I will do that, sir," he said and withdrew.

"Your Excellency," Burke said as they both sat, "permit me to explain the purpose of my visit."

"Before you do that, and I apologize if it is rude to interrupt you in this way, do you have any news of General Washington?"

"I have not seen him. I hear only that he is being held in the Tower, is uninjured and comfortable. He is even able to walk about some parts of the Tower grounds."

"I have demanded to see him, or if not him, Lord North first and then him, but been given evasive answers."

"Not surprising. A trick of this government is to make people wait. You shouldn't shy from insisting on your right to see each of them, and promptly. Or you will cool your heels here for weeks while your general rots in the Tower."

"I shall take your advice. But if you hear any news of him, will you let me know immediately?"

"Of course, Excellency."

"There is no need to call me Excellency. I would be pleased to be called simply Abbott, especially by so eminent a person as yourself."

"Sir, I would not give up the moniker of Excellency so easily were I you. Titles go a long way in this land of lords, earls, barons, knights and what have you. And your title also puts forward the seriousness of your mission and the scope of your authority."

"I will follow your lead, then."

"And also, and in any case, we do not often use even unadorned last names amongst us, except when we're children, when we use Christian names, unless the other child is titled."

"True in my country as well, except that we don't have aristocratic titles."

Burke raised his eyebrows. "Your country. You already think of yourselves as a fully separate country?"

"Yes."

He pursed his lips and shook his head slowly up and down. "Well, I suppose you do, I suppose you do. The time when we might have worked something out and remained one country may be in the past now, although it saddens me."

Abbott chose not to respond directly and said instead, "I have read and admired many of your speeches, Mr. Burke, especially the one you gave some years ago on American taxation. It was reprinted in full in our newspapers, as your speeches continue to be with regularity. All of us appreciate your support for our independence."

Burke smiled. "Ah, there are those who read what I say that way. But, to be clear, I didn't support your independence as much as support your rights as Englishmen to have authority over your own taxes and certain aspects of governance, including representation in Parliament. But not to gainsay the absolute sovereignty of Parliament over every part of the Empire."

"I see. But in any case, you are greatly more of a supporter of ours than is Lord North."

"That most certainly."

"Let me ask, if I may be direct, the exact purpose of your visit."

Burke rose and went to stand with his back to the fire. "Please forgive my standing. I am now past fifty years and find myself cold all winter long."

"Yes, it's not only cold here, but damp to boot. Worse even than Philadelphia."

"Before I get to my purpose in coming today, may I ask how you lost your leg?"

"At Saratoga."

"Ah, that was a loss my fellow members of Parliament found

hard to grasp. It was a shock to them. And to me as well, I would admit."

Abbott stretched out his leg, so that the metal tip on the end shone in the firelight. He laughed. "To me, too, but in a different way."

Burke stared for a few seconds, then said, "You asked the purpose of my visit. I am here because it is being bandied about that the King—and perhaps Lord North, too—want to see General Washington tried for high treason and have imposed upon him a gruesome traitor's death. If that be true, an investigation by the Solicitor General will soon be launched. General Washington will need a barrister to represent him. The sooner the better."

Abbott smiled. "And I suppose you could be that barrister, eh, Mr. Burke?"

"I could. Although it has been many years since I practised before the courts. These days I largely save my words for the House of Commons."

"And yet you could do it?"

"I believe I maintain the skills, and I have retained a relationship with a barrister's chambers in the Inner Temple, where I was first trained and admitted to the bar."

"Is that enough?"

"I would think so. But more important, I would be known to the judges who will sit on this matter."

"Favourably or unfavourably?"

"There is that. In candour, it depends."

"Will this be a jury trial?"

"Most certainly. Unless you waive the jury, which I would not advise."

"How do you do with juries?"

"I always did well. At least when I was on my best behaviour—not sarcastic and not quite so openly treating my opponents as fools. As they so often so richly deserved to be treated."

"I still wonder if that is enough."

There was a gentle knock on the door and Jarvis reappeared. "I should like to enquire again if you gentlemen desire tea or some other libation?"

"Thank you. I think I *will* have a cup of tea," Burke said.

Abbott pondered it for a few seconds. Would being out of Pennsylvania, where the drinking of tea had become an act of near treason, absolve him of his pledge? He thought not. "I no longer drink tea," he said.

Burke smiled a broad smile. "Of course you don't. Hard as it is to believe, I had almost forgotten about that little tea party you had in Boston." He looked back at Jarvis. "On second thought, I will pass. I don't think we'll be much longer."

"I'm not in need of anything," Abbott said.

Jarvis withdrew from the room again, and Abbott continued. "We were discussing your trial skills."

"My trial skills are not what's relevant here."

"What is?"

"My political skills."

"Why would those be of importance? You're, as I understand it, a Whig, a member of the opposition, and thus not in position to make things happen."

"Abbott—I think I will call you that since you invited it, and you may call me Burke—you don't yet understand the game that is afoot here. Lord North did not bring Washington here to see him executed."

"What for, then?"

"To use as a bargaining chip to extract from your Continental Congress what we have not been able to achieve by either military gains or negotiation heretofore."

"Which is what?"

"To have you stay in the bloody Empire and recognize the sovereignty of Parliament over you."

"What is on the other end of the bargain?"

"Whatever you want. The power to tax, the right to have your own assembly make your laws. Even representation in Parliament if you can find anyone willing to cross the Atlantic twice a year in order to listen to endless prattle."

"And if that deal is not struck?"

"Washington will hang by the neck until he is dead."

"Which you claim is not North's intention."

"I am sure it is not. He wants out of this war, even though he in large part caused it. But this kidnapping is the type of thing that, once launched, can slip a man's control."

"Meaning if we don't agree, they will have to carry out the threat implicit in the trial."

"Yes, and with the King egging him on."

He had his instructions, of course. But he didn't want to give them all away. So he said only, "Well, we might stay in the trade arrangement. But I am afraid they will have to cede our full independence."

"The King will never agree to that. If you are insistent on it, you may have to decide what General Washington is really worth to your country."

"I see."

"But in any case, while the game is being played, there is no person better than I, steeped now for almost two decades in the politics of the American rebellion—a leading opponent of the war—to support that negotiation on your behalf, while formally serving as the General's lawyer."

Burke had presented him with a difficult choice. Abbott had no interest in committing to any course of action in the spur of the moment. But he also wanted to avoid offending Burke, who might prove a powerful ally. He temporized. "Which lawyer to hire is, of course, a decision for His Excellency."

"There would be no need to hire me. I would represent him without fee." He moved away from the fireplace and began to pace around the room, hands behind his back. "Please forgive my walking about. I am afraid this weather stiffens my joints."

"I will put your suggestion to His Excellency."

"There is only one problem with regards to my representation, Abbott. I am not permitted, as a matter of barristers' practice, to solicit clients. Even by coming here and making the suggestion, I may have crossed the line."

"How would it normally be done here, then?"

"A solicitor would procure my services on behalf of his client."

"Am I equivalent to a solicitor?"

Burke grinned. "Are you a lawyer in your own city?"

"Yes."

"I see no reason that you could not instruct me. You don't have to be a member of the bar to instruct. Having a legal education in order to fill that role is more a tradition than an absolute requirement. In any case, you have a legal education, acquired in this same Kingdom, albeit at a distance."

"True. Rest assured I will bring up the entire topic with the General—just as soon as I'm able to meet with him. Perhaps you can find a way to speed it up, Burke." He rose from his chair—something he had discovered in his law practice to be a polite way of bringing a meeting to an end. "I thank you very much for your visit."

"It was my pleasure," Burke said. "There is one other thing, by the way."

"Which is?"

"I am sure you're very comfortable in this dwelling—" he waved his hand about as if to take in the entire house "—capacious, well-furnished, with many servants. And with multiple fireplaces, well-lit and warm."

"Yes."

"But you will be constantly spied on here. That man Jarvis? He is likely a spy. I wouldn't be surprised if he were listening on the other side of the door this very moment. Even if he is not, your movements will no doubt be reported to the government on a daily if not hourly basis."

"I had intended in any case to spend only a few days here. And there is, Burke, a possible solution." He told him about Franklin's friend Mrs. Stevenson.

"I was aware Dr. Franklin knew her," he replied. "And that he resided at her home with her family. I have not made her acquaintance personally, but I will endeavour immediately to contact her on your behalf. I'm sure that once she hears that you know Dr. Franklin, even if you do not have a letter of introduction directly from him, that you are likely to be welcome in her home."

"I would be most grateful."

"Once those arrangements are made, I would make haste to leave here."

"I will."

As he approached the door to the room, Burke turned and looked at him. "What *is* General Washington worth to your country, do you think?"

"Everything."

"Then you had best find a way to resolve the negotiation before your general is convicted."

"Why?"

"Because if he is convicted of treason, the mandatory sentence is death by hanging, usually cut down and disembowelled before the prisoner is actually dead. And then the body is quartered, and the head removed."

Abbott had not been aware of it. "Surely that is no longer done?"

"It has been done well within living memory, and the punishment is still very much in the statute books."

"But I assume he could be pardoned as part of a final settlement."

"I wouldn't count on it. Once he is convicted and sentenced, only the King can pardon him."

"The government has no power over that?"

"It does. In reality it more or less controls pardons. But Lord North would pay a high political price for trying to arrange one unless he got something in exchange. And he is not a strong man when it comes to the King's wishes."

"I see."

"I hope you do see, and see the peril your great man is in—and he is a great man." Without waiting for a response, he opened the door, turned again to look directly at him and said, "Just so you know, if the prisoner is quartered, it is up to the King to dispose of the parts."

Abbott said nothing.

"He will likely give one to the French King, save one each for Dr. Franklin and Mr. Adams and perhaps give you one, too."

Then, with a quick half-smile, he was gone.

32

The next day, early in the afternoon, as Abbott was preparing to go directly to the Tower and demand of the jailer to see Washington, a messenger arrived for him with a note from Mrs. Stevenson. It said that a friend of both Dr. Franklin and Mr. Burke was certainly a friend of hers and that he was most welcome to lodge with her family for as long as he found it convenient. It begged him to send his man with his things as soon as possible. Supper would be awaiting him that evening.

He made the arrangements with Mr. Jarvis, who told him that Mr. Sellars would take his trunks to Mrs. Stevenson that afternoon.

"I assume," Jarvis said, "that Your Excellency will want your manservant to continue to attend to you once you are there. I doubt the government will have any objection."

Did Burke's warning extend to a manservant employed by the government? It would, of course, be useful to have Sellars in his service. On the other hand, he could no doubt obtain someone elsewhere who was not beholden to the administration. Or just do the things that needed to be done himself.

"I think not, Mr. Jarvis. My needs are simple, and I'm sure Mrs. Stevenson can make what other arrangements I might need. Please be sure that Mr. Sellars is given a proper gratuity, my thanks for his service and an indication that, should he be in need of a reference, I will be pleased to supply it, even though his services to me have been of short duration."

Jarvis did not look happy. "Very well, Excellency." He bowed his head slightly and departed.

By 4:00 p.m. a carriage, compliments of the government, was waiting outside to deliver him to Mrs. Stevenson's house, which turned out to be conveniently located at 7 Craven Street, not far from Charing Cross. It annoyed him that he had to arrive at her home in a vehicle bearing the Royal Arms on its side, but he seemed to have little choice at the moment.

Mrs. Stevenson was there to greet him and showed him up a stairway to a well-appointed room with a pleasant view of the street. Over dinner she asked for the latest news of Dr. Franklin.

He was disappointed that Polly was not at dinner, but Mrs. Stevenson explained that she was away for a few days visiting the parents of her late husband.

Towards the end of dinner, a servant appeared and announced that a letter from the First Minister's office had been delivered for His Excellency. He handed Abbott an envelope embossed with the Royal Arms, in red. He opened it, and since Mrs. Stevenson had bent her head forward, clearly interested in the contents, he read aloud:

"My Dear Sir,

It is my pleasure to inform you that you may meet with George Washington at the Tower at your convenience.

Kindly present this letter to the Governor to obtain the right of entry.

I trust you will advise him of his need to select an attorney since the Solicitor General was here during the day to advise His Excellency Lord North that the treason investigation has begun and is progressing rapidly.

I have the honour to be, &c.,

Jacob Hartleb"

"What do you make of that?" Mrs. Stevenson asked.

"I am pleased, obviously. For the most part. But I find it distressing that he did not use my title in addressing me. Even though I've had that title only a brief while, I take his having failed to use it a form of insult to my country."

"What else?"

"That he referred to His Excellency, General Washington, only as 'George Washington,' which is also a way of avoiding acknowledgement that he outranks all but the most senior generals in the British Army."

She laughed. "You can hardly expect anything else, Mr. Abbott. As you must surely be aware, but there have been raging debates, both in the government and in Parliament, as to whether your Continental Congress, your generals, your governmental officials or anyone else in rebellion should be acknowledged as having legitimate authority or should simply be treated as something other."

"The something other being?"

"Rebels needing to be hanged as soon as the government can get its hands on them."

"I see. Well, it is quite odd, because when the Carlisle Commission came to Philadelphia two years ago to try to negotiate an end to the Revolution, the commission members dealt for months with men who were delegates to our Congress."

She shrugged. "Politics is a strange and off-putting business.

That is why I tend to avoid it, at least in what I say in public. When will you go to see General Washington?"

"I am inclined to go tonight, before they change their minds."

"I will lend you our driver and carriage. It is not fancy, but it will take you there."

"Why, thank you, Mrs. Stevenson. It is much appreciated."

With dinner over, he excused himself and went upstairs to change into his best clothes. He rejected wearing a peg and instead strapped on the cleverly built leather-and-wood leg and foot. When a silk stocking was pulled over it, it was hard to tell that he was wearing an artificial leg at all. And then he went down to say goodbye to Mrs. Stevenson—who wished him good luck—and boarded the carriage, which was waiting for him out in front.

He had rehearsed many times in his mind how to approach General Washington when he finally met him. He had seen the man at a distance a number of times, both before the war in Philadelphia and in the army after Abbott enlisted. But he had never met him in person. Should he be entirely formal? Should he be open about his instructions or keep them to himself? He had thought about it incessantly on the ship, as well as in the guest house as he tossed and turned while trying to fall asleep. Now he was thinking about it again as the carriage bounced along towards the Tower. As he approached the Tower gate, he was still undecided.

And there was one more issue that had been added to his list since he arrived in England. Clearly, some in the government were not interested at all in a negotiation. They just wanted Washington to hang. How candid did he need to be about that? He was, of course, doing exactly what he routinely did as a lawyer on first meeting a new client. He was trying to decide how much to tell the man and how much to hold back. If you were too optimistic, the client would likely sense you just wanted to handle his matter, no matter what; too pessimistic and he would go elsewhere.

But Washington was not his client. He was instead the man on whom an entire nation being born had pinned its hopes. In a way now, those hopes were on him. He shivered at the thought.

33

Abbott had half-expected to find difficulty in gaining access to the Tower and to Washington. But he did not. The guard in the small booth just outside the main entrance seemed to be expecting him, and when he showed the man the letter from Hartleb he was ushered immediately through the portcullis gate, and taken by another man along a stone walkway with a crenellated wall to his left, and finally to a stone-floored small room with the door standing open.

"There he is," the man said. He pointed into the room and left. A tall man had been standing at the barred window, looking out. He turned quickly around at the sound of the guard's voice.

So far as Abbott could tell at a glance, Washington was none the worse for wear—still very tall and very large in every proportion—strong neck, broad shoulders and huge hands. He was, however, dressed in an American uniform that had one epaulette missing and was otherwise almost in tatters.

"Excellency, please allow me to introduce myself. I am Ethan

Abbott, and I am most honoured to meet you." He nodded his head slightly and started to continue, "I am…"

"I know who you are, Colonel. A hero of Saratoga. I wasn't there, but General Gates told me later of your bravery, and how your actions under fire saved so many others but cost you a part of your leg. It is I who am honoured to meet *you*. I thank you for your service to the army and to our country and for the glory you have bestowed upon them both."

Washington's words took him aback. He had not expected the General to know anything at all about him. "Thank you, Excellency. I simply did my duty like any other soldier."

Washington glanced at Abbott's lower leg. "I see you disguise your injury rather than flaunt it."

"I flaunt it when I need to."

Washington smiled. "In any case, as pleased as I am to meet you, Colonel, no one told me you were coming, and I do not know why you are here. Can you enlighten me?"

"Yes, of course. I have been appointed by the Continental Congress as an Ambassador Plenipotentiary to negotiate your release. But first, I must ask if you are in good health and well treated."

"I am well, thank you. When I arrived I was examined by a physician from the Royal College of Medicine, who pronounced me fit. The food is good and I have not been ill-treated in any way."

"I am pleased to hear that. I am prepared to share my instructions with you and take your lead on how we should go about our negotiation."

Washington nodded and pointed at the room's side walls, which appeared to be made, not of stone, as Abbott had expected, but of wood.

"We should of course discuss your instructions," Washington said. "But we should do it elsewhere. Because they recently brought in two new prisoners, neither looking very much like a felon, and placed them in cells to the left and right of this one. And I note their doors are not locked at night."

"Spies, in other words."

"Yes. And if you peer down from my window you'll see a man down below pressed up against the wall, no doubt hoping to hear some words of mine transported to him on the breeze."

Abbott walked to the window and looked down. There was indeed a gentleman below leaning against the wall, trying to make his presence look casual.

"This is ungentlemanly," Abbott said.

"I think the British left that concept behind long ago, at least as concerns our Revolution. And there is one more thing. The man who captured me—Colonel Black—is also lodged here in the Tower, although in a different part."

"You've seen him?"

"Not only have I seen him, but he has come by to visit with me. Twice."

"And you treated with him?"

"Yes, of course. We had cordial enough relations from the moment he seized me at my headquarters until we disembarked from the ship at Portsmouth. He seems not even to begrudge me my attempts to escape, agreeing with me that it is a soldier's duty to try."

"Did he say why he comes to see you now?"

Washington grinned. "I think he has been appointed by someone to make certain I don't try to escape again."

Abbott walked over to the door and examined the lock, a very large metal bolt, turned by key, and designed to fit into a hasp on the doorjamb. "They lock you in at night?"

"Always before midnight. Sometimes sooner."

"Are you permitted to leave the room during the day?"

"Oh, yes. There are a few areas which I'm forbidden to visit. Otherwise I seem to have freedom during daylight to go where I wish. They refer to me as a guest."

"A guest who is locked in at night and cannot leave."

"Precisely. Which is why I am always followed by at least two soldiers." He gestured into the adjoining hallway, and Abbott noticed for the first time two soldiers with bayonets loitering at a distance.

"There are only two?"

"Sometimes there are more. I have tried to befriend them. I have been friendly and talked with them when they wanted to talk."

"You'd best be careful they are not also spies."

"I am. Let us stroll together upon the parade, where I think we will be less likely to be overheard."

"Of course, Excellency."

They moved to the parade, a long broad stone walkway, which was overlooked on the one side by the White Tower and on the other by a storehouse of some sort. "I must warn you," Washington said. "Yesterday, they permitted individuals into the storehouse and they stood in the windows and threw fruit and eggs at me as I walked along here."

"You joke."

"No. When I first arrived at the Tower there were crowds waiting outside, and they were friendly, cheering me actually as I entered. But now someone within the government has decided to show me the other side of British hospitality."

"Perhaps, Excellency, they will not be there now, it being night."

"We shall see."

"Before we discuss my instructions, Excellency, please permit me to ask another question of you first. If you have been well taken care of since your arrival, why have they not provided you with suitable clothes?"

"It is my choice. I wish to wear my uniform, and all that they have offered me are civilian clothes."

"We must find a solution to that."

"There is an easy one, I think. For many years, my supplier of fine English goods, including fine cloth, was here in London. His name is Richard Washington."

"Is he a relation?"

"No. But assuming he is still amongst the living and still in business, he might yet have my measurements." He laughed. "Although the finished clothes he shipped rarely fit well, so in the end he just sent the cloth. He can come here with a *good* tailor. If he is willing."

"I believe I have enough funds to pay for at least two uniforms, so I will see to it first thing tomorrow."

"You won't likely need to use your funds, which I assume are limited. Upon the outbreak of the Revolution, I was unable to take delivery on several things I had on order from Mr. Washington at the time. He wrote me and said the amount I had paid him in advance would remain on account as a credit."

"And if the authorities will not permit you to receive those clothes from him?"

"Then I will eventually need to appear in my undergarments. The embarrassment will be theirs, not mine. And if I do manage to get a new uniform, I have promised the soldiers each a button from this old one." He laughed. "I am apparently famous, even here."

There was a shout from the second story of the warehouse. "There he is!" A piece of fruit smashed against the stones near them, then a second and third, their pulp splashing on the ground. It seemed to Abbott, however, that those who were throwing did not intend to hit them, which they could certainly have done had they wished to do so. The shouting grew louder, a chorus of voices yelling, "Traitor! Hang him! Hang him high!" There followed a volley of eggs.

Washington seemed unmoved by the tumult. "Over there," he said, "is a niche at the base of the storehouse where their projectiles can't reach." He pointed.

They moved into the niche, and Abbott said, "This is unpardonable. You must be correct that the government is behind it. I will let Mr. Hartleb, who is Lord North's assistant, know and protest in the strongest terms."

All of a sudden, the shouting stopped and the fruit stopped flying. "Perhaps now we can discuss my instructions," Abbott said.

"What are they?"

"I am to insist on full independence no matter what, but agree to stay within the Empire for purposes of tariff-free trade only for a period of ten years. Twenty years if I can do no better. We are to receive all British lands as far west as the Mississippi, but they are to keep the Caribbean islands, Florida and Canada and we are to promise not to invade them."

"And in exchange?"

"You are to go free and be permitted to return to America."

"Is that it?"

"No. You are to be permitted to negotiate different terms so long as full independence is one of them."

"Colonel Abbott, I can see how those terms might make sense to the faraway Congress. But they make no sense to me. I do not wish to be the gold chip on the gaming table in any kind of bargaining."

"What do you mean?"

"I mean that the British must gain no advantage by having captured me. If they want to keep me until the war is over, they can do that. After all, I am a prisoner of war. If they want to exchange me for a general we might capture, they can do that. But nothing else."

Abbott steeled himself for what he needed to say, took a deep breath and said it. "But, Excellency, they plan a third choice. To try you for high treason and hang you." He decided to leave out the part about quartering. "Or at least that is what the King desires."

"Let them. I will go honourably to the gallows, and in the

fullness of time, the gods of history will frown down upon them, and especially upon the tyrant who calls himself their king."

"There are those who think—and I am one of them—that you are needed in America to bring the war to a favourable end."

"There are others who can accomplish that."

"I do not agree, Excellency."

"Even if there are not others who can accomplish it, and the war is lost, it will be lost only for the moment. There are not enough British soldiers, nor enough money in the British treasury, to subdue the spirit of liberty that has been unleashed in our land. Their soldiers will be fired at for years—decades if needed—from behind every rock and tree and every house and barn. Eventually they will give up and go home."

"You will not defend yourself in a trial, then?"

Washington was quiet for a long time. Abbott could sense he was thinking how to respond to the question. He took a deep breath and said, "I *will* defend myself. It will present an excellent opportunity to argue our case directly to the British people, who, by the way, have many similar complaints about their own loss of liberty."

"In that case, you will need a lawyer to help you make your case most effectively."

"I am not sure I need one, but perhaps you are right. You are a lawyer, are you not?"

"Yes, but obviously not admitted to the bar here."

"Who, then?"

"Edmund Burke stopped by to see me yesterday to volunteer for the role, without pay."

"Now, that is an astonishing thing, I must admit. And flattering. But he is only partly on our side. He defends us but insists Parliament must remain sovereign over us even if it does nothing—for now—to bring that sovereign power to bear."

"You will reject his offer?"

"Yes. With thanks, of course. Instead, I want an American. Someone born over there but admitted to the bar here."

"I know of no such person."

"I am aware that there were many Americans here studying to be lawyers when the war broke out. Some of them must by now be members of the bar. Or others who came before. Go find them."

34

It was a beautiful, sunny winter day, and Abraham Hobhouse, gazing out the window at the green lawn that stretched away from his office, felt content. He had recently become a full partner in the barristers' chambers of which his father-in-law, Samuel Fletcher, was the head. And Abraham's wife, Abigail—Fletcher's only daughter—was three months pregnant with their first child. It was perhaps regrettable that the child would be born in England and probably raised there, too, and not, like himself, born and raised in America. His life was otherwise on the path to success that he had long envisioned for himself, even though it had taken a turn he had not anticipated.

His original plan, after receiving his barristers' training in England, had been to return to Philadelphia, the city of his birth and upbringing, and establish a law practice there as a lawyer trained at London's prestigious Lincoln's Inn. All of that had been upended by the rebellion, of which he had had only an inkling when he departed Philadelphia for London at the age of eighteen in 1761. Nor had he planned, when he started as a pupil at Fletcher Chambers at Lincoln's Inn, to one day fall in love with Abigail when she came of age.

His reverie was interrupted when his secretary entered and handed him an envelope. It was addressed to him personally and bore a printed return address—*Continental States of America*—which he had never on stationery before seen, although he had read in the newspapers that the rebel assembly in Philadelphia was calling itself by that name.

Upon reading the message within, he bolted out of his chair and practically ran down the hall to the office occupied by his father-in-law. After giving a perfunctory knock on the open door and watching Samuel Fletcher turn around to face him—he was sitting, as usual, in his well-worn brown leather chair with the carved wooden arms—he said, "Mr. Fletcher, I received a note from a Mr. Ethan Abbott. If I do not mistake, he's the man the papers say is here as the Ambassador Plenipotentiary from the rebel assembly to try to negotiate George Washington's release. He wants to meet with me."

"He may be looking for personal legal advice," Fletcher said. "The newspapers say that the government has treated him shabbily. Both Lord North and Lord Germain have declined to meet with him. Instead they have sent an untitled assistant. Quite insulting, really, even though I may not have much sympathy for his cause."

"But as you have taught me so well, we don't give personal legal advice to people. We represent them in court only after they have been charged with a crime or sued."

"True. Yet perhaps that is not what this is really about," Fletcher said. "We don't know yet."

"We may not know, but I strongly suspect Ambassador Abbott is looking for a barrister to serve as General Washington's counsel in a trial should he be indicted. To undertake such an engagement, we require a solicitor to retain us and then instruct us on how to handle the case. The papers say that Abbott is a lawyer. But that doesn't make him a solicitor, or at least not in this jurisdiction."

"Son, the man who brought me up in this business, may he rest in peace, always said, 'Never turn a potential client away without hearing him out.' Meet with him. And now let me ask, how is Abigail doing?"

"She seems fine, if suffering from a bit of distress in the mornings, which seems to be declining as she moves on in term."

"Her late mother had much the same problem."

"I should meet with Mr. Abbott, then?"

"Yes."

"Do you want to join?"

"No, certainly not."

Abraham smiled. "So as to blame any problems that develop on me?"

"What else are young partners for, eh?"

The meeting with Abbott was quickly arranged for the next day.

Hobhouse had to admit that he was surprised when Abbott arrived wearing elegant business attire, including a soft brown leather coat. He had expected, not exactly a rube, but certainly not someone dressed at the height of fashion. Almost twenty years in London had apparently turned him into something of a snob.

After they had made their introductions, he saw no harm in commenting on it. "I must say, Mr. Abbott, I'm admiring of your fine suit. I myself am originally from Philadelphia, and I don't recall having been able to purchase that kind of thing back there. Much as I would've liked to do so."

As soon as he said it, he realized how awkward it had sounded, although Abbott seemed to take no offence and said simply, in response, "I was somewhat limited in what I could bring with me due to the haste of my departure on this mission. Once I arrived here, I took some time to look for something more in fashion."

"And you found it, obviously."

"Yes. In Aldwych. I located a tailor who by happenstance had in stock a suit of clothes in my rather tall size that had for some reason been rejected by another customer. He lent them to me while he is making something bespoke for me. Well, more than one item, actually."

Hobhouse had learned, also from his father-in-law, that clients, especially potential new ones, often enjoyed engaging in some conversation about personal things before getting down to business. It made the transaction seem less commercial, especially if they were in distress and in need of help and, really, friendship. And that was what he and Abbott were doing. But interested as he was in Abbott's fashion needs—for the man seemed almost to be dressed for an evening out—he wanted to get down to the real business at hand. "I'm happy to hear you're finding what you need in London, Ambassador," Hobhouse said. "But what can we at Fletcher Chambers do for you, since we are hardly an emporium?" He smiled in a way he hoped would communicate his inherent scepticism about what Abbott might want.

"They are going to put General Washington on trial, and he will need a barrister."

"Really? The newspapers have reported that the government is intending to use his capture to grease the wheels for a quick settlement of your Revolution."

"Is it not your Revolution, as well? You are by birth and upbringing an American, are you not?"

"Yes, I am, but I admit to mixed feelings about the rebellion. On the one hand, I can understand how people in the colonies feel that their liberties are being trampled, particularly in the area of taxation."

"But on the other hand?"

"On the other, now that I have resided here these many years, and have an English wife and English in-laws, I can understand that the mother country has spent a great deal of treasure defending the frontiers in America against the Indians and the French. It should be paid for, at least in part, by those who are being protected."

"Shouldn't the needed taxes not be voted on by those people themselves?"

Hobhouse laughed. "Perhaps, but as you must know, the people themselves have refused to vote in those taxes, or at least so I have read."

At that moment, the door to the small room in which they were meeting opened, and, to Hobhouse's astonishment, Samuel Fletcher himself walked in, carrying a tray which held a teapot, two cups and a plate of small cakes. Both he and Abbott stood up, and Hobhouse said, "Mr. Abbott, allow me to introduce the head of our chambers, Mr. Samuel Fletcher."

Fletcher put the tray down, extended his hand and said, "Welcome to Fletcher Chambers, Ambassador."

Abbott extended his own hand, shook and said, "So pleased to meet you, sir."

"It's a cold day and I thought I would bring you some hot tea and some cakes and make sure that Mr. Hobhouse is getting you what you need. And I also have to admit to curiosity about how you came to know about us."

"I am lodging with Mrs. Margaret Stevenson, and she recommended you. I believe she knew your father when she was a little girl."

"Ah, yes, that is so. In any case, Ambassador, I just wanted to be sure you are getting what you need from Mr. Hobhouse."

"Yes, most definitely," Abbott said. "Although I don't think we've yet gotten to the meat of it."

"I will leave you to locate the meat, then. Please let me know if you need anything," he said and withdrew.

After Fletcher shut the door, Abbott asked, smiling broadly, "Does the senior partner always serve tea?"

"I've never seen it before, Mr. Abbott. I suppose he just wanted to set eyes on you. May I pour you a cup?"

"No, thank you. I no longer drink tea, and I think I will pass on the cakes as well for now."

"Coffee if we have it?"

"There is no need."

Hobhouse poured himself a cup and said, "Let us return to the topic at hand. If you know, what is the charge to be brought against Mr. Washington?"

"Not mister, *General* Washington, or more properly, His Excellency."

Hobhouse laughed. "If you wish, although he is usually called General only in Whig newspapers. But in any case, with what crime are they planning to charge His Excellency?"

"High treason."

He lurched back. "Well, that truly astonishes. And makes little sense unless the government is intending to execute him, enrage the Americans and then spend even more blood and treasure to try to crush the rebellion in a way we've not yet figured out how to do."

"I have been given to understand this involves not so much the wishes of the government but those of the King."

"I don't know who has told you that, Mr. Abbott, but the King in our system has very limited powers. It is the *government* which decides with what crimes people are to be charged."

"I was told that by an assistant to Lord North, and His Excellency has already been interviewed by the Solicitor General."

"He will then need an excellent barrister immediately. We can certainly recommend a chambers skilled in defending treason and sedition cases."

"No, I've come to determine if your chambers, and you in

particular, would be competent and willing to undertake His Excellency's defence."

Hobhouse had learned from his father-in-law not to respond instantly to propositions that he found surprising. He just sat there for a moment, saying nothing. He saw, though, that Abbott was willing to wait just as patiently for him to respond.

He got up, began to pace around the room, finally turned towards Abbott and said, "Sir, I have defended many serious felony cases, but never a high treason case. Such cases, which are fortunately rare so far this decade, usually involve politics or religion, and we here at Fletcher try to avoid them."

"I see."

"I am flattered—*we* are flattered—but surely there are any number of the other chambers here at Lincoln's Inn, or at one of the other Inns of Court, who would be much more suited."

"General Washington insists on having an American-born lawyer, and there are very few Americans associated with chambers that carry the reputation for excellence that I have learned this one does."

"Again, I am flattered. But without agreeing to undertake this representation at your behest—and I understand that you are a lawyer, albeit not exactly an English lawyer—let me ask you, what is the defence?"

"That the rebellion, as you call it, is not a rebellion at all but rather a lawful attempt by the people of America to retrieve liberties that have been taken away from them."

"That is not a defence, just an excuse for unlawful activity."

"Perhaps so, but if you accept this representation, your job will be to find a way to turn my argument into a winning defence that will allow His Excellency to walk free."

35

Hobhouse and Abbott then conversed further about a variety of things, including fees, which Abbott assured him he was prepared to advance. Hobhouse cautioned Abbott, as the ambassador prepared to leave to go back to Mrs. Stevenson's, that the decision whether he would be permitted to represent Washington was one that would have to be made by the entire partnership of Fletcher Chambers. There was no guarantee that the vote would be favourable.

As soon as Abbott left, Hobhouse walked down the hall to see his father-in-law. The truth of the matter was that it would be Fletcher and Fletcher alone who would make the decision, even though he was almost eighty. The views of the other partners were only advisory, if Fletcher even bothered to consult with them.

Hobhouse found him sitting in his office, smoking a pipe and reading the *London Advertiser.* Fletcher looked up from his paper and said, without removing the pipe from his mouth, which tended to muffle his voice, "It says here that this fellow Abbott is trying to negotiate a resolution to the war—Washington's freedom in exchange for the colonies staying in the Empire. It would be interesting to participate in that negotiation. Not to mention fame-producing for our chambers."

"For certain it would be that," Hobhouse said. "But the dead fly in the ointment is that, according to Ambassador Abbott, General Washington has no real defence, or at least nothing we would think a defence."

Fletcher took a long pull on his pipe, blew the smoke out again and finally said, "A losing proposition, I'd think. And one in which he will be wagering with his life."

"Likely so. But the urgent question before our firm is, shall we take the case?"

"You mean, should *you* take the case. It is you he wants, I assume, because you are an American."

"Yes."

"Well, I leave it to you, Mr. Hobhouse. If you want the case, the chambers will support you with all we have."

"Thank you, Mr. Fletcher."

"You realize, I assume, Mr. Hobhouse, that if you win, fame and glory will descend upon you, and you will in the future have every wealthy client in London beating a path to your door."

"Yes."

"But if you lose and your client is executed..."

"You well know that I have had that grim experience once before."

"I do know. I simply mean to remind you."

"I need no reminding, Mr. Fletcher."

"No, I suppose you don't. There is one more thing, however."

"What is that?"

"Being with a famous American, and all who will surround him, you will, in a fashion, be reacquainting yourself with the land of your birth."

"In a sense, yes."

Fletcher turned his pipe upside down and tapped it against the large ashtray that sat on a table next to him. "That kind of thing can create the strong pull of nostalgia. Promise me that you will not, when the rebellion ends, decamp to America and take my only living child with you, along with my first-to-be-born grandchild."

"You are serious, aren't you?"

"Yes, Mr. Hobhouse, I am."

"I promise you I will do no such thing."

"Good. Well, then, what is your next step?"

"I must visit the client and see both if he wants me and if I want him."

Gaining permission to visit Washington in the Tower took some effort. Despite Abbott having written him a letter of explanation and introduction, Hobhouse still needed to secure permission from the First Minister's office, which proved no small task. Finally, though, on the morning of the third day after he had first met with Abbott, Hobhouse finally had what he needed and approached the guard at the Tower's portcullis gate. The man seemed already well aware of who he was. He glanced quickly through the papers Hobhouse had brought with him and then led the way. "I see you have come to see our most famous guest," he said, as they walked along.

"Yes," Hobhouse replied. "Is he doing well?"

"Oh, yes, and he's quite friendly, too. When I was off-duty I dropped by his room to chat. I have a nephew in Virginia, you see, and I thought there was always the chance His Excellency might have made his acquaintance."

"Had he?"

"No, but he promised to look him up when he returns."

"I notice that you call him Excellency. Does everyone?"

"Most do. After all, we call all others who visit here by their titles. Lord this and that. Lady so-and-so." The man grinned. "Baron Humbug, and so forth."

"Is there really a Baron Humbug?"

"No, of course not. But the way some of these people put on airs, there might as well be."

"Has His Excellency had other visitors?"

"Yes. Quite a few Americans live in London or nearby, you see, and several have come by to look in on him, all of them bringing food and drink, which he has been kind enough to share with the guards on occasion. And some retired British generals have been by."

"A remarkable man, it would appear."

"Indeed. And here we are." They stopped in front of a room with a wooden door, which stood open. "I will leave you here and trust you can find your own way back out."

"Thank you. May I enquire of your name?"

"Certainly. I am Robert Denam."

"Very pleased to meet you, Mr. Denam. Thank you for escorting me."

"My pleasure, sir."

Washington had been sitting at a small desk, quill pen in hand, writing something on a sheet of paper. When he saw Hobhouse and Denam appear, he got up, came over to the door, nodded at Denam and said, looking directly at Hobhouse, "And who might you be, sir?"

"I'm Abraham Hobhouse. Mr. Abbott suggested I call upon you."

"Ah, yes. I have been expecting you, Mr. Hobhouse. I am General Washington." He extended his hand and they shook. "Welcome to my small world. Please have a seat." He gestured at a small chair, one of a pair that had their backs to the window.

Hobhouse sat down in one; Washington took the other.

"As you probably know, Your Excellency, I am a barrister."

"Yes, Mr. Abbott came by and explained who you are and

to expect you. He also acquainted me with your reputation and that of the chambers in which you practise."

"Then you know that, assuming you approve, I have been hired to represent you in the event you are a defendant in a criminal trial."

He laughed. "Mr. Hobhouse, I am almost certain to be a defendant in such a trial. The Solicitor General himself has come by to question me, as have two of his assistants in succeeding days. They would not have been here but for their desire to burden me criminally."

"What did you tell them?"

"Nothing."

"What did they want to know?"

"They wanted to know about my activities in supporting the Revolution."

"I am perhaps surprised you refused to speak to them. Mr. Abbott suggested to me that you wish to shout your Revolutionary views from the rooftops."

"I do. As a young man, I was somewhat of a hothead and would doubtless have done so. In the fullness of time, I have learned that there is a time and place for everything. The time to shout my views about the way in which your king and your Parliament have abridged our liberties will be in a courtroom, before a jury. I will have a jury, will I not?"

"Yes, although the judges have many powers to control their courtrooms. And your opportunity to give a speech may turn out to be very limited."

"You sound like most lawyers I know," Washington said. "Careful to be precise."

"I do try. But now I'd like to go over the evidence they might present against you for high treason, which is defined as, amongst other things, waging war against the King." He gestured at the walls. "But I understand from Mr. Abbott that there are prisoners on each side of you who might want to listen in. Perhaps it would be best if we walked upon the parade."

"Those prisoners have been moved for some reason. So far as I know, there are no prisoners in the adjoining cells, and there is rarely anyone nearby in the hall. We are free to talk. Before we do, though, I am thirsty for coffee. Would you like some?"

"I am astonished that as a so-called guest here you can call for coffee."

"Being cordial with people can work wonders, Mr. Hobhouse." He went to the doorway of the cell, leaned out and looked down the hallway to the right. "Mrs. Crankshaw!" he said, raising his voice. "Could you please bring us a pot of coffee and two cups?" He paused, clearly listening for a response. "Thank you." He returned to his chair and sat back down.

"While we wait for the coffee, let us review the evidence against you," Hobhouse said.

"For waging war? It is plentiful. I have been leading the army chartered by the Continental Congress for almost five years. We have fought against soldiers wearing the King's Arms and killed them. We have taken property carrying the King's seal and made it ours. We have seized the King's soldiers who spied on us behind our lines, convicted them in our courts and hanged them."

"Like Major Andre."

"Yes, hanging him was a pity. But it had to be done."

"Is it likely that anyone alive today in England personally saw you doing all those things?"

Washington thought for a moment. "Possibly, although I can't immediately think of anyone. Perhaps British officers who have returned who personally laid eyes on me."

"There you have it. Unless they find such officers, we may be able to challenge their evidence as being second-hand."

"There might be recruiting posters put out in my name."

"Signed personally by you, in the printer's plate from which they were made?"

"Of course not."

"That you did not sign the originals might be at least a small help."

"Perhaps so. But, Mr. Hobhouse, I have also signed many hundreds of military orders, directing my officers to attack various British units."

"Are any American officers who received those orders now prisoners of the King?"

"Yes, but so far as I know, most are not held here in England. They are for the most part held in America."

"There is that, then. Even if the British have those orders and they might not—they may have difficulty getting them received in evidence without some way to prove that the signatures are actually yours or that you authorized your signature to be put there. Your officers will likely not testify against you. And who knows who may have put your supposed signature on the orders?"

Washington got up and went to lean against the wall. "You will forgive me, but these old bones sometimes have difficulty sitting for long periods."

"I understand, Excellency."

"I hope you also will forgive me for saying that these lawyerly arguments you wish to make seem quite thin to me."

"They are what we have."

"Well, Mr. Hobhouse, unfortunately, you have not covered every possibility of evidence here in England that might be used against me. For example, there are also any number of British officers now residing here who opposed me in America. General Howe amongst others."

"Did he personally see you take ups arms against His Majesty?"

He thought for a moment. "Perhaps not, although I am not certain of that. But I did correspond with him on numerous occasions about matters in the war." He smiled. "And it was quite clear whose side I was on and under whose authority I was acting."

"Which you would put how?"

"Under the authority of the Continental Congress, which the British government refers to as an unlawful rebel assembly."

"I will give thought to how we might deal with that."

"Mr. Hobhouse, you are seeking to build a case out of straw. I *did* take up arms against the King. Every day."

"Your Excellency, forgive me, but you perhaps do not understand a barrister's craft. If the jury is friendly, an acquittal can be woven out of the thinnest straw."

They spent the next hour or more discussing other evidence the Solicitor's Office might bring forward, with Hobhouse explaining how each piece might be challenged or belittled. Not long after they got started, a woman whom Hobhouse assumed to be Mrs. Crankshaw arrived carrying, in one hand, an elegant, rococo silver coffee pot and, in the other, two rather dainty china cups on a tray.

Hobhouse immediately recognized the rounded coffee pot as one in the *epouseé* style favoured by the prominent London silversmith Charles Wright. A similar one had been given to him and Abigail as a wedding gift by Lord Dandridge.

"That's a beautiful coffee pot," he said. "I am surprised they would provide you with such a lovely piece to use here, let alone serve you coffee instead of tea."

"Oh, it is mine," Washington said. "From amongst the gifts with which I have been inundated. Quite a few British officers I served with during the French and Indian War are retired here in London, and several have come by to see me. They all brought gifts."

"So the coffee pot is a gift from one of them?"

"No. Americans from a neighbouring plantation, Lord and Lady Fairfax, brought it. They moved to England several years before the Revolution began in earnest and have regrettably not returned to America. They live in Bath now, but happened to be in London. They are close friends."

"Are they Loyalists?"

"We carefully avoided discussing their political views."

"I see."

"Mr. Hobhouse, putting the no doubt interesting subject of silver coffee pots aside, I am inclined to retain you as my barrister. If you wish to be retained, that is."

"I do. But you have said you are *inclined*. Is there something else needed before you decide for certain?"

"Yes. I need to know about your own attitudes about the Revolution."

Hobhouse had concluded in the course of the conversation that he very much wanted the case. Not only because it would be perhaps the greatest case of the age, but because he was impressed with Washington. But he needed to answer Washington's question directly.

"Excellency, I am a Whig, and Whigs generally despise the government's pursuit of military force in America. But I am nevertheless of two minds about the rebellion because I can see both sides of the argument. I can recite those for you if you wish."

"No need. I might have been troubled had you said you were wholeheartedly for it, because it would have seemed false given your long-time residence here with, apparently, no intention to return to Pennsylvania."

"In truth, I feel very much an Englishman. I intend to remain. But on the other hand, when I hear people here disparage America as a place filled with uncouth, uneducated barbarians, it makes my blood boil."

Washington smiled. "I can understand the conflict within you. Twenty years ago, I would have said that *I* was an Englishman. Indeed, both my brothers were educated here. I missed out on that only because my father died, and we could not afford it."

"I had no idea."

"There is more. I once avidly desired to be appointed an officer in the British Army. It didn't happen primarily because my patron, General Braddock, died before it could be accomplished."

"Will you retain me, then, Your Excellency?"

"I will. I want, however, to give you my instructions and be sure they are agreeable to you."

"What are they, sir?"

"You may pick at, belittle, question or otherwise attack the government's evidence of my supposed guilt, as well as its witnesses, but only so as to argue that the government has not proved my guilt or that they have not met the standards of the treason statute, whatever they are."

"I am agreeable to that." He took a sip of his coffee. "I sense there is something else, though."

"Yes. You may not apologize, say, suggest or hint that I am sorry for my actions, or suggest in any way that the colonies should not be free and fully independent states, or that I desire *any* compromise. It is either full independence or fight them in the swamps and forests for however long as it might take."

"I will strictly adhere to your position on this, Excellency."

Washington took another sip of coffee and said, "Now let me ask you something that Mr. Abbott seemed unwilling to address in detail. People have told me several times that I may suffer a *traitor's death*. I believe I know what that involves, but I am not certain. Please tell me exactly what that means."

Hobhouse swallowed hard, then said, "The mandatory sentence for high treason is to be drawn to the gallows standing in an open cart, hanged, cut down before you are dead, disembowelled, your head cut off and then your body either quartered, with the parts distributed as the King might wish, or dissected in public."

He looked at Washington to see if he gulped. He didn't, but said only, "And they call this a civilized nation."

"There is more, Excellency. When they beheaded the leader of the Jacobite rebellion, back in the '40s, they put their heads on pikes at Temple Bar. Two of them were still there as recently as ten or fifteen years ago."

"If it will secure the independence of my country, they may put my head where they please."

He hardly knew what to say in response, so said only, "Are there other instructions?"

"No, but I do have another question. Is the condemned man entitled to make a speech as he stands on the gallows?"

"I believe so."

"Good, because if I am to be executed, there will likely be a large throng, and people from all the newspapers in England there."

"And America, too, no doubt."

"It will be an excellent opportunity to make the case for my country to the people of England, and remind them that our cause for liberty and freedom is also theirs."

"I will do my utmost to prevent your having the opportunity to make that speech, Excellency."

"Thank you. There is one thing, though, that we have avoided discussing."

"Which is?"

"What Colonel Abbott is doing. If I understand correctly, he is going to attempt to negotiate a settlement of the Revolution, in some fashion that will provide the King with a better outcome than he will get on the battlefield."

"Mr. Abbott came to hire our chambers for your defence, in what he anticipates will be a treason trial. But he did not share with me even one bit what his instructions are with regard to any negotiations with which he's been entrusted."

"I see. Well, know this. Congress is a lawful body, and it may do what it will to resolve or not resolve the issues that gave rise to our Revolution. But you are not to suggest to anyone, English, American, French or Spanish, that I give one whit about what happens to me personally. Nor will I, as I told Colonel Abbott, be a willing chip in a bargain."

"What is the practical import of that for me, as your lawyer?"

"It is simple. If, for example, there is a treason trial, and someone should say to you that if this or that condition be met by my country, I will be released or treated more leniently, you are to reject any such bargain."

"Is that really realistic, Excellency? From what I have read, the people of the colonies look to you for leadership, and not just military. Really, who else is there? I suspect they fear that without you, all will be lost, and that they might well wish to make such a bargain."

"There may be those who think that, but it is not true. Some equally talented—or more talented—man will arise from amongst our great people to lead us on to victory."

"I do not suppose the men who sent Mr. Abbott to try to resolve these problems likely agree with that. Indeed, Abbott has told me that your leadership will be even more sorely needed when the war is ended."

"The people who desire that of me will end disappointed. If I don't die here, I intend at war's end to return to my wife and family at Mount Vernon and live out my life there as a simple farmer."

"I can understand that."

"This reminds me, Mr. Hobhouse. I have penned a letter to my wife. I wonder if you would be so kind as to see it delivered. She has no sure way of knowing if I am dead or alive. I do not quite trust the authorities here to make certain it is dispatched."

"Whether they see to its delivery or not, they will certainly read it."

"They may if they wish. I have said nothing in it that is secret or scandalous." He went to the small desk, opened a drawer, removed an envelope sealed with red wax and handed it to Hobhouse.

"They have provided you with all the writing paper and other implements you need, I see."

"Yes. And it is quite odd," Washington said. "Because I have asked several times to see President Henry Laurens, who is also imprisoned here under suspicion of treason, although I do not think he has been indicted. But I have been denied permission to see him."

"Of what is he the president?" Hobhouse asked.

"Of the Continental Congress, a post he stepped down from and was then appointed a diplomat charged with negotiating support from the Dutch. On his return from his mission to Holland he was captured by the British on the high seas and brought here."

"Is he treated well?"

"No. A guard explained to me that the poor man, who is in ill health, is being held in close quarters, and able to see only a few visitors. Even his own son was granted only a half hour. He has even been denied pen and ink for writing. He must use a pencil instead."

"How long has he been here?"

"I am not sure, Mr. Hobhouse, because I don't know when, exactly, he was captured or when, exactly, he was brought to London. At least many months, I would say. But I do not understand why I may write with pen and ink, and he may not." He motioned at his writing table, on which sat a quill and inkpot.

"General, they no doubt wish you to write as much as you would like. And to whomever you wish."

"Why?"

"So that they will have samples of your writing and your signature to show a jury to compare with whatever supposed treasonous orders they may get their hands on."

"I see."

"Hence, I advise you to keep no diary, to write only when I am here in your cell and to hand over to me whatever letters you write. I will then see to their delivery by means not likely to be discovered. I do not think, as your attorney, I will be searched on leaving."

"Thank you, Mr. Hobhouse, for your sage advice. I had not thought on what you have mentioned, although I certainly ought to have. I will do as you suggest."

Hobhouse left happy with himself that he had thought of the risk of Washington putting pen to paper and alerted him. But he also thought that Washington was deluding himself as to how easy it would be to avoid being a chip, as he called it, in some arrangement that ended the rebellion. But at least his own instructions were clear. He was to find a way—a miracle, in truth—that might get Washington acquitted. But he, Hobhouse, was to take no role in arranging any grand bargain.

And he would not. Hobhouse was a man who believed in taking a client's instructions seriously. Even if, in the usual case, those instructions were often delivered to him by a wealthy man's solicitor rather than, as here, by the client himself.

His first task would be to use the substantial contacts of Fletcher Chambers to see if he could find out what was taking place in the Solicitor General's office. Was a high treason indictment imminent or was the game to be played at a slower pace?

36

Mrs. Stevenson had very kindly told Abbott that he might use her side parlour—situated just to the right of the front door as one entered the house—as his office. She also located an old oak desk and leather desk chair and added them to the room's furnishings, which already included an overstuffed couch and a large table, surrounded by four wooden chairs. "Voila, Mr. Abbott," she said, dusting off the desk. "Welcome to the very *first* American Embassy in London."

She had also provided him with a box of watermarked paper, a writing box containing three quill pens and a blotter and an ink stand with two full ink jars. There was even a supply of red wax, so that he could seal his letters. Fortunately, he had thought to bring along his own seal, which said *Ethan Abbott, Esquire*. He would need soon to acquire one with his proper title.

The day before, he had sent off two letters, both by messenger: a letter of introduction for Hobhouse to Washington, and a carefully worded one to Edmund Burke, explaining that while General Washington was deeply appreciative of his offer of representation, Washington thought an American-born barrister would be most appropriate to the defence argument he planned to make. But, he added, they hoped to seek Burke's advice going forward.

Then he'd gone to see Washington a second time, but, except for letting Washington know he'd located a good barrister, it had been very much a repeat of their first meeting. Except that the produce thrown at them as they walked upon the parade—Washington again insisted on walking there for privacy—seemed to have switched from small dried fruit to small vegetables. Washington had said, "Perhaps whoever is paying for this is running out of money to purchase quality imported produce from warmer places."

Using messengers, Abbott had again, through Hartleb, attempted to arrange a meeting with North, but had again been put off. Nor, Hartleb said, on enquiry, had the rest of the American delegation arrived. Was it possible no one was coming?

On his first full day in the "Embassy," with little else to do, he had finally succumbed to his desire to explore the city. He had first gone on foot to explore the immediate neighbourhood around Mrs. Stevenson's. Mrs. Stevenson had earlier introduced him to Polly, who had returned home, and he had invited her to go with him.

"And walk?" she said.

"Yes, of course."

"Mr. Abbott, no one walks who can afford to do otherwise. I take either our own carriage and driver or a sedan chair. As you will soon see if you insist on walking, if the streets are not filled with effluent—and it's rare they are not—you will need to step over the dead dogs and cats and move constantly aside to avoid being trampled by cattle, swine and other animals being driven to market."

"Even in this area?"

"Perhaps not on our street, but nearby, certainly. And it is much, much worse elsewhere. Indeed, in some areas the recent construction is so shoddy that bricks fall off the buildings and hit people in the head. Are you sure you don't want to take our carriage? My mother and I have no need of it this afternoon."

"I thank you, but I like to walk."

"Well, then please be careful of footpads."

"What are they?"

"Men who rob you on foot, on the street. Sometimes they will try to reach inside your coat for your wallet. Sometimes they… Well, *do* be careful."

"You think I am a bumpkin, don't you?"

She blushed. "No, no. A man who has lost a leg in battle cannot any longer be that. If ever you were. But you are not knowledgeable about the dangerous ways of this vast city. How many people live in Philadelphia?"

He hesitated. "Perhaps twenty-five thousand people."

"London is said to be almost a million. Many are poor. Many are desperate. It is our shame." She arched her eyebrows. "And you look quite rich, sir."

"I will take care."

"Do, and when you come to your senses, I will be pleased to put convention aside and accompany you in our carriage, even though we are not engaged."

That first day, despite his limp, he had walked about for almost two hours, marvelling at the dozens of buildings that crowded together but reached four stories into the sky, the bustling crowds, the street peddlers with baskets hung around their necks selling everything from buns and meat, pies and pickles, to hats and cheap jewellery. There was even a man who sang ballads for a farthing. Nothing untoward had happened to him.

The next day he decided to try to locate one of the specific Friends of America whom Charles Thompson had mentioned. And he wanted to walk there, despite how sore the previous day's walk had made his leg. After so many days and weeks cooped up on the ship, his walk of the day before had felt exhilarating.

He recalled that one of the Friends, a man named Joshua Laden, had been listed as living on Cedar Lane. After much searching of a newly printed map of London Mrs. Stevenson had lent him, he found that Cedar Lane was on the other side of London Bridge, in a placed labelled Southwark.

The first part of his walk was easy going, although he continued to run into the same distractions as the day before, including vendors selling tasty salted meats. When he finally reached London Bridge it was so crowded that he had to thread his way forward amongst sets of slowly moving shoulders.

In the middle of the bridge he felt someone reach into his waistcoat and grab at the leather wallet that he had placed in an inner pocket. Instinctively, he swung his wooden leg sharply to his right and heard it connect with a crunch to what was likely the shin bone of the man who was trying to rob him. He turned in time to see the man grab the bottom of his leg and crumple to the ground, screaming. Another man, apparently a companion, was moving towards him brandishing a raised club. Abbott tried to hurry away as quickly as his leg would permit, shoving aside people who blocked his way.

When he looked behind him, the man with the club had closed the gap and was almost upon him. No one else on the bridge, if they noticed at all, appeared to care. Suddenly, two large men, whom he judged from their dress to be constables, appeared out of nowhere, and one of them tackled the man with the club.

Abbott started to approach the two constables to offer a few coins in thanks, when the one who was still standing upright said, "No need, sir. We saw what happened, and we will deal with it from here." The man tipped his hat as if that was the end of that.

After a second's hesitation, Abbott turned and pressed on across the bridge. Polly had been right. He was a fool for having ignored her. This was neither his city nor his country, and it would behove him to listen more closely to people who wanted to help him.

He reached Laden's place on Cedar Lane without further incident. The address housed a haberdashery. When he went in, there were hats, stockings and other clothing items stacked on wooden shelves that reached almost to the ceiling. There was a boy—Abbott judged him to be perhaps sixteen—standing behind a counter.

"May I help you, sir?"

"Yes. I am looking for a Mr. Laden. Is he in?"

"I'm afraid he is out of the city for the day, sir. Replenishing our inventory. May I enquire of your name and whether I might be of assistance?"

"Certainly. I am Ethan Abbott. I have a letter for him." He saw the boy's face fall and immediately added, "Don't worry. It is good news. If you would be so kind as to deliver this to him, it would be much appreciated." He handed the boy the letter he had so carefully penned, folded and sealed that morning.

"Of course, sir."

"And may I enquire of *your* name?" Abbott asked.

"My name is Robert Laden."

"Ah, then Mr. Laden is your father?"

"No. He is my uncle. My father's brother."

Suddenly, Abbott spied, on one of the upper shelves, something he'd been looking for—a three-cornered hat, with only one corner cocked. "If you don't mind, I'd like to try out that hat there." He pointed.

Robert, using a hook, took it gently down from the shelf, handed it to him and said, "With only the backside cocked, this one is called a Monmouth. It's made of beaver fur. We have other styles as well if this one fails to please."

Abbott tried it on, inspected his image in a small mirror that hung on a nail protruding from a shelf and said, "I will take it."

They dickered about the price for a few moments, reached

agreement, and Abbott paid. As he was about to leave, he handed Robert a small coin and said, "I will ask a favour of you, Robert. Please do not volunteer to anyone, other than your father, that I have been here. I'm sure your uncle would not wish anyone to know I had come."

The boy raised his eyebrows, gave Abbott a knowing look and said, "My uncle has shared his interests and views with me. I will keep your confidence, sir."

"Thank you. Now of course, there is a chance that someone saw me come in and may make enquiries. If that occurs, please tell them only that I came in, bought a hat and left, but did not tell you my name. They may already know my name, but you do not."

"May I tell them which hat you bought?"

"Of course. Be sure to say it was very stylish." He winked, and the boy laughed.

Abbott left, walked to a nearby main street and decided, in part because his stump had begun to ache, to hail a sedan chair for the trip back to Mrs. Stevenson's.

On the morrow, he resolved, he would ask Polly to join him for a trip in the carriage. Perhaps to Vauxhall Gardens. A small London guide Mrs. Stevenson had lent him, published by a man named Fielding, called it one of the liveliest places in London.

37

As the afternoon wore on—darkness came quite early in London in winter—North found himself once again slouched on the oak bench that stretched round the old holly tree in the yard behind 10 Downing, staring morosely at the gate in the wall. He was bone weary, so much so that he could hardly find the energy to push back against the King, who had now written him three letters suggesting various strategies by which Washington could be quickly tried, convicted and executed.

The Washington plan was not shaping up as he had hoped. Truth be told, he had not planned carefully for the game that would need to be played out upon Washington's capture and return to England. It had seemed so unlikely to succeed when he'd authorized it—he'd assumed that most likely both Black and Washington would die in the attempt—that careful planning hadn't seemed pressing. Now it had become a lark that had come home to roost. He smiled at his own mixed avian metaphor.

He could hardly remember what he had expected to happen if the kidnapping succeeded. But the gist of it was that Washington would be returned to America as part of a grand bargain that would give the colonists most of what they wanted in exchange for their staying in the Empire, at least for now. But he had certainly expected someone like Dr. Franklin to arrive as the prime negotiator, not the overly tall fop, Mr. Abbott, whom he'd not yet met in person but had had described to him in sufficient detail such that he already disliked him.

"First Minister? May I interrupt you?"

It was Hartleb.

"Yes, of course. What is it?"

"The two gentlemen you asked to see are both here."

"You've put them in separate rooms, as we discussed?"

"Yes, of course."

"Good. I will meet first with Mr. Abbott. You can bring him to the library. I will arrive after he's been seated and served. Have you had him followed, as we discussed?"

"Yes."

"And?"

"He has been exploring London, as one might expect of someone from a provincial place coming to this great city for the first time."

"You know, Hartleb, there are those in the Foreign Office would like to see him restricted to the guest house."

"I know, but I think your idea to let him have his freedom here, so he can get a sense of this great city and what belonging to the Empire means, makes sense."

"Thank you. Has he engaged in any entertainments?"

"He has been to two plays, neither one of them especially ribald."

"Anything else?"

"He has gone into some of the less savoury areas of the city, across London Bridge, into Southwark."

"He's had no trouble yet?"

"Almost. He was accosted on London Bridge by a man who

apparently tried to snatch his wallet from inside his coat. And he was about to be clubbed."

"And?"

"Our men intervened."

"Do you think Abbott suspects the men were ours?"

"Our men say he gave no hint of it. They pretended to be constables who just happened to come upon his troubles."

"Perhaps he will now realize the danger he puts himself in by walking about like that and use coaches or chairs."

"I suspect Philadelphia is much safer, although he has certainly now learned his lesson about *this* city, and he has so far avoided going out at night."

"Where was he going south of the bridge?"

"He went to a hat store on Cedar Lane. He was hatless when he entered and, after only a few minutes, left with a three-cornered, cocked hat."

"That was all?"

"When our men went inside, there was only a young boy at the counter. He said the man had come in, bought a hat and left. He said the man didn't volunteer his name, and that he had never seen him before."

"It's passing odd to travel all that way to buy a hat. Perhaps we should look into that store and who owns it and frequents it."

"I've already examined the property tax records to confirm the name of the owner. He is not on our list of those helping either the Americans or the Irish."

"How good are your lists?"

"Quite good, I think, although we are always adding to them."

"Where is Abbott dining in the evenings?"

"He's with his landlady, Mrs. Stevenson—Dr. Franklin's former landlady—and her daughter."

"All right. Please put Mr. Abbott in the library. I shall arrive shortly."

38

North had given careful thought about how to approach a negotiation with Abbott, a man unknown to anyone in the government and, so far as he could determine, a man with no diplomatic experience. It would have been so much easier to deal with Dr. Franklin, even though he could be underhanded and difficult, while capable at the same time of charming the fur off a rat.

He had decided to make Abbott feel at ease and important while simultaneously making it clear that Washington's life was at grave risk if an agreement wasn't reached quickly. He knew his enemies might call his strategy manipulative and cynical, and perhaps they were right when they argued those qualities were his stock-in-trade. But he judged his approach had served both his King and the Empire very well indeed.

The library, a small room on the second floor, was the perfect place to begin the wooing of Abbott. North had created the room and caused it to mimic the inner sanctum of a posh London men's club like White's—glass-fronted bookshelves, deep leather chairs, side tables in rich, carved woods, with large glass ashtrays for those who might wish to indulge in a cigar. A small marble bar filled one corner. Only gaming tables had been omitted.

North waited a bit before entering, to be sure Abbott understood who was waiting for whom. When he finally strolled in, Abbott was seated in one of the big chairs, a glass of sherry already in hand. The man wore an elegant black velvet waistcoat, topped by a maroon coat of wool with silver buttons and, below, leather breeches. A cocked hat, presumably the one he had bought in Southwark, lay on a table. A silver-headed, ebony cane was leaning against his chair.

On seeing him, Abbott put down his glass, stood up and said, "Good afternoon, your Lordship. It is indeed a pleasure—and an honour—to make your acquaintance." He bowed slightly.

What struck North was how large the man was. He had been prepared, from Hartleb's account, to meet someone tall, but not someone who looked as if he could break your neck with his bare hands.

"It is a pleasure to make *your* acquaintance, Ambassador. My thanks for coming on such short notice, and when night is almost upon us." Abbott was not, of course, an ambassador from anywhere. He was the representative of a great treason, but why not use his rebel title if it would flatter him?

"It was no trouble coming at this hour, my Lord. My lodgings are in any case not far."

"You are comfortable there, I hope?"

"Yes, quite."

"I'm sorry you felt you needed to leave the guest house. We thought to provide you every service you needed. Was something amiss there?"

"No, no, nothing like that. I am just more comfortable in an environment with a family."

"I see."

North walked over to the window and said, "Come join me

here, Ambassador." The invitation was another part of his technique. He had learned over the years that men of great power could flatter those without it by inviting shared intimacies, especially of physical space.

Abbott came over and stood beside him.

"I like standing here sometimes," North said. "Looking out into the street. You see real life down there—pedestrians walking, people passing by in carriages, vendors selling food." He sighed. "So real compared to life in here at 10 Downing, surrounded by dozens of ministers and subministers, and more dozens of assistants who toil for them."

"Do you also live here?" Abbott asked.

"Yes. Unlike many of my predecessors, I have chosen to live here with my family. The benefit is a very short walk to the office, and that I can sometimes put my work aside and see my children, although as they get older, less and less."

The truth was, of course, that he sometimes worked late just to avoid seeing his older children, who told him at every opportunity that his handling of the American war was appalling and that he should just grant the colonies their independence and be done with it.

"Speaking of work, Ambassador, let's not beat about the bush. I want to make a proposal to you."

"Directness is an approach I like, my Lord. It has always served me well."

"Good. This war is costing both the colonies—your *country*, if you prefer to call it that—and mine—thousands of dead and wounded and treasure almost beyond measure. Would you agree?"

"Certainly."

"Thus the war needs to end."

"At some point I hope it will, my Lord."

"Well, to bring its end about sooner rather than later, I have a proposal for you."

"I long to hear it."

"It is this. Parliament will revoke each and every law that affects you, including all taxes, and will withdraw all troops from the colonies except those you request. All trade rules will remain as they were before or more favourable, to be negotiated."

"In exchange for what?"

"Only in exchange for formally recognizing the continued *theoretical* sovereignty of Parliament."

"A kind of empty sovereignty that will just lie there on the shelf, unused?"

"Something of that nature. You might still need to show our sovereign on your money and official stamps and the like. But who would object to that?"

"Many, now that so much blood has been shed."

"On both sides, I would remind you."

"That is so, including some of mine. But let me ask you this, my Lord. Would you withdraw even those laws that purport to prevent us from settling west of the Appalachians?"

"Show me on the map exactly what you refer to," North said and led Abbott over to a large map of North America that hung, framed, on the opposite wall.

Abbott pointed to the Appalachians and ran his finger down the map, from the Province of Massachusetts to the Royal Colony of Georgia. "Settlement to the west of this entire chain of mountains to the Mississippi River is what we desire," he said. "British law currently prohibits it."

"With no limit on your settlement?"

"Obviously, some of the land beyond the river is French, so that would be a natural limit."

"You would otherwise not care that you would be invading Indian lands currently protected by solemn agreements?"

"Candidly, my Lord, no."

"Withdrawing that law could be a bit more contentious, only because it affects our relationship with the French power. But that could be done, too, I'm sure." He sighed, intending that his sigh be heard.

"Without that assurance, we could never reach agreement."

North continued to stare at the map. "You know, Ambassador, I have dealt for many years with the affairs of the rebellious colonies, even though I have never set foot in any of them. Nor has any senior member of my cabinet."

"No one?"

"Not one. Which is perhaps in part why we so misjudged the ferocity of your rebellion. I suppose at this point, I never will get there."

"Well, my Lord, if this war can soon be terminated by our joint efforts, I will invite you to visit Philadelphia as my personal guest."

"Does that mean you are inclined to accept, in principle, my outline of a settlement?"

"No. For one thing, it sounds very similar to the proposal your so-called peace commissioners, led by Lord Carlisle, presented when they came to Philadelphia two years ago, back in '78. A proposal the Congress roundly rejected."

"There are two large differences."

"Which are what, my Lord?"

"First, I am making the proposal as First Minister, not young Lord Carlisle, who had limited authority to bargain. Second, we now have your General Washington in hand, and I assume your Congress and your country would like to have him back." He hoped that was true. Washington, he knew, had enemies, and there was always a risk they would manoeuvre to reject any settlement so as to *not* get him back.

"I suppose those are differences," Abbott said. "But I doubt very many delegates to the Congress will want to give up our claim to total independence. There are too many bodies buried far from home for that. They will have died in vain."

"Let's sit back down, Ambassador," North said. "It sounds as if we may be here awhile."

After they had moved back to the chairs, and a servant, without being asked, had refilled Abbott's glass and handed a full one to North, North said, "General Washington—I will afford him your preferred title in our private conversations—is unfortunately the major impediment to any deal we may reach, even if we somehow find a solution to the problem of independence."

"Why?"

"Because his position is, apparently, that he will take no part in any negotiation that results in anything less than your full independence. Without regard to whether he is threatened with execution. If he openly opposes any accord, your Congress will not confirm it."

"You are no doubt correct, my Lord. But without saying one way or another whether I think those might be his actual thoughts, what leads you to believe they are?"

"He was overheard to say them."

"His Excellency was spied on?"

North raised his eyebrows. "Ambassador, I assume your shock is feigned. When a man, while imprisoned, speaks of such sensitive matters next to a wide-open cell door, unless that man is a fool, he expects to be overheard. Perhaps even intends to be overheard. Do you think General Washington is a fool?"

"No, of course not, but he took precautions when I was there—on two different occasions—to avoid being overheard. We talked only while we walked outside his cell."

"Well, he didn't always take those precautions. Indeed, I believe it was an issue in this case of *wanting* to be spied on."

Just then, without knocking, Hartleb entered the room, walked over to North, bent down and whispered in his ear.

"Please excuse me for a moment, Ambassador," North said. "I must attend, very briefly, to an affair of state." He stood up and, with Hartleb in tow, left the room.

When he reached a reception area that led into the library, he made small talk with Hartleb for a few moments, then said, "I think that is long enough," and returned to the library. When he re-entered, he said to Abbott, "I have received a most unfortunate letter from the King. He has heard that Washington is having, to use his words, 'too fine a time' in the Tower, and wants him moved to one of the prison hulks in the Thames." It had not been exactly a lie because there had indeed been such a letter from the King, received the day before.

"And will you move him, my Lord?"

"Not right away, if I can avoid it. But it may depend on whether I can tell the King you and I are making progress."

"I would like for us to make progress, obviously. I have, however, no authority to agree to give up my country's demand for complete independence, with or without General Washington's encouragement. But perhaps in the fullness of time, these things might somehow be worked out, although I don't know how. Perhaps other members of my delegation will have some thoughts on the matter when they arrive."

"Unfortunately, Ambassador, we may not have a great deal of time." North picked up a small gold bell that had been sitting on the table next to him and rang it. A servant appeared almost instantly. "Mr. Townsend, please bring me the piece of paper that I left sitting in the middle of my desk."

"Yes, my Lord."

39

A few minutes later, Townsend returned and handed North a piece of paper.

North took it from him and said, "The Solicitor General informs me that the evidence of General Washington's guilt is so overwhelming that he has already completed his investigation and drawn up the draft of a formal treason indictment. Here, I will read it to you." He placed a pair of spectacles on his nose, held the paper out in front of him and read aloud:

"'George Washington, of His Majesty's colony of Virginia, being the subject of our said sovereign Lord George III, by the grace of God of Great Britain, France and Ireland, King, defender of the faith, etc., and George Washington, not having fear of God before his eyes, nor weighing the duty of his allegiance, was moved and seduced by the instigation of the devil, on 3 July in the 15th year of the reign of our said sovereign Lord the King, in the city of Cambridge in the County of Middlesex, in the year of our Lord 1775,

> in the Province of Massachusetts Bay, and on that day did George Washington unlawfully, maliciously and treacherously compass, imagine and intend to traitorously raise and levy war, insurrection and rebellion against our said Lord the King within the King's colony, with force and arms.'

"It goes on at some length if you'd like me to read more."

"No need right now," Abbott said. "The devil, really?" He laughed.

"It is just the way these things are written," North said.

"And the date? They would focus the indictment on the day General Washington took command of the Continental Army?"

"Apparently. As you might imagine, that date is not burned into my memory as it seems it is into yours."

"My Lord, the Solicitor General, if I understand properly, is subordinate to you, and in any case, before an indictment can issue, General Washington would first need to be examined by the King's Privy Council. Why can you not simply instruct the Solicitor to hold up on the examination?"

North was taken aback. He had expected Abbott to be ignorant of the niceties of English law. Apparently he was not.

"The Privy Council can be skipped if the evidence is overwhelming," North said. "As for the Solicitor, he imagines himself independent. I could nevertheless instruct him but for the second problem."

"Which is?"

"The King. Unfortunately, General Washington's statement suggesting he wants to make a grand speech on the gallows has reached the King's ears. The General was, ahem, overheard. The King's reaction upon hearing it was, crass as it may seem to you, 'Let us begin to lay out the small cakes for the crowds who will come.'"

"And yet, you, as the First Minister, must still consent to the handing down of an indictment."

"I will almost certainly be able to delay it. But only for so long. I serve at the pleasure of the King, so I cannot do so forever. If I delay for too much time, His Majesty can try to dismiss me and replace me with someone more bloodthirsty than I, who will agree to bring your general to trial quickly. One of the main powers remaining to the King in our system is to choose the First Minister, although only from amongst those who can receive majority support in the Parliament."

"Would the King really seek to replace you over that issue?"

"Yes. And in the hothouse of our current politics, there are some in Parliament who would wish to take my place and do the King's bidding, and perhaps be able to bring the support of enough members to form a government."

"Why does the King find himself so intent on this?"

"It has in part to do with what was written about him in your unfortunately worded Declaration of Independence. It calls him a tyrant. He thinks of himself as an enlightened monarch with limited powers. It would be so much better if the document had stopped before it got to the part about despotism instead of filling it with so much blather long after it made its initial point about natural rights."

"Washington did not write any of that, nor even sign it."

"I know he didn't write it. Even the King knows that. But Washington has waged a bloody war to make independence happen. A war in which thousands of British soldiers have already died, and on which we are spending tens of millions of pounds a year."

"And what is to be done about that, Lord North?"

"In the King's view, what can be done is to provide Washington a traitor's death."

"I see."

"So, Mr. Ambassador, I will do what I can. But I trust you will now understand our mutual problem. If Washington's mind cannot be changed, there is little point in a negotiation. It will come to naught."

"There must be a mutually agreeable solution to be found," Abbott said.

"There might be, if Washington can be persuaded to take at least a neutral position in any negotiation." He picked up the small bell and rang it. Again. Townsend reappeared within seconds.

"Mr. Townsend, please bring in the other gentleman, who has been waiting so patiently."

"Yes, my Lord."

A few moments later, Abraham Hobhouse entered the room.

After an exchange of the customary greetings, Hobhouse said, "Excellency, I believe we have met once before, at the dinner to honour the recently retired Solicitor General."

"Yes," North said, "I do recall that. Please do have a seat, Mr. Hobhouse. Might I offer you something to drink?"

"No, thank you. Not for the moment. I am most curious to learn why you've summoned me." He glanced over at Abbott. "And even more curious as to why I'm here with His Excellency, Ambassador Abbott."

"It's about your new client, Mr. George Washington. Or at least I assume from the visitor list at the Tower that he's now your client."

"I can certainly confirm that I now represent His Excellency, General Washington," Hobhouse said. "But I'm still not certain why I'm here."

"I will get directly to the point, sir," North said. "Although we are at a very early point in our discussions, I think that Mr. Abbott and I might well be able to reach an agreement that would end the rebellion on terms agreeable to both sides." He looked over at Abbott, waiting to see if he would disagree, but Abbott said nothing.

"After more than five years of war, that would, I'm sure, be welcome news on both sides," Hobhouse said. "But I'm still not sure..."

"Why you are here."

"Precisely."

"It is because I believe that Washington would prefer to go to the gallows rather than support any agreement short of total independence, and that his open opposition to any other kind of deal would scuttle it."

"On what basis, First Minister, do you believe General Washington would oppose any agreement?"

"What he has said."

"To you, my Lord?"

"No. To *you*, Mr. Hobhouse. You were overheard."

There was an uncomfortable silence in the room. Finally, Hobhouse said, "By Mrs. Crankshaw, the woman who served us coffee?"

North was tempted to tell him exactly who had overheard what. Mrs. Crankshaw was not their only informant in the Tower. And then he would add that as a barrister he ought to be more careful about being overheard. But he thought better of it and said, simply, "Sir, I don't concern myself with who does what at those low levels. I just know what I know."

"Well, First Minister, be that as it may, I am certainly not prepared to breach the trust my client has placed in me by disclosing his confidences."

"I don't expect you to."

"What do you expect of me, then?"

"To inform your client that Mr. Abbott and I are approaching an agreement, one that will save thousands of lives and hundreds of thousands of pounds on both sides by ending this war now. I am asking you to persuade him that it is his patriotic duty to support an agreement we reach or at least to remain silent about it."

"Patriotic as regards which country?"

North hesitated for a moment. The question went to the heart of the sovereignty issue. "Both, if you must."

"And if he does?"

"He will be free to return to America, whether a final agreement is ultimately signed or not."

"When?"

"When an agreement in principle is initialled by me and Ambassador Abbott."

Hobhouse looked over at Abbott, who had said nothing. "Is this also your desire, Mr. Abbott? That I try to persuade the General?"

Abbott shrugged. "I do not think we are quite so close to an agreement as the First Minister thinks. He and the King insist we first acknowledge the sovereignty of Parliament, even if it turns into an empty sovereignty, of which they agree to make no use. I have no authority to agree to that."

"But what of my question? Whether you think I should try to persuade the General to go along?"

"I have no position on that, one way or the other...at the moment," Abbott said.

Hobhouse stood up and addressed North directly, "Normally, my Lord, to leave a meeting such as this without your Excellency having first invited my departure would be the height of impertinence on my part. But I am increasingly uncomfortable with the idea of being a message bearer from you and the King to my client. My job is to defend my client, not to bargain with you about using him as a golden chip in your plans. With respect, may I take my leave?"

"Of course, Mr. Hobhouse. Be aware, though, that the Solicitor General was here this morning and informs me that he now has enough evidence to ask the grand jury to indict Mr. Washington for high treason and, unless I tell him not to, will have that accomplished within days."

"I appreciate your letting me know that. Of course, a trial

need not take place immediately upon indictment, isn't that correct?"

"That is correct."

"And so let us be clear, then, First Minister. *If* there is a trial, or *when* it takes place if there is one, are matters entirely in your hands." Without waiting for a response, Hobhouse turned and headed for the door, which was opened by Hartleb—who had apparently been eavesdropping—even before Hobhouse reached it.

After he was gone, Abbott said, "I don't think we are anywhere close to agreement, my Lord. And in any case, I cannot even begin to think about entering into an agreement until the rest of my delegation arrives. And until after you make a formal opening offer and we have the type of serious and detailed negotiations necessary to an agreement between nations."

North smiled. "There is good news about your delegation. The rest of them arrived in London today. Here is a list of their names." He took a piece of paper from his waistcoat pocket and handed it to Abbott.

"Just arrived, or arrived many hours ago?" Abbott asked.

"This morning, I believe."

Abbott managed to hide his irritation by reading quickly down the list. "Some of the names are familiar to me, but I don't personally know any of them."

"Two have described themselves to us as clerical—scribes and the like. And I suppose their presence in the delegation is intended to indicate the seriousness of the mission. For why would you need scribes unless there is going to be something important to scribble down?"

"That's logical," Abbott said. "Who are the others, if you know?"

"Henry Pierce and John Brandywine, who presented commissions designating them as deputy Ambassadors, subordinate to you. And one man, John Forecastle, who describes himself as Washington's personal physician."

"I see. But again..."

"You don't know of any of them."

"No."

"Do you recognize any of those names as possibly being delegates to your Congress, Ambassador?"

"They are not."

"The make-up of the delegation that has arrived is quite unusual for this kind of affair. I would have thought that at least *one* person sent would be experienced and high-ranking. No offence meant to you, of course, Ambassador."

Abbott was about to respond with the diplomatic "no offence taken," but at the last second decided to forgo it and asked simply, "Where are they staying?"

"At the same guest house where you were lodged when you first arrived."

"I will need to meet with them."

"When you have met them and had the opportunity for discussion among you, may I suggest we try to start a formal negotiation very soon?"

"Of course."

"The odds of success are small, Ambassador, but for the moment, the cabinet is in my corner in terms of trying to end the war. But if we do not act soon, the forces of our corrosive politics will erode the consensus that now exists. Please let your delegation know that."

"With regard to my delegation, my Lord, it is highly regrettable that I was not informed immediately upon their arrival. Very regrettable. I will take my leave of you now and go to see them without further delay. Perhaps I'll find amongst them someone who can meet your expectation of *high-ranking.* Good day to you." He was sorry there was no door to slam as he left.

40

Once outside 10 Downing, Abbott hailed a sedan chair and soon arrived at the guest house. He rang the bell and was greeted by Mr. Jarvis.

"Ah, Ambassador Abbott, how nice it is to see you again. How may I be of assistance?"

"I have just come from 10 Downing, where the First Minister informed me that more members of my delegation have arrived and are lodged here."

"Yes, that is so."

"If you could inform either Mr. Pierce or Mr. Brandywine that I am here, I should like to see them."

"Of course."

Jarvis led him to the parlour—the same room in which he had met with Burke—and bid him make himself comfortable. Abbott noted that he had not been offered anything to drink or eat. He was just to wait.

Time went by and neither Jarvis nor anyone else appeared. There was a large grandfather clock in the room, and, by its dial, almost half an hour had gone by since his arrival. He found himself becoming annoyed. As he was about to get up and leave in something of a huff, Jarvis reappeared.

"My profound apologies, Excellency. I had difficulty locating either Mr. Pierce or Mr. Brandywine, who have apparently gone to bed, even at this early hour. The long trip from Portsmouth has apparently tired them greatly."

"What about the others?"

"Ah, I did locate the physician, Mr. Forecastle, and he asks if you could meet with the entire delegation day after tomorrow."

"Whatever is wrong with tomorrow?"

"Ah, I could check, but Mr. Forecastle did mention that they must spend the morning unpacking and getting settled and that he hopes to see General Washington in the morning, being that he is his physician."

"This is outrageous!" Abbott said.

Jarvis cleared his throat and said, "Actually, Ambassador, the problem is that two of them have the flux. Acquired on the ship, I'm afraid. They are required to spend much time with the privy, but hope to be better by day after tomorrow."

Abbott was taken aback by the turn of events. He even momentarily regretted no longer being lodged at the guest house because he could have gone and knocked on their doors, their flux be damned. But since he was no longer residing there, there was nothing to be done. "All right, if it cannot be tomorrow, then let us make it day after tomorrow at 2:00 p.m."

"I will let them know."

"Thank you, Mr. Jarvis."

He returned to the Stevensons and arranged to borrow their carriage and driver for the next day. Between the arrogance of Lord North and his delegation's apparent decision not to meet with him immediately under a pretext of fatigue, it had not been a good day. He hoped tomorrow would be better.

★ ★ ★

The next morning, he dressed down—a brown ditto (which was what Mrs. Stevenson had told him the locals called an outfit, all the pieces of which were a single, boring colour), no wig, no powder and no hat—climbed into the carriage and said to the coachman, "I would just like to be taken on a tour of London this morning, starting with London Bridge."

"Do you want us to cross the bridge, sir?"

"No, please just pass by the north end of it. And if you would, please let me know what we're seeing as we drive along. It would be very much appreciated."

"Of course, sir."

They had driven along for about an hour, with the coachman stopping the carriage from time to time, pointing out various landmarks. Abbott glanced to the rear from time to time and noticed that the same carriage seemed always to be behind them. When they reached London Bridge, Abbott said to the coachman, "Excuse me. I'm feeling rather ill at the stomach suddenly. The motion perhaps."

"I'm so sorry, sir. Is it the route we've taken? I know our roads can be rough and cause too much motion inside the coach."

"No, no. I was often ill on the ship from America even with very little motion, and I seem not to be entirely over it."

"We can stop for a while, sir."

"I think better would be to just drop me right here, by the bridge. I can make my own way home later."

"Are you quite sure, sir? I can wait for you."

"Quite sure. I may take the opportunity to look into some shops."

"Very good, sir."

The carriage came to an abrupt halt, and Abbott, after tipping the driver, said, "Please give Mrs. Stevenson my thanks for lending me her carriage and my thanks to you for driving."

Abbott opened the door and stepped down. They were only

a few feet from where the roadway began to slope upward to the bridge. He glanced quickly behind him, saw no one climbing down from any following carriage and immediately plunged into the crowd.

As he inched his way along, sometimes pushing people rudely aside to make progress, he kept glancing over his shoulder but could detect no one following him.

After spending considerable time on the south side of the bridge, where there were many shops, he hailed a sedan chair and asked the driver to take him back across the Thames via the Blackfriars Bridge, which was further to the south, and to drop him a few blocks from St. Paul's.

Once he was dropped off, he took Mrs. Stevenson's guidebook from his waistcoat pocket, walked slowly along and consulted it constantly as he stopped to admire various structures. Once he arrived at the cathedral itself, he craned his neck and looked conspicuously up at the dome, then went inside and examined the interior features of the church while looking down at the guidebook. Finally, he headed down the stairway to the crypt. After a bit of searching, he located the black marble slab that marked the grave of the cathedral's storied architect, Sir Christopher Wren. He stood for a while, examining the crypt, consulting the guidebook (but no longer really reading it) and wondering how long he could stay there without attracting undue attention. As he was about to give up hope, a man of middle height and middle years with unpowdered greying hair, dressed all in black, came up beside him and said, "I am Joshua Laden. I hope you have not had to wait here too long."

Abbott stood silent for a moment, considering the risk that his message had been intercepted, and the man next to him was not Joshua Laden. And did he even have immunity from prosecution? Given that his country was not recognized by the government, it seemed unlikely.

Finally, and despite that, Abbott said, "I am Ethan Abbott. You received my note, then?"

"Yes. And I know who you are. Your mission has been much in the newspapers. Who recommended me to you?"

"Charles Thompson. Do you know his middle name?"

"Yes, Elihu. I know him from two trips I made to Philadelphia before the Revolution began."

"To which you are favourably disposed?"

"Yes. Because we here in England need to have our liberties restored, too. The right to vote must be extended to all men, not just to those of property. And members of Parliament must be elected from real towns, not from those of yesteryear that no longer have any people in them and thus allow the government to choose who will be elected."

"You cannot vote?"

"No, I am not a landowner—a freeholder."

"And yet you own a shop and employ people."

"Ha! If my shop were north of London Bridge, I would be in the haberdasher's guild and could vote. But as my shop is south of the bridge, I can do neither."

"Our needs are in some ways similar."

"Yes, and also the death penalty must be restricted to serious crimes, and not applied to petty things, as now."

"You perhaps risk the death penalty for yourself just by meeting with me."

"My wife and three children died in the smallpox two years ago. I would just as soon join them in heaven if it comes to that. And my nephew, whom I believe you met, will inherit my business."

"He is young to inherit."

"My brother will be his guardian till he is of age," Laden said.

"Is there somewhere more private we can talk?"

"Yes, there is a coffee house nearby that has a back room we can use."

"Before we go, Mr. Laden, my Latin is poor. What does the epitaph carved above Wren's tomb say?" He pointed to it and read it aloud, haltingly: *"'Lector, si monumentum requires, circumspice.'"*

"It means, 'Reader, if you seek his monument, look around you.'"

"Ah, and what do you expect *your* epitaph to say, Mr. Laden?"

"'Stylish hats, reasonably priced'?"

They laughed together.

"And yours, Ambassador?"

"That depends on the outcome of my mission here. If I even have a marked grave, most likely it will say, 'Failed his country in London.'"

"Pessimistic."

"The situation is not good," Abbott said. "Let us find that coffee house and put some plans in place."

41

The place was called Daughters Coffee House and was only a few blocks from St. Paul's. The ground floor of the building held a bookstore. The coffee house itself was up a rickety set of steps on the second floor. When they entered, Abbott beheld a large room crowded with perhaps two dozen men sitting at long, wooden tables, some intent on conversation, some reading newspapers and almost all drinking what he assumed to be coffee from a large, tapered mug. A few were smoking long-stemmed pipes, leaving the room redolent with the aroma of pipe tobacco.

Abbott felt drawn to sit down amidst them and discuss the events of the day, as if he were an ordinary Englishman. But he couldn't, of course.

Shortly after they entered, a grizzled man with a head of grey hair, who looked to be in his sixties, approached them. He glanced quickly at Abbott, started slightly—Abbott assumed he'd been recognized—and said to Laden, "I think I have a place for you gentlemen that you will find amendable to your needs."

"Thank you, Mr. Collins."

They followed Collins to a back corner, where a carved wooden door led into a small, square room with four upholstered, high-backed chairs set around a low, round table. Once they were seated, Collins said, "If you desire coffee, we have a new shipment, just arrived, of special Arabian."

"I like the sound of that," Laden said.

"I do, as well," Abbott added.

"Good. I will bring you each a mug. May I also suggest some chocolate?"

"Yes!" Laden said. "I have a craving that needs to be satisfied."

"I will fetch that, as well. In the meantime, I will leave you gentlemen to your privacy."

After the door had closed, Abbott said, "Are you confident Mr. Collins will not report my presence here to government spies? I have begun to notice articles appearing about me in the newspapers, and I believe I have been followed on at least one occasion and possibly recognized when we came in here."

"I have seen those articles. Even one describing your, ah, usual mode of dress and making reference to the fact that you stick out in the crowd above most other men. But not only will Collins not report you, he takes care to exclude from his establishment those who would."

"He has an interest in our Revolution, then?"

"No, his interest is in complete independence for Ireland, but he sees the two as linked."

"Isn't it sedition to talk favourably about either?"

"The line between talk and sedition is a thin one. Right now, so long as you don't try to gather people about you who try to do something about independence, or get up on a box and proclaim your ideas to a crowd, and so long as you take no action, the government will let you sit at a table here and discuss it until you are hoarse."

"If questioned, I will say we did nothing more than discuss our mutual annoyance with the government," Abbott said.

Laden smiled and said, "Ambassador, before we get down to discussing all of that, let me first ask you, do you think you were followed to St. Paul's?"

"Perhaps initially, but I took precautions after that, so I think not in the end. And I wore less, ah, flamboyant clothes than usual, so I more easily disappeared into the crowd on London Bridge today. Although I can't do anything about my height."

Just then there was a knock on the door. Collins came in carrying a tray that held steaming mugs of coffee and two pitchers of warm chocolate. He set them all down on the table and asked if they needed anything else. They said no, thanked him, and he left.

"Now that the preliminaries are out of the way, what can I do for you, Ambassador?"

"General Washington is spied on inside the Tower, day and night. And reported on to the authorities. I would like to place someone I can trust within the Tower who can tell me what is being reported about the General and, specifically, to whom. And who goes there to try to see him. If that is possible."

"I see."

"Do you have a friend of America you could somehow place there?"

Laden paused and said nothing for many seconds. Abbott waited, understanding that Laden was trying to decide how much to say.

Laden poured chocolate into his coffee, took a sip and said, "Ouch! Too hot, scalding really." He put the cup back down. "We already have someone in the Tower who can do what you wish."

"I don't need to know the person's name."

"I would prefer you do know it, so we don't all step on one another's toes. Her name is Mrs. Crankshaw. She serves coffee, cleans the cells and the like. She already reports to me what the General says and to whom. And who comes and goes."

"Is she able to tell you who in the Tower is reporting to the government?"

Laden laughed. "Yes. She herself is doing the reporting."

Abbott raised his eyebrows. "She is a double spy?"

"Precisely."

"Why is she willing to risk such a thing? They will hang her if they find out."

"Her only son was in the British Army. He was killed in America."

"Isn't she very pro-British, then?"

"They think so, which is why they trust her. But in fact she believes the war is being fought for foolish reasons by foolish men. She thinks her son gave his life for no reason."

"Ah, I see."

"There is more. She is angry his body was not shipped home to her. She didn't realize that they do that only for officers."

"But the smell?"

"They store the bodies in rum aboard ship."

Abbott wrinkled his nose.

"Is there anything else you might need, Ambassador?"

"There is one more thing."

"Which is?"

"The crowds outside the Tower are hostile to General Washington. For example, they throw fruit and vegetables, and sometimes eggs, at him when he walks upon the parade."

"There is no way to prevent that."

"But there is perhaps a way to cause others, more friendly to him, to appear, too. If there is a trial, they will be needed in the streets. Or even before that, as an indication of popular support for our independence."

"Do you expect a trial very soon?"

"I expect an indictment soon. But a trial? No."

Laden raised the coffee to his lips again, blew on it to cool it a bit, waited a few seconds and drank some. Finally, he spoke. "Now you are asking that I engage in sedition. The government does not like crowds who gather for political purposes. Were I to arrange it, they might well come after me. It is not as if I am unknown to the authorities."

"You can't do it?"

"I didn't say that. Let us leave the topic for now and return to it another time. If the trial is far away, we have some time."

"All right."

"Drink your coffee. It's amongst the best in London and it should finally be cool enough it won't burn your mouth."

"At least it's not tea, although truth be told, I miss it."

Laden laughed. "If you come here and order tea, no one will tell the Continental Congress." A broad smile cracked his face.

"Speaking of Congress, Mr. Laden, I feel quite cut off here in London from news of what is happening at home."

"You are not accustomed to the weeks and weeks that must go by before news from America arrives?"

"No. Even when I was in Saratoga, which is hundreds of miles from Philadelphia, it was at most ten days before I got news from home."

"There is no ocean to cross in America, Ambassador."

"Of course. But I would like to know whether you receive information about events in America that is somehow more current or more detailed than what I can find in a newspaper or learn from someone in the government."

"No, alas, I do not. But in recent years our newspapers—we are in the midst of a veritable explosion of new newspapers—have become very adept at ferreting out what is happening in the government, and the government knows better than anyone else what is going on in America." Laden pointed to a table set against the far wall, which held a stack of perhaps ten newspapers.

Abbott walked over and rifled through them while Laden

waited. "I can see that there are many articles about the war," Abbott said. "And I take you at your word, that these papers have good information from the government. But it would not be as good as what the Americans themselves know." He walked back to the table, sat down and added, "Nor as good a source as those the Americans might consult about their plans."

"Ambassador, if you are suggesting that Mr. Thompson or others might forward secret information to me or advance plans for operations, they do not. Nor could they without great risk."

"Of course." Abbott paused. "Well, I already buy one or two newspapers every day and I will continue to do so, of course."

"Which papers do you read?"

"It varies."

"My advice would be to read at least four each day."

"Any four?"

"No, I would advise you to read the *Public Advertiser*, the *Evening Post*, the *Morning Post* and the *Daily Advertiser.* The first two are anti-North, Whig-leaning papers. They are opposed to the government and the war, although that doesn't necessarily mean they are in favour of independence. The latter two might just as well be published by the government itself, like the *London Gazette*, which is in fact the government's official paper."

"I will endeavour to obtain them."

"One word of warning, Ambassador."

"What might that be?"

"Don't believe everything they say. Their main goal is to sell newspapers."

42

The next day, Abbott again took a sedan chair—he didn't want to abuse the privilege of using Mrs. Stevenson's carriage—and paid a call on Richard Washington, the General's London tailor. The man was stunned to see him but confirmed, after burrowing into some old records, that His Excellency did indeed have a substantial credit balance on his account. He also confirmed that while he had at first made uniforms for the General, in the end he had simply sent fine cloth to him in America to be shaped by a tailor there. However, if he could gain access to the General, he could certainly go to the Tower with a bespoke tailor, measure him and get new uniforms made.

After some negotiation about price—Abbott saw no reason to waste the General's money—he ordered three complete uniforms (a blue wool coat with buff waistcoat and knee breeches—the colours His Excellency normally wore), all with gilt buttons, as well as appropriate shirts and undergarments. He also ordered three sets of epaulettes, two without any stars and one with two stars sewn in.

"Are you sure you want three sets of everything?" the tailor asked. "It will take up most all of the credit."

"Yes," Abbott replied. "You see, I suspect that at a trial, the government may at some point attempt to embarrass him by taking away his uniform and putting him in prisoner's clothes. I want to have a spare to use in that event."

"All three are to be delivered to General Washington?"

"No, two are for him—the two with the starless epaulettes—and are to be delivered directly to the General in the Tower. The third is to be delivered directly to me for safekeeping. I will give you the address."

Abbott handed him a folded letter he had prepared earlier in the day, anticipating it might be needed. "Here is a letter that you may show to the jailer to permit entrance to the Tower and access to General Washington."

"Thank you, Ambassador. I must ask, though, is any part of this transaction to be considered confidential?"

Abbott thought a moment before answering. "The fact that I have been here to order new uniforms is not. The fact that I have ordered a spare is."

"Is there anything else, Ambassador?"

Abbott thought about the two additional suits of clothes he had ordered from the other tailor, but the man had seemed a bit stuffy, and he also wanted something truly à la mode, so he said, "Yes, I would like a suit for myself in the *very* latest fashion."

"You have come to the right person for that. I will need to measure you, of course, and learn exactly what type of thing is of interest to you."

"Of course. By the way, the suit I have on is a bit tight. I have gained weight since getting off the ship. Please make the new one for me a bit larger. I like some room in my clothes, and I seem to be eating well here, so I'll probably go on gaining weight."

As Abbott was measured, and they discussed styles, the tailor asked, “Are you interested in being dressed in the macaroni fashion?”

“You mean like the fops I’ve seen who return from the Grand Tour in Italy and dress in outlandish colours—pink waistcoats and bright green coats, with a mass of flowers on the lapel and a ridiculously high wig?”

“Yes.”

Abbott laughed. “No, I’m definitely not. Just something that’s the latest fashion, on the bright side, but *not* macaroni.”

“The green waistcoats are really quite attractive.”

“All right, I will have the green waistcoat, but not the colourful coat.”

“Excellent choice. And new wigs, too, perhaps? You are not wearing one at the moment, I see.”

“Also a very good idea. I managed to pack only two in my trunks, and they are rather old and I see now hardly stylish enough for this city. Do you have a suggestion of where I might procure them?”

“Yes. Try Ravenscroft’s at 3 Serle Street. They make fine wigs, including for high-placed barristers and judges.”

When the tailor had finished taking his measurements, he said, “Very well, Ambassador. I assume you will want all of these as soon as possible. And, of course, speed can cost extra.” He smiled.

“Prompt will be fine. And you can always deliver the first one for the General before the other two sets are ready.”

“Of course. I just thought extreme haste might be needed.”

“Why?”

“You have not seen the latest edition of the *London Advertiser*?”

“No.”

The tailor reached behind a counter and handed Abbott the paper.

The lead reported, “Mr. George Washington, an American rebel leader from the colony of Virginia, has, this day, been indicted for high treason." It went on to quote Lord North as stating that, although he had met with the American Ambassador Plenipotentiary, who was now in London "suing for peace," regrettably, "negotiations for an end to the conflict do not appear promising." Abbott realized as he read it that Laden was correct. He would need to read the papers every day, without fail.

Abbott thanked the tailor, handed the paper back and said, "I think the General would like his order expedited."

"And your own, too?"

Abbott thought for a second. He would certainly want to be well dressed for the trial. "Certainly. If there is not enough money in General Washington's account to cover the expectation, you can just add it to my bill." Abbott thanked the tailor again and left.

As he walked down the street, he asked himself, had he misheard North? Had not the man said quite clearly he'd try to delay the indictment? It was not until he was far down the block that he uttered the longest stream of profanity he'd used since the pain of his amputation.

He came upon a bootery, went in and ordered three pairs. He had failed to ask Washington his boot size, so he just guessed it was about the same as his. If they didn't fit, he could bring them back.

He walked aimlessly for almost an hour, thinking through what he had to do. Then, realizing that the stump of his leg had again begun to ache—it seemed to be happening more and more frequently—he hailed a sedan chair and took it to the government guest house for his meeting with his delegation. It was almost two o'clock.

When he arrived, they were all waiting for him in the parlour—the same one where he had met with Burke at a time that now seemed like a year ago, even though it had been only a few days.

Four of the five members of the delegation were there—the

two clerks, as well as Henry Pierce and John Brandywine. The physician, Forecastle, was not present.

Before they had even had a chance to fully introduce themselves, Brandywine—a man of middle years whose flushed face and rosy cheeks seemed to communicate a love of both products reflected in his surname—said, "Mr. Forecastle regrets his absence from our meeting. He examined General Washington late last night and wanted to see him again this morning."

"Is he ill?" Abbott asked.

"Perhaps so," Brandywine said. "Forecastle did not really say."

"Did he mention the General's condition to any of the rest of you?" Abbott asked.

All shook their heads in the negative.

It seemed odd to him that none of them had enquired of the physician after His Excellency's health, but he let it pass.

Just then, Jarvis, preceded as usual by only a perfunctory knock, entered and asked, "Would any of you gentlemen like tea or some other beverage?"

To Abbott's relief, no one did.

As soon as Jarvis had shut the door behind him, Abbott said, "I do not think our conversations here are likely private." He gestured at the door. "I suggest we reconvene at the home in which I'm staying. The guest house has a carriage here that I expect they will let us use. It can hold several of us, and the rest can follow in sedan chairs."

As they departed, Abbott turned to Jarvis, who had been hovering by the front door entreating them to stay and arguing that they would be much more comfortable at the guest house, and said, "When Mr. Forecastle returns, would you be so kind as to ask him to join us at Mrs. Stevenson's? I assume you know the address."

"I do know it, Excellency, and I will direct him there."

"Thank you."

On their way there, Abbott chose to share the carriage with

Brandywine and Pierce, while the others took chairs. Brandywine, he learned, had been the long-time secretary to one of the delegates who served on Congress's Committee of Secret Correspondence. That committee, Abbott knew, was initially charged with corresponding with sympathizers in other countries.

"So, Mr. Brandywine, you have some experience in diplomacy, then," Abbott said.

"Yes, you could say that. Indeed, I wrote some of the letters that went to our various friends in England."

Abbott thought of asking him if Laden was one of those friends but decided against it until he could get to know Brandywine better. And trust him. There was something odd about Brandywine, indeed about the entire delegation, but he couldn't quite put his finger on what it was.

Pierce was something of a mystery. He said that he was really not a diplomat but had been sent in case Abbott and the others needed protection.

"From what?" Abbott asked, although he was beginning to think protection might indeed be needed.

"From whatever you might need to be protected from here," Pierce said and flexed his biceps, which Abbott could see bulge even through the man's jacket.

Abbott looked up to see if the coachman was within earshot, but he appeared not to be. Nonetheless, he decided to ask no more questions as they bumped along, and they remained mostly silent until they arrived at Mrs. Stevenson's.

43

To Abbott's amusement Mrs. Stevenson had hung a small sign on the parlour door that said, "American Embassy." By the time everyone finally arrived, she had found additional chairs so all could gather around the table, and shortly thereafter brought in coffee and small cakes.

"Mrs. Stevenson," Abbott said, "in due course my government will want to reimburse you for the refreshments, and so forth."

"There is no need for that, Mr. Abbott. I am not political, but yours is a cause I know Dr. Franklin supports, and so it is one I am pleased to support, as well. I need no reimbursement for these small favours. I will now leave you gentlemen to your work." She left and closed the door behind her.

"What news do you bring from home?" Abbott asked of the group. "And how many days after I left did you depart?"

"We left four days later," Brandywine said. "And as the news of His Excellency's kidnapping has spread, so, too, the outrage has spread apace. If we do not resolve this war here through negotiation, then no matter what the outcome on the formal battlefield, the war will go on forever."

"Has politics intervened as yet?" Abbott asked.

"No," Brandywine said. "So far, all are united in demanding Washington's return without conditions. Only *then* people say should we negotiate."

"And the army?"

"Our generals, of whom we seem to have a plethora, are already jockeying for the position of commander-in-chief even while saying out loud that the rank should be left vacant until His Excellency returns—that only he can lead us to victory."

"That is to be expected. Was that all between the time I left and the time you left?"

"No," Brandywine said. "In the days before we sailed, there was a furious battle being played out in the newspapers. Radicals were demanding some kind of retaliation, although no one said exactly what. Cooler heads were arguing that we should first give your mission a chance to succeed."

Abbott scrunched up his brow in puzzlement. "Since we are already in a war with Britain, what kind of retaliation could they possibly be talking about?"

Brandywine shrugged. "One newspaper demanded that captured British officers be investigated for spying and hanged. Like Major Andre."

"If they do that, it will not make our mission any easier," Abbott said.

"No, and many people made that very point in response."

"What about the Congress?" Abbott asked. "Is the battle being played out in the newspapers being played out there, too?"

"We do not know," Brandywine said. "They had not yet formally reconvened, and members were still arriving back from the faraway states. But we would expect so."

There was quiet in the room. Abbott knew that they were

likely all wondering the same thing: Would those demanding action win out, and what kind of action would be undertaken?

Brandywine broke the silence. "We also have additional instructions for you, Excellency."

"In writing?"

"No, it was thought too risky for us to travel with them in that form. They are instead in our heads."

"What are they?"

"That if Washington can be paroled to a neutral country, as part of the bargain we may agree to stay in the Empire for twenty years, so long as we are independent in all but name."

"What does that involve?"

"No British troops on our soil unless we request them, no taxes imposed on us, no legislation to be passed affecting us without a vote of all the colonies approving it, all trade benefits to which we were entitled before the war began restored and freedom to settle west of the Appalachians."

"I think, from my conversations with Lord North, that we can achieve all of that," Abbott said. "But we don't have much time. Perhaps you have not heard, but General Washington was indicted today for high treason."

There was a stunned silence around the table. They had not heard.

"I fear the trial will be held very soon," Abbott said. "With His Excellency held hostage to a quick outcome to these negotiations."

There was a knock on the door. "Please enter," Abbott said.

It was Mrs. Stevenson. "There is a gentleman here saying his name is Mr. Forecastle, that he is General Washington's physician and asking to join you."

"By all means, send him in," Abbott said.

A few seconds later, Abbott watched as a man he assumed was Forecastle walked into the room. He was a big man with a vivid red scar across his face. Was it a war wound? And why would a doctor have one? If he could do it discreetly, he would try to find out. But after introductions and for the moment, Abbott merely said, "It is a pleasure to meet you, sir. As the head of the delegation, I welcome you."

"Thank you."

"How is His Excellency?"

"He is doing well, although he has some anxiety, which is not at all his usual disposition. He usually shows no signs of it, even amidst the worst of things."

"Did you see him after the news of his indictment for treason was announced?"

"Yes. But I am not thinking that is the problem."

"Perhaps even His Excellency might fear death," Abbott said. "Especially so far from home."

"Ambassador, I have seen him astride his horse, in the lead as the musket balls fly by. I never saw him hide himself or even flinch. If he now has a fear of death, it would indeed be something new to him."

Abbott could have pressed the issue. The type of death Washington faced was quite different than one found in battle. He chose instead to take the conversation back to the problem at hand.

"Mr. Forecastle, I will want, myself, to see Washington again soon. It has been several days. But for now, please join us around the table."

"I would be delighted to do that."

"There is an extra chair over there in the corner," Abbott said. "We are discussing how to negotiate something with the British that will assure our independence while still meeting some of their needs and allowing His Excellency to go free."

The conversation about what to propose went on for almost two hours. In the end, it was Brandywine, the only one amongst them with anything approaching diplomatic experience, who suggested the way forward. "What we need to do is to agree to stay in the Empire, but to slice the concept of 'stay' very thin," he said.

"How thin?"

"I propose to go back to the guest house and work with Mr. Pierce to try to outline a plan to slice it up."

"That's good," Abbott said. "But as that place is, I believe, a den of spies, you should ask one of our scribes—" he nodded at the two scribes, who had said nothing at all during the meeting "—to stand guard outside the door of whatever room you're working in."

44

The meeting with Lord North had unnerved Hobhouse. It was dark that night by the time he left 10 Downing, and he had gone directly to his club, where he drank a good deal more than he normally did, until he was well into his cups.

What had bothered him so? He judged that he had acquitted himself well in that he had not betrayed his client to North, and had been firm about it. Perhaps it was because, despite having seen such people across the room or uttered a brief greeting, mostly at functions he was taken to by his famous father-in-law, he was hardly accustomed to mingling with them, let alone confronting one of them one-on-one and then walking out on him.

What had really unnerved him, though, if he were to be honest with himself, was that a situation he had regarded as very likely to be resolved short of trial and simply make him better known might well turn into a high-stakes treason trial. He would be representing the most famous man in the world and would likely lose. Because there was no real defence.

★ ★ ★

Two days after the meeting with North, Hobhouse's fears were made manifest when one of the other young barristers walked into his room in chambers, dropped a copy of the *London Advertiser* on his desk and pointed to an article on the front page. Hobhouse read it and blanched. It was time to see Washington again.

He travelled to the Tower not long after that. For the first time, the paperwork he carried which permitted him access to the Tower and Washington was examined by the guard with some care before he was admitted.

When he arrived at Washington's cell, the General was gazing out the window. Hobhouse watched him for a few seconds—Washington had apparently not heard him approach—and marvelled again at the man's size and bearing.

To call attention to himself, he knocked gently on the open door and said, "Your Excellency, excuse me for interrupting."

Washington turned around and said, "Ah, Mr. Hobhouse. I have had many visitors so far today. You are the first one whom I find welcome."

"If I may ask, Excellency, who were the others who came to see you today?"

"The Solicitor General, Mr. James Mansfield, was one, trailed by a flock of assistants who flew in with him. He came in order to serve me with an indictment for high treason."

"The Solicitor is aware that I represent you, or at least I assume he is since Lord North is aware. But they did not have the simple courtesy to let me know directly about the indictment before serving it on you. I had to read about it in the newspaper."

"I don't expect there will be many courtesies extended to us in this matter hereafter, Mr. Hobhouse."

"Did they leave you with a copy, Excellency?"

"Yes." He picked up a piece of paper from a small table and handed it to Hobhouse.

As soon as Hobhouse touched it, he realized it was parchment, an expensive medium used only for very formal governmental documents intended to stand the test of time. When he was done reading it, he looked up and said, "This is more or less the standard form, to my understanding."

"I am surprised it mentions…"

Hobhouse interrupted him. "Excellency, I think it might be prudent to continue our conversation as we walk upon the parade so we are not overheard." He motioned towards the door with a tilt of his head.

Washington smiled. "Yes. They have probably heard enough at this point."

As they exited the cell, Hobhouse thought he saw someone disappear around a corner. But he could have been imagining it. As soon as he and Washington were out of earshot of anyone who might be lurking in the hallway, Hobhouse said, "Excellency, I have reason to believe that Mrs. Crankshaw overhears what you say and reports it."

"I suspect so myself, Mr. Hobhouse. Perhaps I even intended that she hear and report certain things." He smiled again, showing, to Hobhouse's mind, a set of shockingly bad teeth.

"In any case," Washington added, "Mrs. Crankshaw makes very fine coffee."

"Earlier, in the cell, Excellency, I interrupted something you were about to say."

"Yes. I was about to say that there is something in the indictment that surprises me. It mentions specifically only my taking command of the Continental Army in Cambridge in '75. Yet while it speaks broadly about my continuously taking up arms against the King, it mentions not a single battle in which I commanded the army. Of which there have been dozens."

"They may think, Excellency, it will be easy to prove that

you took command of what they call a rebel army. They may fear that if they bring in witnesses to specific battles you led, it will give you the opportunity to bring in witnesses of your own to testify to your personal heroism in those battles. They would certainly prefer the judges and jury not hear that, even though it is hardly relevant."

"I see."

"Besides handing you the indictment, Excellency, what else did the Solicitor say or do?"

"He said how serious it all is, let me know the penalty, and so forth. It was mostly legal prattle."

"That was all?"

"No. He found every opportunity to bring up former General Arnold."

"Former?"

"Yes. By my order, his name was struck from the records of the American army, so he is certainly no longer any kind of general on our side. And we do not recognize the rank in the British Army he paid for with his bloody treason."

"Why do you think they brought him up at all?"

Washington pursed his lips, then shrugged. "Perhaps it was intended as a broad hint that if I changed sides, I, too, could be demoted to become a lower-ranked general in His Majesty's Army and obtain a rich lifetime pension."

"Was that your entire conversation with them?"

"No. They also asked me many questions about my role in the Revolution, and I politely declined to answer, as I had when they first came to question me several days ago."

They continued walking upon the parade for almost an hour and, blessedly, no one threw any fruit at them. Not even an egg. Towards the end, they reviewed, as they had at their first meeting, witnesses whom the government might be likely to call during the prosecution's case. They also made a list of those who might appear in Washington's defence. That list was thin indeed.

Hobhouse summed it up. "They won't need to put themselves to too much trouble to prove you took up arms against the King. And I fear that our argument that the King had by his actions taken away your liberties as an Englishman will be likely ruled irrelevant."

"There is nothing else?"

"Unfortunately, all of our remaining arguments will be technical in nature and not very strong and must in any case be made to the judges. The jury will not get to rule on them, although they may get to listen."

"What is the best one of those?" Washington asked.

"That the indictment is flawed because it was not handed down after you had appeared before the King's Privy Council to argue your case."

"I know enough to have made that very point to the Solicitor myself."

"How did he respond?"

"He said there is an exception when the investigators for the Crown have found evidence showing guilt is obvious. And I responded that the entire point of the Privy Council proceeding is to let the prisoner plead his case to them and point out why guilt is not at all obvious."

"A very good response, Excellency."

"Do you think it a winning argument, Mr. Hobhouse?"

"Treason is a charge in which the Crown has given itself every procedural advantage, so I wouldn't hold out great hope for it."

"I sleep well at night with or without hope. If I am executed—and I well understand the gory nature of the execution—the fury at home will only assure our ultimate victory. I will go to my grave—if there be one at all—happy in the knowledge that my death will only have made our independence arrive more quickly."

Hobhouse really didn't know what to say in response. Finally, he said, "Excellency, there is one more thing. I am a good lawyer, but not by any means the most experienced criminal barrister in London, and as I told you when we first met, I have mostly experience with important civil cases and felony cases brought against the rich in matters of commerce."

Washington said nothing in response, so Hobhouse continued. "I have not much experience with felonies that carry the death penalty and none at all with high treason cases. Now that it appears that a treason trial will actually occur, perhaps you will want to consider replacing me."

Washington stopped walking, put his hands on Hobhouse's shoulders and said, "Mr. Hobhouse, I want a lawyer born and raised in America. Only such a person can really understand the need for our Revolution and represent me well and truly."

"Surely there are others."

"There are, but it seems most are unwilling to represent me. You will represent me superbly, I am sure. And I am deeply appreciative of your willingness to put your own reputation at risk in this matter."

"Thank you, Excellency. I will work hard to reward your confidence."

They resumed walking. Eventually their walk took them back to the door of Washington's cell. After they had said their farewells, and as Hobhouse turned to depart, another man appeared—tall, spare and with a vivid red scar across his cheek. Washington introduced him as Mr. Forecastle, his physician.

As Hobhouse left, Forecastle and Washington were deep in conversation. It didn't seem to Hobhouse as if Forecastle was about to conduct a medical exam. Indeed, his entire bearing shouted *soldier*, and Hobhouse thought that a small jerk of Forecastle's hand showed he had been about to salute Washington but at the last instant thought better of it.

Hobhouse left and noticed a coffee house nearby with a view of the gate. He would wait there for Forecastle to come out so he could ask him what was going on. Intuition told him something was. He found a table near the window, ordered a coffee, paid for it immediately, sipped and waited.

He didn't have to wait long. Forecastle emerged only a few minutes later. But instead of hailing a carriage, he walked slowly down the street, stopped about one hundred feet away and loitered there, reading a newspaper. Perhaps he was meeting someone. Hobhouse continued sipping.

After a while, Mrs. Crankshaw also came out of the gate and raised her hand to hail a carriage—it was of interest to Hobhouse that she could afford one. She suddenly seemed to notice Forecastle. Whereupon she abandoned her effort to get a cab and instead walked slowly down the street towards Forecastle, who was still reading his paper.

When Crankshaw drew even with him, she simply kept on walking. Forecastle waited for her to move some distance beyond him. At that point, he started to walk, too. He quickly caught up with her, but slowed a bit as he was about to pass. The result was that they walked side by side for a very short while, something that might have appeared to a casual observer as a coincidence.

Hobhouse could tell from Forecastle's head motion as he passed Crankshaw, and her slight nod in response, that Forecastle had said something to her. He then watched Forecastle move quickly off down the street while Crankshaw soon came to a halt and resumed her efforts to hail a carriage.

Hobhouse continued to sip his coffee and wait. In not too long, he was rewarded by Forecastle's return. He left his coffee on the table and went outside. Approaching Forecastle, who appeared ready to re-enter the Tower, he said, "Mr. Forecastle, forgive my intrusion, but what did you say to Mrs. Crankshaw?"

Forecastle just stared at him. "If I said anything, what business is it of yours, Mr. Hobhouse?"

"My client is about to be tried for high treason, with his very life at stake. Everything that is said to him or possibly about him is now my business. And his."

"You can take it up with him, then."

"I will. And with Mr. Abbott, as well."

45

Abbott listened attentively to Hobhouse's report of what he had seen—they were seated across from one another at the conference table in the "American Embassy"—and finally said to him, "Mr. Hobhouse, I am as much perplexed as you are. I have never had any reason to believe that Forecastle is other than who he says he is."

"Do you know, then, why Forecastle might have reason to exchange words with Mrs. Crankshaw?"

Abbott pursed his lips. Hobhouse already knew, of course, about Mrs. Crankshaw's role as a spy for the British. Should he now also tell him about her role as a double spy? Perhaps not.

"I do not know any reason Forecastle should talk with Mrs. Crankshaw," Abbott said. "I shall ask him why he did that. But let me now, if I might, change the topic to the trial, which it appears to me might come sooner than I thought."

"Why?"

"Because of what Lord North said to us both the other day and because this morning we reached a perhaps final impasse in the negotiations. We have been able so far to agree on many things—the recognition of our Congress as a legitimate elected body able to make laws and lay taxes, borders, trade, fisheries, the permanent withdrawal of British troops and much more. But for one thing."

"Independence."

"Quite right. We want it made clear that we have sundered our relationship with the Empire. They want us to acknowledge that it continues. We have proposed many solutions, as have they, but nothing has been accepted. Late in the morning today, we agreed to take a few days off and then start again."

"I thought, Ambassador, that you were prepared, somehow, to find a compromise on the issue of independence. Did I misunderstand?"

"No, you did not. But His Excellency does not favour that."

"What now, then?" Hobhouse asked.

"Now the action will switch to you, sir. Because I assume they will sooner than we expected put His Excellency on trial for high treason. And then try to use his conviction to pressure us into conceding on the independence issue. Or maybe dangle a possible pardon by the King to get us to concede it."

"The King does indeed have an unlimited power of pardon."

"Is there any chance at all His Excellency will not be convicted in a trial?" Abbott asked.

"There is always a chance, but the odds are heavily against acquittal. He is charged with treason for levying war against the King. And he did. Publicly and continuously. Even though we might deny to them, through technical arguments, the right to put into evidence some of the most obvious examples of his guilt, in the end the Crown should not find it so difficult that they cannot prevail."

"Are there no good legal arguments you can make, then? Ones that somehow avoid those bad facts?"

"The best one is that Washington could not have betrayed

the King," Hobhouse said. "We would argue that His Excellency is no longer His Majesty's subject, the King having given up his sovereignty over the colonies by his illegal actions and the colonies having declared themselves independent. One cannot betray one to whom one owes no allegiance."

"If that were true, what crime would His Excellency have committed?" Abbott asked.

"None. He would simply be a prisoner of war."

Abbott smiled and raised his eyebrows. "You might be thought treasonous yourself just for making that argument."

"Perhaps so," Hobhouse said. "But I will lack an opportunity to do so, at least directly to a jury."

"Why?"

"I do not know how it is in Pennsylvania, Mr. Abbott, but here the prisoner's lawyers are not always permitted to make either an opening or a closing statement. We may only examine and cross-examine witnesses."

"But a skilled lawyer could hint at that argument by the questions you ask."

"Yes, if I am clever enough and the judge doesn't stop me."

"Can the Crown prosecutor directly address the jury?"

"The Lord Chief Justice will be one of the judges in this case," Hobhouse said. "I doubt he will permit anyone to argue to the jury, but we shall see."

"There are no other arguments in your basket, then?"

"There are a few others, but they are technical attacks involving the statute of limitations and such. Also, the Crown will surely call at least two witnesses to testify to General Washington's making war against the King, as required by the treason statute. We will contend the two must have witnessed the very same act."

"Is that what the law provides?"

"It is a point in dispute in the law."

"Is that a promising argument, then?" Abbott asked.

"No. None of our legal arguments is promising. I will try with every skill I possess to make at least one of them succeed, but you should prepare to lose."

Abbott got up, moved over to the window and looked out into the street. "It is strange, Mr. Hobhouse. The scene out this window is not so much different from what I would see if I looked out my own window at home in Philadelphia. We speak a common language. We read many of the same books. We sit in the same type of chairs while we read them, and we laugh at many of the same jokes. At heart we are all Englishmen. Brothers and sisters, or at least cousins raised in the same household."

"That is all true," Hobhouse said.

"So I ask myself every day why we have fallen to fighting so."

"The fight is about a principle, I think," Hobhouse said. "Those kinds of disagreements often yield the most bitter of wars and are the hardest to resolve."

"You are perhaps correct." Abbott stared out the window for another little while, then returned to the table and said, "How long will the trial likely take, Mr. Hobhouse?"

"They are usually short. An hour to choose the jury, half a day for the testimony perhaps, however long it takes the jury to deliberate. It could all be over in a day. Two at the most."

"And if His Excellency is convicted, how long before he is sentenced?"

"If he is convicted of high treason, sentence is usually immediate, or at least within a day or two. The judges have no discretion in what the sentence will be. General Washington will be sentenced to a traitor's death."

"There is no delay for another court to reconsider?"

"If there is a serious question of law, the trial judges can delay sentencing, especially an immediate execution, and refer the legal question to what we call the Twelve Judges. They are all of the judges of the three common law courts in London. They resolve the legal question. Sentencing could be delayed a few weeks while we await the answer."

"How likely is that to happen?"

"Very unlikely."

"How long before the sentence is carried out?"

"A day or two at most, unless the King pardons him."

Abbott wanted to ask Hobhouse if he knew where prisoners were held after sentencing and how they were moved to Tyburn for execution. But then he thought the better of it. The man had a family.

"Thank you for coming, Mr. Hobhouse. If there is anything I or the rest of our delegation can do to assist you, please let us know. Anything at all. I am trained as a lawyer, you know."

"I have thought on that. But I have enquired and learned that the judges will only permit you to be a spectator, not to assist me by sitting at counsel table or even close by. Perhaps if you'd been educated here…"

"I understand, but I will be in the courtroom in any case."

As he prepared to leave, Hobhouse asked, "If His Excellency is convicted and there is no pardon from the King, what will you do?"

"If His Excellency wishes me to stay and witness the execution, I will do so. Otherwise, I will depart beforehand. It may be cowardly, but I would rather not bear witness to my failure."

"I understand," Hobhouse said.

"But all of this is theoretical, until there is a trial," Abbott said. "When is the trial likely to be?"

"Whenever the government wants it to be. You've been negotiating for many weeks now. I think the government is hoping that your negotiations will at some point yield a settlement and avoid the necessity for a trial."

"But we've made so little progress."

"Perhaps they are delaying for other reasons."

"Such as?"

"Looking for witnesses in America, and having time to bring them back. The rumour is that none of the British Army officers in London will testify against him."

"Let us hope they fail to find a single one."

46

North had returned to the family quarters at 10 Downing after another short, but nonetheless deeply frustrating, session with Abbott and his delegation in one of the large conference rooms. It was already early April, and after well over two months of on-again off-again negotiations between them, some of them intense and lasting far into the night, they had failed to reach an agreement. The demand of the Americans for acknowledgement of total independence and its refusal by North and the majority of his cabinet—not to mention the King—was a Gordian knot neither side seemed able to cut. Both sides had clearly hoped that news would come from the battlefront in America—some sharp decline in the fortunes of the other side—that would shift the argument in their favour. But so far, no news of something like that had arrived. Of course, the news was always at least four to five or more weeks old, so they really didn't know the exact state of affairs across the Atlantic.

Towards the end of the morning, North had decided to put the talks in abeyance and arrange for an immediate trial in the expectation that finally putting Washington on trial would somehow force the Americans to abandon their unyielding position on independence. Or so he hoped. Or so he prayed was perhaps a more accurate way to put it.

He didn't know what the Americans were really thinking. Maybe they thought it was truly over and were planning to leave their beloved general to his fate. Indeed, Abbott had even asked about obtaining a laissez-passer for the entire delegation, so they could travel to France and depart for home from there, leaving only Washington and his physician behind in London.

That very same day, not more than an hour after returning to his office, North found himself standing before the King, who was seated on his throne, feet firmly planted on the purple, velvet-covered footstool in front of him. It was not the casual setting in which his audiences with the sovereign usually took place.

He had been notified only shortly after the noon hour of the demand to appear and been instructed to bring no one with him. He assumed one of the King's many friendly ears had told the sovereign of the apparent failure of the negotiations.

That he had been asked to bring no one with him did not mean they were alone. At least half a dozen members of the royal household stood along the sides of the room. North assumed the King had permitted them to stay, for what would normally be a private audience, to demonstrate that despite recent troubles he still had what it took to dress down the head of government.

"You are the one who originated the idea of kidnapping Washington, are you not?" the King said.

"Yes, Your Majesty, I am. Although he was not kidnapped. He was lawfully arrested by an officer of Your Majesty's Army on a charge of high treason, pursuant to a duly issued warrant."

"You may call it what you will, my Lord, but we have now spoken with four senior army officers just returned from New

York. They say the people of our colonies call it a kidnapping and are enraged. So enraged that there has been a threefold increase in the number of men signing up to join the rebel army. And four colonial assemblies—so far—have been called into emergency session to vote more funds for the war and more taxes to raise those funds."

"I have heard the same reports, Sire. But those reports, even though freshly delivered here within the last few days, are at least four to five weeks old."

"Do you imagine the reports would be more favourable if we could by some miracle cross the ocean in only a day and observe for ourselves what is happening in Philadelphia right now?"

"I do not know, Sire. Sometimes these things yield a sharp passion that dies away as quickly as it arises." He glanced over at the factotums who lined the walls, who were not normally present when he met with the King. "Sire, I would speak candidly, but would prefer not to be overheard."

It was not as if the men along the walls were complete strangers to North. They were all minor functionaries of the royal household, each wearing a colourful coat, and each with some medallion or other dangling from his neck. North well knew why they wished to stay. They lived for gossip and hoped to trade an account of North's dressing-down by the King for some other tasty morsel from someone else. The one whose function he well knew but to whom he referred in private as "the fat one" glared at him, no doubt unhappy at possibly being deprived of so delicious a treat.

The King seemed to ponder North's request for a moment, glanced briefly at the lined-up men and finally waved his hand in dismissal. The men instantly disappeared through wooden doors along the wall. North imagined they had not gone very far, but were instead just the other side, ears pressed to the wood.

"You may speak freely now, my Lord."

"My apologies that this arrest has not gone as planned."

"Nor has anything else you and your cabinet have done in this war."

Did he dare contradict the sovereign? He did dare, and he would. "With all due respect, Sire, some things have. We took New York, for example. And things go very well in the South with General Cornwallis."

"Did the blockade of Boston Harbor, in '74, to retaliate for what the rebels call the Tea Party, go well? No. It just stoked the embers of the rebellion into open flame."

He was tempted to point out that the King had been an enthusiast for that action and more, but he said nothing.

The King was not done. "Did the plan to have Burgoyne meet up with Howe and seize the Hudson River Valley, thereby winning the war for us, succeed?"

"No, Sire, it did not. It resulted in our loss at Saratoga."

"I could go on."

"I will offer my resignation."

"We are not inclined to accept it. We are inclined instead to hear a sensible plan from you and your ministers to make use of General Washington's captivity here in London to advance our goal of winning the war."

Dare he correct the King? It would not profit them to have Washington referred to at court by any title other than *mister.*

"With due respect, Sire, we labour to avoid conceding him the title of General."

"My Lord, all the officers with whom we spoke yesterday called him by that title. And our spies in the Tower say that everyone, from the Governor of the Tower to the maids, refer to him as General."

"And yet..."

The King was not to be interrupted. "And his army, which you and others assured me five years ago was nothing more than a barbarian rabble that would soon collapse, and which has instead fought us to a draw, refer to him as *His Excellency, General Washington*."

The King paused, his face flushed. "I propose to call him General until you tell me you have found some way to bring this war to an end."

"Including no independence?"

The King sat bolt upright. "Never! Not while I remain on this throne. I would rather abdicate."

"We will put him on trial, Sire. And try to use that as leverage."

"A trial of the traitor will be most welcome. I might even attend."

North blanched.

"You look distressed at the very thought, my Lord. I will of course not attend, but I enjoy seeing your reaction when I say I might. You are dismissed. Please go."

North bowed slightly and backed out of the room. As he did so, he watched all of the wooden doors spring open, as the various retainers began to return to their places.

47

North left the palace and returned to his carriage, which was waiting for him in the courtyard. He was relieved that the audience was over, and hoped not to see the King again for a long while.

When he arrived back at 10 Downing, he found Hartleb waiting for him in the street, directly in front of the famous front door, which was most unusual. "I wanted to greet you before anyone else finds you," Hartleb said.

"Why? Has something happened to someone in my family? Or one of my ministers?"

"No, my Lord. Something happened in New York five weeks ago that has just been reported to us by the Admiralty. They themselves learned of it only a few hours ago from a report carried by a fast packet-ship, one that arrived in Portsmouth within the last two days. The newspapers will soon be after us for comment."

"Well, tell me!"

Hartleb glanced at the men guarding the front door. "As soon as we have gone inside."

One of the guards opened the door, and North and Hartleb passed through it.

As they mounted the stairs and walked towards the library, Hartleb said, "A navy ship, HMS *Lightning*, a bomb ship, exploded in New York harbour. It's a ship with two mortars at the front for shelling targets on shore."

"What happened?"

"The gunpowder room exploded. It destroyed the *Lightning* and set two nearby ships of the line ablaze. They both burned down to the waterline and sank."

North took a deep breath. "How many dead?"

"At least a hundred on the bomb ship, many dozens on the ships nearby and dozens more on the docks. Well over two hundred in all. A group we have never heard of before, calling itself the Fathers of Liberty, has claimed responsibility. Within the hour, flyers asserting the group had blown up the *Lightning* were posted on walls all around the port area. The posters said it was done to retaliate for Washington's kidnapping."

"Do we believe them? Or are they just taking credit for an accident?"

"The navy doesn't know yet. A confidential source told a pro-Patriot newspaper that still exists in New York that members of the group had somehow gotten hold of uniforms that matched those of the ship's crew and pretended to be drunk sailors returning from a late-night liberty. They supposedly killed the men guarding the gunpowder room, set a slow fuse to the powder and got out before the explosion. The packet brought a copy of the posters and the newspaper. I have ordered them brought here."

"Is there any evidence that story is true?"

"No, my Lord. The men who guarded the powder room are all dead. But there were survivors, one of whom was on the ship's watch late that night. The report says he doesn't recall seeing any drunk sailors returning to the boat."

North grimaced. "Or he didn't wish to admit that he had allowed sailors aboard the ship who had no right to be there."

"That may be the case, my Lord."

"But let us assume instead, Mr. Hartleb, that this was an accident for which this new group is taking credit, hoping, perhaps, to cause outrage here and interfere with our negotiations."

"Perhaps. But the flyers, which were printed, were posted almost immediately."

"Printing can be done quickly in this day and age."

"That is so."

"I will need to meet with my senior cabinet tonight, Mr. Hartleb. Please arrange it. Tell them we will have dinner."

"I will see it done."

North sighed again. "Those who oppose the negotiations will be much cheered by this, although they will no doubt shed copious false tears for the dead."

"What is your own thought about it, my Lord?"

"I will need to reflect on it because I am torn. Part of me is as outraged as I was by the events in Boston in '73. Another part of me is uncertain whether we did the right thing in response. I am glad of one thing, though."

"What is that, my Lord?"

"That I did not know of this when I was with the King earlier."

"Should I also arrange an immediate audience with His Majesty?"

"No. I am in no especial rush to see him. He will without doubt summon me at some point. I will be quite content to wait." He paused and said under his breath, "Or maybe I can find in it an excuse to resign."

"Is there anything else, my Lord?"

"Yes. Send a messenger to Ambassador Abbott and ask him

to come here tomorrow at 11:00 a.m. If he reads the morning papers, as I am sure he does, he will know before he arrives why I have summoned him."

"I will see that done."

"Also, Mr. Hartleb, when the newspapers hound us for comment in the next hours, as they most certainly will—this will not long be a secret—tell the reporter for the *Morning Post* that I will see him in person if he will call on me late this afternoon, before the cabinet meeting."

"What about the other papers?"

"They can wait."

48

With the negotiations in abeyance, and an April trial soon upon them, with the burden of preparation falling on Hobhouse, Abbott had permitted himself to sleep late on some days and had begun to explore London a bit more. He felt some guilt about it, but assumed the negotiations would resume at some point, whether during the trial or at its conclusion. He had seen Washington several times in recent days, and they had been in agreement that, no matter Hobhouse's skills, the verdict would almost certainly be *guilty*, but that a guilty verdict would put greater pressure on the North government to make more concessions. They both were of the belief that the last thing the government wanted was to go forward with an execution.

He went down to breakfast, where he found Mrs. Stevenson sitting at the table, reading the *Daily Advertiser.* A second paper, the *Morning Post*, sat next to her on the table. The newspapers had no doubt been purchased by Mrs. Stevenson's porter, who had been kind enough to venture out twice a day, morning and evening, and buy the four papers Abbott had taken to perusing daily.

She looked up as Abbott entered the room. "There is grim news this day," she said. She folded the paper and handed it to him.

Abbott quickly spotted the article to which she was no doubt making reference, read it and blanched. "Oh, my God, what a horrible thing."

"You're not happy that all those English sailors were killed and three of His Majesty's ships destroyed?" she said. "It is a war after all."

"I'm not sure. It says many civilian workers were killed on the docks, although I do wonder what they were doing there so late at night. For a second thing, if it is believed that this was the work of Patriots, the outrage here may keep our negotiations from ever recommencing, which is the very point the article makes. But another part of me is glad of it."

"Is resumption of the sessions what you have been hoping for?"

"Planning on, really. Did you read far enough into the article to see what they are calling the event?"

"Yes. The New York Gunpowder Party." She raised her eyebrows. "You have to wonder who exactly made that name up. The men who did this awful thing or the newspaper."

"Or perhaps it was made up by Lord North's government," Abbott said. "Yet the *Daily Advertiser* is anti-North. If they wanted to enrage the King and cause North's government to fall, stoking rage about this, and encouraging people to compare it to the Tea Party, might be a way to accomplish it."

"Yes, although the *Daily Advertiser* also supposedly wants the war to end," Mrs. Stevenson said.

"Let's see what the *Morning Post* says. It is so pro-government that it might as well be North himself speaking." He picked up the *Post*, read it and passed it to Mrs. Stevenson.

"As you'll see, they make no mention of the civilian casualties, don't call it any kind of party and say nothing at all about its possible effect on further negotiations. They don't even use the word *accident*, but are calling it a 'misfortune of war.'"

Mrs. Stevenson read it. "You're right. It's almost as if they are trying to shrug their governmental shoulders and move on."

"Well, at least it explains why I received a message from Lord North last night asking me to come to call on him at 10 Downing this morning at eleven."

"A question before you go, Ambassador. Do you think this could possibly have been the work of your Congress, in retaliation for the kidnapping and for putting the General on trial?"

"I think not. I have been sending regular reports to the appropriate committees since I arrived here and they have been responding. The reports to me have said nothing at all about the reaction in America to Washington's kidnapping. And they have been nothing but encouraging about the negotiations, so long as we obtain independence, of course."

"How do those reports get delivered in time of war?"

Abbott smiled and said only, "By various means, some open, some not so open."

She smiled back. "Of course. If it is not a secret, was the letter you received yesterday correspondence from them?"

"Yes."

"And *yesterday* for you was actually four or five weeks ago for them."

"That is true. And when they receive correspondence from me, it is even longer out of date—six or seven weeks. Hence, they have not even learned yet that Lord North has put the negotiations in abeyance. And if the negotiations resume and we fail, Washington might well be executed before Congress is able to learn about it."

"That must be a lonely feeling for you."

"At times it is. Although I do have my delegation to assist me."

"Do you think the British read your dispatches?"

"I assume so. I mark them as confidential diplomatic correspondence and word them carefully, but I cannot imagine they do not read them, and the responses, too." Abbott rose from the table. "If you will excuse me, Mrs. Stevenson, I must go now and dress for my meeting with Lord North."

"But you have not eaten any breakfast."

"I will get something later. If truth be told, I am not very hungry."

"I can understand that. Please feel free to use my carriage for your meeting."

"Thank you. I am most obliged and will do that."

Abbott went up to his room, changed into something less ostentatious and started to read a book. He had, months ago, borrowed *The Sylph* from the government guest house, in what seemed now almost a long-ago life, but had still not finished it. He found himself unable to concentrate on the book. He couldn't go to see North undecided about his own position. As he had said to Mrs. Stevenson, there was a part of him that felt good about what had happened in New York. Given the devastation that the British had brought to America over the past six years—the deaths, the destruction of property, the sundering of families—perhaps all those who died, even the civilians, who were likely there working on British ships, deserved it. The bomb ship, after all, had been designed to shell not other ships, but towns. Another part of him, having seen war close-up, deplored the mindless death that went with it. And still a third part reminded him that he was a diplomat with a task to accomplish.

Finally, he went downstairs and took the carriage to 10 Downing, still undecided.

49

When Abbott arrived at the First Minister's, he was greeted, as usual, by Mr. Hartleb and led to the library. Lord North was standing beside one of the two large chairs. He gestured at the other chair and said, "Please sit down, Ambassador," although he did not take a seat. "And please forgive me for not offering you anything to eat or drink. I do not think I will need to impose upon your time for very long."

Abbott sat down and said, "I take no offence, my Lord. How may I be of help? Are you perhaps prepared to resume the negotiations?"

"No, not yet. I assume you have read the morning papers?"

"Yes."

"And so you know about the terrible tragedy in New York."

"Yes, and may I say I regret so much loss of life." That was a good way to put it, Abbott thought, because it let open the possibility that he didn't regret all the loss of life.

North smiled. "But not the damage to the ships?"

"That might be much harder to regret, my Lord."

North moved to the window, clearly, Abbott realized, his favourite place in the room, and looked out. Without turning, he asked, "Did you have any foreknowledge of this event, Ambassador?"

"None at all."

"Was there any indication in any way from your Congress or others in America that this type of event was being planned or even contemplated?"

"Not in any way. And besides, I assume you have read my correspondence with the Congress."

North did not respond one way or the other to Abbott's statement. Instead, still facing away, he said, "I know that you have contacts here in London who are perhaps in touch with the rebels in America in different ways than you might be."

It was Abbott's turn not to respond directly to the question. Instead, he said, "I have acquired no knowledge of this act from anyone, anywhere, at any time. And might I add that Congress may be outraged at the kidnapping of General Washington, but they are aware we are in the midst of delicate negotiations, which I remind you they have authorized me to participate in. It would be foolish to approve, or even encourage, an action such as the one in New York, and they are not fools."

North turned around. "No, they are not." He returned and took the chair opposite Abbott's. It seemed to Abbott that he looked careworn.

"Mr. Ambassador, we had a difficult cabinet meeting last night. Some of my senior ministers want to retaliate as best we can. By sending more troops, or more ships, or opening a new front in the war, in addition to the one being carried out in the South."

As if, Abbott thought, you could afford to do any of that. One of the things he had learned since coming to England was that the British Treasury was near to bankrupt from the costs of the American war and the costs of the wars with the French and Spanish that had been loaded on top of that. But he kept that thought to himself and said only, "I would hope we could instead turn our efforts to resolving the conflict as it is."

"That is the approach that prevailed," North said. "But barely, and for the moment."

"What exactly is that approach, my Lord?"

"That we will treat this terrible incident as an accident, and that we will say there is no evidence whatever that your Congress or any American was involved in any way. We will launch an investigation of how powder stores are managed on His Majesty's warships. This was clear mismanagement."

"I see," Abbott said, wondering why North was telling him this in such detail.

His question was soon answered. "I need your assistance in preserving that approach," North said.

"Before I ask how I might be of help in that, if I want to, I must ask you a question, my Lord."

"What is it?"

"Why are you taking the position you are with regard to the incident? It might be very popular to take a punitive approach."

"I would put it this way. When the tea incident occurred in Boston—oh, let me just call it the Tea Party, we have found no better term for it—we took a distinctly punitive approach. The Parliament passed the Coercive Acts, closing the port of Boston and so forth."

"We called them the Intolerable Acts."

"I know. But call the Acts what you will, many of us are now persuaded that it was a mistake. And as the old saying goes, which was at least popularized, if not invented, by Dr. Franklin, a spoonful of honey will catch more flies than a gallon of vinegar."

"Well, I suppose I ought to be offended at our being referred to as flies to be caught," Abbott said and smiled. "But I take the sense of what you're saying. How may I be of help, assuming I decide to help?"

"You are likely to be approached for comment by our various newspapers, Ambassador. I know you have so far scrupulously refused to talk with them and forbidden your delegation from doing so."

"That is true."

"I might suggest you relax that rule and speak to the papers on this one matter. Although you only, not your delegation."

Abbott paused. "And tell them what?" He felt a possible trap opening up.

"Tell them what you truly think about the incident in New York."

Abbott laughed. "I sense you are going to suggest to me what I truly think."

North laughed, too. "Only that your government—it is a concession on my part even to call it a government—regrets the loss of life and had no role in the incident. And you might avoid using the phrase 'gunpowder party' in describing it."

"Is that all?"

"No. If you feel comfortable saying it, please say although all the evidence suggests it was a terrible accident, in the unlikely event any American was involved in any way, they will be prosecuted."

"I don't have that authority."

"Mr. Ambassador, one of the things I have learned after many years here is that authority flows to those who assert it."

"What will the Congress say when they hear what I have said?"

North shrugged. "They will not learn of it for at least six weeks, maybe more, and by that time, I hope our negotiations will have proved successful."

"And if not?"

"You may end up being disavowed by those who claim the

right to direct you. But candidly, being disavowed may be a shock to your system the first time, but after a while you come to regard it as just a cost of governing effectively."

"I am not a person who governs."

North raised his eyebrows. "Having watched you these many weeks, I think you have both a taste for it and a talent for it. But we shall see."

Abbott did not respond.

After a small silence, North said, "Well, you will do what you will do. I thank you for coming on such short notice. I think by now you can find your own way out." He gestured at the door.

"I will carefully consider what you have asked," Abbott said.

He turned and was about to leave when he had a thought and turned again towards North, who was still sitting in his chair. Hartleb was in the process of putting some sort of drink in front of him, even though it was not yet noon.

"My Lord, if I may, you would catch a great many more flies if you were to release His Excellency, at least to a parole, while we resolve our final differences."

"Ambassador, for political reasons, we must at least begin the trial first. Then, I hope, we will be able to get to where you and I both want to go and use honey liberally."

On the way back to Mrs. Stevenson's, Abbott decided that—at least for now—he would comply with the first part of Lord North's request about the American government having played no role in the event. But he would certainly not assert that guilty people, if found, would be prosecuted. When the negotiations resumed, as he assumed they would, his cooperation was something he could remind the First Minister about when he was in need of a concession. And in the end, what he said to the London press would likely make little difference to the actions of the Fathers of Liberty—if there really was such a group.

50

Hobhouse and Washington were once again walking upon the parade of the Tower, the better to avoid being overheard. It had become almost a daily occurrence as they prepared for the trial. Fortunately, the throwing of fruit had become infrequent, although there was still the occasional egg. Hobhouse was not sure whether fruit had simply become harder to obtain or eggs more dear, or whether the authorities had simply tired of finding people willing to stand in the storehouse windows and throw and shout.

"The trial, Excellency, is tomorrow," Hobhouse said. "We have discussed the strategy now many times, but there are two things I must confirm with you."

"What might they be, Mr. Hobhouse?"

"First, it is still the case—and this was confirmed to me yesterday by Lord North himself, who sought me out to tell me—that if you publicly support the various terms—borders and troops and trade and so forth—upon which the government and the American delegation, led by Ambassador Abbott, have so far tentatively agreed, the indictment will be dismissed, subject to being refiled if things do not work out. You will also, at the very least, be permitted your liberty here in London or, more likely, paroled to a neutral country. All this while awaiting Congress's formal approval of the agreement."

"It is still, I presume, an agreement which fails to confirm the independence of the United States."

"It does not acknowledge the independence of the United States."

"What is your advice, Mr. Hobhouse? You have worked enormously hard on this matter, and it would be untoward of me not to ask."

"I would advise you to accept it. It is an excellent outcome considering the potential evidence against you and the penalty. But, of course, I cannot weigh in the balance the independence of the United States. It is a political matter on which I, as a lawyer, can have no useful view in advising you."

"Thank you, sir. But I can *never* support what has so far been agreed to, no matter what other terms the agreement might contain and no matter how beneficial they might be to us. Independence is our right, and it ought not to be gainsaid because I myself may face death."

"Very well, Excellency. I apologize for needing to ask you again, but it was my duty to do so."

"I understand that. What was the second thing you feel you must tell me again?"

"It is more what I must ask you. We have discussed before that you may have the right to speak in your own defence. But I remind you again that it would be unsworn testimony because here in England, as I understand the law also to be in America, prisoners cannot testify in their own defence under oath. They are not sworn."

"A jury takes such testimony less seriously?"

"Yes, Excellency, in my experience that is the case."

"Mr. Hobhouse, it would be foolish for me to deny that I have been for more than five years, and still am, the Commander-in-Chief of our army. Were I to say otherwise, sworn or unsworn, it would be immediately apparent to the whole world that I have uttered a bald-faced lie. The lie would dishonour not only me but the army and the people I serve."

"I understand your position."

"If I decide not to testify, will I still have the opportunity elsewhere in the trial to state my reasons for leading the armed forces of our Revolution?"

"Yes. If you are convicted, you will, at your sentencing, be able to speak your mind about why you have done what you have done."

"Good. I will prepare something. Although I must say, Mr. Hobhouse—" he smiled his usual tight-lipped smile "—I have been so impressed with your insights and skills that I will not be shocked if I am acquitted."

"To be candid, I will be so shocked I am likely to fall over," Hobhouse said. "Acquittals in felonies are not unheard of. In treason trials, they are rare as hen's teeth."

"Wasn't Lord Gordon acquitted of high treason in his trial in February?"

"Yes, but on a technicality that doesn't apply to you."

"Have you been able to learn who the government's witnesses against me might be?" Washington asked.

"No, and they are not required to disclose them in advance. Their peculiar reasoning is that more truth will arrive if we are surprised by the witnesses."

"Perhaps they will be able to find some British officers who fought against me who are willing to testify. Despite what was said by the ones who came to visit me."

"I recall that you mentioned their visits. Do you think they will come to the trial to show their support, even if they do not testify?"

"I asked them. They will not. But I am sure they will not testify against me. They gave me their word. And whatever else officers of the British Army might be, they are, in my experience, men of their word."

As he was about to leave, Hobhouse said, "Ah, Excellency, there is one other piece of news I had meant to convey to you. Do you recall our discussing, many weeks ago now, that in mid-January, your American troops had defeated British troops in a major battle at a place in South Carolina called Cowpens?"

"Yes, I recall it. Led by that excellent soldier General Morgan."

"One of the morning papers reports that the British general who forwarded the report of the battle to the government had neglected to mention something."

"What was that?"

"That each time the British attacked the American line, the American troops shouted your name."

Washington smiled his usual close-lipped smile. "That is flattering to hear, Mr. Hobhouse. Which paper reported that?"

"The *Daily Advertiser*."

"Which is an anti-North paper, according to what I am told."

"Yes."

"Well, even if we assume that story to be true, it was our troops who won the battle. They are so much better trained now than they were at the beginning, when raw courage was what drove their success. So I must assume they would have won that victory even without my name to inspire them. If that is truly what really happened."

"You doubt it?"

"It sounds like the type of story that circulates in armies and, over time, is expanded beyond all recognition. As will no doubt happen with the facts of my trial, no matter what the outcome."

PART III

April 16, 1781

51

Hobhouse walked into the Old Bailey courtroom in which Washington was to be tried and looked around. It was a familiar place, one he had first set eyes on the day after his twentieth birthday. Back then he had been only a pupil and had watched and learned as others from Fletcher Chambers tried cases.

When he got his own cases, they had been simple misdemeanours for charity clients. Later, after he had been formally admitted to the bar, he had moved on to trying high-value civil cases and felonies for wealthy merchants or aristocrats who could afford what Fletcher Chambers charged. Very few had been charged with capital crimes.

But then there was the client who had been so charged, and had been convicted and promptly executed under the "bloody code," the draconian law that sentenced so many to death for so many crimes. Samuel Fletcher had insisted that Hobhouse attend the man's execution, saying, "You attend the parties that celebrate the acquittals. Now you must also go to this. We represent our clients unto the grave."

With that one exception, Hobhouse's cases had played to a largely empty room. Today, by contrast, the courtroom was abuzz with spectators talking and laughing. Every seat in the public galleries, which rose up in rows at the back and on the sides, was filled, including a small section set aside for reporters for British, German and even a few enterprising American newspapers, who had found the trial so important that they had hired British subjects to send them reports, day by day, ship by ship. And, of course, the daily British papers would be transported to America every day on the very same ships.

The judges' seats were as yet unoccupied. But instead of the usual three chairs, there were four. Because this was a treason trial, the fourth would be occupied by the Lord Chief Justice, William Murray, the Earl of Mansfield. A former Attorney General, he had a reputation as a legal reformer. Indeed, nine years earlier, in Somerset's case he had effectively abolished slavery in England by holding that it had no basis in English law. And only two months earlier, he had presided over Lord Gordon's acquittal. His presence on the bench gave Hobhouse hope.

The counsel tables were in front, below the bench. The right-hand one was already occupied by the Crown Prosecutor, who in this case was the Attorney General for England and Wales himself, James Wallace, who had been only recently appointed to the post and had been a Member of Parliament for almost fifteen years. Wallace had been in office less than nine months and Hobhouse knew very little about him except that he was rumoured to be in poor health. Next to the Attorney General were four assistant prosecutors. Hobhouse was to be the sole barrister at his own table, although he had brought along a scrivener to take notes and a barrister in training—a pupil—from Fletcher Chambers.

Once Hobhouse had seated himself, he twisted around to look back towards the dock, the mid-courtroom raised platform on which the prisoner, unless infirm or elderly, stood during trial.

To his surprise, it was empty. Usually, the prisoner was brought into the courtroom before the proceedings began.

A moment later, the clerk announced the Lord Chief Justice, who strode in and took his seat, followed in turn by the other three judges. When all were seated, the Chief Justice said, "This court is now in session. The spectators are admonished to maintain their silence. Please bring in the prisoner."

Moments later, Washington, surrounded by six guards, was escorted to the dock. He had been permitted to wear his uniform, but it still had no insignia of rank or country.

The Chief Justice said, "Mr. Washington, are you represented today by counsel?"

Washington stood mute. The Chief Justice tried again, but still got no response.

Hobhouse sucked in his breath, stood and said, "My Lord, the problem arises because the prisoner in the dock is a general and regrets, with all respect, that he is unable to respond when addressed as *mister.*"

The Chief Justice blinked and said, "Well, this is indeed a new kind of problem. Mr. Attorney General, will the government concede the gentleman his claimed rank?"

The Attorney General stood and said, "My Lord, the government will not so concede. The prisoner in the dock is associated with a ragtag rebel army to which the government accords no official status."

The Chief Justice had a reputation for both eloquence and dry humour, and did not disappoint. "Would that ragtag rebel army, Mr. Attorney General, be the same one that defeated His Majesty's Army at Saratoga?"

The Attorney General, clearly nonplussed, said, "Yes, but that makes it no less a rebel army, whose so-called officers are not officers of any recognized sovereign, but just especially impertinent traitors."

The Chief Justice said, "I see. Well, isn't the gentleman sitting there in the back—" He pointed to Abbott, who was dressed in his usual finery, although to Hobhouse's eye, his clothing looked even finer and more flamboyant than usual. "Isn't he the man who styles himself the Ambassador Plenipotentiary from the Congress that has appointed those very officers?"

"Yes, so I understand."

"And isn't he also the man with whom the First Minister has been negotiating an attempted end to the war being waged by those rather effective *impertinent traitors*?"

"Yes," the Attorney General said again. "But that makes Mr. Washington no more a general than the man in the moon."

The Chief Justice smiled. "Are you suggesting that the First Minister thinks he is negotiating with the man in the moon?"

"No, my Lord, of course not."

"I will confer with my colleagues on the issue of how the prisoner in the dock is to be addressed."

He turned first to the two judges on his right and whispered with them, then to the judge on his left. While he conferred the buzz in the courtroom rose again.

Finally, he looked up and said, "Silence, please," and when the room had quieted continued, "We cannot resolve this issue right at this moment, but we in any case do not see a need to resolve it...*right at this moment.* Mr. Hobhouse, if you will confirm that the prisoner in the dock was born George Washington, and that you are his counsel in this trial, we can proceed without resolving the *General* question, which we leave for a later time."

"To my understanding, he was indeed born George Washington," Hobhouse said. "And I do represent him." He glanced back at Washington, who had a bemused smile on his face.

The Attorney General had started to rise, clearly intending to say something, but the Chief Justice cut him off mid-rise. "Mr. Attorney General, we have resolved the issue for now. Please stay seated."

"Thank you, my Lord," he said and fell back into his chair.

"We will now proceed with jury selection," the Chief Justice said. "Bailiff, please bring in the first twelve juror candidates from the pool and seat them in the jury box."

Hobhouse glanced over at the jury box, which consisted of three rows, each with four chairs. There, he thought, will soon sit the men who will determine the fate, not only of General Washington, but perhaps of the war and the entire American nation.

Now he would be called on to decide which prospective jurors to approve and which to challenge. He would be permitted thirty-five peremptory challenges. For those, he would need provide no reason. As soon as he uttered his challenge, the man would be gone. The Crown, by contrast, needed to show cause for any challenge, although it could wait until the end of the trial.

He watched the first twelve file in and occupy their seats.

52

The first juror to present himself was Edward Hults. Under questioning by the Chief Justice, he said he lived on Queen Anne Street and was a freeholder—he owned the home he lived in. That made him eligible to vote and serve. He said he was "in trade." Hobhouse judged him to be around forty years old.

"Does either counsel have questions for Mr. Hults?" the Chief Justice asked.

"I do not," the Attorney General said.

"I do," Hobhouse said. "Mr. Hults, do you have any sons, grandsons or nephews who have served in the army or the navy or who are serving now?"

The Attorney General was on his feet. "Objection, my Lord. These are not proper questions."

"Why are they not?" the Chief Justice asked.

"Because the direction of these questions suggests that military service is a disqualification to serve as a juror. Which would be an insult to the nation."

"I have said no such thing," Hobhouse said. "I have simply asked a question."

"I will wait until Mr. Hobhouse receives his answer and either challenges this juror or does not before I rule on your objection," the Chief Justice said.

While the colloquy had been going on, Hobhouse had been reflecting on an earlier conversation with General Washington on the subject of jurors with military service. They had agreed that they could not possibly exclude from jury service all those who had served in the military or had family members who had. Not counting veterans, there were currently over one hundred thousand soldiers from England and Wales in the army alone.

"Mr. Hobhouse, please resume your questioning."

"My question, sir, to remind you before we were interrupted, was 'Do you have any sons, grandsons or nephews who have served or are serving in the army?'"

"No, I do not. Although I myself was a soldier in one of our wars in Germany, about ten years ago."

"Thank you for serving your country," Hobhouse said. He glanced up at Washington, still standing in the dock, who gave a slight nod of his head.

"My Lord," Hobhouse said, "we have no objection to this juror."

Looking to Washington with each juror choice was something they had worked out in advance. Most prisoners in the dock were seen by jurors as cowed. Washington thought giving his visible consent to each juror would show him as strong and in charge, but help make the juror feel a friend.

"Mr. Attorney General, do you have any objection to Mr. Hults?" the Chief Justice asked.

"No, my Lord, we do not."

"Well, Mr. Hults, you are our first juror. Please remain in your seat while the questioning of others continues."

They ran with fair speed through another fifty-two prospective jurors. Twenty-five were routinely eliminated because they were not landowners, and another sixteen were dismissed when Hobhouse exercised some of his peremptory challenges. These included one man who was the fifth generation of his family to serve as an officer in the navy and one man who announced that if Washington was not a traitor, then he didn't know what the word might mean. Of the others Hobhouse challenged, he just had a bad feeling about them. For a few of them, it was their body language. In ways he couldn't quite articulate they seemed to walk and talk like sure guilty votes. For others, it was irrational superstition. He challenged one juror with red hair simply because he had never gotten a favourable verdict from a jury that contained one. Washington had permitted him his head on the peremptories.

When they were down to only twelve remaining in the box, all of whom had been questioned and drawn no objection from Hobhouse, the Chief Justice said, "Mr. Attorney General, do you have objection to any of the gentlemen who remain in the box at this point?"

"No, my Lord, the Crown has no objection to any who remain."

Hobhouse read the Crown's failure to lodge a single objection as a strategy to tell the jury of the Attorney General's supreme confidence in his case. The jurors who remained had been able to observe as juror after prospective juror was objected to only by Washington's side. It was not a good thing, but there was nothing to be done about it. And he was satisfied with the jury they had chosen.

"Let us take a brief respite," the Chief Justice said. "Please return when the clerk goes out into the hallway and calls you back. The prisoner is to remain in the dock."

As Hobhouse turned towards the dock, intending to talk to Washington, he saw Forecastle enter the courtroom, presumably to pretend to check up on his supposed patient. Washington's guards seemed to know the man and paid him no attention as he approached the General.

Hobhouse had months ago concluded that whatever Forecastle was, he certainly wasn't a physician, or at least not only a physician. He watched as Forecastle started to talk to Washington. At the same time, though, Forecastle kept glancing around the courtroom, almost as if he were studying its layout. Even more curious, another man, a British Army officer in uniform, came in, stopped dead in his tracks and stared fixedly at Forecastle for a few seconds. Almost as if he recognized him. A distressed look crossed the man's face, and he bolted from the room.

Hobhouse walked up to the dock, greeted Washington and then said to Forecastle, "Did you notice the British Army officer who was staring at you just now? The man in uniform?"

"No, I didn't," Forecastle said. "What did he look like?"

"Trim, dark hair, maybe in his early thirties."

"It does not remind me of anyone I know," he said.

"Excellency, did you see him?"

"No, I did not."

"If I see him again, I will point him out to both of you," Hobhouse said.

Forecastle left shortly after that and Hobhouse said, "I think, Excellency, that we have chosen a good jury."

"Which doesn't mean you believe I will be acquitted, does it?" Washington said.

"No, Excellency, it does not, but I will try my best."

"You are doing a fine job, Mr. Hobhouse. Whatever happens, I am grateful. As I have no doubt the American people are."

"You distinguish them from the people of Great Britain?"

"I do. We are all members of the great English-speaking peoples. But we are now separate."

Just then the clerk began to call people back into the courtroom. With everyone seated again, the judges took the bench.

"We will now resume," the Chief Justice said. "Let us swear in the jury."

After that was done, the Chief Justice addressed the clerk. "Please read the indictment, and please stand while you do so, so the jury might hear clearly."

53

The clerk stood and read in a loud voice:

"Gentlemen of the jury, the indictment preferred against George Washington by the Grand Jurors for our Lord the King, sitting in the City of London, upon their oath, present..."

What Hobhouse heard as the clerk read on was nearly identical to the words in the draft indictment Lord North had given him to read in the library at 10 Downing. And also identical to the copy that had originally been served on Washington in the Tower. Except for two things, both of which he had noticed when Washington, just a few days earlier, had been presented with a revised indictment. They were important changes, which he would use to move to dismiss the case as soon as the clerk stopped reading.

When the clerk finished, Hobhouse rose and said, "My Lords, I move to dismiss the indictment against the prisoner on two grounds."

Hobhouse thought the Chief Justice looked annoyed, but he

nevertheless said in an even voice, "What are they, Mr. Hobhouse?"

"Thank you, my Lord. First, the original indictment spoke only of the allegation that General Washington had taken up arms against the King on July 3 in the year of our Lord 1775. The statute of limitations for high treason is three years from the date of the alleged treasonous act, and the act alleged took place five years ago."

"You are bringing a motion to dismiss on that ground?"

"Yes."

"And yet, Mr. Hobhouse, the superseding indictment, as revised, adds to the phrase 'rebellion against the King with force and arms' and the new phrase 'and continuing to the present day,' does it not?"

"Yes, my Lord, but that is not sufficient. It must specify with particularity the acts that are claimed to continue."

The Chief Justice looked down at the Attorney General and said, "What says the Crown to that, Mr. Attorney General?"

"The Crown contends that the addition of the phrase 'continuing acts' is enough so long as actual evidence of continuing acts is presented during the trial itself. The Crown will present copious evidence of such continuing acts. The original indictment was drafted in haste and by lawyers for the Crown less skilled than those currently here."

The Chief Justice raised his eyebrows, presumably, Hobhouse thought, at the rare admission of error by counsel for the Crown.

The Chief Justice said, "The motion is denied, without prejudice, Mr. Hobhouse, to your renewing it later if the Crown fails to prove up sufficient additional acts that took place within three years past of the date of the indictment."

"Thank you, my Lord," Hobhouse said.

"You have a second motion, I believe you said?"

"Yes. As your Lordship is no doubt aware, an indictment for high treason requires two witnesses to the alleged acts of treason, and the witnesses must be named. The original indictment named no person at all, and this revised one names only one witness, someone named William Alwick. In addition, the revised indictment says nothing about who Mr. Alwick is or where he might be found, and neither I nor General Washington know who Mr. Alwick is."

"Have you made enquiry?"

"Yes, diligent enquiry, including of counsel for the Crown, who has, as of this hour, not responded."

"Mr. Attorney General, what say you to that?"

"First, the case law, as it has evolved to give detailed meaning to the spare words of the treason statute, whose most recent enactment is now almost eighty years behind us, provides that it is sufficient to name the witnesses to the treason *during* the presentation of evidence. Which is what the Crown will do."

"I think, Mr. Hobhouse, that he is correct about that," the Chief Justice said. "Nor need the Crown provide you any information about witnesses before they testify. You are, of course, free to enquire of a witness's background when the man is in the witness box."

"Thank you, my Lord," Hobhouse said.

Then the Chief Justice gave Hobhouse a small gift. "Now that we have disposed of the law here, Mr. Attorney General, the court would like to know why you have refused to give the prisoner and his counsel any information about this man Alwick, who is named in the superseding indictment. It seems at best somewhat rude."

Clearly taken aback for the second time that day, the Attorney General started to say something that Hobhouse was not able to hear because he mumbled his words. Then he began again and said simply, "Although Mr. Alwick is named in the indictment, we have only within the last day or two gathered sufficient facts from him and about him to allow us to put him on as a witness.

I will be glad, before he testifies, to inform Mr. Hobhouse of what we have learned."

"Is he your first witness?" the Chief Justice asked.

"Yes."

"Mr. Hobhouse, how would you like to proceed?"

Hobhouse had not expected to win either motion. Rather he had brought them so the jury could begin to see how unfair the proceeding was. For reasons he had never understood, the jury was not excluded from the courtroom while the lawyers made their legal arguments to the judge. He always tried to use the opportunity to begin to argue his case to the jury.

Hobhouse sighed audibly, looked over at the jury as if to say, "See what I have to put up with?" and said, "To save the time of the jury and the court, my Lord, I will instead question the witness about his background while he is on the witness stand."

"Very well," the Chief Justice said. "Mr. Attorney General, please call your first witness."

"I would like to be able to make an opening statement, my Lord."

"I think not. Permitting opening and closing statements is discretionary with the court. This is a simple case, with a clearly stated indictment. Let us just go forward. Please call your witness."

"With all due respect, my Lord, I am not aware of a case in which the Crown has not been permitted to make an opening statement. A prisoner, perhaps, has been denied that opportunity. But I represent the King and Sovereign."

"This is not the first time, Mr. Attorney General, that I have denied an opening statement to the Crown. Please call your witness."

"Very well, my Lord."

54

"The Crown calls Mr. William Alwick," the Attorney General said.

Hobhouse watched an elderly-looking gentleman—almost bald, not very tall and with a distinctly crooked nose—rise from one of the benches near the front of the courtroom and walk unsteadily to the witness box, relying on a cane. He stood, kept upright only by leaning on his cane, and the clerk administered the oath.

Hobhouse had never set eyes on the man before. He looked over to Washington, still standing ramrod straight in the dock, who just shrugged.

When the clerk had finished with the oath, the Chief Justice said, "Mr. Alwick, would you prefer to sit on the bench that is there in the box? We ask witnesses to stand so that all may hear easily, but you look uneasy on your feet."

"Yes, my Lord. I would be pleased to sit down, if it would not offend your Lordship."

"Please do so, then."

"Thank you, my Lord."

"Where do you live, Mr. Alwick?" the Attorney General asked.

"I live at number 22 Berners Street."

"Have you always lived there?"

"No. Until three years ago—1777, if I recall right—I lived in the city of Cambridge, in His Majesty's Colony of Massachusetts Bay. In that same year I came here, to London."

"Why did you move?"

"Many years ago my daughter moved here with her husband, who is in business here. When the Revolution—I mean, the rebellion—broke out, she insisted I come to London. She said it was much too dangerous to stay in Cambridge." He smiled. "There was a hell of a lot of shooting around there, you know."

The audience tittered and someone said, not so sotto voce, "Still a hell of a lot."

Hobhouse glanced up at the Chief Justice to see if he was going to take umbrage at the use of profanity in his courtroom by the witness, but he said nothing. Age excused many things.

"Were you still living in Cambridge in 1775?"

"Yes. And I saw…"

"Just a moment, Mr. Alwick, until I ask you another question. Do you remember any excitement in July of 1775?"

"Well, no. The excitement was way back in April of that year. That's when the redcoats—I mean, the British troops—got into trouble on their way to Lexington."

"Yes, of course. But try to think whether anything exciting happened in July."

"Oh, yes, there was something all right. General Washington took the oath to take command of the army started by the Continental Congress."

"Did you see that event?"

"Yes. You see, I lived on a street right near the Commons.

And one day I heard a crowd, and I went out and there he was, big as life."

"Who?"

"Why, General Washington, of course."

"Do you see him in this courtroom?"

"Yes, the prisoner in the dock over there." Alwick pointed at Washington.

"Are you sure it's the same man?"

"Very sure."

"Did you hear what he said when he took the oath?"

Alwick scrunched up his face. "I think so."

"What did he say?"

"He raised his right hand and swore allegiance to the American states. I think he called them the United States or the Continental States. I'm not sure."

"Did he say anything else?"

"That they were independent. And sovereign. Or words like that."

"Anything else?"

Alwick looked around the courtroom, almost as if looking for guidance, and said, "I do not wish to speak ill of our king."

"You may say it here in court without fear, Mr. Alwick."

"All right. He said the states were no longer to follow George III and instead oppose him. Or words like that."

"Did he say what he was doing there?"

"Oh, yes. He said he was taking command of the army."

"Did he say which army?"

"Yes, the army our Continental Congress had chartered."

"Thank you, Mr. Alwick. I do not have any more questions."

Alwick started to leave the box when the Chief Justice said, "Please wait one moment, Mr. Alwick. Mr. Hobhouse might have questions for you."

Hobhouse glanced at Washington, saw no expression on his face that would have instructed him one way or the other and said, "I have no questions of the witness, my Lord. Thank you for coming today, Mr. Alwick."

As he spoke, Hobhouse heard a slight stir in the courtroom, as if the audience had expected him to attack Alwick's clearly coached memory. But he had seen no benefit in doing it. Alwick had described a true event, and Hobhouse's strategy was to show that the Crown could not produce two witnesses to the *same* treasonous event. He would then argue that the law ought to require there be two.

There was a pause as almost all in the courtroom turned and watched Alwick hobble out of the room. When the door had closed behind him, the Chief Justice said, "Mr. Attorney General, please call your next witness."

Hobhouse spoke before the Attorney General could respond and said, "My Lords, before the next witness appears, I move that Mr. Alwick's testimony be excluded from consideration by the jury. The alleged act to which he testified took place six and a half years ago, and the three-year statute of limitations for high treason has long ago expired."

"My Lord, the act testified to by Mr. Alwick is the start of a continuing series of actions leading down to the present," the Attorney General said. "And we will show that."

"The motion is denied for the moment," the Chief Justice said. "Mr. Hobhouse, you are welcome to bring it again, if you choose, at the close of the Crown's evidence. Let us now have the next witness."

55

"The Crown calls General Benedict Arnold."

At the mention of the name, there was a tremendous stir in the courtroom, until finally the Chief Justice, with a sharp tone, silenced everyone. The Attorney General, in an act of showmanship Hobhouse assumed he had thought out well in advance, nodded to one of his men, who was standing by the rear door of the courtroom.

The man opened the door, and General Arnold stepped through, wearing the standard blood-red coat of a British officer, with the single star and crown of a brigadier general on the epaulettes. He struck Hobhouse as slightly shorter than average height and somewhat stout. He was dark-skinned, with a rather prominent nose and a florid complexion. His hair was black, powdered, but without either wig or hat. Yet he didn't cut an athletic figure, as Washington did, and despite walking assisted by a cane, he nonetheless walked with supreme confidence, greeting people left and right as he made his way to the witness box, almost as if he were a war hero. Which perhaps he now was to some in Britain.

Hobhouse looked over to Washington, who had Arnold fixed in a hard stare, but otherwise showed no emotion. Arnold, he noticed, avoided looking directly at Washington as he moved forward, although he seemed to cast an occasional glance at the man in the dock out of the corner of his eye.

How had Arnold got here? The last Hobhouse had read, months ago, he was leading British troops somewhere in the colonies. Creating time to get him back to London must have been the real reason North had several times delayed the trial. It had not been, as he had claimed, to give the negotiations still more time.

Hobhouse felt duped. But maybe there was advantage in it. No one liked a traitor.

After Arnold was sworn, the Attorney General said to his witness, "What is your profession?"

"I am a professional soldier. A brigadier general in His Majesty's Army."

"Have you always been a soldier in His Majesty's Army?"

"No. I was for a time a soldier in the rebel army in America."

"How did it come to be that you transitioned from one to the other?"

"I had always felt an allegiance to His Majesty, a pull, if you will, of loyalty, and I finally realized that that was where I belonged." He paused. "And that was where my true liberties would be best protected."

The Attorney General had, as Hobhouse and his fellow barristers liked to say, pulled the sting on his witness, bringing out the bad things himself so that Hobhouse couldn't do it later.

Hobhouse looked over to Washington. His face was red and his lips were compressed in a hard line. It was perhaps a good thing that the General was being guarded by soldiers. The look on his face suggested he might otherwise leap out of the dock and throttle the witness with his bare hands. It was the only time Hobhouse had ever seen the General come close to losing his composure.

Arnold was continuing to testify. "...and in terms of liberties, I came to realize that although, while living in America, I had no direct vote for members of Parliament, and in fact Parliament represented all of us, whether we were living here or in the colonies. Like a father looking after all of his children."

Hobhouse stifled a laugh. The Attorney General was putting the government's political arguments into the mouth of his witness. In a normal case, Hobhouse might have objected to the testimony as being far from relevant to the proceeding. But he would let it go and see if he might make use of it in the cross-examination.

"General Arnold, did you spend time with George Washington during the years 1778, 1779 and 1780?" the Attorney General asked.

"Yes."

"Do you recall any specific times?"

"Yes. In late May of 1778, I met with Washington in a Pennsylvania town called Valley Forge. It was not long after the Americans had won a battle against the British, and Washington was joyous."

"Do you recall anything in particular he said to you?"

"Yes. But to repeat it, Mr. Attorney General, I feel I must seek leave, for it was vulgar." He glanced up at the bench.

The Chief Justice, without waiting for the Attorney General to respond, said, "You are under oath, General. You must truly state what he said, and we will forgive any vulgarity you repeat."

"Thank you, my Lord," Arnold said. "Washington said to me, 'We have struck a blow against the bloody King. When we finish this war, let us hope he will no longer even retain his throne.'"

Hobhouse glanced at the jury. They did not look especially shocked at the use of the vulgarity. Probably, he thought, many of them used it not infrequently themselves. But in private. To use it publicly about the King might well get you whipped.

Washington, however, was not able to contain himself. "That is a damnable lie," he said. "He has made it up."

The Chief Justice looked at Washington. "The prisoner is not to speak unless the court calls upon him to do so."

"My apologies, my Lord," Washington said.

The Attorney General resumed his questioning. "General Arnold, do you recall any other instances in which you met with Washington in person in those years?"

"There were dozens of meetings. Another I recall well was upon assuming command of the rebel forces in Philadelphia in May of 1778. Shortly after, I met with Washington to discuss the defences of the city."

"Do you recall any of your conversation from that meeting?"

"Yes. I recall that he said, 'The King's men have run away from here, and with God's help we will run them from every one of our cities.'"

When Hobhouse looked over to Washington, he was shaking his head back and forth and clearly having difficulty complying with the Chief Justice's instruction to remain quiet.

The Attorney General went on to elicit from Arnold several more supposed meetings with Washington in which he had allegedly said things suggesting that he was at war, not just with Parliament and its policies, but with the King himself.

Finally, the Attorney General said, "I have no further questions of the witness, my Lord."

"Mr. Hobhouse, I assume you have questions," the Chief Justice said.

"I do, my Lord, but I function under a burden. This witness is a complete surprise, and he is testifying about conversations with my client of which I have no knowledge. I therefore respectfully request a brief adjournment so that I may have the opportunity to consult with General Washington about the veracity of Mr. Arnold's testimony."

Hobhouse noticed that his use of *mister* in place of *General* had caused Arnold to scowl.

"I think we can improve upon your situation," the Chief Justice said. "I have not failed to notice that Washington is in effect instructing you and that you have no actual solicitor in this matter. If the prisoner can restrain himself, I will permit him to sit on the solicitor's bench behind you so that you may more easily consult with him."

"That would be most appreciated, my Lord."

The Attorney General rose. "I object, my Lord. This is most unusual. The prisoner could be a physical threat to all of us."

The Chief Justice raised his eyebrows. "He will continue to be guarded by the soldiers who have guarded him so far. Your objection is overruled. And, Mr. Hobhouse, you may take a few moments after the prisoner is moved to consult with him with regard to your cross-examination. The court will be in recess while you do that."

"Thank you, my Lord," Hobhouse said. "I will be prepared to cross-examine the witness when the court returns."

56

Hobhouse's conversation with Washington took a while, as Washington told him about Arnold's history in the American army as well as the plot to turn over West Point to the British. They had just finished as they heard the clerk calling everyone back to order. Washington told Hobhouse, "I would avoid belittling him. He takes offence easily and it will likely be more effective to get him to admit what he did and let it speak for itself."

"I might want to belittle him and get him to explode."

"Ah, I see. Well, I leave it to you, then."

"Did he describe his meetings with you accurately?"

"What he said about our meetings had the ring of truth because we did meet when he says we did. But I am quite certain I did not mention the King. My effort was and is to defeat the British Army. I have never thought the King was truly our personal enemy."

"Yet you were leading a war against the King."

"Yes, of course. He is the sovereign who must be defeated if we are to be free."

"I want to show that Arnold is a turncoat and not to be trusted. I want the jury to dislike him and disregard what he says, be it true or false."

"A turncoat and a traitor, most certainly. Indeed, the rumour was that he was planning to turn over not only West Point to the British, but me as well, in some sort of trap."

When, a short while later, all had reassembled, with the judges back on the bench and Arnold in the witness box, Hobhouse rose and said, "Mr. Arnold, what was your rank in the *rebel* army, as you have called it?"

He saw Arnold stiffen, presumably because he had addressed him as *mister.* He felt Washington tap him on the shoulder.

"Concede him his title, Mr. Hobhouse," he whispered. "He is no longer a general in our army, but he is in theirs. And he was once a great one. Civility will profit us here."

Hobhouse resumed. "Pardon me, sir. General Washington has instructed me to address you as *General.*" He could feel the tension drain out of the courtroom. "General Arnold, what was your rank in the *rebel* army?"

"I was a general."

"What rank of general?"

"I was a major general."

"And in the British Army?"

"I am a brigadier general."

"A demotion?"

"I would not put it that way. The British Army is much larger, so there are more people ahead of me in seniority than there were…previously."

"Would it be fair to say you switched sides?"

His mouth twitched. "I might put it differently."

Hobhouse had been taught never to give a witness an opening to talk at length. Only to answer yes or no questions. But he decided to risk it.

"How would you put it, General?"

"I would say I recognized who was the true sovereign of our country and came back to him, with regrets that I had strayed."

"But before you came back you were, just months ago, waging war against that very king to secure the independence of the colonies, were you not?"

"Yes, but no longer. Now I am waging war to preserve His Majesty's kingdom against a rebellion."

"You came back here, crossing an entire ocean, solely to testify against General Washington, did you not?"

"I would not put it that way. I was leading troops in the colonies when I was recalled here. I didn't know the purpose."

"But now you do, don't you?"

There was no answer, and Hobhouse chose to press the question differently.

"While you've been here, have you been assigned any task other than testifying in this trial, General?"

"Not yet."

"Have you been ordered to return to America when this trial is over?"

"Yes."

"Thank you. Now let's talk about something else. How long were you a general in the rebel army?"

"I don't recall exactly."

"Would it have been from 1776 to September 1780?"

"That sounds correct. Before I resumed a path of loyalty."

"Other than the rank of brigadier general, did you receive anything else when you chose what you call the path of loyalty?"

"I'm not sure I understand the question."

"Did you receive any money?"

"I received a pension."

"For how much?"

The Attorney General rose. "My Lord, I object to this line of questioning. It has become wholly irrelevant to what I asked this witness, which was about his meetings with Washington and what Washington said in those meetings."

"It's entirely relevant, my Lord," Hobhouse said. "It goes to this man's character and his reputation for truthfulness, which this jury is certainly entitled to consider as it weighs his testimony."

"Your objection is overruled, Mr. Attorney General," the Chief Justice said.

"I believe the question pending, General Arnold, was the amount of the pension you received for changing sides," Hobhouse said.

"It wasn't for changing sides. It was for information."

"Fine. How much for the information?"

"I was promised an annual income of several hundred pounds and an annual pension of 360 pounds."

"I noticed you walk with a cane. Is that from a war injury while you were serving on the rebel army side?"

"Yes, I was wounded."

"At the battle of Saratoga?"

"Yes."

"Was General Washington involved in that battle?"

"Yes, although he wasn't personally present."

"He was the Commander-in-Chief, is that correct?"

"Yes."

"And you were a general there?"

"Yes."

"So you collaborated with him on overall plans for that part of the war, even though he wasn't personally there?"

There was a pause, as Arnold considered the question, clearly wondering if the unusual wording was somehow a trap.

The Attorney General started to rise.

"Please sit down, Mr. Attorney General," the Chief Justice said.

Hobhouse knew—and assumed that the judge and every other

lawyer in the room knew—that if Arnold and Washington were collaborators, Arnold's testimony would require another witness to corroborate his story in order for it to be used as proof of treason. The Attorney General had presumably planned to find a way, via an objection, to let Arnold know that.

Finally, Arnold said, "Yes. We were."

Washington whispered something in Hobhouse's ear. Hobhouse nodded and said, "General Arnold, when you were serving in what you now call the rebel army, was that what you called it?"

"No."

"What did you call it?"

Arnold paused, not answering.

"I would remind you, General, that you are under oath."

He heard someone in the audience mutter, "Not that his oath matters much," followed by laughter. Hobhouse glanced over to see if the jury was laughing. One was. The rest were not.

Finally, Arnold, ignoring the tittering, said, "Sometimes we called it the Army of the Continental States of America. Sometimes we called it the Army of the United States of America."

"Did you ever just call it the American army?"

"Occasionally, yes."

"In 1778 did you stand up in public and swear an oath of loyalty to the states, swearing to do everything in your power to protect them from King George III and to support their independence?"

"Yes. But even then I had my doubts about the rebellion, about the way Loyalists were being treated by the so-called Patriots, which was poorly and unfairly."

"You took the oath with reservations, then?"

"You could say that."

"Did you take your oath today with any reservations?"

"No, because it was to our king, the true sovereign."

"One final thing, General. You planned, did you not, to

hand over the plans for the defence of West Point to the British Army?"

"Yes."

"Did you also plan to find a way to hand over General Washington himself to the British?"

"No, I did not."

"It was only one act of treason you meant to carry out, and not two?"

"I will not answer that."

"I didn't think you would. I have no further use for this witness, my Lord."

The Chief Justice looked down at the Attorney General. "Do you have any questions of the witness?"

"Yes. General Arnold, you mentioned poor treatment of Loyalists. To what did you refer?"

"Loyalists, even if they had done nothing but refuse to sign an oath to the rebellion, were beaten, tarred and feathered, forced from their homes, had their property confiscated and sometimes hanged. Amongst other terrors visited upon them."

"Thank you. I have no further questions."

"Nor do I," Hobhouse said.

"You may be excused, General," the Chief Justice said.

As Arnold walked past the Attorney General's table, Hobhouse heard him say, quite distinctly, "I told you this was a poor idea." Hobhouse looked over to the jury to see if they'd heard it. But if they had, they gave no sign of it.

Actually, Hobhouse thought, it was a truly stupid idea. They must be desperate because no other officer could be found to testify. He began to wonder what it would be like to win.

57

The Crown's next witness was a gentleman named Joseph Pickles, who had been a common soldier in the British Army, now retired to the town of Chester, north of London by, he testified, "about three days' journey if the weather be good."

He served in America and claimed to have seen Washington on a white horse, leading his "rebel troops" in battle against Pickles's British infantry unit "somewhere in New Jersey" late in 1778, which would have put the action well within the three-year statute of limitations. To prepare to cross-examine him, Hobhouse reminded himself what he had been taught about cross-examination in his first year as a pupil in Fletcher Chambers—question the witness's ability to perceive, question the quality of his recollection and try to show his bias. Fortunately, Mr. Pickles, however he had appeared earlier in his life, by then looked old and doddering, which should, Hobhouse thought, make for a fine, if delicate, cross-examination.

"It is your witness, Mr. Hobhouse," the Chief Justice said.

"Thank you, my Lord. Mr. Pickles, were you on the front lines during the battle you described?"

"No, my Lord. As I said earlier, I was a cook. Well behind the lines."

"I am not a lord, Mr. Pickles. Addressing me as 'mister' will do quite fine."

"All right."

"Mr. Pickles, how far from the man on the horse were you when you say you saw General Washington astride that horse, leading troops in battle?"

"Well, he might have been two hundred yards away."

"That is quite a long distance, would you not agree?"

"Yes, my… Mr. Hobhouse. It is. But I saw what I saw."

"Could you see his face clearly?"

"Maybe not so clearly. But he is a big man—" he gestured at Washington "—and the man on the horse—a white horse—was very big."

"Are there any big men in the British Army?"

"A few, yes."

"Did you ever see any other big men in the American army?"

"Well, probably I did."

"Did the man you saw have on the same uniform as General Washington does today?"

Pickles looked again at Washington. "I…am not sure. He was far away." And then, realizing how he had just damaged his own testimony, said, "But not so far away I could not see who it was."

Washington leaned over and whispered to Hobhouse, "I did lead my troops in battle like that at times. It helped inspire them. But he is no doubt remembering a battle in New Jersey in late 1776, not 1778."

Hobhouse glanced over at the jury. They seemed attentive, and he wished there was a way to prove to them—and to the court—that the battle in question had taken place in 1776. But Hobhouse had no witness from whose mouth he could elicit that testimony. Certainly, it would not be worth having Washington testify for that point alone. There was too much risk he'd be asked whether he was at the time leading the American army there, no matter what the date. So he tried the "are you sure" approach. Once in a while it worked.

"Mr. Pickles, are you sure the battle you remember was in 1778?"

"Yes."

"You never confuse dates?"

"Not usually."

And then Hobhouse decided to take a risk. "Mr. Pickles, what year is it right now?"

"1780. I'm sorry—I mean 1781."

Hobhouse glanced over at the jury. None looked impressed at Pickles mistaking the year when the old year was less than four months behind them. It was a common mistake. If only he'd said it was 1779. Hobhouse moved on.

"Mr. Pickles, how far away from London is Chester, did you say?"

"It is about a three-day trip by coach."

"Did you pay your own way here?"

"No. The government gave me a stipend."

"To cover the coach, meals and lodging along the way and your meals and lodging here in London?"

"Yes."

"Do you expect to have any left over by the time you get back to Chester? And let me remind you that you have taken a solemn oath."

"Well, yes."

"Quite a lot?"

"Maybe not by the standards of a high-placed man like you, Mr. Hobhouse, but by mine, yes, certainly."

"Did your wife come with you?"

"Yes."

"I have no further questions, my Lord."

The Attorney General asked only one question and it was, Hobhouse thought, the only one really open to him.

"Mr. Pickles, are you certain you saw Mr. Washington on a horse leading his troops in battle in 1778?"

"He was a general, not a mister, but yes."

After that, the Crown produced two more retired witnesses, who were also retired army cooks and who, like Mr. Pickles, purported to have seen Washington on his horse in the exact same battle, from the same distance away, but also placing it in 1778, and not 1776. Of the last witness he had asked as his final question, "Were you all cooking together?"

"Yes, sir," the man had said. "We was all cooking up a very big pot of beans."

"Were you not, then, looking into the pot instead of at the battle?"

That got a laugh from the jury, but the witness was clever enough to respond, "No, sir. The battle was getting close to us, and we was watching it and talking whether we should pack up and move back. That's when we saw that man—" he pointed to Washington "—on his horse."

In the end Hobhouse judged he had managed to cast at least some doubt on the testimony of each of the cooks. Unfortunately, it was not much. Also unfortunately, they were all old soldiers, which had made them risky to attack aggressively. In truth, he had kind of liked them himself, and that was a bad sign.

Finally, the Crown attempted to introduce a series of captured battle plans and orders, purportedly written in Washington's own hand and dated 1779. But Hobhouse managed to show that while Major Temple, the Crown witness who proffered the documents, could say from whom he had gotten the documents (a clerk at the War Department), he could not say where the clerk first obtained them or where the documents had been in the two years since they'd been written if the dates were to be believed. Nor could the Crown produce a witness to persuasively authenticate Washington's signature or handwriting. The court, as a result, excluded all of the orders from evidence. Of course, the jury had heard the whole thing, and when Hobhouse looked over at them, a couple of them were whispering to one another. But it was hard to tell if it meant anything. On the other hand, the exclusion of the documents by the court might mean he'd be able to win the case on legal arguments alone.

The Crown rested its case, and the Chief Justice said, "Mr. Hobhouse, I assume you have motions you want to make before you put on your own witnesses."

"I do, my Lord."

"Let us hear them."

58

Hobhouse rose from his seat.

"My Lord, the prisoner, General Washington, moves to dismiss the charge of treason lodged against him by the Crown on the grounds that the Crown's evidence does not prove the elements of the crime of treason, as stated in the Treason Act of 1695, 7 and 8 William 3, chapter 3, as amended in 1708, 7 Ann, chapter 21. Each and every element of the crime must be proved by the Crown in order for the jury to find the prisoner guilty, and the Crown has not done so."

"All right, please let us hear your argument."

"First, the jury should be instructed to entirely disregard the testimony of Mr. Alwick because the alleged events he described—General Washington supposedly taking command of the American army—took place, by Mr. Alwick's own testimony, in 1775, well over three years ago. That is outside the three-year statute of limitations for treason."

"What about the indictment's assertion of continuing acts, Mr. Hobhouse?"

"Ah, yes, the Crown has cleverly inserted the words *acts of* continuing *treason* in the indictment to try to get around the problem of evidence that is too old. But there is nothing in the statute or the cases to suggest that an act that took place more than three years ago can for some reason be considered just because there are other acts brought up that are within three years."

"All right, Mr. Hobhouse," the Chief Justice said. "But what about the other four witnesses we have heard, all of whom testified to events that are less than three years in the past?"

"The first of those, General Arnold, was by his own testimony quite clearly a collaborator of General Washington. Under the clear law of treason, there must be a second witness to corroborate his testimony if the collaborator's testimony is to serve as the basis of a conviction."

"Wasn't it corroborated by the testimony of the three retired soldiers?"

"No, my Lord, the prisoner contends the General's testimony was not corroborated because those three witnesses testified to having observed different acts than General Arnold did. It is the prisoner's contention that the corroborating testimony must be to the *exact* same act as the one that General Arnold allegedly observed. They contend they saw something different."

The Chief Justice said, "Even if the prisoner's arguments in this regard are persuasive—and I am not saying they are—what of the act the three retired soldiers witnessed? They all testified, it would seem to us, to the same exact act—the General on his horse, leading a battle. All within the last three years."

"Their testimony was from two hundred yards away. Who can identify someone on a horse at that distance? We contend their insistence on the cooks' near-miraculous eyesight was testimony purchased by the Crown through bribes given to the witnesses in the guise of expenses. The prisoner urges the court to instruct the jury to ignore entirely the testimony of those witnesses."

Hobhouse paused, turned to look at Washington, who was sitting behind him and, seeing no sign that Washington wished him to make any further argument, said, "Those are the prisoner's arguments to dismiss, my Lord."

"Thank you, Mr. Hobhouse. Mr. Attorney General, do you have any arguments in response?"

"I would, my Lord, add three considerations to those the court has already so ably noted. First, there is at least one case, Bradley v. Bomler, in which a court held that the statute of limitations could be extended backwards to permit the jury to consider testimony about acts of treason which took place prior to three years before the indictment—so long as at least one of the other treasonous acts alleged in the indictment was less than three years old and part of a pattern of conduct."

"What year was that case decided, Mr. Attorney General?"

"1710, my Lord."

"Seventy years ago?"

"Yes."

"All right, please go on."

"I would add, my Lord, that there is nothing in the law of treason to suggest that the testimony of an alleged accomplice can only be corroborated by the testimony of someone else who observed the exact same treasonous act. Testimony about activities fitting into a pattern of treasonous conduct will do."

"What about Mr. Hobhouse's argument on behalf of the prisoner that the testimony of the three retired soldiers should be entirely disregarded?"

"We could all see that Mr. Hobhouse enjoyed trying to bring down those three old men who had so ably served their country. The decision as to whether to believe them or not is entirely up to the jury."

"We will now retire briefly to deliberate," the Chief Justice said.

Hobhouse did not anticipate a victory. But the motions had been worth making because the jury got to hear them.

Very quickly, the Chief Justice and his colleagues filed in and resumed their seats.

The Chief Justice, reading from notes, said, "On the motion to exclude the testimony of Mr. Alwick, we grant the motion on the ground that the alleged act of treason testified to by him was in 1775, clearly beyond the three-year statute. Nor can the Crown bring that alleged act within the statute of limitations by citing other acts that took place later, especially if they did not include the same set of actions."

He paused and continued, "We next turn to the motion to exclude the testimony of General Arnold. We conclude that General Arnold was a collaborator and further conclude that collaborating testimony must be to the same act. There was no such testimony. The jury will accordingly be instructed to disregard the testimony of both Mr. Alwick and General Arnold."

Hobhouse was stunned. He had argued many motions of dismissal in his career, but had won only one. His victories had always been given to him by juries. This victory was against the Crown, which rarely lost such motions. It could turn out to be a hollow victory because the three retired soldier-cooks had testified to Washington's having carried out a clear act of making war against the King. But because he had no *legal* arguments to exclude their testimony, it would all come down to whether the jury believed they were at least trying to tell the truth, that they remembered the year correctly and that at a distance of two hundred yards, they would really have been able to positively identify Washington.

He was brought back to reality by the Chief Justice saying, "Mr. Hobhouse, does the prisoner have witnesses to present?"

Hobhouse twisted around so that he could see Washington. "We are still agreed that you will not testify?"

"Correct."

He turned back to the Court. "The prisoner has no witnesses to present, my Lord."

"Very well."

The Attorney General rose and said, "I am prepared for closing argument, my Lord."

"One moment, Mr. Attorney General." The Chief Justice bent his head to confer with his colleagues, first on one side then the other. Turning back to the courtroom, he said, "We have decided to dispense with closing arguments. The case is simple and straightforward, and through their motions, with the jury listening, counsel has made, we believe, the same arguments they would make in a closing."

"Thank you, my Lord," the Attorney General said and sat back down, showing no emotion. Hobhouse assumed that he was in fact quite angry. He had no doubt looked forward to condemning Washington in ringing terms and seeing it written up in the newspapers. As for Hobhouse, he thought the Chief Justice was right. The jury had already heard all of the arguments.

The Chief Justice addressed the jury. "Gentlemen, I shall now instruct you on the law and sum up the facts. The law of treason is not complicated. To take up arms against His Majesty, the King, or to lead others in doing so is high treason. Attacking His Majesty's Army is as much high treason as attacking the King himself."

He looked down at the jury as if trying to discern if they had understood. Not that Hobhouse had ever seen a judge actually ask the members of a jury if they had truly understood the instructions.

Seemingly satisfied, the Chief Justice continued. "The facts here are also quite simple. First I instruct you not to consider the testimony of Mr. Alwick or General Arnold, or anything concerning papers allegedly written by George Washington. No persuasive proof was brought forward that he wrote them. Thus, you may only consider the testimony of the three retired soldiers. To convict the prisoner, our treason law requires that you believe the testimony of at least two of them.

"Each of the three testified, in remarkably similar words, that they saw the prisoner on a white horse, leading troops in battle against British forces—in the same battle. If you find their testimony persuasive, the prisoner is guilty of high treason.

"To be persuaded of that you must believe *both* that they were actually at the battle and, if so, in a position to see that the man on the horse was the prisoner. The prisoner contends none of the three could see well enough to tell because they were two hundred yards away."

Hobhouse felt his heart beat faster. He had never before heard a judge, in summing up the facts for the jury, remind them of the main argument made by the prisoner's lawyer.

The Chief Justice finished up. "You must of course have some standard by which to decide. I would put it to you this way. If the scale should hang doubtful in your mind, and you are not fully satisfied that the prisoner is guilty, you ought to lean on the favourable side and acquit him. But if you are fully satisfied in your conscience that the witnesses told the truth about who they saw on the horse, then you should convict."

Hobhouse was pleased with that instruction. It emphasized, much more than those given by most judges, the need for conscience to play a role. That at least hinted to the jury to consider matters beyond the evidence. Such as how they felt about the rebellion.

"Gentlemen of the jury, I now send you to deliberate," the Chief Justice said. "The clerk will hand you a form in which you are to fill in a unanimous verdict of guilty or not guilty. If, after deliberating in all seriousness, you are unable to reach a unanimous verdict, you should tell the Sheriff and he will notify me. The Sheriff will now escort you to a room for your deliberations. Let no one interfere."

Everyone watched as the jury filed out.

Hobhouse turned to Washington and said, "Excellency, there is little point in leaving the courtroom. Your guards would go with us, and then, likely, bring us back very soon thereafter. These deliberations do not usually take very long."

"How long is not very long, Mr. Hobhouse?"

"For felony cases, it is often no more than a quarter of an hour. Treason might take a little longer."

"What is your sense of the case?"

"I think there is a possibility of an acquittal, but it is a small possibility."

"I think there is no possibility at all," Washington said.

The jury was out for almost an hour. After they were led back in by the Sheriff, the judges returned to the bench, and the Chief Justice asked the man whom the jury had selected as its foreman if they had reached a verdict.

"We have, my Lord," he said.

"Please give the paper on which you have written your verdict to the clerk, who will read it."

All eyes in the courtroom watched the transfer of the paper to the clerk, who read it to himself and handed it to the Chief Justice, who read it, handed it back to the clerk and said, "Mr. Clerk, please read the verdict."

The clerk read, "'We the jury, in the charge of high treason against George Washington of His Majesty's colony of Virginia, for taking up arms against His Majesty, said sovereign Lord George III by the grace of God of Great Britain, France and Ireland, King, defender of the faith, find George Washington guilty as charged.'"

There was a rustle in the courtroom as all the heads, which had been facing the bench, turned in a breath to stare at Washington, who showed no reaction.

Hobhouse felt slightly sick.

The Chief Justice gave no indication whether the verdict had surprised him or not, or pleased him or not. He simply said, "The Sheriff will take the prisoner to a place of confinement, to be designated by the Attorney General. Sentence will be imposed at a time to be specified by the court. We will in the meantime consider whether to recommend clemency to the King."

The guards immediately surrounded Washington. As they began to lead him away, he turned to Hobhouse, bowed slightly and said, "Thank you for your efforts, Mr. Hobhouse. They were much appreciated."

59

North had wished fervently to attend Washington's trial in person. Unfortunately, that would have been seen as highly inappropriate. Instead, he had had to wait impatiently in the library for reports. But with the Old Bailey almost two miles down the river from 10 Downing, the trial news brought every hour by messenger was always stale.

The report that had interested him most was about the testimony of General Arnold. The messenger reported that Arnold, in his own view and the view of others seated near him in the courtroom, had been bested by the prisoner's lawyer and made to admit his own treason.

"And, my Lord," the man had said, "those around me in the gallery expressed amazement that the Crown had permitted Arnold to be called, given how easy it would be—and was!—for the prisoner's lawyer to throw his own treachery back in his face."

"We had our reasons," North said. "Thank you for your report."

"Thank you, my Lord, for giving me the opportunity to be of service to you."

Later in the day North received the news that Washington had been convicted of high treason. The verdict came as no surprise. What did surprise was that the court had delayed sentencing so that it might consider whether to recommend clemency. Clemency?

Why would such a traitor be even considered for clemency by an English court? He could not fathom it. He sighed. Clemency, if recommended, would come formally from the King. But the decision whether to grant it would in truth be the government's. In other words, his. But to grant it would take away all of his bargaining power with the Americans.

Not long after, as he sat contemplating the situation, Jacob Hartleb knocked and entered. "My Lord, Colonel Black is here and wishes to see you. He apologizes for having no appointment."

"It must have importance. Please show him in."

After Hartleb left, and North and Black had exchanged greetings, Black declined an offer of something to drink and said, "I saw something in court today that I thought you should be made aware of."

"In the testimony? Or in the verdict?"

"Neither. It was a man that I saw talking to General Washington."

"You accord Washington his title?"

"He is deserving of it, I believe. My apologies if that offends."

"It does not. Washington somehow exudes that he is a great general. Who is this man you speak of?"

"I don't know his name, but he has a vivid scar across his cheek."

"Ah, yes. I met him briefly when he attended a negotiating session. I believe he is Washington's personal physician. Forecastle, I think his name is. He arrived with the second boatload of Americans. The one that came in January, a couple of months ago, not long after Abbott arrived."

"I doubt he is a physician. Or at least I doubt that he is only a physician."

"Who is he, then?"

"He is a senior member of Washington's personal guard."

North sat bolt upright. "What?"

"Yes. We encountered him in the woods a couple of days before we reached Washington's headquarters. He was on horseback, wearing the plumed helmet of Washington's Commander-in-Chief Guard, leading a patrol."

"Are you certain? There are many men with bayonet scars from war."

"Quite certain. He menaced us back then, and I shall never forget him. After I saw him today in court, I left the courtroom. But I returned later for the rest of the trial in order to be absolutely certain I was not mistaken."

"Did he see you?"

"I think not. I came in through a side door, and I could see the side of his face, although I doubt he could see mine. And I don't know if he would remember me as strongly as I remember him."

"From the log of Washington's visitors I have been shown—which includes a remarkable number of retired British officers, I might say—Forecastle has been to the Tower almost every day. It is surprising the two of you have not crossed paths."

"My Lord, I've visited Washington mostly in the mornings, before visitors are permitted. I check the visitor log each day at day's end, and have never seen the name of any person to cause concern. I would have no reason to suspect an entry that said only, 'Forecastle, physician.'"

"I am not criticizing you, Colonel." North got up, walked to the window and looked out for a few moments. Eventually, he turned and said, "Colonel, this explains, I think, a great deal."

"What does it explain, my Lord?"

"We have been receiving reports from our agents within the Tower that they see signs of a plot afoot to rescue Washington. Visitors to Washington are appearing, as if by accident, to take the wrong exit route, almost as if they were exploring. Still other visitors talking with him in hushed tones, as if they were intent on not being overheard. But our agents have not been able to decipher the details, or deduce who the leader might be."

"You think Forecastle might be the one?"

"If he is who you say he is, yes."

"Is there anyone else?"

"For reasons I cannot put my finger on, the first would be Mr. Abbott, their so-called Ambassador."

"Any others?"

"Also Mr. Pierce, a member of their delegation who is pleasant enough and claims to know about border issues, but isn't in fact very knowledgeable and has little to say. But he looks as if he could break your arm with his bare hands."

North returned to his chair, took a sip from the sherry glass that was on the table and decided to let Black know a few more details. "Colonel, we have several spies within the Tower. One is Mrs. Crankshaw."

"The woman who cleans and also serves coffee?"

"Yes. Her son, a soldier, was killed in the war by the rebels. She detests their rebellion."

"Are you certain of her loyalty?"

"Very." He smiled. "And to assure that, we pay her very well."

"There must be many ways to interrupt the escape plot, my Lord, and prosecute those who are planning it."

"There are. But I am inclined to let it go forward without trying to kill it in its infancy."

"Why?"

"An attempted escape might aid my own escape—from a political box I am stuck in. Albeit a box I constructed for myself."

"I don't understand."

"The box is this. I want to settle the war. I had thought that capturing Washington would make that possible. We would settle the war on terms agreeable to all, in exchange for the Americans getting him back. When it became clear that was not going to happen, I finally had Washington put on trial to increase the pressure."

"Isn't settlement still possible, my Lord?"

"Only, it seems, if we grant them full independence. While Abbott is the supposed ambassador with plenary authority, Washington has turned out to be the one who really has final authority. And he will not countenance anything short of full independence."

"Which your cabinet will not agree to?"

"Precisely, Colonel. Nor will the King. At least not unless we suffer a huge military defeat. And even then…"

"Why is it a box, then?"

"If Washington is executed, he will become a martyr. The resulting rage, both over there and over here, will likely turn the forest fire of the rebellion into a conflagration that will burn down the entire Empire, including Canada and Ireland before it is put out." He paused. "If it can be put out."

Black raised his eyebrows. "Are you certain?"

"Certain enough. The reports I receive from our agents in the colonies and—" he sighed "—from the King himself, who appears to have his own informants there, is that the rage in America over what we have done is already building. I have also, in these last weeks and months, for the first time talked with many people who have spent considerable time in the colonies, and I have come to understand it better."

"I still don't understand why that is a box."

"If he is acquitted or even if we instruct the King to pardon him, we will look weak, and the embarrassment will cause my ministry to fall. I fear that the cabinet that replaces mine will do no better, and the war will just go on with even more ferocity on both sides."

"I see. How can I be of help?"

"An escape could get me out of the box...in certain ways."

"Won't an escape be even more embarrassing than an acquittal or a pardon?"

"Only if it succeeds." He smiled. "A failure on the Americans' part, particularly after the escape was well under way, might be perceived differently."

"You want me to foil an escape plot, but not in advance?"

"You should interpret what I say according to your own lights, Colonel."

"My Lord, I would like to ask a question that is perhaps impertinent. If so, please stop me. When you sent me to capture General Washington, did you expect him to be killed in the attempt?"

North paused for a long time to consider his answer. He could hear the ticking of the grandfather clock as Black waited politely.

"Let me put it this way, Colonel. I would not have been surprised if both of you had died in the effort. Or at least Washington."

"And instead you were surprised that I returned, not to mention with him alive and well."

"Yes, and by the way, your well-earned appointment as a brigadier, together with an appropriate medal, should be announced shortly. My apologies for the delay."

"No need for an apology, my Lord."

"You look troubled, Colonel."

"With due respect, my Lord, if Washington is killed while trying to escape, won't that cause just as large a political ruckus in America as if he were executed?"

"Perhaps, Colonel. But perhaps not. We will be in control of the facts, and I'm sure we could make it look as if the Americans themselves were somehow responsible. People are killed every day by overturned carriages. We have such bad roads."

Black nodded his head, although North could tell he was not convinced.

"We will let Mrs. Crankshaw know that you will need her cooperation," North said. "On your way out, Mr. Hartleb will meet with you and tell you some more things we have discovered that make us think there is a plot."

"Thank you. I will do my best for you."

"I'm sure you will. And, Colonel, it will not be helpful if our conversation about any of this becomes known outside this room."

"I will not speak of it to anyone, my Lord. But I will act on it."

"Hartleb will meet with you now. Thank you for coming. And for your extraordinary service to your king and to your country."

60

Later, North stood at the library window and watched Abbott descend from his carriage. Abbott was limping, perhaps more so than when he had first arrived in London, now months ago. His assignment had clearly been hard on him, and he must feel on the precipice of failure. North felt a pang of sorrow for him.

When Abbott was ushered in, North said, "I have tired of meeting in this room. Let us move to the garden."

"Of course, my Lord. I didn't even know 10 Downing had a garden."

"It is a place to which I retreat when I want to try to leave the world behind or meet with someone in a setting more conducive to candid conversation. It is unusually warm for a spring day in London, and I hope it will be pleasant." The truth was, of course, that he used the garden when he wanted something from someone and the casual setting sometimes made it easier.

When they stepped into the garden, North saw that it had been set up exactly as he had directed—two chairs around a small round table, covered by a white tablecloth. A Wedgwood teapot with matching cups, saucers and plates, all in their trademark blue with white edging, were on the table. Small cakes were out on a large platter.

After they were seated, and a servant had poured tea for North and offered coffee to Abbott, North said, "With yesterday's conviction, we are at the end, I think."

"When will the sentence be imposed?" Abbott asked.

"Tomorrow, and the mandatory sentence is a traitor's death. To be carried out within days."

Abbott sipped his coffee. "So I have been told. Is there no chance of the court recommending clemency?"

"Ambassador, would you expect a military tribunal in America to recommend clemency for General Arnold should he be returned there and court-martialled for treason?"

"I take your point, my Lord."

"And yet, in my experience as First Minister, I have observed that sometimes, when things seem at their nadir, there is an opportunity to find solutions that have eluded people before that."

"You refer here to the pressure of an imminent execution?"

"Yes. There is an advantage for both of us from the threat of that, and I have a proposal for you."

Abbott put down his coffee cup, leaned back in his chair and said, "I am listening."

"We have worked out *almost* everything. Your Congress making your laws and passing your taxes, the western border running to the Mississippi, the withdrawal of British troops, your pledge not to invade Canada, trade, fisheries and so forth. The list of things agreed is very long."

"Yes, everything except the one thing."

"Precisely. My proposal is this. Both sides will sign an agreement that confirms our accord on all of the other issues, but ignores the issue of independence."

Abbott was silent for a long moment. Finally, he said, "What would that mean?"

"That Parliament would not assert any sovereignty over you, or try to control what happens in your country in any way or insist that symbols of sovereignty appear on your money or your postage or on any building. The governors' palaces might remain standing, but there would be no one appointed to occupy them."

"Would that be put in writing anywhere?"

"No. It would be an unwritten, oral side agreement, at least for the moment."

"And what would be expected on our end?"

"You would not assert your independence, at least formally."

"What of our Declaration of Independence?"

"It would remain, but it is not, to my understanding, a legal document. It doesn't set up a government."

"Would we be able to appoint ambassadors to other countries?"

"You could send people to other countries, as you have done during the rebellion, but you would call them something else. At least for a few years."

"Could you persuade the Parliament of this?"

"I believe so."

"What of the King?"

"I can persuade him, as well."

"With what leverage?"

"I will threaten to resign if he does not agree. He intensely dislikes those who might replace me."

Abbott picked up his cup and took a sip of coffee. Then a second sip.

North recognized it as a technique he had used himself. Drink to delay while you gather your thoughts about you.

Abbott put his cup down and said, "There would be many, many things to ignore, my Lord. Perhaps too many. But I would be glad to put the proposal to my delegation if it will delay His Excellency's execution."

"I would suggest you first put it to General Washington himself since he is the one, let us admit, with the final authority here. And the one with the most at stake."

"I will. But I have two requests."

"What are they?"

"First, I want to delay the imposition of sentence."

"That may be difficult. The judges are very much in charge of when that takes place. They do not like to delay very long after conviction. So sentence will be imposed tomorrow. But I can delay the carrying out of the sentence for as long as we need."

"By what means?"

"The judges announced they are considering whether to recommend clemency to the Crown. They are not apolitical in matters like this, and they will no doubt see the dangers in killing the hero of what you call the American Revolution. I suspect no one of them wants his name associated with that."

"Will the King agree?"

"A pardon or reduction of sentence is done in the name of the King, but he expects—and follows—guidance from the government. As he would here, I am sure. It might take us a while to decide what is to be done."

"I see."

"What is your second request?"

"It is paltry. General Washington wants to have a bust of himself done for his wife. Something to remember him by. He has never had one done."

"If we fail in our endeavour, there will hardly be enough time for him to sit for a sculptor. It takes many sittings to ensure the sculptor can render a good likeness in clay, then cast it. If we succeed, there will be plenty of time for that. So for right now I will have to say no and deny Mrs. Washington the pleasure of receiving the bust."

"But, my Lord, there is a solution. Are you acquainted with the name Patience Lovell Wright?"

"The American artist here in London who sculpts in coloured wax?"

"Yes."

North sighed. "I know of her. She is infamous for pursuing famous people as subjects of her art, even if they wish to have nothing to do with her."

"She wants to do a head of Washington."

North kept himself, barely, from saying out loud that Wright could perhaps just be patient for a few days and obtain Washington's actual head. Instead, he said, "Even she would not have time to do a proper bust."

"She has come to see me, my Lord, and told me that she has already prepared one from drawings of him she has seen. She claims it needs only a day's sitting to complete."

"Very well, I will give consent for her to see him. For one day only. You may choose the day. If we fail to reach agreement and he is to be executed, she must complete what she is doing by two days before the scheduled execution. Because he will be moved then from the Tower to a different place. And he may be moved even before a date for execution is set."

"I have heard it said, my Lord, that General Washington often does not make up his mind about momentous things until the very last moment. Moving him the day before the execution—or at all—may make it even less likely he will agree to what you propose."

"I will give that consideration. If he is executed, do you plan to stay to watch the execution?"

"No. I could not bear it. But do *you* plan to watch? Even if you don't drop the noose around his neck yourself, you will be the hangman. That is how you will be remembered."

He had a point, but it was not one North wanted to reply to. Instead, he said, "My office has caused to be issued, as you requested, a laissez-passer for each member of your delegation to leave the country."

"Thank you."

"I have also granted permission, as you requested, for a French *civilian* ship to come into Portsmouth to transport you to France."

"Thank you, my Lord." Abbott rose from his chair. "And thank you for the coffee and the cakes. I will do what I can to persuade General Washington to at least consider your plan. I think it is a good one if it is left amorphous enough. I do fear the details if we are forced to delve into them."

"There is one more thing, Mr. Abbott."

"What is that?"

"I have reason to believe that the physician, Mr. Forecastle, is not a physician at all, but a member of General Washington's Commander-in-Chief Guard."

Abbott's head snapped back in apparent shock, and he said, "I was not aware of that."

North could not tell whether Abbott had truly been surprised or not and said, "Whether you were aware or not aware, I must warn you against any attempt at rescue. It will be met with lethal force."

"I am not aware Mr. Forecastle is anyone other than General Washington's physician. Nor do I know of any plot to rescue His Excellency."

"I take you at your word."

"Thank you."

"I must warn you, though, that if such a plot is attempted, you and your delegation will not be protected by any imagined immunity based on your contention that you are diplomats. You will all be locked up and tried for sedition."

"I understand your position," Abbott said. "But I am offended that you think I, as a credentialled Ambassador, would try to evade the judgement of a lawful court here, no matter how barbaric I think your law in this area might be." He got up and left with only perfunctory words of goodbye.

North was quite pleased with himself. Letting Abbott

know the government suspected that an escape plot was being hatched ought to accelerate it and bring it into the open, so that Black could act.

61

The very next day—the day after the trial—Abbott learned from Hobhouse that the court had sent notice that Washington would not be sentenced immediately, as had been expected. The delay might be as much as a week. That kind of delay, Hobhouse had said, was "unprecedented" in his experience and added, "Something must be going on."

Abbott knew, of course, what the something was. He and Lord North had met again briefly and agreed that they would make one last attempt to bridge the divide between the Americans and the British on the independence issue, using North's suggestion of simply putting the issue of independence to the side for the time being. The negotiations, which they expected to take days, would be held at the palace. North was of the view that the setting would impress on the participants the importance of what they were trying to achieve and might lead to the agreement that had eluded them.

The negotiations were attended by Abbott's entire delegation, save Forecastle, as well as by North himself, two other members of his cabinet and several undersecretaries. The discussions were civil, but difficult. It turned out that there were dozens, perhaps hundreds, of ways in which each side would have to agree to do something or not do something, to assert something or not assert something, if the question of independence were to be put to the side and saved for another day.

Hovering over the entire gathering, though, was the understanding that Washington himself would end up with the final say on the matter.

At the end of the second day of negotiations—they always finished their sessions in time for afternoon tea—things seemed to be progressing in a heartening way. For one, they had worked their way through a list of dos and don'ts, which included what images would appear on money in the colonies during what they had come to call the cooling-down period. Flowers, trees, farm animals, crops and Greek gods unrelated to warfare had all been proposed. The fact that it was being called the cooling-down period was, of course, a recognition that at some point in the future, the issue would have to be faced again.

Towards evening, Abbott took a chair to the government guest house, found Forecastle and invited him to go for a walk. He had put off confronting Forecastle, but the time had come. As they walked along, Abbott said, "Mr. Forecastle, quite a while ago you were seen talking with Mrs. Crankshaw on the street in what the person who observed you thought was a suspicious manner. My apologies for being blunt, but what were you discussing?"

Forecastle, without even breaking stride, said, "If I'm recalling the same incident you are making reference to, she simply greeted me as she passed by and wished me a pleasant evening. We have seen each other many times inside the Tower and established a cordial relationship."

Abbott was struck by the fact that Forecastle seemed to know exactly what meeting with Mrs. Crankshaw he was referring to, which was hardly proof of it having been an innocent encounter. He considered whether to tell Forecastle what he knew, and decided he should. "Are you aware she is a spy for the British inside the Tower?"

This time, Forecastle stopped walking, faced Abbott and said, "No, I wasn't aware of that."

Abbott judged from the flush on Forecastle's cheeks that the man was lying. He pressed on. "Lord North informed me that he believes you are not a physician at all, but instead a member of His Excellency's Commander-in-Chief Guard."

Apparently deciding that there was no point in further hiding the truth, he said, "I am trained as a physician, but I have spent most of my adult life as a soldier. I am a lieutenant in the Army of the Continental States and a member of His Excellency's Life Guard."

"Are you involved in a plot to rescue His Excellency?"

"Yes. But I do not believe that sharing the details with you would be prudent, lest you are tortured for the information."

"I do not need to know the details right now. Is this with or without General Washington's knowledge?"

"With."

"Are you going to try to spirit him out of the country or hide him?"

"Perhaps both."

"Has His Excellency changed his mind, then?"

"He believes that his escape will be a very large embarrassment to Lord North's government and will cause it to fall. And to be replaced with one more amenable to agreeing to our independence."

"I thought he wanted to make a speech from the gallows."

"Our plans are not inconsistent with that."

"If you are planning to rescue him from there, many people are likely to die."

"If British soldiers die, so be it."

"What about the others who are there?"

"If they have come to see His Excellency be hanged and butchered, let them die, too."

"I will need to confirm all of this with His Excellency."

"I hope you will do so. I will warn you, though—do not get in our way."

"Mr. Forecastle, perhaps you have not noticed, but I was a soldier in our army once, too. It's not wise to threaten me."

The two of them parted without a word of goodbye.

62

Abbott went the very next morning to the Tower. He asked the guard if Washington was there and was told that he was. Abbott was then searched much more thoroughly than he had ever been before, and he was also accompanied to Washington's cell by a guard rather than being permitted to find his own way.

Washington was indeed in his cell and greeted him as if nothing had changed.

"Excellency, there are two things we must discuss urgently," Abbott said. "For both, we might walk upon the parade."

"All right. Let us go. It is perhaps too early in the morning for the fruit throwers to be in place. Or perhaps they don't toss fruit at the condemned."

As they walked, Abbott said, "We have reopened the negotiations with Lord North, based on a proposal he made. I call it the 'set the issue to the side' approach."

"Which issue?"

"Independence." He explained it to Washington and said,

"We have met for two days now and made good progress. We are scheduled to meet again this afternoon."

Washington stopped, folded his arms and faced Abbott. "It is a trick and a trap. If we should settle with them without formal independence, they will sooner rather than later enter into a peace treaty with France. Whereupon they will invade us again, but we will have no French arms, men or ships to help us. Which, let us agree, have been our saviour in this war."

"If that were to happen, we would have our own professional army to resist their invasion, unlike in 1775."

Washington laughed. "As soon as peace is declared, the Congress will disband the army. They fear a standing army, and even if they did not, they do not want to pay for it. It has been hard enough, when our liberty is at stake, to get even our current army funded."

"Are you instructing me to abandon the negotiation?"

"No, Colonel. You should continue. I quite understand that it will delay my execution, and a few more days on earth in this glorious English spring will please me, certainly."

"We should start to walk again, Excellency, and just not stand here, where we will attract attention."

"All right."

As they walked further along, Abbott said, in as low a voice as he could muster and still be heard by Washington, "I learned certain things, confronted Forecastle, and found out, not only who he really is, but that he is planning your escape. He refused to tell me the details."

"I do not know them either. We thought it best that way. It will come as a surprise on the day of the execution."

"You know nothing else at all of the plans, other than that they will attempt it on the day of the execution?"

"Only one other thing—that they plan to spirit me out of the country."

"Excellency, you have told me many times you preferred

death, even the horrible one inflicted on supposed traitors, to any kind of compromise, so that you might make a speech on the scaffold. One you hoped would rally the people of Britain to our side, bring down the government and lead quickly to independence."

"I judge that my escape, right under their noses, will be such an embarrassment to them that it will have an even larger effect. If things go well, I can return to America and lead our army to victory. *Then* we will have true independence."

"I have a perhaps better idea, Excellency. One that will enrage them even more. I will explain it to you and you can tell me to abandon it or to go forward." He explained it in detail.

When Abbott had finished, Washington, looking thoughtful, tilted his head back and forth as if weighing the options. "It would, then, Colonel, take place the night before the execution?"

"Yes."

"Thus, if it fails, it will not interfere with Lieutenant Forecastle's plan."

"It would seem unlikely to interfere. But for it to work, you must stay in the Tower until the day of execution. If you are moved earlier, Forecastle's plan—whatever it is—may still work, but mine will not."

"I have no way to assure they will keep me here."

"You do, Excellency. You must at all times indicate, by word and deed, that you are still possibly open to Lord North's suggestion. But only if a few more changes are made."

"Why will he care?"

"I believe he is desperate, Excellency, not to execute you. But he seems to feel boxed into a corner politically. He cannot wait forever."

"Who has boxed him in?"

"The 'never independence' members of Parliament." He paused. "And the King."

"I know what was said in the Declaration about the King, but I have always thought that the King was led around by the nose by Parliament."

"I think that is true and not true at the same time. But whatever the formal relationship, the situation seems to have left the King unhinged from logical thinking on the subject. At least if Lord North is to be believed."

"You have gotten to know North?"

"When you spend a long time with someone locked in a room, it breeds familiarity."

"Some would say it can breed contempt."

"I don't have contempt for him. I see him as a man with a problem, partly of his own making, who would like mightily to resolve it but has been unable to find a way. Or perhaps lacks the political skill to find a way."

"The fact that his *problem* is my pending death makes me less understanding of him, Colonel."

"Of course, Excellency. I did not mean to turn it into a philosophical conversation."

"Where are you going next?"

"To meet with a friend of America, whose help I will need."

They said their goodbyes, and Abbott added, "I will see you again very soon," and left.

The afternoon before, right after his meeting with Forecastle had ended on such a sour note, he had returned home. Once there, he had prevailed on Polly to travel to the haberdashery and return his tricornered hat and to explain that, through no fault of his, it had shrunk. He instructed her to give it only to Mr. Joshua Laden or his nephew who ran the shop, and that they should credit his account rather than return his money. He assumed Polly would not be followed, and that even if she were, her errand would seem innocent enough and fall well within the persona he had established for himself.

Now he would go to Daughters Coffee House.

63

He went to Daughters via the same circuitous route he had used before—across London Bridge, down the Thames, then back across the river using Blackfriars Bridge and finally to the coffee house. The proprietor, Mr. Collins, recognized him and said, "He is in the back room. I will take you there."

"Thank you."

When Abbott opened the door, Laden was sitting at the table with a steaming mug of coffee in front of him. There was also a quill and ink set, as Abbott had requested.

"Welcome, Mr. Abbott. I almost didn't look inside the hat. Fortunately, I did, and here I am."

"Thank you for coming. I have a plan which needs your help."

"I will try to help so long as it does not put me or my family at risk."

"It should not. It can be done in the open and has nothing of the untoward about it."

"Then why meet here in secrecy?"

Abbott smiled. "I came openly into this place, as did you. What is secret about it?"

"That might be funny, Mr. Ambassador, if this meeting didn't reek so with the odour of sedition."

"Here is what I need, and you can judge the smell for yourself."

"Go on."

"But for a miracle, I expect General Washington to be executed."

"Yes, so I understand from the newspapers."

"I will not stay for the execution. It would be unseemly for the American delegation to watch Lord North's government carry out what we consider to be a crime against the law of war."

"Are you in need of assistance for your departure?"

"Yes. The night before the execution—there will be plenty of public notice of the date—I will need three coaches, each to hold two people, lined up outside the Tower of London starting at eleven o'clock. They should be ready to travel to Portsmouth, with whatever changes of horses are needed along the way. If you let me know the charge, I will pay you."

"Who are they for?"

"My entire delegation will go to the Tower to say goodbye to Washington. When we emerge, we will take the coaches to Portsmouth, where a ship will be waiting."

"Innocent enough."

"Yes, and as it is a two-day journey, we will need a place to stay. As soon as the execution date is announced, please send someone ahead to an inn that is about halfway to reserve beds for the night of the scheduled execution for six people. I will give you the funds so you can pay for them in advance."

"Most country inns will not reserve rooms."

"They will if you offer to pay them more than their posted rate and tell them that if no one arrives to take the rooms they may keep the money."

"In whose name shall I reserve it?"

"Brandywine."

"All right."

"Have you arranged for what comes next?"

"I have, and Collins has his instructions as to how it should happen."

"Thank you."

"I will take my leave now, Ambassador, and wish you Godspeed."

"And to you, Mr. Laden, and I convey to you the thanks of the people of America for your help. When this war is ended, I hope you will visit me in Philadelphia as my guest."

"I will. Goodbye and good day."

He left the same way as he had come in.

Abbott waited. After not too long, the door to the room opened, and there stood Mr. Collins with Mrs. Crankshaw. She took a few steps forward and shrieked when she recognized Abbott.

"Why are *you* here?" she said. "I was to meet Mr. Laden. No one told me you would be here. Where is Mr. Laden?"

She turned to flee the room but found the door locked.

"Please sit down, Mrs. Crankshaw. No harm will come to you, I promise."

She stared at him for a moment, but finally walked over to the table and took a seat.

"Would you like some coffee?"

"Certainly not. I would prefer to go."

"After you hear me out. I know you are spying for Mr. Laden, who is a friend of America, and at the same time for the British, telling them what Washington and others are doing in the Tower."

"This is not true."

"Which part?"

"The part about the British."

"Mrs. Crankshaw, there is no point in lying to me about this. I know it to be true from Lord North himself." That was not quite the case, of course, but it would do.

"What do you want, then?" She had turned pale and was shaking.

"Eventually, General Washington is going to be executed. The execution date will be announced. The night before, towards midnight, I am planning to visit him. I want you to arrive there two hours beforehand."

"To what end, sir?"

"To inform any person who wishes to see Washington that he is praying on whether to approve the agreement that has been reached with the British and is not to be disturbed for any reason."

"And if someone tries to enter his cell?"

"Block their way. Most people will refrain from hitting a woman."

She looked at him with an expression he could not read. It was certainly not one of acquiescence. They stared at each other in silence until Mrs. Crankshaw finally said, "I am not usually in the Tower at night."

"Do what you need to do to change that. Tell them you like General Washington, and he has asked you to make him coffee as he awaits his execution. Or whatever you need to say."

"All right."

Abbott reached inside his waistcoat and withdrew a handful of gold and silver coins. He put them in front of her and said, "If you need to, you can use these to help gain access to the Tower."

"What if I don't use them?"

"You can keep them."

She counted them out. "It is more money than I make in a year."

"Yes. I understand you have children. I'm sure it will help."

In bribing her he was, of course, taking a great risk should she decide to turn on him, even with his assumed limited immunity. A seditious conversation could be denied. Her possession of so much money would be more difficult to explain away. But he had concluded that a threat softened by a bribe would work better than a threat alone. He still needed to deliver the threat.

"Mrs. Crankshaw," he said, "if you do not do exactly as I have asked, or if you should tell anyone else about our conversation, I will make certain that Lord North learns about your treason."

"How will that assist you?"

"It won't. General Washington may hang, and I may hang. But so will you."

"You won't be able to bring Lord North proof of anything."

"Ah, but I will. I must have from you a receipt for the coins." He took from a second inside pocket of his waistcoat a pre-written-out receipt. He handed it to her, pointed to the quill and ink and said, "I think you'll find the amount correct. Please sign."

"I can only make an X."

"I know that not to be true, Mrs. Crankshaw." He had seen her write something in the Tower. "Please sign or I will turn you in now."

Reluctantly, she signed her name and said, "May I be permitted to leave now?"

"Yes. Please exit via the back stairway." He pointed to a door at the rear of the room. As she reached the door, Abbott said, "Oh, Mrs. Crankshaw, there's one more thing."

"What is that?"

"General Washington thinks you make superb coffee."

64

Black had grown up on his father's estate hunting deer. Tracking them and tracking people turned out not to be so different. Instead of hiding behind trees or bushes, he used doorways and pillars. Nor was Abbott particularly careful to cover his steps. Black easily followed him through his circuitous route until he disappeared up the stairway to Daughters.

Black considered following him into the establishment, but thought better of it because he'd then be unable to see who came and went. He stationed himself across the street and waited.

Over the next hour, he saw only one person he knew go in—Mrs. Crankshaw, the woman who served food and made coffee in the Tower for guests favoured by the Warder of the Tower, which had never included Black, despite his having made a number of requests to be added to the list. She went up the steps, but despite Black waiting awhile for her, she didn't come back down.

After waiting a moment or two longer, it occurred to him that there might be another exit. He walked around to an alley that ran behind the building, just in time to see Mrs. Crankshaw descend a back stairway that hugged the outside of the building. She departed down the alley in the opposite direction.

He went up the back stairway, opened the door and stepped into an empty room with a large table in the middle. He tried to open the door that clearly led into the coffee house itself, but it was locked. He rapped on it, and when no one came, he pounded on it. Rather quickly, a middle-aged gentleman opened it and said, in a fairly heavy Irish brogue, "May I help you? The entrance to the restaurant is around the front. If you would kindly go down the steps you came up and go around and come in proper, it would be vastly appreciated."

"I am an officer in His Majesty's Army investigating a possible crime, and I will come in this way."

He brushed past the man, who said, "Well, Colonel, you've come to a pub where the Irish like to gather. I don't suppose you'll be too popular here, especially if you say who you are, but suit yourself."

"Do you know a Mrs. Crankshaw?" Black asked.

"No, I don't suppose I do."

"I am told she comes here often."

The man sighed. "This is a coffee house frequented by the people in the neighbourhood, by people coming and going to whatever they do to earn their daily bread, and by people from all around London because it is one of the finest in London."

"Do you know if Mrs. Crankshaw was in the room behind me today?" Black asked.

"Since I don't know her, I couldn't say. A while ago, I was in there m'self doing the books for m'business and drinking coffee. Before that, two hours ago, there was a card game."

"Do you know Ambassador Abbott?"

"The man who they say is trying to negotiate an end to the American war?"

"Yes, that one."

The man laughed out loud. "Now, why would I know such a high-born person, Colonel?"

"Do you know him, or not?"

"Neither in person nor by sight."

Black looked around the place, saw no one he knew and stomped out via the front stairway.

Perhaps tracking people was not so easy as tracking deer. At least he had added Mrs. Crankshaw to their list of suspects.

It was now clear to him that if he were to have any chance at all of foiling whatever escape plot might be under way, he would need assistance. He went immediately to 10 Downing to try to see Lord North, but did not succeed. Instead Hartleb greeted him and told him North was at his home in the countryside. He would pass on the request, but in the meantime Black should just go forward as best he could.

After he left Daughters, Abbott went to the home of Patience Lovell Wright. They had corresponded, but never met. She greeted him warmly at the door and offered him coffee. Abbott was surprised at her appearance. For some reason, he had expected a younger woman. Mrs. Wright instead turned out to be a woman in late middle age, to whose long face time had applied deep creases.

After they had exchanged greetings, Abbott said, "Lord North has agreed that you may have access to the Tower to complete your bust of Washington. But for one day only."

"I would like to have more time, but I can complete it in a day."

"Mrs. Wright, I am given to understand from a mutual acquaintance that you are a strong friend of our Revolution."

"I am an American, born and bred. I came here less than ten years ago. Our country deserves its independence."

"Are you willing to take a risk for your country?"

"I have taken many already. Some of which badly damaged

my business. What is one more? What do you propose, Ambassador?"

"Is it true that your bust of General Washington is almost complete, but that you need one live sitting to finish it?"

"Yes."

"In that case, please come to the Tower for His Excellency's sitting two days before his scheduled execution. No earlier, no later."

"Is the day already known?"

"Not yet. But when it is set, it will be announced publicly, I am sure."

"Is that your only request?"

"No. I assume the busts you make are hollow. I need there to be, inside the bust of Washington, a small, hidden shelf on which something a half foot long can be stored."

"I do not understand."

"A shelf that dips down from a ridge so that whatever is on it cannot easily be seen when you look inside, but must be felt for."

"Something that might hold a weapon?"

He shrugged. "Something that might hold something a half foot long."

"I can do that. Do you want the bust delivered somewhere afterwards?"

"No. I want you to leave it in His Excellency's cell, in a corner. If you are asked, you will say you need to do still more work on it. The guards will not know that you are limited to one day."

"At what time on that day am I to arrive?"

"I will be in touch and let you know."

"What if he is never executed?"

"The bust will be returned to you, and I will find a way to be sure that, should you return to America at war's end, you can sculpt not only Washington, but Jefferson, Adams and perhaps even Franklin." He had no idea how he would accomplish any of that, but he would try.

She smiled. "I have already sculpted Dr. Franklin, but I would be highly pleased to do a new one of him and to sculpt the others, as well."

They spent almost an hour after that discussing news from "home," as Mrs. Wright called it. She was of the opinion that the London papers did not report fully on the military successes of the American side in the Revolution.

As Abbott prepared to leave she said, "Ambassador, when times improve I would be pleased to sculpt you, as well. Without charge."

"I would be pleased to accept," Abbott said.

Abbott then returned to Mrs. Stevenson's. There were other things to attend to if his plan was to succeed.

65

The negotiations dragged on for several more days. By the end, they had reduced to a six-page list the things the American and British governments would agree to do or not do in order to ignore the issue of independence, at least for the time being.

After the last negotiation session closed, with the final draft in hand, Abbott found himself once again in the library at 10 Downing with North.

Over sherry, North assured Abbott that he could secure the consent of both his cabinet and Parliament to the overall agreement, including the list.

"What of the King, my Lord?" Abbott asked.

"If he will not accept it, I will resign."

"In which case you will be off at your country house, but His Excellency will be on his way to the gallows."

"My friend—and I hope I can call you that now—I expect to be able to persuade the King. You and I have had faith in each other over many things these past weeks and months. I ask you to have faith in me for this, too."

"All right."

"Now it is your turn. Can you persuade Washington?"

"I believe I make small progress each time we speak. I will see him later today."

"If he consents, can you persuade your Congress?"

"I think so, even on the issue of the currency." That was a reference to something they had struggled over in the negotiations. They had agreed that while the British would issue no special notes to circulate in America, neither the states nor the Congress would put any image or words on money, whether paper or coin, that glorified the rebellion, those who led it or fought in it, nor buildings, places or ideas associated with it. Images must be limited to anodyne things, such as the Greek gods or landscapes.

They parted with warm assurances of mutual respect, and Abbott went to see Washington.

As was typical in recent weeks, he was thoroughly searched on entering.

He presented Washington the final agreement, and Washington sat down at the small table in his cell, put on his reading glasses and studied the document for quite some time. Finally, he handed it back and asked, "What news is there of the Revolution?"

"I have written to the foreign affairs committee of the Congress every week, Excellency, telling them, in guarded terms, of our progress. And they have also written back almost every week, in the same tone. We are all, I think, aware that, despite being in sealed pouches, the British are reading every word."

"What do you learn from those reports, even if carefully worded?"

"From those and what I read in the London newspapers, as well as a few American newspapers that have been brought here, the war is much the same as when you were kidnapped. It is something of a stalemate, although the British have won a major victory in the South at a place called Guilford Courthouse."

"What of the French alliance, Colonel?"

"The French fleet is still eagerly awaited but has not yet come in force."

Washington pointed at the papers still held in Abbott's hand. "Perhaps then, these terms are the best we can do if we do not want the war to go on for many years, killing our people and emptying our treasuries."

"That may be, Excellency."

"Colonel, on many levels, the terms are acceptable—the border arrangements, the withdrawal of British forces, the trade agreement. It lacks reparations for all they have done to us, but that might be overlooked in order to end the war."

Abbott felt his face flush. Was Washington about to bless the terms?

"But the list of dos and do nots is not practical and will surely lead to endless disputes and, in the end, to renewed war."

"To what type of practicality do you make reference, Excellency?"

"Will the British send commissioners to monitor that our printing presses are not about to turn out money with the wrong images? Will we in turn station people at Portsmouth to be sure British warships are not heading to our waters instead of to France?"

"These are practical matters that could be worked out, Excellency."

"Perhaps so. But the real problem is that agreeing to this list of dos and do nots is beneath the dignity of a great nation, which we are and shall be. The list is so constraining that it screams out that we are *not* independent. I will not countenance it."

Abbott sighed deeply. He found it difficult to speak.

Finally, Washington said, "I know you have poured your heart and soul into this matter these last weeks, Colonel. You are a hero to me and to your country. I thank you. Now I must begin to work on the speech I shall deliver from the gallows."

Abbott held back tears and said, "Excellency, you must first be sentenced. And there is the chance of clemency. But you will not go to the gallows if either I or Lieutenant Forecastle have any say in it."

"I have given my consent for your efforts, and if they succeed, they do. If they do not, they do not."

"For the sake of the Revolution, they must."

66

The Chief Justice called the courtroom to order, announced the case and said, "George Washington, do you have any statement to make before sentence is imposed?"

Like everyone else in the courtroom, Hobhouse waited to hear what, if anything, Washington would say. He had offered to assist Washington with his statement, and the offer had been politely declined. He glanced around and saw that the courtroom was full, with an entire section set aside for reporters. He also saw Abbott, wearing a bright green waistcoat; North's assistant, Hartleb; and, to his surprise, Edmund Burke.

Washington had been granted permission by the court to be seated in the dock. Now he rose and said, "My Lord, I have been brought here against my will, captured at my headquarters. I am a prisoner of war, not a criminal, engaged in lawful combat for my country, much as every general who wears British red is doing at this very moment across the sea in America.

"But if I must nonetheless provide a defence for my actions, it is this. Every Englishman born in the King's realm is guaranteed certain rights of life and liberty. In America, those rights were taken from us, and that sundered the bonds that once connected us, and made His Majesty's former colonies into free and independent states."

Hobhouse looked over at the Attorney General, who looked apoplectic that this treason was being spoken aloud in a British courtroom for all the world to hear. The Chief Justice could stop it as inappropriate, of course, but he did not.

"The King," Washington continued, "whom I respect and honour in his person, acting through his government, which I concede he does not entirely control, being a limited monarch, has taxed us without our consent, cut off our trade with all parts of the world, suspended our legislatures and our laws, quartered armed troops amongst us and in our homes, and deprived us in many cases of the precious right to trial by jury."

He paused. "I commend this court for providing me the sacred right to a jury trial, although I am being tried for a crime I could not under law have committed. I am a soldier of another country, now a prisoner of war, arrested for the lawful act of defending that country."

Hobhouse was impressed. Washington had managed to list many of the main grievances set forth in the rebels' Declaration of Independence while moving the blame away from the King. Were the court to recommend clemency to the Crown, it might well help persuade the King to sign the document. But blaming the government, which was actually in charge of granting clemency, might do exactly the opposite.

Washington was finishing up. "For those who wish a complete list of the grievances which have sundered our relationship, you need look no further than our Congress's declaration of our independence, which was promulgated in July of 1776.

"I thank the court for its consideration for me and its kindnesses, including permitting an ageing man to stay seated during the trial. God bless you and God bless the King." He sat down.

Hobhouse smiled. He had always known that Washington was a great general. He had not known that he was also a wily politician. No speech could have been better crafted to persuade the judges to grant clemency while letting the King off the hook. Indeed, he knew that was so because three of the four had spoken privately of their support for the rebels' cause. His father-in-law, who dined regularly with many of the judges who sat in the Bailey, some of whom were old friends, had told him so. In the meantime Washington's speech would encourage British reporters to go and read the Declaration of Independence again. Washington had in effect repromulgated it to the world.

The Chief Justice said nothing in response. As he was about to speak, presumably to hand down the sentence, the Attorney General, without rising, started to say something that Hobhouse could not make out. The Chief Justice must have heard, though, because he said, rather sharply, "Mr. Attorney General, the Crown is not entitled to make a reply to a prisoner's statement before sentence is imposed.

"I will now impose sentence. The prisoner will please rise."

Washington rose and looked, so far as Hobhouse could tell, at peace with himself and with the world. Hobhouse felt as much as heard a hush descend on the courtroom.

The Chief Justice looked down at a piece of paper in his hand, as if the sentence were unfamiliar to him and he needed to remind himself of it. He looked directly at Washington, standing now in the dock, and said, "George Washington, you have been found guilty by a jury of the crime of high treason against our sovereign Lord George III, King, by the grace of God of Great Britain, France and Ireland, as the crime is stated in the treason statute of 1708, 7 William III, chapter 3.

"The court chooses, due to the severity of the offence and the need to make an example to others, not to recommend clemency."

He paused, looked down again at the paper and said, "Pursuant to our laws, you are to be drawn to Tyburn three days hence and there hanged, cut down before you have died, disembowelled until you be dead, quartered, your head severed, the parts to be distributed according to the wishes of the King."

Hobhouse looked at Washington and saw only calm in his face.

The Chief Justice said, "Does the prisoner wish to say anything further?"

"No, my Lord. I have said what I wished to say."

The Chief Justice looked to the Sheriff, who was in the courtroom loaded down with all of his silver and gold medallions and seals of office, and said, "The Sheriff is to take the prisoner to a secure place and remove him three days hence to Tyburn for the sentence to be carried out at dawn. God save the King."

Hobhouse watched Washington being taken from the dock under guard. He knew Washington would be going back to the Tower. Abbott had told him earlier that morning that he had persuaded North there was still a chance, if Washington were treated with great respect until the end, that he might change his mind and bless the agreement.

The courtroom was by then in an uproar of noise and argument. Hobhouse heard one man say to another that Washington's speech had been a masterful statement of the colonists' case, while at the same time contrite. The man he was talking to laughed uproariously and said, "Contrite? No, it was a simple 'I spit on your laws.'"

For himself, he could only think that his chambers's tradition would require him to go and witness the gory event.

67

Black had, the day before, attended Washington's sentencing. He had known from a young age what a traitor's death entailed—the children in his school had even joked about it, as children will—but he had never before heard the sentence visited upon someone he knew. Indeed, upon someone with whom he had come to have, from his near-daily visits, if not a friendship, at least an involvement in an odd kind of joint endeavour that would affect them both, for however long each might live. In Washington's case, that was, of course, not likely to be very long.

So far there had been no real sign of any escape plan. Other than seeing Mrs. Crankshaw go into Daughters Coffee House after Abbott did, and then apparently leave via a rear stairway, nothing had seemed out of the ordinary. Perhaps both Crankshaw and Abbott were at Daughters at the same time by coincidence. Perhaps customers often used the back steps.

The incident had caused him, after the sentencing, to seek out the Warder to ask about Mrs. Crankshaw. When Black had enquired, the man looked uncomfortable and said only, "Mrs.

Crankshaw? A very good worker. Gets along well with the guests. Arrives when she says she will. Stays late if needed. If you want to know more, I'd suggest you talk to Lord North's office."

Black realized that the Warder had just not very subtly told him that Mrs. Crankshaw *was* a spy, which he already knew. He asked if he could see Mrs. Crankshaw.

"Not here today," the Warder had said. "She asked for two days off. She'll come in the afternoon two days from now and work until midnight."

"The night before Washington's execution?"

"Perhaps she wants to say goodbye to him. I think she's become quite fond of the man." He paused. "As have we all, frankly."

He was right. Black realized that he too had become quite fond of the man.

At the sentencing, Black had seen Hartleb and approached him again about needing assistance. He had again been put off. It gave him to wonder if they were planning to frame him for Washington's murder. After all, didn't he need at least some kind of death warrant or written direct order from North in order to shoot Washington lawfully?

The day after the sentencing—two days before the scheduled execution—Black faced a choice. Either use his room in the Tower as a base from which to patrol inside to try to see what was happening there or sit in the coffee house across the street and watch who came and went, with occasional forays back into the Tower to check it out. He chose to station himself in the coffee house. Since his formal red officer's uniform would have made him stand out, he wore civilian clothes, but tucked a small pistol into a sack he carried.

After only an hour of keeping watch, he was rewarded when a middle-aged woman, accompanied by two men, appeared carrying a lumpy object hidden inside a cloth sack. After three guards inspected the contents of the sack the trio was admitted, with one guard accompanying them. Black had been unable to see what was in the sack.

Black walked over to the guard, whom he knew from many casual conversations as he had gone in and out, and asked who had just entered, and what was in the sack.

"Oh, that was the sculptor Patience Wright. She makes coloured wax heads of the famous," the first guard said. "Washington wants one for his widow. Well, tomorrow's widow, we should call her." A sad look passed over his face.

"No, you dunderhead," the second guard said. "It's the day *after* tomorrow. If I can get the day off I'm going to go."

"I thought you liked him," the first guard said.

"I do, I do. But that is no reason to be denied a public entertainment. I'll take my children so they may see why they must stay on the straight and narrow."

"If we could go back to what was in the sack?" Black said.

"She's already almost finished the wax head," the second guard said. "That's what was in the sack."

"Did she bring tools—knives and chisels and that kind of thing—with her?" Black asked.

"We counted them," the first guard said. "When she comes back out, we'll count 'em again. Mr. Sergeant escorted her to Washington's cell, so she won't get into any trouble along the way."

"Did you search *her*, too?" Black asked.

"No, but a matron will before they get to Washington's cell."

"What about inside the sculpted head? I assume it's hollow."

"I looked there, too," the second guard said. "There was nothing."

"Will you let me know if anything's missing when she comes back out? I'll be over in the coffee house."

Black went back to his table. Something about the sculptor seemed not quite right. It might do to find out more about her. But when? There was very little time left.

After a few hours had passed and Patience Wright's two assistants had emerged from the Tower, but not her, Black decided to visit Washington in his cell. When he arrived, Washington was sitting in a chair and Patience Wright was looking back and forth between him and a wax head she was working on. The head looked, he had to admit, a great deal like Washington. Wright was surrounded by tables that held small knives, chisels and a small metal device clearly intended to heat wax. There were also fine-tipped painters' brushes and pots of colour in small glass jars, much like those he had seen women use for make-up.

Washington, upon seeing Black, said, "Colonel Black, may I introduce you to Mrs. Wright, who is doing my portrait in wax. Mrs. Wright, permit me to introduce Colonel Black of His Majesty's Army, the man who kidnapped me."

Black cringed slightly and said, "In point of law, arrested. And pleased to meet you, Mrs. Wright."

"Colonel," she said, "I have little interest whether it might have been a kidnapping or an arrest, but I really need General Washington to keep still and not talk, much as if I were a portrait painter in oil." She sighed. "Those of us who work in wax are so underappreciated."

"Perhaps I can speak with you later, Colonel," Washington said. "Although there may not be many *laters* available." A wry smile played on his lips.

"Please, General," Mrs. Wright said. "No smiling."

Ignoring her, Black said, "But, General, the newspapers say you are still considering approving the agreement, which would provide you many more laters."

"Yes, I am, and edging closer to approval," Washington said. "But perhaps edging more quickly towards the gallows."

Black bid them both a good day and returned to the café. In late afternoon, Mrs. Wright emerged with a small bag, but without the wax head. Black watched as the guards searched the bag and counted the items inside.

After Mrs. Wright stepped out into the street, Black crossed over and accosted her.

"Mrs. Wright, may I enquire why you don't have the head with you?"

"How nice to see you again, Colonel Black. Thank you for bringing General Washington here so that I might sculpt him from life. I have wanted to do so for many years."

"I assume you are jesting, Mrs. Wright."

"How may I be of assistance, Colonel?"

"Why didn't you bring the head out with you?"

"Two reasons. First, General Washington wants his wife to receive it, and this way he can arrange that. He has assured me Lady Washington will pay me if I will send her a bill."

"And the second reason?"

"There is still a small bit of work to do, and I am hoping to receive permission to return tomorrow to complete it."

"May I look into your bag of tools?"

She pulled apart the drawstring that closed the bag and held it out to him. He peered inside and saw only a jumble of the same items he had seen in Washington's cell. If the guards had counted the same number of items going in and coming out, he supposed he had to be satisfied, although he was bothered by the entire thing.

"Thank you," he said.

"May I go now, Colonel?"

"Of course, and a good day to you, Mrs. Wright." He returned to the café.

By evening, he had seen Forecastle and Abbott come and go, each for a very short period of time. But nothing else and no one else of interest. He had considered following Forecastle, but that would leave the Tower unwatched, so he chose to stay where he was.

Towards midnight, he gave up and went back to his quarters

in the Tower to sleep. As he fell asleep, he was still trying to figure out what was wrong.

When he woke the next morning, he knew what was wrong. He got dressed and went to find the guards. It was the same crew who'd been on duty when Mrs. Wright had arrived the day before.

After appropriate greetings, he said to the first guard, "If you know, who searched Mrs. Wright yesterday?"

"Why, like we told you, Colonel, it was a matron."

"Yes, but who?"

"I imagine it was Mrs. Crankshaw. She's what usually does it."

"Bloody hell," Black said. "I thought she took a few days off."

"You'd have to ask the Warder 'bout that," the first guard said.

"She was here on and off all day yesterday," the second guard said.

"I am going to find her," Black said. "Do not let her leave before I speak with her."

"How will we know, Colonel, whether you spoke with her?" the first guard said.

Black rolled his eyes. "I will come back and tell you."

He went off in search of Mrs. Crankshaw.

68

Black looked for Mrs. Crankshaw all through the next day, without any luck. Finally, from his perch at the café, where the owners had begun to grumble about his taking up a table without spending much, he saw her enter the Tower. It was already dark.

He jumped up and followed her inside.

"Mrs. Crankshaw, might I have a word with you?" he said.

She turned and said, "Well, of course, Colonel. What about?"

"Did you search Mrs. Wright the other day, when she came to sculpt the head of General Washington?"

"Yes."

"Did you search her thoroughly?"

"Thoroughly enough that I think I embarrassed her. Why?"

"I am concerned that she might have hidden in her clothes something to deliver to the General."

"If she did, it was so well hidden, we would have had to strip her naked to find it."

"Good that you were thorough, then."

"What business is it of yours, Colonel, if I may ask?" she said.

"If you must know, Lord North has asked me to be sure nothing will interfere with the lawful execution of the General." It was not quite the truth, but close enough.

Her mouth turned down into a frown. "You kidnapped him and now you want to make sure he dies?"

"Frankly, your question makes me wonder if you are somehow working with the Americans."

He watched her face closely as he said it, hoping to see a glimmer of guilt. All he saw was astonishment; whether feigned or real, he could not tell.

"You must be daft," she said. "My son was killed by the Americans. I have no love for them."

"And yet you like General Washington."

"It is different, I think, when you get to know a man, even if he is on the other side. I have observed you with him, too. Do you not feel the same way?"

She had asked a good question, but Black did not feel like answering it.

"It is I who am questioning you, Mrs. Crankshaw, not the reverse."

"If you have no more questions, Colonel, I would like to return to my job here."

"You may go."

A voice from behind him said, "Do you suspect her of something, Colonel?"

Black turned and saw that it was Abbott. He'd only ever seen Abbott before from the distance of the coffee house or the back of the courtroom, but his clothes marked him quite clearly. They were even more outlandish than usual, including a ridiculous high wig and a bright green waistcoat. He could not imagine anyone of character wearing such a thing to so solemn an occasion.

Although Black couldn't be sure of it, he assumed Abbott

had overheard most of his conversation with Mrs. Crankshaw. Perhaps all of it.

"I don't believe, Ambassador, that we've ever formally met," Black said. "I am Colonel Black."

"You are correct," Abbott said. "We have not met before. Permit me to introduce myself, as well. I am Ethan Abbott, and as you apparently already knew, the American Ambassador Plenipotentiary."

"Ah, yes," Black said. "Just as I assume you already knew who I am since you called me by my rank even though I am out of uniform."

"I do, at least by reputation. I could not help but overhear you accuse that poor woman of working with us. Pray tell, other than to make General Washington's last day on earth more pleasant by bringing him his favourite coffee, with what do you think she might be helping us?"

"Helping General Washington to escape."

Abbott laughed. "Have you not noticed? The Tower is now surrounded by troops, and there are soldiers at the entry to every corridor. Even if Mrs. Crankshaw were helping us, which she is not, what could she possibly do?"

"That is what I have been trying to determine."

"Perhaps she is a witch and will turn General Washington into a bird so he can fly out the window of his cell."

Black ignored the sarcasm. "Why are you here, Ambassador? This is all but over. General Washington will be roused before dawn, taken to Tyburn and hanged. Rumour has it that you plan to leave before that, not having the stomach to remain and watch."

"It has not so much to do with stomach, Colonel, as with refusing to dignify an illegal act by the presence of an ambassador from the country whose honour and dignity are being trampled."

Black smirked. He should have ended the conversation, but

the soldier in him could not resist, and he said, "I say you are a coward."

"Say it how you will, I will now go to see General Washington."

"To what point?"

"To the point that Lord North has made a last-minute proposal on the independence issue that might move General Washington to relent and approve the agreement we have reached."

"And if he does not agree?"

"I will leave at midnight and never return," Abbott said.

"I wish you a pleasant trip home."

"Good day, Colonel," Abbott said. "I hope you enjoy the execution. Just remember as you watch that, in the end, you caused it, and you are the one who will be judged for it, even if not here on earth."

Black watched him walk away, annoyed at himself for not having responded to the last remark. The truth was that he hadn't known what to say.

Black patrolled the Tower for much the rest of the evening, alternating between watching the gate, where, as Abbott had said, there were ranks of soldiers guarding the building. He also walked the corridors and dropped by Washington's cell multiple times. Each time he arrived, there were two soldiers stationed to each side of the door. He asked them the same questions each time and got the same responses.

"Who is in the cell?"

"George Washington and Ambassador Abbott."

"Can you hear what they are saying?"

"No, Colonel. They are talking in low voices, and we cannot make out what they are saying."

Each time, Black looked through the small, rectangular grille on the cell door and saw the two men sitting face-to-face on straight-backed wooden chairs.

The last and final time Black visited the cell, it was close to midnight, and he found the door to the cell still guarded, not only by the soldiers, but by Mrs. Crankshaw. She stood there, arms folded, blocking the view into the cell.

"Stand aside, Mrs. Crankshaw," he said. "I wish to look inside."

"No, Colonel. They are in prayer and have asked not to be disturbed. By you or by anyone."

"I will ask again—stand aside."

"I will not. Have you no respect for a man's last night on earth that he might, with a friend, spend it with his God?"

Black was weighing whether to just shove her aside when the door to the cell opened and Abbott stepped out. He nodded to Black, shut the door gently behind him and limped away, head down and shoulders hunched. Even his bright clothing failed to hide his distress.

Black watched him go, then said, "Now I will look inside, Mrs. Crankshaw." He peered into the cell through the small window. The room was lit only by a single candle, but he could nevertheless see the entire room and see that Washington was lying in the bed, face to the wall.

"It is still there," he said.

"What is still there?" Mrs. Crankshaw asked.

"The wax head."

"Where did you expect it to be, Colonel?"

Black felt foolish and mumbled his reply. "I don't know." He paused and finally spoke up. "I expected the wax head somehow to be in the bed maybe, substituted for General Washington, designed to trick us while he escaped."

"You have been to see too many plays," she said.

"Perhaps so, and I am tired. Goodnight, Mrs. Crankshaw."

He went out through the Tower gate to watch Abbott's departure. He saw three coaches just starting to move off down the road, the horses' hooves drumming on the cobblestones, the clatter of the metal-rimmed wheels echoing in the cold night air. He didn't know whether he wished Abbott and his delegation well or ill, but he did wish he were going with them, somewhere far away.

69

Black arose before dawn and dressed himself in his full red officer's uniform, complete with campaign medals and a brigadier general's star on the epaulettes. He had received his promotion via letter, without ceremony, three days before.

Although he had not yet been assigned to any particular role in the King's Guard, in which he had always been an officer, and although he had no command of his own, he could still requisition his needs from them because they were based in London. As a general, even if a new one, he could take what he wanted. He chose a good horse and saddle, preferring to ride to Tyburn rather than walk behind the prisoner's conveyance, usually an open cart.

He rode back to the Tower gate and waited. It was still dark. In not too long, a phalanx of soldiers carrying bayonets emerged from the gate, marching in step, followed by Washington, surrounded by still more soldiers. Black could barely make him out in the crowd but could tell that he was wearing his uniform and his wig, whereas usually a condemned man was forced to wear a white linen shirt over his clothes and a cap on his head. Lord North must have given his permission.

As Washington walked along, Black caught another glimpse of him amidst the soldiers and saw that two stars had been sewn onto his epaulettes. Perhaps that was what Abbott was taking care of when the cell door was blocked.

To Black's surprise, Washington was ushered not into a crude wooden cart but into a highly polished coach drawn by four horses. Four soldiers got in with him and two more stood on the running boards. A priest got in on the other side. Perhaps Lord North hoped that if Washington were treated to not only prayer but kindness on his way to his death, he might change his mind about the agreement at the last moment.

Black kept looking for signs of a planned escape but saw nothing, although he did notice Forecastle, also riding a horse, keeping pace with the coach that held Washington and the soldiers who were guarding it.

Black rode behind the coach until it reached Tyburn, some five miles distant from the Tower. When they arrived, he saw that a newly built wheeled platform, set very high above the ground, had been positioned to sit beneath the gallow tree, which was next to the platform, its multiple nooses hanging down above it. It looked as if Washington would be moved from his coach and made to stand on the platform, which would then somehow be pulled out from under him, leaving him dangling. Black was amazed at the trouble they'd gone to. Usually, the condemned man or woman was simply drawn to the place of execution while standing on a crude wooden cart. Then the noose was draped around the prisoner's neck, and the cart pulled away from the gallows by the same horses that had brought it there, leaving the poor soul to strangle on the rope. The large platform would be harder to move, and Black looked around for the team of horses that would be needed. He didn't see them. Perhaps they would be brought in later.

Black had been to several executions—there were usually dozens in London every year to choose from, almost all public—but the sight of the waiting nooses always turned his stomach, no matter how horrendous the crime that was being avenged.

The crowd was huge. Perhaps ten times the size of the crowds he had seen before at Tyburn. It seemed divided between those who wanted to see Washington die and those who did not. He could hear people chanting, "His liberty is our liberty" and the treasonous "God damn the King!" While others screamed a more direct "Hang the traitor! Kill him!"

It was quickly becoming a mob, being held in at the back and front, but not at the sides, by soldiers with fixed bayonets.

Black positioned himself, still astride his horse, to the side of the platform. No one challenged him. He assumed his general's star worked as a kind of shield against enquiry. He looked around for Forecastle and found him, still on horseback, close to the platform. Washington had in the meantime left the coach and, with a soldier's bayonet in his back, mounted the steps to the platform. His hands were now tied behind his back, his wig still on. The buttons on his crisp, clearly new uniform glinted in the rising sun. The boards of the newly built platform were rough and uneven, and Washington at one point stumbled slightly, then recovered his balance. The hangman began talking to Washington and placed a blindfold around his eyes. The priest started whispering in his ear.

It looked to Black as if Washington was having trouble standing upright. Was it nerves? Suddenly his right leg collapsed, and he fell on his back.

At the same instant he saw Forecastle signal to someone, and half the mob began to push out through the sides, where there were no soldiers, and storm the platform. So here it was, Black thought. They were going to grab Washington and spirit him away. If he got a chance, he'd just shoot him and foil the plot.

Black manoeuvred his horse closer to the platform, where the hangman and the priest were trying to get Washington back on his feet. Black noticed immediately that the heel of the General's right boot had apparently caught on the edge of one of the rough boards as he fell, and had been pulled completely off by the force of his backward motion. It was then Black saw, sticking out from Washington's right pants leg, the longer wooden leg he had been told that Abbott wore when he wasn't sporting a peg.

It came to him in an instant. Abbott and Washington had switched clothes the night before, and their similar height and bulk had made it possible. That was why Mrs. Crankshaw had blocked his view into the cell. Black, like everyone else, had been so fixated on Abbott's outrageous clothing that he had not looked closely at "Abbott's" face as he left the Tower the night before.

He moved his horse ever closer to the stage, pushing screaming people aside, many of whom were now fighting and starting to hit each other with sticks.

The executioner and the priest seemed not to have noticed the wooden leg. They had stood Abbott back up, and the executioner, trying to get it done before the mob made it impossible, was putting the noose around Abbott's neck. Part of Black wanted to let Abbott die. Another part of him wanted Abbott tried for treason and to suffer his very own death. Right up against the platform now, he shouted, "That's not Washington. It's Ambassador Abbott!"

The executioner heard him, looked more closely at the face of the man with the noose around his neck and pulled off Abbott's wig. He stared for a moment, consulted the priest and then announced to the crowd, although most likely hardly anyone could hear him, "I do not have a death warrant for this man. I cannot execute him."

Black yelled to Abbott, "Where did he go?"

"To London, to London to buy a fat pig," Abbott said, grinning.

Black thought about it. There were many ports from which

the delegation could sail to France, but Portsmouth was the most likely since they had a laissez-passer that was good there.

He thought of telling others, but he knew they would dither, and precious time would be squandered. And besides, it had been his job to keep this from happening. He wheeled his horse around, moved away from the platform and headed out at a fast trot. They had a good eight hours on him, but they would have to stop somewhere along the way for the night. If he rode hard he had a decent chance of catching up. Horses were faster than loaded coaches.

On his way out of London, he stopped by his unit's armoury and picked up a long gun. It was a rifle, not a musket, similar to the type introduced by Major Ferguson several years earlier. He had practised with the rifle before, and it was breech-loading, which meant it could be reloaded and fired far more rapidly than a musket. It was also more accurate at long range. He also took with him a flask of the high-quality priming powder the rifle required plus a pouch of the specially sized balls the weapon used.

70

He rode hard and had time to think. Why didn't the soldiers who took Abbott from Washington's cell to the coach see he wasn't Washington? The two men's faces were quite different. Washington had ruddy cheeks, whereas Abbott's were pale. Maybe it was because the soldiers had never before set eyes on either Abbott or Washington. But what about the priest?

By late afternoon, he and his horse were both very tired even though he'd managed along the way to exchange his horse twice for a fresh one. The first trade was easy since his horse was so clearly superior. For the second trade he had to add a few silver coins.

In mid-evening, he arrived at an inn in a small town. There were no coaches out front, but he noticed fresh tracks in damp soil, leading to a barn. He rode around the back, peeked through a crack in the door and saw three coaches.

He loaded his pistol with powder and ball, went around and knocked on the front door. He had his pistol in his right hand, not levelled but not pointing at the ground, either. The door was opened by a matronly woman who said, "They have been more or less expecting you, General, although perhaps not quite so quickly. They are in the parlour." She pointed to a room to the side. "You can put your weapon away. They guarantee you no harm and, in any case, General Washington is not here."

He walked into the parlour, where all of the remaining members of the delegation were seated, all looking rather the worse for wear. This was hardly unexpected. They had spent all day bouncing up and down in a coach being pulled along on bad roads, which pretty much described almost all of the roads in England outside of London and even many in London.

"Who amongst you is the leader?" Black asked.

"That would be me, I suppose," a portly man with flushed cheeks said. "I am John Brandywine." The others did not introduce themselves.

"I wish I could say it is a pleasure to meet all of you," Black said. "But this is not the occasion for niceties. Where is General Washington?"

"We don't know," Brandywine said. "He didn't tell us where he was going."

"How long ago did he leave here?"

"Perhaps four hours ago," Brandywine said.

"Was he riding a nag or a fast, fine horse?"

"The latter. It was waiting for him here. And he has money to buy others."

That meant, of course, the owner of the inn was complicit in the escape, but that could be dealt with later. There was no time for that now.

"Where are all of you going now?"

"To Portsmouth. But two of our three coaches have broken axles and we are waiting for someone to come and repair them."

In other circumstances, he would have arrested all of them on the spot, as they were also likely complicit in Washington's escape. But there was no time for that either. Instead, he said,

"I hope that happens soon, and I wish you a pleasant journey back to your…country."

"You'll never catch him," Brandywine said. "He is said to be the finest horseman in the Continental Army."

"I have personal experience with his horsemanship."

Black went to find the innkeeper. "I would like to have some bread, dried meat and ale and a few dried apples if you have them," he said to her.

"I don't know if I wish to give it to you, given your mission."

"Madam, you are clearly involved in helping Washington escape. I may yet turn you in for treason, but if you want me to give it some thought before I decide to do that, you'd best give me some good food and drink."

She did.

Black rode out thinking that if Washington had a four-hour head start on him on horseback, he was unlikely to catch up. Perhaps, if he guessed right which port town Washington was heading for, he could persuade the harbour master there to bar the departure of his ship. Although there were also places along the coast where a rowboat could be landed on a beach and Washington rowed out to a waiting ship.

About an hour later, he heard the whinny of a horse far behind him, carried on a gust of wind. He rode off the road into a thicket of trees, tethered his horse and gave him one of the dried apples to eat, hoping it would keep him quiet. He loaded both his pistol and his rifle.

Not long after, he saw a man on horseback galloping down the road towards him. He recognized the man easily. It was Forecastle, who had a long gun slung across the saddle in front of him. In other times and places, Black might have tried to parlay with him and take him prisoner. Not this time. He raised his rifle as the man approached, took aim, tracked him and shot him full in the chest at close range. Forecastle fell from his horse, which continued down the road without him.

Black walked up to him. He was mortally wounded but not yet dead. "Did you know of this plot, this switch?" Black asked.

"No," Forecastle wheezed. "I organized the riot."

"Where is Washington going?"

"I don't know."

"If you tell me I will let you live and tell the next house to send a physician to your aid."

"I still don't know."

Just then, Forecastle's horse returned. The long gun that had been across the saddle was missing, no doubt fallen off somewhere along the way.

"I am sorry to do this," Black said. "But there is no point in leaving you alive to report to others about any of this."

He searched Forecastle, found his pistol and loaded it with power and ball from the man's own saddlebag. He put Forecastle's hand into the grip of the pistol, put it to his head and helped him pull the trigger. He dragged the body a little way into the woods, put the pistol back in Forecastle's hand and left the body where it lay. There was no time to cover it up with leaves. He soon got under way again.

By midnight, he was exhausted. He moved far off the road into the woods and found a deep depression in the ground in which he could shelter himself. Fortunately, it was not a cold April.

He woke up at first light stiff and sore. He ate a small amount, quenched his thirst and started out again with his rifle freshly loaded. He could only hope Washington had also had to rest.

Suddenly, the wind changed direction and he could smell the sea. That meant, he recalled from knowledge he had acquired during military exercises in the area, that he would soon come to a major fork in the road, where one direction led west and then south towards Portsmouth and its naval base, the other east and south towards the small village of Langstone. In Langstone there were several places at which a small boat could be landed and take Washington out to a waiting ship. He sat for a moment, thinking. What would he do if he had been planning Washington's escape? It seemed logical that Washington, as a fugitive, should be told to head for the less-populated place. The only question was whether those who had actually aided his escape had been able to arrange for him to be met at the chosen place by those who would spirit him away to France, or wherever it was they intended to take him.

When he reached the fork, he took the road to Langstone.

He rode hard all day, pushing the horse, and knew he was getting close when the smell of the sea, which had been coming and going with the breeze, changed to steady and grew ever stronger. Finally, he crested a hill and could see a man in an outlandish costume about to board a small rowboat that was pushed up on a narrow beach. It had to be Washington. He was less than a hundred yards away.

Black took the rifle from the saddle, lay down on the ground, snapped the frizzen back, refreshed the priming powder from the flask and closed the frizzen. Then he pulled the hammer back to full-cock position and raised the gun to his eye. He was a good shot, and he had practised marksmanship with an identical rifle the year before. He looked down the sights on the barrel and fixed his aim on Washington's back. There was no wind, and the man was standing still, presenting an excellent target. He placed his finger on the trigger, paused for a second, then moved his finger away.

He remained there on the ground, looking through the sights, watching as Washington boarded the boat. He stayed that way until he saw the oarsmen begin to pull the boat out to sea. Then he rose, dumped the powder out of the rifle, blew out the small amount that remained and put the gun back across the saddlebag. He mounted and turned his horse back towards London.

If he had later been asked his reasons, he would have said that while the King could lawfully kill Washington for having committed treason against him, he, personally, had no such reason. Nothing had been done to him, and he had become ever more revolted at the idea of serving as Lord North's personal assassin. Besides, having captured Washington in the first place, it seemed like it ought to be his right to set him free.

On the way back to London, Black stopped again at the inn where the delegation had been staying. To his surprise, they were all still there, waiting for someone to come and repair their broken coaches. Black told Brandywine that he had been right. He had not been able to catch up with the General.

Over dinner, he asked them a question. Had Washington told them how he and Abbott had managed to make Abbott look like Washington and vice versa when they each had such different colouring?

"He did explain it," Brandywine said. "They put rouge on Abbott's face and a kind of white powder on Washington's, using a small brush."

"Where was the brush hidden?"

Brandywine hesitated. "General, I will tell you, but only if you swear on your honour as an officer that you won't tell anyone else."

"I won't. I swear."

"All right, then. In the hollowed-out interior of a wax head that was in Washington's cell, there was a small shelf carved out that was hard to find unless you knew it was there. It held a small brush, which the artist—I think her name is Mrs. Wright—had concealed in the bottom of her shoe and left on the shelf."

"And the rouge and white powder?"

"Smeared on red and white areas of the wax head, so they weren't able to be detected unless they were touched. All Abbott and Washington had to do was put a little spit on the rouge and rub the brush across it. The powder needed no moisture. They touched up their lips, too."

Black smiled. "I knew there was something about that head. But here's my final question. Why did Washington agree to escape? He seemed bound and determined to make a grand speech and become a martyr to the cause."

"His Excellency told us Abbott persuaded him he would be of much greater use to our country alive than dead."

"Anything else?"

"Abbott told him his plan smacked of vanity. The General apparently likes to think he is not vain." They all laughed uproariously.

"What happened to Abbott?" Brandywine asked. "Washington told us Abbott had solemnly promised not to let the charade get too far, to reveal to the executioner who he really was before they put the rope around his neck."

"He let himself get a lot closer to death than that," Black said. "But when I left he was alive and well, although presumably now in prison."

After a fine dinner and a good night's sleep, Black headed back to London. He and North dined at 10 Downing upon his return and imbibed a not-insubstantial quantity of fine wine. After both the food and the wine had dwindled down, North said, "You're absolutely sure he escaped?"

"Very sure, my Lord."

"I still don't understand exactly how the two of them did it. Do you really not know, General?"

"I truly have no idea, my Lord. However they did it was well plotted and well hidden from us until the last moment, although it is being investigated."

"Well, it's more or less what I wanted, really. And the news from Cornwallis is good. He has prevailed in a major battle in South Carolina at a place called Guilford Courthouse. I think victory is finally near." A broad smile crossed his face.

Black at first said nothing in response but instead cast his mind back to their first meeting, in what now seemed a faraway time, albeit in a room not fifty feet away from where they were dining. Then they had known each other not at all. Now they had achieved the sort of intimacy that comes about when one man has, in however guised a form, asked another man to kill for him. So Black didn't think it would be out of place to ask a question of the First Minister that had been gnawing at him. Had the mission to America made the King any more sovereign in the colonies than on the day Black first set foot aboard the *Peregrine*? Then again, as he thought about it, the answer was so obvious there was no point in asking.

Black suddenly realized that his failure to respond aloud to North's statement of confidence in ultimate victory was fast becoming awkward. North was sitting there, staring at him, twirling the stem of his wine glass in his hand. Black raised his own glass high and said, "To victory, and to the King, our sovereign, long may he reign over us." Whoever *us* was now, or might one day be.

★★★★★

HISTORICAL NOTES

Independence of the United States

In October 1781, the American army, led by George Washington, defeated a large British army under the command of Lord Cornwallis, who surrendered on October 19. The band played "The World Turned Upside Down," but the war did not end immediately. It dragged on in one way or another for almost two years.

In September 1782, Henry Laurens was prisoner exchanged for Lord Cornwallis, left the Tower and went to France to join Benjamin Franklin, John Adams and John Jay as peace commissioners.

Finally, on September 3, 1783, the United States and Great Britain entered into the Treaty of Paris. The peace commissioners, Benjamin Franklin, John Jay, Henry Laurens and John Adams, negotiated it on behalf of the United States; David Hartley and Richard Oswald on behalf of Great Britain and King

George III. It was signed for the United States by Franklin, Adams and Jay. Laurens was too ill to attend the signing.

Article 1 of the treaty says:

> His Britannic Majesty acknowledges the said United States [there follows a list of the states] to be free sovereign and independent, that he treats with them as such, and for himself, his heirs, and successors, relinquishes all claims to the government, propriety, and territorial rights of the same and every part thereof.

There were no conditions or restrictions placed on the independence of the United States. Article 1 is the only portion of the treaty still in effect.

George Washington (1732–1799)

It is said that sometime in 1783, almost two years after the Battle of Yorktown but before the formal signing of the Treaty of Paris, George III was sitting for a portrait by the American painter Benjamin West. The King asked West what Washington would do after the colonies achieved independence. West supposedly replied, "They say he will resign his commission and return to his farm."

West reported that the King had said, in response, "If he does that, he will be the greatest man in the world."

Although Washington delayed returning permanently to his farm for quite a few years after the Revolution ended, he proved himself indeed the greatest man in the world, not only by resigning his commission as commander of the armed forces of the United States in 1783 but, later, by stepping down from the presidency at the end of his second term in 1797 and retiring to Mount Vernon, where he died on December 14, 1799, at the age of sixty-seven.

The idea of kidnapping Washington during the Revolutionary War may not be entirely fiction. In June 1776, Thomas Hickey, a member of Washington's Commander-in-Chief Guard (sometimes called the Life Guard) was court-martialled, tried for mutiny and sedition and hanged in front of a reported twenty thousand spectators in New York City. His crimes involved passing counterfeit money and planning to defect to the British, along with others. There were rumours at the time, however, that he was involved in a plot to assassinate or kidnap Washington. These rumours were later promoted and expanded by historians of the nineteenth century.

But the kidnapping pendulum swung both ways during the Revolution. In September 1781, Prince William Henry, the eldest son of George III, was serving as a midshipman aboard the British battleship HMS *Prince George*, the flagship of Admiral Digby. At some point that month, it docked in New York. An American spy, Colonel Mathias Ogden, reported to Washington that the Prince, who was sometimes quartered ashore in Hanover Square, was not well guarded. He proposed that the Prince be kidnapped, providing Washington with a major asset to trade in a prisoner exchange. Washington, by letter dated March 28, 1782, praised Ogden's "spirit of enterprise" and authorized him to attempt to carry out the plan. Washington cautioned, though, that the Prince was to be treated with "all possible respect." However, the plot was discovered and foiled by increasing the guard, and the Prince eventually returned safely to England. Many years later, in 1830, he succeeded his father and reigned as William IV.

George III (1738–1820)

Until Queen Victoria, George III was the longest-reigning monarch in British history, having reigned from 1760 until his death in 1820. In the later years of his reign, he suffered from recurrent mental illness, and a regency was finally established in 1810, whereby his eldest son ruled as Prince Regent. Based on the King's reported symptoms, many modern physicians believe he was likely suffering from a hereditary blood disease called porphyria, although there are dissenters from that diagnosis.

The King was never fully reconciled to the independence of the American colonies. Indeed, in March 1783, some six months before the Treaty of Paris was signed, the King drafted an abdication notice, but never delivered it.

Frederick, Lord North (later 2nd Earl of Guilford) (1732–1792)

Lord North stepped down as First Minister in March 1782. He returned to an influential role early in 1783 as Home Secretary, in a coalition with his old enemy, Charles James Fox, a Whig. That ministry fell in late 1783, but not before it had managed to negotiate and sign the Treaty of Paris, thus truly ending the American war. North, who never regained power, began to go blind in 1786 and died in London in August 1792 at the age of sixty. He thus presumably lived to hear about the accession of George Washington to the Presidency of the United States. I could find no record of what North may have thought about that event.

Henry Laurens (1724–1792)

Henry Laurens was the fifth President of the Continental Congress and presided over it during the adoption by the Congress of the Articles of Confederation in 1777 (the Articles were not fully ratified by the thirteen states until 1781). He resigned that position and then went to the Netherlands on a diplomatic mission and was captured by the British on the high seas. He was charged with treason and imprisoned in the Tower of London, where he was held under harsh conditions. After the Battle of Yorktown, he was prisoner exchanged (in a deal he brokered himself, with assistance from Edmund Burke and Benjamin Franklin, amongst others) for Lord Cornwallis. Cornwallis had been paroled to England after the Battle of Yorktown, having agreed as a condition of his parole not to participate in any military actions against the United States. Laurens eventually went to Paris as a peace commissioner to help negotiate the Treaty of Paris. He returned to the United States after the treaty was signed and largely retired from public life in 1784. He died in 1792 at the age of sixty-four.

Samuel Huntington (1731–1796)

Samuel Huntington was a Connecticut lawyer who served as President of the Continental Congress from 1779 to 1781. He was a signer of both the Declaration of Independence and the Articles of Confederation. After the Revolution, he served as the Chief Justice of the Connecticut Supreme Court and as the governor of the state. Huntington County, Indiana, is named for him.

Charles Thompson (1729–1824)

Charles Thompson was the permanent secretary of the Continental Congress. His name is affixed to the first published version of the Declaration of Independence, as Secretary of the Congress.

Although not a delegate, he was integral to its functioning, having served in the role for the entire fifteen years of the Congress's existence. He also had a significant role in foreign affairs and has been said by at least one biographer to have served as a virtual prime minister. Earlier Thompson had been a leader of the Philadelphia Sons of Liberty. He fell out with some of the other Founders over various actions and issues and never obtained an office in the new federal government.

Patience Lovell Wright (1725-1786)

The wax sculptor, Patience Lovell Wright, was a real person. She practiced her craft in New York, Paris and London.

Her wax sculpture of Prime Minister William Pitt, the Earl of Chatham (done after his death) can be seen in the Westminster Abbey Museum. She died in London in 1786.

ACKNOWLEDGEMENTS

I am deeply indebted to the many people who have helped me write this novel. Chief among them are my wife, Sally Anne, for her encouragement to get going on writing it when it was only an idea bumping around in my head (not to mention her excellent editorial comments on each chapter as it was written, as well as her comments on the finished manuscript); my son, Joe, who also bugged me to write it and whose comments on structure and arc, once I got started, were extremely helpful (not to mention that he came up with the title!); my editor, Peter Joseph, who not only acquired the book for Hanover Square, but whose careful edit of the manuscript has improved it greatly, in ways both large and small; and Gina Macdonald, my excellent copy editor, who not only did a terrific job smoothing grammar, syntax and text and bringing the manuscript into compliance with the style manual, but also checking many hard-to-find facts and ferreting out a variety of anachronisms that had escaped me, despite my earlier efforts to find them all. I also want to thank the proofreader, Katie McHale; the publicist, Shara Alexander; Mary Sheldon, Natalie Hallak and the entire production crew at Hanover Square. Last, but hardly least, I am indebted to my wonderful agent, Erica Silverman, without whom this novel would never have seen the light of day.

A special note of thanks is also owed to Jacque BenZekry, who has been such a great cheerleader for the project as it has gone forward.

Various other friends have not only read the manuscript and given me their notes on it but, in the process, lent me their particular expertise—thank you, Roger Chittum and Mike Haines, for your knowledge of ships under sail; Clint Epps, for your insights into Revolutionary War weapons and culture; Brinton Rowdybush, for your knowledge of American diplomacy in the eighteenth century; Amy Huggins, for your knowledge of eighteenth-century costuming; John Brown, for your comments on New Jersey geography; Jeff Davison, for pointing out that no one could have drunk from a bottle of beer in America in 1780 since the first bottling in the United States didn't take place until much later; Maggi Puglia, for your great tour of the Dey Mansion and your knowledge of how Washington's headquarters functioned while he was there; and Gemma Smith, for your informative tour of the Benjamin Franklin house in London (now listed at No. 36 Craven Street, but numbered as No. 7 during the time that Franklin lived there). And last but not least, Diana Wright, for your help with my website and all things social media.

Whatever errors might be in the book are, of course, mine alone.

As always, still other friends and colleagues have given unstintingly of their time to read early drafts and provide general comments or to support my efforts in other ways. They include Melanie Chancellor, Dale Franklin, Lorie Stromberg, Tom Stromberg, Sam Ahn, Mi Ahn, Daniel Wershow, Alison

Balian, Roger Toll, Mary Menzel, Dan Martin, Jack Walker, Belinda Walker, Wendy Joseph, Marty Beech, Hwa Kho, Ping Lee, Miriam Singer, Linda Brown, Maureen Gustafson, Elaine Katz, Lauren Gwin, Deborah Coontz, Maxine Nunes, Joel Davison, Jessica Kaye, Richard Brewer, Gayle Simon, Maryglenn McCombs, Tyson Butler, Carolyn Denham, Prucia Buscell, Deanna Wilcox, John Shelonko, Bob Vanderet, Mindie Sun, Diana Wright, Dick Birnbaum, Pamela Okano, Annye Camara, and all of those Facebook friends who suggested names for the ship.

I have had an interest in the American Revolution since grade school, when my fifth-grade teacher had me memorize Longfellow's poem "Paul Revere's Ride." Over the years since, I have read dozens of books and articles about the Revolution, some of them now lost to memory. The research on this novel involved reading dozens more. I was, however, particularly impressed by what is "out there" now that wasn't when I first began to read on the subject: online resources, which are today quite amazing. Those I found particularly useful included the digital resources at the British National Archives, Founders Online (supported by the US National Archives), as well as the website of Mount Vernon.

I must also mention Wikipedia. I know that it is often criticized and can sometimes fall short of pristine accuracy, that it can be guilty of bias or miss important facts. But, carefully used, it makes possible an initial dive into a pool of knowledge that is both broad and deep. And its footnotes frequently lead to specialty books and articles that would otherwise be difficult to find. I am grateful to the Wikimedia Foundation for supporting it, along with the thousands of volunteer contributors and editors who strive to make it an ever more useful tool.